That night their positions became re-versed.

She was no longer the mistress and he the slave. In this close communion he be-came the master and *she* the willing slave, doing his bidding . . .

At dawn he was sleeping, and in the still dark cabin his face was only a black smudge on the whiteness of her skin. She hastened to get into her clothes before he woke up.

"Get up, Colt!" Her words were peremp-tory, leaving no doubt that she was a mis-tress, *he* a slave. "Get up and get out! And remember! You keep your mouth shut about everything if you want to keep the meat on your back!"

The Falconhurst Series:
(*in the order of the stories*)

FALCONHURST FANCY 13685-X $1.95
MISTRESS OF FALCONHURST 13575-6 $1.95
MANDINGO 23271-9 $1.95
FLIGHT TO FALCONHURST 13726-0 $1.95
THE MUSTEE 13808-9 $1.95
DRUM 22920-3 $1.95
MASTER OF FALCONHURST 23189-5 $1.95
HEIR TO FALCONHURST 13758-9 $1.95

Fawcett Crest and Gold Medal Books
by Lance Horner:

CHILD OF THE SUN (*with Kyle Onstott*) 13775-9 $1.95
THE BLACK SUN (*with Kyle Onstott*) 14034-2 $2.25
GOLDEN STUD 13666-3 $1.95
THE MAHOUND 13605-1 $1.95
ROGUE ROMAN 13968-9 $1.95
THE STREET OF THE SUN 13972-7 $1.95
THE TATTOOED ROOD
    (*with Kyle Onstott*) 23619-6 $1.95

FALCONHURST FANCY

Lance Horner
and
Kyle Onstott

FAWCETT GOLD MEDAL • NEW YORK

FALCONHURST FANCY

Published by Fawcett Gold Medal Books,
a unit of CBS Publications, the Consumer
Publishing Division of CBS Inc.

ISBN: 0-449-13685-X

Printed in the United States of America

40 39 38 37 36 35 34 33 32

FALCONHURST
FANCY

A PROLOGUE

Chapter I

"HE BIN OUT afore now," the storekeeper said. "Nothin'
to get all het up 'bout. He'll come back."

"He bin out, yes, but not fer two weeks—over two
weeks, a-goin' on three." Young Ransom Lightfoot leaned
against the wall from the upturned keg on which he sat.
"An' all the cotton gittin' in the grass. T'other times he
bin out, 'twere lazy times like jest afore pickin' o' somethin' when he wan't a-doin' aught 'cept eatin'. This time
he needed bad. He a monst'ous big man. Why that black
bugger, he kin hoe more cotton'n three common niggers.
That is when the lazy bastard a-workin'. Take a driver
wid a cowhide to keep him a-goin' 'n' a-hoein'."

Bannion, the storekeeper, nodded in agreement, not
that he was particularly interested but it was something
to talk about and topics of conversation were at a premi-
um between Ransom and him. He could not understand
what it was that brought the boy almost daily to the store
unless it might be, and probably was, the grog he sold
and to which occasional and infrequent visitors treated
the young fellow. Lightfoot was grown—as mature probably as he would ever be. Although his smooth, unlined
face was immature, there was a thickening of the blond
hairs on his cheeks and chin. He appeared only fourteen
or fifteen, certainly not the eighteen years Bannion knew
him to be. Ransom's mind was far less developed than his

7

body but, regardless of his immaturity, and although his trade was small, Bannion rather liked to have him around; he was at least company and Bannion's customers were few. His trade was mostly at night when the chores on the farms were over and the men congregated in his store for grog. During the day, people seldom stopped, and although Lightfoot's conversation was limited, it was at least the sound of a person talking and it helped pass the time. Their talk rarely strayed beyond the minor gossip of the immediate neighborhood—the petty occurrences in the vicinity, the state of the crops, the weather. Today, for a change, it had to do with something of more importance—the disappearance of a slave from Elm Grove Plantation some ten miles to the west, owned by one Macklin. He had, so it was commonly known, had difficulty from time to time with a stalwart black slave named Jem. This Jem was in the habit of disappearing from the plantation for some three or four—once even five—days at a time, after which he would return of his own accord, accept whatever punishment was meted out to him, and resume his life with his assigned mate, or "wife" as he called her, and take up his wonted labor. He was not classed as a runaway but was merely thought of as *out*. His punishments, which took the form of progressively more severe floggings, impressed themselves upon his memory only long enough for the lesions on his back to heal; soon he would be missing again only to reappear when he became sufficiently hungry or cold or lonesome to return. This time, however, he had been gone long enough to be considered a runner and to become a subject of comment and interest in the community.

"Mista Macklin too goddam easygoin', too lenient." Bannion hoisted himself up from his chair by putting two hands on the rough counter. "I'da took him to the blacksmith long 'go 'n' put a three-prong collar on him 'n' burned 'n 'R' on his face so's anyone a-seein' him would of knowed he a runner."

"Hearin' he go 'roun' a-pesterin' the wenches on other plantations 'n' they a-likin' it so much they ain' a-tellin' he a-bin there," Ransom snickered, moistening his lips. "Mista Jenkins down at Stony Creek nigh to caught him

8

one night a-comin' outa one of his wench's cabins but that Jem, he light out for the woods like'n unto a scalded cat 'n' nobody kin git no trace o' him."

"Whoppin' don' do that bastard no good, seem like. Goddam, I'd shore a-cut him. I'd a-nutted him long time 'go 'n' stopped his tom-cattin'." Bannion brought his fist down on the counter, causing the collection of jugs and bottles to jump.

Ransom sucked in the thread of saliva that drooled from his lips. The conversation was taking a turn that excited him. "Seems a shame tho' ter nut a nigger what so powerful's him. 'Thout nuts he ain't no good. I'd just ring him 'n' that don' need no blacksmithin' neither. All Mista Macklin gotta do is make a couple o' holes 'n' solder a ring through him. Cain' pester no woman but still got his nuts if'n he a-needin' them. Cain' pester none if'n a nigger's ringed, kin he?" A brightness in Ransom's otherwise dull china-blue eyes anticipated Bannion's answer.

Bannion answered Ransom's question with a shake of his head, then nodded vigorously. "Perhaps better jest ter ring him, like yo' say. Macklin'd lose money if'n he nutted him. That Jem he got hisself a wench over on Elm Grove what brings in a sucker a year. She what brings him back. She'll be fetchin' him back afore long. Guess that why Macklin never did have him ringed nor nutted. 'Sides, take the sap right outa him to nut him. Go to sell one, cain' hardly git nothin' fer him. House servants dif'rent though. Al'ays best ter nut house boys fer protection to white women folk. Onct them nigger bastards gits hot they don' care where they put it. Gelded boys, specially if'n they's yellow, bringing good money now but has to be done while they's young. Ain' so dangerous that way. Jem he too old ter nut now."

"All them floggin' whales on a nigger's back cut his price near's much's nuttin' him, I'm a-thinkin'." Ransom was loath to drop the subject, which he found pleasantly erotic.

"Not on no common fiel' han' tho'." Bannion considered the matter thoughtfully as though he were an expert on the subject. "Don' make so much dif'rence on him but

9

on a fancy yeller, 'specially a wench. Ain' nobody a-goin' ter pay fancy prices fer a whaled-up back. But on a fiel' hand, 'n' it a buck, yo' cain' hardly fin' 'em 'thout whaled-up backs. Doubt if'n there's a dozen in the county. Goddam lazy bastards won't work 'thout'n a little touch o' cowhide now 'n' then."

"That Jem o' Mista Macklin's got whales all over him —back, belly, legs 'n' ass 'n' everything," Ransom said. "Seen him myself onct a year back when Mista Macklin's driver was a-ticklin' the varmint wid a blacksnake. Plum nekkid, he was, hung up by his wrists 'n' covered with whales what make him look like a corduroy road. Mista Macklin's nigger driver was a-whalin' the daylights outa him and that Jem a-howlin' like a painter wid his tail in a trap. Fust time I'd ever seen a nigger whaled and it right comical, it was. Cain' never fergit it, I cain', but a-wishin' it'd been a wench I'd a-seen whaled. Shore like to see that. Aimin' someday ter get me a wench—a right purty mustee one mos' white—'n' if'n she do anything, I'm a-goin' ter strip her down 'n' cut the meat off'n her back myself. Ain' a-goin' ter let nobody else do it neither." His eyes were half closed and his breath was coming faster. "Yo' ever seen a wench whaled, Mista Bannion?"

"Seen plenty"—Bannion grinned and pointed to Ransom—"but ain' a-goin' ter tell yo' 'bout them much as yo' a-wantin' ter hear." Ransom ducked his head shamefacedly so that Bannion could not see the crimson spreading over his cheeks.

"High time, boy, yo' went 'n' got yourself a woman 'n' got it outa yore system. Too bad yo' ain' got no wenches up to your place. Cain' yo' git yore mama to buy yo' none? Ain' scarcely fittin' fer young fellers like yo' 'n' yore brother Jonas not ter have a wench ter drean yo' right often. Jonas he al'ays a-tom-cattin' to all the quarters fer miles 'round a-seekin' wenches. Seems like the suckers birthed 'round here got that Lightfoot yeller hair. Whyn't yo' go 'long wid him?"

"Jonas he ain' a-lettin' me. He a-sayin' I too young 'n' 'sides, I ain' never had no hankerin' fer black wenches. Wantin' me a white one or a mustee for my first one."

"Damn few white ones 'round here what's yore age."

10

Bannion poured out a couple of fingers of corn into a tin cup and handed it to Ransom, then filled his own to the brim. " 'N' not no mustees neither, 'cept my Fronie 'n' she most white 'nuff ter be a mustee. Drink up 'n' cool yo'self off."

Ransom gratefully accepted the liquor, staring at it in anticipation before he drank, then sipping it slowly to make it last. Concerned with their drinking, neither man spoke for a while.

The cabin of logs that housed Bannion's store sat some fifty yards back from the main highway that crossed the eastern part of Mississippi territory in what was shortly to be Alabama. It was an approximately equal distance from the western shore of a small stream called Falls Run as it was from the road, with a much rutted crossroad, tributary to the main road, running between. Nobody knew nor cared how Falls Run got its name, whether from some early settler named Fall or from some supposed falls in the tiny creek itself. None was, however, apparent in the sluggish rill in the vicinity of the un-named crossroads store, although it did widen out, far-ther along, before it joined the Escatawpa River.

Behind the cabin that housed the store was another, somewhat smaller one, that served Bannion and his wife as a dwelling and also housed their slaves, Netty and Fronie, along with Netty's latest infant son. The whole household lived, ate, and slept in the single room of the rough, dirt-floored cabin. Both cabins, the store and the house, were enveloped at the rear by a fine grove of na-tive trees, and one magnificent elm stood in a clearing before the door of the store. A sign, all but defaced, its paint graying and peeling, proclaimed the single word "S-T-O-R-E" over the doorway, although it was en-tirely superfluous since the neighborhood for miles around knew of its location. Although Bannion's store was a prototype of most crossroads stores of the time, his chief stock in trade was corn whisky; but he did purvey, if any-one wanted to buy, a miscellaneous assortment of mer-chandise such as sugar, molasses, flour, meal, salt pork, lard, and bacon, together with a few bolts of printed calico, some pins and needles and thread, and a meager,

11

shopworn and bedraggled assortment of vari-colored ribbons. Most of the stock was stale, dirty, or faded and Bannion made no effort to sell it. His trade, such as it was, was in the corn whisky of which, however, he was one of his own best customers.

Across from the store and a short distance down the highway were two log buildings, now fallen into ruins, that had once housed a blacksmith's shop. An anvil and the remnants of a forge were still to be seen within one of the tumbledown buildings, while bits of misshapen metal protruded from the high grass. Occasionally a piece disappeared when it could be used to mend a wagon, but as nobody owned the place, nobody objected, least of all Bannion, who might have claimed some proprietary interest in the place, merely from its proximity.

Although there were no other buildings within sight of the store, it was far from being situated in a wilderness, since Alabama was starting to fill up. That part of the territory was fertile and a fair amount of people lived and farmed within a trading radius of the store. Bannion managed to make a living out of it, for it supplied him with his own whisky and apparently supported his household, although he begrudged the food necessary to feed the two slaves and the child that appeared yearly. The original slave had been a wedding present to his wife from her parents—a black wench of some Congo stock, thick of lip and flat of nose, with great open nostrils. When she had become nubile, Bannion had denied her access to any bucks, preferring to sire her child himself. He pretended to his wife that he would take no pleasure in such a distasteful chore and thereby won her permission; she, in fact, convinced of the superior value of light-skinned progeny, encouraged him. The issue had been Netty, and the black wench died in having her.

Netty was of a yellowish-brown color, less amorphous and far less Negroid than her mother had been, but when Netty came to maturity, Bannion had refused to lie with her. To be sure, he was far more tempted than he had been with her mother, but the fact remained that she was his daughter and he was prejudiced against incest. Not

12

that his scruples were moral ones; he simply believed that such a mating would result in misshapen, deformed, or witless progeny. Consequently he had solicited the services of three vigorous white men who were his customers, bribing them at different times with corn whisky that they might permit him to witness the proceedings. He was never entirely sure which of the three was the sire of Netty's daughter, but as she grew older she developed a likeness to Enoch Lightfoot, the now dead brother of Ransom Lightfoot, his current guest and loafer. The child has been so light in color, so robust and spirited that he had kept her and named her Sophronia, a name long since replaced by her current appellation of Fronie. That had been about thirteen or fourteen years ago when Ransom Lightfoot was a mere child. Now Fronie had grown into an early nubility, a comely quadroon child with small bones, amber skin, slightly curling hair and, barring the faintly thickened lips, features that approximated Caucasian. All of Netty's subsequent children had been sold, as they were boys and useless for Bannion's purpose. Being her brothers, he could not mate them to Fronie, and the money he received for the children, little though it was, helped him to stave off his creditors. Fronie and the unweaned baby that Netty now nursed—who, Bannion suspected, had probably been sired by the wandering Jem because he was far blacker than Netty herself—were all that remained of her brood. Bannion planned to sell the baby as soon as it could be taken from its dam and some trader came along to buy it. Negroes were going up in price and he regretted now that he had not reared the others and sold them for real money. The only reason he had retained Fronie was that she could be expected to have a child every year and he knew that he would have no difficulty in getting white men to sire her progeny. The results of these matings would be octoroons and should bring a high price on the fancy market.

Ransom Lightfoot finished the meager cupful of whisky and passed the cup hopefully back to Bannion who, much to Ransom's disgust, made no offer to refill it. Instead he handed Ransom a piece of horehound candy which the boy accepted willingly. Anything that cost

13

nothing was always welcome. As he crunched it in his jaws he peered out the door.

"A-gittin fearful dark, ain' it. Guessin' we goin' ter have a storm." Not waiting for Bannion to express an opinion, he continued, "Whereat that Fronie wench o' your'n? Ain' sold it yet, hev yo'?"

"Ain' sold it 'n' thinking I ain' a-goin' ter. Come 'nother year 'n' I kin be breedin' her. Ought ter bring me in some good mustee suckers if'n I kin get a good strong white feller ter sire them. But jest don' know if'n I kin keep her. Goddam factors a-gettin' so urgent 'n' all 'n' she bringin' such a good price, seein' as how she's virgin, so ter speak. Ain' no man ever mounted her." Bannion, watching Ransom's jaw working on the horehound, bethought himself of a chew of tobacco.

"Ain' she 'bout ready?" The turn of the conversation was serving to excite Ransom again.

"Ready fer what?" Bannion expectorated a stream of amber liquid.

"Ready fer me, that's what." Ransom leaned forward, eagerly pointing to himself. "Who else yo' reckon? She nigh growed up, ain' she, 'n' I white."

"Not by a damn sight, she ain' growed up 'nuff yet. 'N' besides, in the fust place yo' too goddam much fer her, she so little 'n' all. Heered all 'bout yo'. Second place, yo' too goddam young; ain' got no good fertile seed in yo' yit. 'N' third place, yo' her uncle cause yore brother her pappy." Bannion spat again with sufficient vehemence to conclude the conversation.

"Ain' no dif'rence," Ransom persisted. He was anxious to make his point, for this was something of paramount importance to him, the subject of his secret dreams for a long time. "Ain' no dif'rence at all. She not a-knowin' if'n I her kin or not 'n' niggers don' care none anyway. They screw jest like animals anyway. Ain' I a white feller? Ain' that what yo' a-wantin'? Shore I'se big like yo' say but I ain' goin' ter rip her 'n' I sure got plenty o' sap. Just a-goin' ter waste it is. Could git yo' a nice, bright-skinned sucker outa that Fronie fer yo'. Mayhap it have yeller hair like me 'n' be extra fancy."

As though she had been listening to them discussing

14

her, which probably she had, Fronie chose that moment to slink into the store as unobtrusively as possible. She well knew that her presence in the store was forbidden, but she had noticed Ransom's horse at the hitching rack and was drawn to him. His long yellow hair and his blue eyes had always fascinated her. Bannion, noticing her, began to upbraid her for her presence.

"What in hell yo' a-doin' in here?" he demanded, expecting no reply. "Yo' know yo' ain' got no call a-comin' in here. Now scat!" He clapped his hands together, making the girl jump.

"It a-rainin'," she whined, holding up her wet dress to prove her statement. It was merely an excuse to justify her presence and certainly not the reason for her intrusion.

"That case . . ." said her owner, going toward the open door, for there were no windows through which he might observe the weather. "Not rainin' much but it comin' up, sure's hell it is. Goin' ter be a hell-raiser of a thunder shower."

Ransom leaned back on the upturned keg, spreading his legs wide apart and beckoning to the girl with one hand.

"Come on over here, Fronie. Got something fer yo', I have."

A flash of brilliant lightning illuminated the June skies and was followed by a reverberating clash of thunder to which Ransom waved his hand with a warning gesture. "Yo' be safe here wid me. Ain' no thunderin' nor lightnin' a-goin' ter harm yo', yo' bein' here alongside me."

The bashful girl wanted to obey this youthful white demigod with the yellow hair and was intrigued by his invitation, but she was undecided whether or not to go to him. He leaned forward until his hand clasped her wrist and pulled her, not ungently, to him. She was still fearful, but seeing that Bannion was not looking, she edged coyly toward Ransom and let him draw her to him. Once before him, he drew his legs around her, pulling her up tightly against him. His fingers removed the remnant of horehound from his mouth and plopped it into hers.

"Ain' that good?" he spoke softly.

15

She nodded her head, sucking on the candy.

"Somethin' better'n that." His hand slid along her bare arm and she, strangely content, snuggled even closer. The rain continued, becoming a downpour, darkening the interior of the store so that it was almost impossible to see except for those brief moments when the flashes of lightning illuminated the darkness. Ransom, entirely oblivious of the downpour and grateful for the darkness, caressed her.

At first he was more or less circumspect, fearing a reprimand from Bannion, but Bannion was still at the door looking out, fascinated by the storm, his back to them. Bannion did not seem to care and, in truth, despite his previous objection to Ransom, he really didn't mind as long as Ransom did not go too far. Consequently Ransom, emboldened by Bannion's tolerance, slid one hand under Fronie's garment and raised it up over her knees, his hand progressing in slow moving circles up her legs. She seemed to relish the contact with Ransom's hand as much as he did himself, but even had she resented it there would have been no recourse. She reached down to touch him. Her fingers, warm and grasping, seemed intrigued with what they had discovered, and presently Ransom's loud moan caused Bannion to turn around. Despite the darkness, he could see what had happened.

"Yo', Fronie, git yo'self away from that white boy 'n' come over 'n' set down o' I'll put yo' out, rain o' no rain. Yo' a-knowin' better'n such goin's-on. Yo' ever done that afore?"

"Ain' never, masta suh, never."

"Ketch yo' a-doin' that 'gain 'n' I'll whale yo'." Although Bannion's scolding was directed against the girl the rebuke was meant more for Ransom, whom he could not censure in front of Fronie. Custom demanded that the white man be blameless. Bannion's objection was not based on any concern for Fronie: his interest was purely commercial. If he decided to sell Fronie she would bring far more as a virgin; if he decided to breed her, he wanted to mate her with an older, more vigorous man than Ransom. He also feared somewhat for Fronie's safety were Ransom to initiate her, for Ransom's excessive endowments had been a joke and a byword in the community ever since he had swum with other boys in the creek. Ransom's interest in the girl had only this afternoon become apparent. Now Bannion suspected the boy's reason for hanging around, and although he did not want to discourage his coming entirely, for his company was welcome, he did want to squelch his interest in Fronie.

"Got myself plans fer that wench, I have, Ransom boy." Bannion smiled to mitigate the implied censure of his words. "Cain' have no horny youngster like yo' a-foolin' 'roun' wid her yet. Promise yo' somethin' tho'. Time a-comin' when I a-goin' ter breed her, mayhap I think 'bout yo'. Keep yo' in mind, I will. She git done havin' her first sucker, yo'll be older 'n' she'll be stretched 'n' no reason why yo' cain' sire her second one. Keep yo' in mind, I will." He winked at Ransom.

Ransom, now momentarily satisfied, had apparently lost all interest in the matter. He rose and stretched, buttoning up his pants, and walked to the door as though planning to leave. When he peered out and regarded the downpour, he decided against it, although he remained in the doorway watching the wind and the rain tear at the trees.

"Shore 'ppreciate it, Mista Bannion," he said listlessly, "if'n yo' lets me, come the time yo' wants me ter." Suddenly he leaned forward, his head out in the rain, his hand shielding his eyes. "Hey, Mista Bannion, someone's a-comin' down the road, wet's a muskrat, he is."

Chapter II

SUCH AN UNCOMMON HAPPENING as a stranger arriving in the midst of a violent thunderstorm brought Bannion to the door and he, alongside Ransom, watched the horseman coming down the road. His horse was apparently spent, for the animal was plodding slowly and the man on his back was slouched forward as much as possible to keep the rain from his face. Ransom, with this new interest in view, abandoned any thought of leaving. A stranger would be fair game to stand him a drink and he watched with interest while the horseman rode up to the store, jumped down, and wound his reins around the hitching rail. With one bound he cleared the steps and entered the door of the store. Bannion, in the meantime, had lighted two tallow dips and stuck them in iron candlesticks on the counter. Their flickering yellow light illuminated the interior with Bannion standing behind the counter, Fronie crouched on the floor beside it in the shadows, and Ransom lounging in the doorway.

"Right bad weather," Ransom greeted the stranger as he entered. "You're soppin' wet. Come to the right place tho'. Nothin like a good swig o' corn ter keep yo' from gittin' the ague," he said hopefully.

The stranger was a tall, well-set-up, handsome fellow in his early twenties. He wore a long, shoulder-caped coat of fawn-colored broadcloth, darker now on the shoulders and skirt where the rain had soaked it but retaining its original color under the arms. He took off his white beaver hat, shaking it to remove as much of the water as possible, and stamped his feet to get the water out of his boots. Looking at Bannion as though requesting permission, he removed the sodden outer garment, disclosing a handsome suit of bottle-green broadcloth and a waistcoat of flowered satin over which a heavy gold chain glinted in the candlelight.

"I do declare." He smiled at Ransom and then transferred his greeting to Bannion. "When I started out this morning the sun was a-shinin'. Purty a day's yo'd want to see. Wonder if'n yo' got a blanket o' somethin' I kin put over my saddlebags 'n kindly pertect them. Ain' mindin' so much about the horse; it warm out 'n he's used to weather."

Bannion had nothing that would serve and said so.

"How fur yo' come?" he asked.

"Fifty o' sixty mile, I reckon," the young man replied. "Nearer sixty. Came from over beyond Highbank." He smiled good-naturedly, showing a row of white, even teeth.

"Quite a piece," Bannion agreed.

"Only jest a-startin' out. Cain' git home till tomorrow night, if then," the youth replied.

"Whur yo' live at, a-comin' so fur?" Ransom was surly. His immediate jealousy of this well-attired young man who was apparently so much more affluent and better-looking than he was manifest.

"Live over to Natchez," explained the young man. "My papa he's a doctor there 'n' he got a plantation nigh to there. Been a-visitin' at my uncle's over in Highbank. Got any whisky? I shore a needin' some after all that rain. This the first place I seen since the rain started up."

Bannion assured him that the whisky was available and in proof poured out a cup and set it down on the counter. The young man eyed it a moment and, noticing Ransom's slavering lips, said, with an all-encompassing wave of his hand, "Whisky fur this young gentleman 'n' yourself."

Bannion eagerly drew two more cups of whisky from

19

the barrel. Handing one to Ransom, he waved at an up-turned keg for the stranger to sit on and a nail on the wall for his wet coat. For a moment, they all sipped their drinks, Ransom tickled to see that his cup was full this time. Bannion paused in his drinking and asked, "How long yo' bin out—from home, I mean?"

"Nigh onto three months," the youth replied casually. "Yes, three months, thereabouts. Mayhap yo' know my uncle where I bin a-visitin'. Name o' Thomas Verder, same's mine. I named after him but everyone a-callin' me Tommy. My uncle's place called Dove Cote Plantation. Ever hear o' Dove Cote?"

Bannion denied any acquaintance, first asking Ransom if he had heard of such a place. At Ransom's disavowal, he answered, "Too fur; too fur 'way. I knowin' everyone 'roun' here but not so fur's Highbank. Name Verder, yo' say?" He rubbed his hand over his bald pate as if trying to recall the name. "Nope, don' know him, I reckon." Then, bethinking himself of the proprieties, he pointed to Ransom, "That there's Ransom Lightfoot, 'n' my name's Bannion."

Tommy acknowledged the introductions with a nod to each of them, and all three continued to drink in silence. As soon as one cup was finished, Tommy asked for them to be refilled, but on the fourth cup he felt himself grow-ing tipsy. He wandered to the door, sickened by the stench of the store and the seminal odor of Ransom's clothes, breathed in deeply of the damp air, and then returned to his seat. The weather showed no signs of clearing, and although the vividness of the lightning and the rumble of the thunder were not so great, the rain continued to pour down. Tommy Verder had never drunk much alco-hol and the drinks under his belt had all but staggered him. They were, however, he assured himself, merely medicinal, purely prophylactic against a cold or lung fever which might result from the soaking he had under-gone. He realized, when he started the fourth cup, that he had drunk enough but he wanted to prove himself as much of a man as the other two and the amount of whisky they had consumed seemed to have no effect on

20

either Ransom or Bannion. Tommy tossed off his fourth cup and immediately ordered a refill all around.

Now, and apparently for the first time, he noticed Fronie sitting in the corner beside the counter, her eyes glued hungrily on him. Tommy rose and took a step nearer to Fronie, squinting down at her in the shadows, then moved the candlestick over on the edge so that the light shone in her face.

"Right nice piece yo' got there." He turned to Bannion. "She your'n?"

Banion nodded in reply.

"She mos' white, ain' she?" Tommy appraised her. "Don' suppose she a virgin tho'."

"Jes what we a-talkin' 'bout afore yo' came in. She shore is," Bannion boasted. "I ain' got the bucks 'n' ain' asked no white man 'roun here to mount her yet. Ransom here, jest a-pinin' ter rip her open but I a-tellin' him he cain' 'cause he her uncle."

Tommy set his cup down on the counter and took a step toward the girl, who stared back at him. The memory of her recent escapade with Ransom was so pleasant that she hoped another such might be forthcoming from this handsome stranger. Tommy reached behind and hitched his keg over nearer to the counter while Bannion, as much for the sake of discipline as to stimulate Tommy's interest in the girl, commanded her. "Yo', Fronie, stand up 'n' show yo'self to the young masta. I got to thresh yo' to teach yo' some manners?"

Fronie advanced slowly toward Tommy, her gaze still fixed on him, but now a strange edge of fear mingled with her admiration for him. Tommy reached out toward her but she drew back from him until Bannion rasped out her name and she stood still. Tommy leaned forward, grasped her upper arm and drew her closer to him, pulling her in between his knees. His procedure, so similar to Ransom's only a few minutes before, led her to expect a like experience, and she placed one hand expectantly on Tommy's knee. Tommy's hands, however, followed a different path from those of Ransom's and ascended from her belly to her breasts. His disappointment showed on his face.

"She pretty goddam small. Ain' titted out 'tall; no bigger'n apples, they ain'."

"What in hell yo' 'spectin'?" Bannion bristled. "She still young, not more'n thirteen. Cain' 'spect watermelons on a young un like that. 'Sides, she got too much white blood to be big-titted."

Tommy shrugged but returned his hands to her arms, felt them, and then ran his hand up along the back of her dress to feel her back. "Back 'pears right clean, I reckon."

"Ain' never been whaled." Bannion's tone was conciliatory now that Tommy's investigation was proceeding. "Never been more'n switched a bit 'roun' the legs with a willow withe. She a good gal, that Fronie is. Ain' never caused no trouble. Right smart too, she is."

Casually, as it were, Tommy picked up a splint from a broken basket which was lying on the floor and, still holding the girl by one hand, he caught the hem of her garment with the stick as if he feared contamination, and lifted the skirt to her shoulders to enable him to see her back for himself. There seemed to be no such fear of contamination with the flesh as with the garment, for Tommy, releasing her hand, ran his fingers down over her back, her buttocks, and her thighs. He felt again the flat, boy-like belly, letting his fingers linger for an instant, but did not explore nor handle her further.

Ransom, from his seat on the keg, clenched his fists and scowled in anger. That another should touch that very flesh he had so recently fondled and which had, in turn, fondled him, rekindled his quiescent desires, and now his lust for Fronie was increased by his hatred for this stranger. That he was doing everything Ransom desired to do and doing it boldly with Bannion's full approval angered Ransom even more. He could have willingly killed this handsome stranger who was so casually examining Fronie, and the whisky in Ransom lent him further impetus to strangle the fellow. Bannion, quite unaware of Ransom's fury, to which he would have been indifferent even had he noticed it, waited for some word of praise or approbation from Tommy. When none was

22

forthcoming, he felt he had to justify in some way his property's good qualities.

"Right nice, ain' she?" he blurted out. "That is, she a-goin' ter be when she asses out 'n' meats up some." Still receiving no answer, he pointed to Fronie. "Whyn't yo' shuck her down? Take off her dress. Yo', Fronie, peel outen your clothes."

The girl was reaching for the only button on her single garment to obey her master's command when Tommy interrupted.

"Wait till I'm comin' back," he explained, " 'n' I'll strip her down then. Thinkin' I mayhap buy her fer the bride I'm a-goin' ter marry me up with. Gotta know if'n she a virgin. Twon't do no good to examine her now, 'cause even if she's pure now, she might get pleasured 'fore I get back. Main reason I a-buying it 'cause she a virgin 'n' if'n she ain' when I come back, ain' thinkin' ter buy her. 'Sides, ain' got 'nuff money ter buy her anyway. Onct I get home, my pappy'll give me plenty but now ain' got too much."

Bannion, believing the sale was falling through, grew angry with Tommy, but he could take his spleen out only Fronie. He grasped her dress by its neck, where it was buttoned, and yanked it off, the loose button coming off in his hand. He slapped her hard on both cheeks and upbraided her with, "When I say peel, yo' peel." He flung the garment to the floor and turned her around to face Tommy. "There she be. Look her over."

Ransom leaned forward, sucking in his breath. "Right purty, ain' she?" He stared at her round-eyed. "Do believe she the purtiest li'l wench I ever did see."

Bannion thanked him with a look of gratitude for his praise, but Fronie burst into tears. She was unabashed at her nudity; up until six months before, she had gone about entirely naked and, as was the custom, had been given a garment only at her menarche. But her cheeks stung from Bannion's slaps and she was unaccustomed to being the center of so much attention.

She has little concept of what it meant to be sold. She realized that it meant going away with the buyer and having a new master, but how these things came about

23

or why she did not know. She did not think it would bring about her separation from her master and mistress or from her mother, and even if she had, it would have been a matter of indifference to her. The life she lived was dull and humdrum. She had never enjoyed any consideration and knew that she was a nigger and a slave —a domestic animal—living at the whim of her master, whom she must obey because there was no other choice. Heretofore such matters had bothered her but little. She had known no other status and aspired to nothing better. Now, from the words and actions of the white man, Fronie gathered hints that she might be sold to this strange gentleman and have to go away with him. This, she considered, despite her show of tears, would be much to her liking. Perhaps he would let her do what Ransom had just taught her. Ransom's heat still lingered in her fingers, but now, looking at him who had been a paragon of beauty with his yellow hair, she could not but compare him to the elegant Tommy Verder, whom she found a thousand times handsomer. She had been exhilarated and ecstatic at what she had done to Ransom, but Tommy's fingering of her breasts had produced an even greater rapture. Now all her desire for Ransom was gone, swallowed up in her admiration for this splendid newcomer with his fine clothes. She was disappointed that she had not pleased him, for she felt that if she had, he would have allowed her to do the same to him as she had to Ransom.

"How much yo' a-wantin' fer her?" Verder seemed interested enough to inquire but quite indifferent as to the answer.

Bannion lost no time in answering. "Seven hundred about, I reckon. That's cheap too but I a-needin' the money. Dirt cheap, that is, her a guaranteed virgin 'n' all."

"Wouldn't take no less?"

Bannion shook his head decisively. "Cain'. Niggers a-goin' right up 'n' this one's a particular fancy. Quadroon, she is."

"Bring more in foal," Ransom said. He was still hoping for the opportunity that was fast slipping away.

Bannion shook his head. "Her maidenhead wuth all o' fifty dollars. Sucker not wuth more'n ten dollars maybe. Nope, she wuth more'n like she a virgin. Wuth fifty dollars ter any man ter bust that."

Tommy Verder took a few minutes to consider the matter, turning Fronie slowly around while he looked at her. She was rather a pretty piece of flesh at that, and the fact that she had never been exposed to a man interested him. By giving her to his bride as a wedding present, he could kill two birds with one stone—make a handsome present to his wife and enjoy Fronie himself. He wanted her and that meant that he must have her. But the unfortunate fact of the matter was that he did not have enough money with him to buy her and, being a stranger, his credit would be no good with Bannion. Finally he nodded his head, as if he had settled the matter in his own mind, and looked up at Bannion.

"Tell yo' what I'll do, Mista Bannion. I'll be a-comin' back this way in 'bout a couple o' months. Like'n I told yo', ridin' back to get married up wid my cousin—the gal o' my Uncle Thomas. Like ter git me a nice young wench for her fer a weddin' present—a light-skinned one such as this. But it got ter be a virgin and pure-like to kindly wait on my wife. Wouldn't buy it if'n it was not."

"Thinkin' she ain' a-goin' ter be pure long onct yo' a-gittin' her," Ransom said, seeing his dream being shattered before his very eyes.

"His property once he buys it," Bannion retorted, hoping to silence Ransom. "Kin do wid it what he likes. Cain' blame him much tho' if'n he wants ter snatch that maidenhead—it mighty temptatious."

"Mighty temptatious, I agree, Mista Bannion, mighty temptatious." The whisky and the desire for the girl were working on Tommy, but he continued to pretend that he was interested in Fronie only as a wedding present to his wife. "But I ain' aimin' ter bust it."

"The hell yo' ain'." Ransom rose from the keg where he had been sitting and walked over to where the naked girl stood and placed his arm around her shoulder as though to protect her.

Fronie, however, wanted no protection from Ransom.

25

She had eyes for no one but Tommy. Remembering how her owner had commanded her to stay away from Ransom, she slipped out from under his arm and walked over to stand beside Tommy, hoping he might caress her. But he, not trusting her propinquity and the desires it might engender, disregarded her and merely ordered another drink for himself and the two men, a gesture which caused Ransom's anger to disappear. He too came over to stand beside Tommy. When Tommy reached for his cup of whisky, his hand was placed directly in the light of the candles, and Bannion and Ransom noticed a strange deformity; the hand appeared excessively broad. Bannion restrained his curiosity, but Ransom was brash enough to ask, "What ail yore hand, Mista? Appear like it ain' like other folks'."

Tommy smiled, somewhat proud of his deformity, and spread his fingers as he replied, "I got me six fingers on my right hand. Yes suh, six fingers! Count 'em! Each one perfect, too." He set down the cup and held up his hand so that the phenomenon might be more readily seen.

Bannion, seeing that Tommy was not averse to a discussion of such an abnormality, said with proper awe, "Well by darn, I never, no, I never saw the likes. Six fingers on one hand."

"Runs in the family," Tommy boasted. "Mos' o' the menfolk in our family has six fingers. My grandpappy he had 'n' my Uncle Thomas, he the one I bin stayin' with and the one who I a-goin' ter marry up wid his gal, he got six on one hand too." Picking up the cup, he walked over to the door, moving slowly so that he wouldn't stagger. "Seem like it lettin' up," he said, studying the sky. "Reckon I kin be goin' now." He hung onto the doorjamb to steady himself.

"Jes' when yo' plannin' ter come back this way?" Bannion asked. "Bin a-thinkin' I cain' really promise yo' nothing 'bout the wench here. Had me some offers fer her 'n' no tellin' when I might sell her 'n' 'sides, she might get raped out in them woods. Cain' tie her up jest ter keep her fer yo'."

"Got ter stay home long 'nuff ter have the tailor make me some new trogs ter git married up in. Take six weeks o' a couple o' months. Bin thinkin' I might go down ter N'Orleans ter find me a tailor. Them up in Natchez ain' up ter snuff."

"Cain' promise yo' nothin' 'bout this wench here," Bannion repeated. The prospect of a sale was uppermost in his mind, and he was determined not to let Tommy get away without some definite commitment. In order to detain him longer, he took the cup away from Tommy and drew him another drink, filling his own and Ransom's cups.

"Mayhap yo' kin make it a little cheaper? Seven hundred seems mighty high, her so little 'n' all."

'Ain' costive fer one like this'n tho'," Bannion rebutted. "She bring yo' a right good bright-skinned sucker every year if'n yo breed her yo'self o' get a white man ter do it." Bannion set his cup down on the counter, pursed his lips, then, as if he had had a sudden inspiration, he announced, " 'Course, if yo' was to make a deposit on her like'n ter bind the sale, I could consider it, but shore a-goin' ter be hard to keep her virgin. Lotsa randy young studs like this here Ransom 'round here. Look, Mista Verder, I ain' being inquisitive 'n' pokin' my nose inter yore business, don' think that, but jest how much a deposit could yo' make ter bind the bargain?"

Tommy gulped his drink, almost retching now at the taste of the whisky. He was anxious to get away, not wanting these men to see him sick, but he was also anxious to get Fronie. He pulled out his purse, opened it, and dumped its contents out onto the counter. The gold pieces glinted in the candlelight and, one by one, Tommy's fingers put them back into his purse as he counted.

"Got me 'bout a hundred dollars here," he said. "Be needin' 'bout twenty at least ter git me home 'n' wantin' ter stop in Natchez 'n' git me some presents fer my family. Gives yo' the rest I will, ter bind the bargain, 'n' I pay yo' the balance when I comes back ter fetch her." Once again he dumped his purse on the counter and counted out the gold eagles and silver. "There 'tis." He put the purse back in his pocket. "But she gotta be pure when I comes back. If'n she ain' yo' got ter give me back my money."

"Tell yer what, boy." Bannion reached for the money, noting Ransom's eyes on it, slitted, greedy, and jealous. "Got a proposition ter make yo'. Cain' guarantee yo' nothing 'bout that wench come two months from now. But why don' yo' bust it right now. If'n yo' a-goin' ter give it ter yore bride, shore be right nice ter have it in foal. Births yo' a nice bright-skinned sucker 'n' be a play child fer yore own child when it comes along. Yore bride never suspect yo' sired it, yo' telling her yo' picked it up 'n' it already knocked up when yo' bought it. 'Course cain' tell if'n it'll take, jest once, but if it do, yo' got a better present fer yore bride. Then too, if'n yo' don' come back fer some reason o' other, I'd have me a pup outa yo'. Ought ter be a goddam good-lookin' one outa yo' 'n' her."

Fronie had understood enough of the conversation to realize that in some way Bannion wanted this young man for her, and as much to please him as to please herself, she insinuated herself between Tommy and Ransom, facing Tommy. Absently he pulled her to him and she snuggled against him.

"Ransom here 'n' I we'll go out," Bannion continued. "Rain's stopped now. Kin take yore coat 'n' spread it out on the floor. Come on, yo' Ransom, let's get t'hell outa here." Bannion dragged Ransom away from the counter and pushed him out the door, closing the door behind him.

"Ain' a-goin' ter stay here no longer," Ransom shouted over his shoulder as he jumped on his small roan gelding. "Ain' fair, yo' a-sellin' it to that stranger 'n' yo' knowin' how I wanted ter bust it. Ain' fair, I tell yo', 'n' me thinkin' yo' 'n' I friends. Ain' never comin' here no more. Ain' never speakin' ter yo' 'gain, I ain'.'" He slapped the horse's rump and galloped away.

Bannion stood on the lower step laughing. "Yo'll be back," he hollered at Ransom's disappearing figure. "Yo' ain' got no other place ter go 'n' ain' nobody'd put up wid yo' if'n yo' did have." He waited until Ransom was out of sight and then walked slowly, so that his steps would make no noise, around the store to where a chink in the logs gave him a view of the candlelit interior. He stood there for a long time, fascinated, hearing Fronie's screams which turned into little whimperings and then subsided. All in all, he might have been there about an hour when he heard the sound of horses out in front of the store. Walking around front with the air of one who had been on some errand of importance, he was surprised to see Ransom and his elder brother Jonas sitting on their horses before the store. It was the first time that he had ever seen the two brothers together. Jonas had never been known to go anywhere with Ransom before. He was considerably older than Ransom and had never wanted him tagging along. But before Bannion could express his astonishment at seeing Ransom back so soon and in the company of his brother, Jonas slid down off his horse and came over to Bannion.

"Ransom here"—he gestured with his thumb in the direction of his brother "—he say he jes' had words wid yo', Mista Bannion. Cain' have that, we bein' neighbors 'n' friends 'n' all. A-bringin' Ransom back to apologize, I am. He too quick-tempered. He's right sorry now, Mista Bannion, ain' yo', Ransom?"

"Right sorry, I am, Mista Bannion. Jonas here he guv me fifteen cents 'n' aimin' ter buy us a drink 'n' one fer yo' too, Mista Bannion, jest ter show yo' I ain' a-holdin' no hard feelin's."

"Cain' go in now, that young Verder he ain' a-finished wid Fronie yet, I don' think." '

"He a-comin' out now." Jonas pointed to the door which was opening and to Tommy Verder coming down the steps.

"Be a-leavin' yo' now, Mista Bannion." Tommy was dressed in his coat and had his hat on. "Was a-thinkin' ter ask yo' fer a receipt fer that money but ain' necessary. Gentleman's 'greement, what? 'N' besides, Mista Lightfoot, he a witness that I paid yo'."

"Gentleman's 'greement," Bannion concurred. "How 'bout 'nother drink?"

"Thank yo' kindly, Mista Bannion, but I'm right anxious ter git started. Got me a lot a miles ter cover so

29

I'll be startin' if'n yo' don' mind. Mayhap yo' kin tell me the right turns ter take ter git ter Tahallawata. Don' want to waste no time takin' the wrong roads."

"Yo' must be the young Mista Verder my brother Ransom a-tellin' me 'bout." Jonas stepped up, smiling. "Ransom he say he not very perlite to yo' 'n' I a-aimin' ter teach him a lesson. Roads a mite confusin' next ten miles o' so. Tell yo' what, Mista Verder. Ransom 'n' I'll ride alongside yo' 'n' keep yo' on the right road fer a spell."

"That's right kindly o' yo' boys," Bannion said, a bit puzzled by Jonas' civility but accepting it.

"Right kindly 'n' appreciated," Tommy said as he mounted his horse.

Bannion waved at their retreating figures until they were out of sight. Reaching in his pocket and fingering the gold pieces, he reentered the store. Fronie had put her dress back on, but was crouched on the floor beside the counter crying.

"What in hell yo' bawlin' fer?" Bannion asked, not unkindly.

"Hurts, I do. Hurts somethin' awful."

"Yo'll git over it." Bannion, in an excess of generosity, gave her a piece of horehound candy. "Don' wonder yo' a-hurtin'. That Verder boy he shore bust yo' good. Better yo' go down ter the crik 'n' wash that blood off'n yore legs."

Dumbly she obeyed him.

Chapter III

THE FOLLOWING DAY Ransom did not appear at the store as he was wont to do, and Bannion wondered at his absence. He was eager to talk over the stranger's visit, his tentative sale of Fronie, and Ransom's and Jonas' departure with Verder. He felt that there must have been some conversation between the three as they rode along together and he was curious about what Verder might have said about him, about Fronie, and about his return. It was Jonas, who however, arrived, seemingly embarrassed, in the late afternoon. He carried a jug which he asked to have filled with whisky. Bannion eyed him sharply before drawing it.

"Got money?" he demanded. "Yo' got money ter pay?" The fact that neither of the Lightfoot brothers ever had any money prompted Bannion's distrust.

"Hell, yes." Jonas assumed an air of belligerence to cover his embarrassment. "Got money I have—plenty." He casually tossed a gold eagle on the counter as though it were an everyday occurrence.

Bannion stared at the gold piece, quite unable to believe he was seeing it, but nevertheless he filled the jug and made change from the wooden box which served him as a till and from a greasy leather bag he carried in his pocket. His curiosity, however, got the better of him, and he could not resist asking, "Whur yo' git all

31

that money, Jonas Lightfoot, whereat it a-comin' from?" The Lightfoots were about the most impoverished of any white folks in the community; the family resources were nothing at all and the few acres on which they lived supplied the family with food and little else. Old Sam Lightfoot, the boys' father, had been a hard worker, and the elder, but now deceased, brother had followed somewhat in his father's footsteps, but the two younger brothers, Ransom and Jonas, had never been known to do a tap of work unless forced to it by their mother. Consequently the fact that Jonas was now buying whisky with a gold piece surprised Bannion and set him to wondering.

"Ransom 'n' me, we stole that foal my mama's bin a-raisin' 'n' sold it. She ain' missed it yet, a-thinkin' it out ter pasture. Hope yo' ain' a-goin' ter tell her."

"Reckon not. Ain' no goddam business o' mine what yo' 'n' Ransom do."

Jonas drew the corncob stopper from the jug and raised it to his mouth for a long swig of its contents, then replaced the cob and wiped his mouth on his shirtsleeve.

"Yo' 'n' Ransom git that Verder feller started on the right road last night?" Bannion asked.

Jonas nodded briefly in reply and then attempted to change the subject. "Ransom 'n' me we ain' mad no more. He's bigger'n me but I'm the older 'n' I kin still lick him anytime I wants. Ransom he all beef 'n' not much spunk. Sometimes I a-thinkin' he not right smart. Thinkin' he touches hisself too much. Heerd that makes a man soft in the head. But he helped me sell that foal so's we friends now. Be comin' in ter see yo' soon. Ransom he got a tech o' misery today so I takin' him this corn ter make him feel better. Soon's he git well, we come." He tucked the jug under one arm and departed.

Ransom did not come to the store that day nor the following day, nor the day after that. There was no obligation for him to come but his visitations were so habitual that Bannion wondered at his absence. While the storekeeper did not particularly care for Ransom, he missed him when he didn't come and worried over Ransom's illness. Left alone too much, he became irascible and vented his spleen on Fronie, slapping her for the smallest carelessness or peccadillo, cursing her and threatening her with the switch without adequate reason.

When at length Ransom did appear, he was accompanied by Jonas, who supplied a kind of moral support for his failure to show up for so long. Ransom assumed a bravado in an effort to hide the sheepishness he felt at his absence from his usual haunt, for he had a feeling that Bannion would not believe his excuse of sickness. They both swaggered into the store, Jonas carrying the whisky jug to have it refilled. Bannion this time did not ask if he had money to pay for the whisky, since he realized there was sufficient change from his first purchase to replenish the jug a half-dozen times or more. However, to Bannion's even greater surprise, Ransom this time produced another gold eagle which he threw down on the counter in exchange for the whisky Jonas had just purchased. Bannion was unable to make the change and unwilling to extend credit to either of the brothers, despite the fact that both had demonstrated their recent affluence.

"Whur all this money a-comin' from? Yo' boys must hev struck a gold mine out on yore place," the storekeeper asked with an attempt at banter. "Yo'uns got more money'n me. Ain' got 'nuff change fer this a-much."

Jonas dug into his pocket and drew out the change from his previous purchase, saying to his brother, "Yo' got ter 'member, Randy, that I paid las' time 'n' now this time, too. 'N' if'n yo' don' 'member, I a-goin' ter give yo' a clubbin' that'll shore put yo' in mind."

"I ain' fergettin'." Ransom pocketed his gold piece and drew a thick silver watch from his pocket which he passed over to Jonas. "Yo' kin tote my watch fer warrantee ter make sure I goin' ter pay yo' back. Yo' always drink more'n I do anyway."

"Watch won' do me no good nohow," the elder brother said, pocketing it nevertheless. "Yo' knowin' I cain' read time 'n' the goddam watch ain' no good 'n' yo' done lost the key ter wind it up with."

Bannion leaned over the counter and pulled Jonas'

33

hand out of his pocket with the watch along with it. "Where yo' git that watch? Ain' never seen yo' totin' it afore now."

"Heired it, I did, from my grandpappy when he die," Ransom explained. "Got me a gol' chain fer it, too. Belonged to my grandpappy, it did, my mammy's pappy. He a Ridgecomb, yo' know, 'n' come from a right rich fam'ly. He learnt me to read time real good ere he died; that's how come he lef' it ter me. Los' the key tho' 'n' cain' wind it up." Ransom's answer seemed adequate to Bannion, who remembered that Mrs. Lightfoot had indeed come from a well-known family.

"Whur-at that Fronie wench?" Ransom sought to change the subject.

"How come yo' askin' 'bout her? She sold, she is. Hopin' she a-knocked up, too. Yo' knowin' all 'bout it. Yo' right here when that Verder feller come. Wantin' yo' ter keep 'way from her now 'n' not plaguing her ter touch yo' 'gain. Tain' fittin'; she bein' sold 'n' goin' inter a nice family 'n' all. What her new masta a-goin' ter say if'n she go 'round doin' that ter all the menfolks whereat he a-takin' her."

Jonas pointed to Ransom with derision. "Randy he right disappointed, he is. He always a-sayin' as how he goin' ter bust her open one o' these days. Wishin' he mighta done it, too. High time he started pesterin' wenches."

"How yo' a-knowin' that she sol'? He ain' come back fur 'er." Ransom resented Jonas' belittling of him and the fact that his long-laid plans in regard to Fronie had gone awry. "Think she git in foal from that little pesterin' that Verder fellow gave her? Didn' look ter me that he had any sap in him 'tall. He so goddam ree-fined 'n' everything."

"She sold all right. Got me the deposit on her."

Ransom pooh-poohed Bannion. "He say he a-goin' ter buy her. He ain' a-comin' back, he ain'. All that big talk 'bout his a-goin' ter N'Orleans 'cause they ain' no tailor good 'nuff in Natchez. He ain' a-goin' ter do nothin', he ain'. He off to N'Orleans ter git himself a wench better'n Fronie fer what he owin' yo'. Got purtier wenches'n Fronie 'n N'Orleans—purtier'n any in these parts."

Bannion shook his head, his lips pursed. "Reckon him an honest feller, real honest, the way him dressed so fine 'n' so nice mannered 'n' everythin'. 'Sides, he shore to come back, 'n' he a-hopin' he got her swolled up and she a-havin' a purty light-skinned sucker fer him."

"I'm a-tellin' yo' that son-o'-a-bitch not a-comin' back 'n' yo' mark my words he ain',", Ransom insisted. "Betcha he ain' never comin' back," he repeated, and then took the whisky jug from Jonas, withdrew the cob, took a long swallow, and passed it to Bannion, who drank and wiped the mouth of the jug with his hand before passing it back to Jonas. It passed back and forth between the brothers several times, Bannion politely refusing another drink while he studied the brothers. Even more specious than their sudden affluence was their new mutual amicability, for Bannion knew there had been bad blood between them for a long time. Possibly it was the money that had healed the breech, or again maybe it was Ransom's growing maturity which had brought him out of the smaller-brother class and made him a peer of Jonas'. Whatever it was, the brothers appeared to be friendly and Bannion was pleased. It meant more trade for him if the boys had money and came together regularly.

The boys were preparing to leave the store when Bannion walked out from behind his counter where he had caught a glimpse of Ransom's feet. "Bin a-gittin' yo'self new boots too?" he asked quite casually, knowing that Ransom usually went bare-footed.

Ransom replied with greater alacrity than was his wont. "Hell, them ain' new. They my dress-up boots, but my mama a-thinkin' since I had the misery I'd 'a' better wear 'em. Hurt my feet somethin' awful they do. Ain' worn 'em in a coon's age."

"Look like new." Bannion studied them. " 'Pears like they jes' as good quality as them that Verder feller had on."

"Ain' new tho'," Ransom insisted. "Goddam nigger he make 'em too tight. Cain' hardly git 'em on my feet. I'd give 'em ter Jonas here only he got feet jes's big as mine. Anyway he not a-needin' them afore winter. Barefoot better in summer."

35

Bannion, still staring at the boots, asked, "What nigger make 'em? Whur at 'roun' here is a nigger shoemaker? Who got un'."

Ransom sought to evade answering. It dawned on him that he should not have mentioned the shoemaker lest he have to identify him and prompt Bannion to make further inquiry about him. "Oh, a feller down Six Mile way own him, a-sayin' the bastard kin make boots. Don' never git him ter make none; he cain' cobble wuth a damn; see what he done to mine."

To avoid further conversation about the boots, Ransom picked up the whisky jug and signaled to Jonas. "Come on, Jon, le's get goin'. Le's get home 'n' go out in the corncrib 'n' get drunker'n a couple o' polecats, yo'n' me." As Jonas turned to follow him, Ransom regarded him with a certain amount of pride—the younger brother at last admitted to the company of the elder. "Jonas 'n' me we a-doin' things tergether these days. He sayin' mayhap he take me over ter Barnsville some day ter see that widder woman over there what charges two dollars. He say it wuth it, tho'."

"Glad ter hear yo' two boys so friendly like, mighty glad. That the way brothers ought to be; not a-fightin' 'n' a-feudin'." Bannion's words were a mere cover-up for his thoughts. The knowledge that the boys had money in their pockets provoked him to try to find a way for them to spend it to his advantage. He had been certain that he would get all of it from the sale of the whisky, but the mention of the Barnsville widow, who was known to sell her favors, made him fearful that someone else might get a share of it. Outside of whisky there was only one thing that would tempt the boys to spend their money—Fronie. "Don' see no sense in yo'-all a-hurryin' today. Plenty o' time fer yo' ter git drunk. Here, let me give yo' a free one. Got something ter talk ter yo' 'bout."

Ransom was immediately suspicious. "If'n it that young squirt what bought Fronie, ain' no sense a-talkin' 'bout him. He ain' a-comin' back."

Bannion proffered the two full cups across the counter and then drew one for himself.

" 'Course he a-comin' back. He got money tied up in

Fronie 'n' a sucker already seeded in her. Leastwise I a-hopin' he has. He a-goin' ter be right disappointed if'n he come back 'n' find she ain' took. But cain' tell jes' that one time he pestered her if'n she took or not. Mayhap his sap not good like'n yo' say. Could be that if'n he come back 'n' finds she ain' knocked up, he ain' going ter take her. So I bin a-thinkin'."

Ransom was far more interested in Fronie than he was in the liquor. That he had never had a woman and had to listen to Jonas' bragging about the wenches he had enjoyed was always a source of irritation to him. Then too, he had arrived at an age where his healthy body demanded one. "What yo' bin a-thinkin'?" he asked.

"Bin a-thinkin' yo' two boys might make sure she knocked up good 'n' proper. Then when he come back he'll be shore ter buy her 'cause he shore it's his own sucker 'n' even if he don', I gets me a good light-skinned sucker ter sell. 'Course I know it ain' right, Jonas 'n' yo' a-bein' her uncles, but if'n he take her, shore ain' my fault if'n the sucker have two heads o' be beast-like, 'n' if'n he don' come back 'n' it not right, we kin drown it. Was thinkin' tho' I should charge yo' somethin' fer pleasurin'. Yo' pays me a dollar 'n' yo' kin both have her till nightfall. Ain' nobody goin' ter be 'round till then anyway 'n' I kin padlock the door. 'Sides, that's a helluva lot cheaper'n that widder over ter Barnsville 'n' Fronie a lot purtier, too."

"Yo' pay him a dollar, Jonas," Ransom answered immediately. "Pay him the dollar 'n' yo' go on home 'n' leave me here with Fronie."

"That be only fifty cents." Jonas looked to Bannion for confirmation. "He a-sayin' we kin both have her fer a dollar. If'n only one that only fifty cents. 'Sides, I aimin' ter have her too. Seein' this yore fust time, I'll show yo'."

Bannion nodded in approval, feeling sure now that he had devised a way whereby all the money that the boys had would eventually find its way into his pockets. He came around the counter to put his arm affectionately around Ransom's shoulders. "Jonas right," he said, "Jonas shore right. Make it more interestin', too. Members when I was a young feller like yo'uns me 'n' my brother Bert always used ter pleasure the same wench. One watchin' t'other keeps yer rarin' ter go. Ain' I right, Jonas?"

"He right, Randy," Jonas agreed.

Bannion slapped the boy's shoulder again. "Jes' chargin' yo'uns a flat rate. Don' make no difference ter me how many times yo' boys make it, long's yo' finish by nightfall. Tell yo' what I'll do. Won' charge yo' no extra either. Leave two candles burnin', I will, 'n' yo' kin see right good."

Ransom was convinced. "Whur's Fronie?"

Bannion stuck his head out the door and yelled for her. She appeared at the cabin door and limped across the path that led to the store. "Wha's the matter wid yo'?" he scowled at her as she came up the steps to the store. "What in hell yo' a-limpin' fer?"

"I'se got a misery," she complained. "Hurt I do. That Masta Tommy he 'bused me somethin' awful."

"Well, yo'd better git used ter it. Yo' got somethin' more a-comin' ter yo'. Member what yore mammy said. She said yo' a-goin' ter love it the nex' time. Well this the nex' time 'n' yo'd better like it. Come in here 'n' shuck down." He pulled the girl into the store and waited for her to take off her dress. She stood there in the middle of the floor staring dumbly at Ransom and Jonas who stared back at her. Ransom's tongue encircled his loose lips and Jonas' beady eyes devoured her.

"I'm a-goin' fust," Jonas said. "I'll get her ready fer him." He grinned at Bannion.

"Like hell yo' a-goin' fust." Ransom gulped down his liquor and set his cup on the counter.

"Better that way, boy." Bannion tried to be conciliatory; he didn't want a fight starting now when he had gone to such trouble to arrange things. "Yo' a-goin' ter enjoy it more, Jonas gittin' her primed up fer yo'." He walked out the door and slammed it behind him, snapping the padlock. Once again, he tiptoed around to peer through the chink in the back.

The sun was setting in a blaze of saffron and amethyst when the two brothers knocked on the door to be let out. Bannion unlocked the padlock, his hand outstretched.

Jonas fumbled in his pocket and withdrew the silver dollar and handed it to him.

"Rightly speaking, Mista Bannion, that Randy he ought ter pay more' half. Guess he plumb wore out that wench. Seems like'n she cain' git up off'n the floor."

Randy swaggered down the steps, chest thrown out, shoulders squared, hands on hips.

While Jonas was trying to think of an apt reply Bannion spoke. "How 'bout yo' boys comin' back tomorrow afternoon?"

"We'll be back." Randy mounted his horse and took the jug from Jonas. "Won' we, Jonas."

"We shore as hell will."

Chapter IV

THE COMPATABILITY between Ransom and Jonas Light-foot lasted only as long as their new-found affluence endured. When the money was gone and they were no longer able to purchase jugs of corn or afternoons of sharing Fronie, their companionship ceased and they went their separate ways as before. They had, however, managed to extend their period of indulgence somewhat by turning over to Bannion a gold watch chain and the nearly new pair of boots, after which their credit was exhausted and Jonas abandoned Ransom, who once more took to spending his time at the store, cadging drinks whenever he could find a victim and meeting Fronie in the high grass behind the abandoned blacksmith's shop until her advanced pregnancy made this impossible.

When two months had passed after Verder's visit, Bannion commenced looking for his reappearance as well as signs of Fronie's pregnancy. After the third month had slipped into the fourth, he was reassured by one fact, at least. Fronie was pregnant, or so Netty had informed him. But there were still no signs of Tommy Verder. Every horseman coming down the road from the direction of Natchez caused Bannion to hurry to the doorway of his store, shading his eyes and straining to identify the figure as that of Tommy Verder. But each time he was disappointed and by the fifth month, albeit regretfully, he was inclined to agree with Ransom's prophecy that Verder would never return. His initial reaction of disappointment gave way to a feeling of satisfaction that Verder was not coming back. He had the seventy-five dollars that Verder had paid him; he still had Fronie, whose market value was only slightly depreciated by the fact that she had lost her maidenhead; and he was now assured of the imminent arrival of a light-skinned whelp, sired by either Verder or one of the two Lightfoot brothers. He hoped it was Verder, from whom there would be no taint of consanguinity, but even if it were one of the Lightfoot boys, the baby would at least be light-skinned and the chances were that it would be perfect. Other owners occasionally bred fathers to daughters and sons to mothers with good results, so he was not especially fearful that the whelp would be either feebleminded or deformed. In addition, he had received a fair amount from selling Fronie's favors to the Lightfoot brothers. All in all, he was sure that he was better off than if Verder had returned, paid off the balance, and taken Fronie and her unborn child with him.

"Ain' lackin' fer tail these days, are yo', Randy?" he asked one day.

Ransom admitted as to how he wasn't.

"Bin 'commending yo', I have."

Ransom nodded his head. " 'Preciate it kindly, I do. Seems like every man fer ten miles 'roun' what got a wench 'n' wantin' a good light-skinned sucker off'n her jes' a-beggin' me ter knock her up. Mista Allen over on Deep Spring Plantation he say I the best stud he ever had. Paid me five dollars ter pester ten wenches. Not that I likes 'em black but business is business 'n' what the hell difference it make when it night. Goin' ter be a helluva lot o' yaller-headed bright-skins 'round here come fifteen o' twenty years. Fetch big prices they will. Thinkin' o' goin' inter the stud business, I am. If Mista Allen willin' ter pay me ter stud his wenches, ain' no reason why others cain' too. Mista Macklin o' Elm Grove, he a-sayin' as how he got five o' six wenches just freshened 'n' he allowin' how he'd like ter git some bright-skinned suckers off'n 'em, seein' as how bright-skins're bringin'

41

high prices these days. Mista Allen 'commended me, a-sayin' six o' his wenches already knocked up. What yo' thinkin' I should charge that Mista Macklin? He too far 'way fer me ter come home nights; gotta stay over there two, three weeks, maybe a month ter be sure all them wenches git took good. Goddam hard work too. Studdin's work—ain' like screwin' fer fun. Got ter have me plenty o' rawr eggs, plenty o' goat milk 'n' plenty o' Jamaicy Ginger mixed in it. Heats up the blood it do. How much yo' think I better charge Mista Macklin?"

Bannion scratched his bald pate, considering the matter. He tried to figure out how he might get some commission on the deal but finally gave it up. He did, however, console himself with the fact that the more Ransom got the more he, himself, would eventually get. He was therefore anxious to make the ante as high as possible. "Yo' havin' ter be away from home 'n' all, think yo' should git at least ten dollars, maybe twelve."

"Gotter finish up them four o' Mista Allen's what ain' tooken yet, then goin' ter ride over ter Mista Macklin's. Guess I'd better be gittin' over ter Mista Allen's now 'n' gittin' started on them four. One she right good-lookin' 'n' she hotter'n the hinges o' hell. Yo'd shore enjoy a-seein' me workin' on her. Let yo' look on, I would, but suppose yo' cain' leave the store."

" 'Preciate it." Bannion smiled in approval of Ransom's thoughtfulness. "But jest cain' leave the store. Mayhap yo' kin tell me 'bout it aterwards. Them wenches young 'uns?"

"Not so young's yore Fronie. All birthed suckers afore but they likes it. That Sue Hannah wench I tol' yo' 'bout, she say I better'n any nigger 'n' truth is, mos' wenches like niggers better'n white men fer pleasurin', so I takes it as a real compliment she sayin' I better. Well, got ter git goin'.'" He swung his foot over the horse and turned to wave back to Bannion.

It was about five miles to Deep Spring Plantation along the same road which some nine months before he and Jonas had traversed with Tommy Verder. On the way, Ransom passed a deep ravine and slapped his horse's rump, making the beast break into a gallop as he passed it. He had been tempted many times to turn off the road and follow the course of the ravine a few hundred yards to see what might still be there but had never summoned up sufficient courage to do so. He kept the horse trotting, after its burst of speed, anxious now to get started on his duties at the plantation. Lately Fronie had been no good to him and his healthy body demanded regular satisfaction.

"Yeah, man! A couple of drinks of Mista Allen's corn 'n' then one o' them four wenches what ain' tooken!" It made no difference to Ransom which one it might be.

He turned off the road, between the two high gateposts, now standing awry from the weight of a gate they no longer supported, that marked the entrance to Deep Spring, and rode up the tree-bordered lane that led to the main house, an unpainted, one-story, shake-covered affair with a wide porch covered by the sweep of roof from the high-pitched gable. It looked like a man with a slouch hat down over his eyes. Mrs. Allen and her fat daughter were rocking on the porch, sewing rags together, in preparation of the advent of the itinerant weaver who would turn them into rag rugs.

"Kin I kindly ask if'n Mista Allen, he at home?" Ransom remembered his manners in the presence of white ladies. As he jerked his head in a quick bow, he briefly inventoried the Allen daughter and decided she was too fat and carrot-haired for his taste. "Like pleasurin' a goddam featherbed," he thought, listening to Mrs. Allen's high-pitched, whining voice.

"He down in the harness shop, t'other side o' the quarters, a-mendin' mule harness." She put down the big ball of rag strips she was winding and picked up a palm leaf fan which she wielded vigorously. "Hot, ain' it?" She clove the air with two more strokes of the fan, then asked, "Kin I offer yo' some refreshment?"

Ransom denied the offer with profuse thanks, having no stomach for her raspberry shrub. With another jerky bow, he left them and rode around to the back of the house, his horse slipping in the muck made by thrown-out dishwater, and down a short lane which meandered between a row of slab-sided cabins. In the dusty roadway, he spied two Negro adolescents playing some game of hitting a round object with sticks. A powerful whack of one stick sent the round white object bowling along the ground toward his horse and the animal shied, with an excess of spirit which Ransom had hardly thought possible, rearing up and nearly throwing him.

"Yo' goddam black varmints, what yo' mean a-foolin' roun' this-a-way? If'n yo' wants ter play, git yore foolishness outa the road. Got a good mind ter tell yore masta what all yo' a-doin'—scarin' my horse. He'll have yo' stripped down, shore's hell."

The boys, frightened at the sudden appearance of a stranger and awed by the fact that he was a white man, froze like two ebony carvings. Ransom leaned down from his horse and squinted at the object which they had been hitting. He called one of the boys over and ordered him to pick it up and hold it so that Ransom could study it. It was, as he had suspected, a skull, and by the teeth it looked like a human skull. Through the gaping eyeholes he could see crawling insects and dirt, although the outside was bleached white.

"Whur-at yo' git that thin'?" he asked the boy who held it.

"Foun' it," the boy mumbled. He was extremely emaciated, with a long thin neck and arms like pipestems.

Ransom lashed out with the willow withe which he used on his horse and caught the boy across the mouth. "When yo' answers a white man, yo' says 'masta', don' yo'?"

"Yes suh, masta suh." The boy tried to wipe away the sting from his face with the back of one hand. "We done foun' it 'n' thinkin' we kin use it ter play with. Don' belong ter nobody, it don'. Foun' it out 'n the woods."

"Whur?" Ransom demanded.

"Up the road a piece." The boy gesticulated, the skull clutched in his long, bony fingers. "Up yonder in that there ravine. Me'n' Tadpole, we foun' it. I tol' him not ter take it but he did. It Tadpole's fault, masta suh."

"Ain'!" The other youth, smaller but stockier, defended
44

himself. "It all yore idea, Yantree. It yo' what said le's take it. He did, masta suh, he shore did."

"Don' make no nevverminds," Ransom replied, relieving them both of responsibility with a wave of his hand. "Yo' find anythin' else thar?"

"Lotsa bones all 'round," the boy called Tadpole answered, looking up and beyond Ransom to where a tall, spare man, clad in loose butternut trousers and a soiled shirt, came riding down the lane.

"Howdy, Ransom." The man reined up his horse. "Pleasured ter see yo, I am. What a-goin' on with these varmints here? That Yantree boy he always a-gettin' inter trouble. If'n they a-sassin' yo', I'll strip the meat right off'n their bones, only ain' much on that Yantree's bones. Skinny runt, ain' he, 'n' him a-eatin' like a horse."

Ransom was willing to make light of the whole matter but Yantree, anxious now to be the center of attraction, held up the skull for Allen to see and, wishing to exculpate himself, he again protested his innocence. "We jes' foun' it, Masta Allen suh. Me 'n' Tadpole jes' found it. Didn' think ter skeer this masta's horse wid it, masta suh; jes' a-playin' we was."

"What ter hell yo' got thar, Yantree?" Allen demanded.

"It's a skull, look like ter me," Ransom answered for the boy. "He say he fin' it down in some ravine nearby. Say they's a lot o' bones down there, too. Yo' think it 'pears like a human skull, Mista Allen?"

"Cain' tell." Allen took the object from Yantree and examined it. "Jes' cain' tell if'n it human o' nigger. Them teeth tho', so good 'n' strong, they don' look like human teeth ter me. Look more like nigger teeth. All there; ain' none missin'. If'n it a white man, must be young but if'n it a nigger, cain' tell 'cause them bastards always got good teeth even when they gits older." He nodded his head appraisingly. "Would say, howsomever, that it 'pears like it ain' human—jes' a nigger."

Ransom breathed easier. "Ain' no niggers missin' 'roun' here, is they?"

"Ain' heard o' none. Nary a one . . . 'cept"—Allen pointed a tentative finger at the skull—"that big black buck o' Macklin's what runned las' year. Ain' never heerd

45

nothin' 'bout him. Betcha that this belong to him—what they call him?"

"That there Jem?"

"Tha's him. Yo' 'member 'bout him a-runnin' 'bout a year 'go?"

"Shore do! Tha's him. Gotta be. Ain' nobody else a-missin', is they?"

"Ain' heard o' nobody. Looks like we better go 'n' see. Yo', Tadpole, climb up here." Allen reached down a hand and hoisted the boy up onto the crupper and, much to the boy's delight, ordered him to guide them to the place where the skull had been found.

When they reached the turn in the road near the ravine, Tadpole directed Allen to turn into the woods and through the brush to the rivulet at the bottom of the ravine where the skull had been found. There they discovered, as Ransom had been sure they would, the dismembered skeleton of a body with the bones picked clean. It was evident that buzzards had done their work. None of the clothes remained and the condition of the bones indicated that the body had been a feast not only for buzzards but for other wild things. The arm bones and the leg bones were all detached except one femur which had disappeared, and other bones were lying scattered a few feet from the body. The spine and rib cage were intact, half filled with dead leaves.

"If'n Ed Harkness' wife hadn' a-heerd from him, would say it might of been Ed, but she got a letter 'n' he in Arkansaw. Shore think it gotta be that of Macklin's Jem. This here lookin' like it be a big man 'n' that Jem were big. Fust time Jem ever runned—al'ays comed back afore. Knowed that Macklin sent Cy Cadman 'n' his dogs out after him but never did pick up a trail. Awful bad on Mista Macklin a-losin' Jem. Heard he bin offered eight hundred dollars fer him, whaled back 'n' all, jes' afore he took off. Guess we better go back 'n' git that skull 'n' take it over ter Elm Grove." Although Elm Grove was ten miles away and Allen was busy on his own plantation, he considered it his neighborly duty to go to the Macklin place and apprise the slave's owner of the death of his property and the finding of his skeleton. He invited Ransom to go with him. After they had returned to Deep Spring, fortified themselves with a few drinks of corn, and got the skull which they placed in a croker sack, they rode off to Elm Grove.

Before they reached the Macklin house, they saw the owner astride a horse in the middle of the field and they rode down through the cotton and the rows of stooping Negroes toward the host.

"Jem is foun'," Allen called out as he approached. "He foun'," he repeated four times before he was heard.

"Whur he be then? Don' see him. Ain' yo' a-fetchin' him alongst?" Macklin inquired. He was a thin under-sized man with a long, drooping pepper-and-salt moustache which was so luxuriant it seemed to have sapped all his strength.

"Done brung him, at least part o' him." Allen waved the bag with a note of triumph in his voice as if he expected Macklin to be gladdened at the news of his slave. He handed the bag to Macklin.

Macklin looked in the bag and the sight of the skull set him off in a fit of coughing, for he was consumptive and far gone with the disease. "What yo' reckon I want with this?" he asked after he had recovered from his coughing, hawked up a clot of bloody phlegm, and spat it on the ground.

"Reckon yo' goin' ter crave ter see it be Jem shore 'nuff." Allen appeared disappointed that Macklin was not excited over the momentous news and the evidence he had brought. "It him, ain' it?"

"Not a-knowin, suh. Cain' rightly tell and the meat all off'n it. Ain' no way o' tellin' if'n it human o' nigger. How come yo' got this, it bein' him o' not him?"

When Allen had explained his and Ransom's finding of the skull and later of the skeleton and had asserted his belief that the skull was Jem's, Macklin began to be convinced even against his will, for he still harbored the hope that Jem would return. He reached into the sack and withdrew the skull, holding it at arm's length and turning it around.

"It shore got a good mouth o' teeth jes' like Jem had. All here jes' like his'n cause he never lose one o' them.

47

No, suh, nary a one. Reckon it him, goddam him." He turned in his saddle and called to his driver who had been standing a few feet away out of hearing. Macklin did not employ a white overseer, but had entrusted the eldest and most responsible of his bucks with a whip and the task of getting a modicum of work—as much as the lash would bring—out of the others, a mixed group of men past middle age, women, and adolescents.

The black approached his master obsequiously. Doffing his decrepit straw hat and winding his whip around one wrist, he intoned his customary, "Yas suh, masta suh, yo' a-wantin' me?"

"Shore as hell do. What yo' think I call yo' fur if'n I not wantin' yo'? Hollered to yo', didn' I?" He extended the skull to the Negro. "That Jem, yo' reckon? Look like him, teeth 'n' all, don' it?"

The slave hesitated a moment to determine his master's desire, whether he wanted an affirmative answer or not. It made him feel more important to be consulted, but he must make certain that his opinion agreed with his owner's. Apparently Macklin wanted it to be Jem so Jem it would be. "Shore, shore, masta suh. Tha's him, masta, that's Jem, suh. Reckernize Jem's teeth anywhur."

"Painter must 'a' got him." Allen seemed relieved to know that the skull belonged to a slave and not to a white man. "Painter shore must 'a' got him 'n' ripped him all ter hell. Both arms 'n' laigs ripped right off'n him."

Ransom sighed deeply. A great weight had been lifted from him, but he said nothing as he listened to Macklin.

"Must 'a' been a painter what killed him. Knew Jem would 'a' come back if'n he could. Jem wan't no runner. Jes' lef' home every once in a while 'cause he wanted a change o' screwin'. Goddamndest buck fer screwin' I ever did see. Kep' all my wenches knocked up 'n' most o' those fer twenty miles 'round. Seem like he never could get 'nuff o' it. Tol' me onct he took on ten wenches in one night 'n' just's strong on the las' as he were on the fust. Don' believe it tho'. Jem he 'n awful one fer braggin'." He looked up at Ransom whom he had

48

apparently not noticed before. "Ain' yo' that Ransom Lightfoot what lives over near Bannion's store?"

"Tha's me," Ransom said. "Don' yo' 'member talkin' with me 'bout three, four weeks 'go? Askin' me if'n I couldn't come over here 'n' stud some o' yore wenches 'cause yo' wantin' ter git some good light-skinned suckers. Mista Allen here 'commended me."

"Kindly ask yo' ter forgive me, suh, fer not a-recognizin' yo'. My eyes ain' too good but kin recognize voices 'n' sort o' thought yo' were he. Needin' some one I am. Since Jem gone ain' got me no good buck fer studdin'. This here Rye he too old; done los' mos' o' his sap 'n' ain' much good. 'Sides, I aimin' ter have light-skins fer my nex' crop. Wuth more."

"This Ransom boy shore good," Allen bolstered his recommendation of Ransom to Macklin. "Studded my wenches 'n' got six knocked up already. He mighty full o' sap, this boy is, jes' full and a-bilin' over. He better'n that Jem claim to be. 'Members as how I 'commended him to yo'?"

"Kindly 'preciate it, I do. Ain' no trouble a-gettin' bucks from other plantations fer studdin' but they don' bring in light-skins." Macklin turned his graying, cataract-scummed eyes toward Ransom. "Now that yo're here, suh, how 'bout yo're stayin' a spell? Too far ter go back 'n' forth."

"Kin right well do that," Ransom answered, pleased that Macklin had brought up the subject and not him. "Kindly like ter know how many yo' got what wants servicin' 'n' how much yo' pays me?"

"Got me 'bout five o' six. One called Pansy, she ain' more'n fourteen 'n' ain never been busted but she ready. Got May-Ann, 'n' Pearl, 'n' Agnes. They all had one o' two suckers already. Got Emma Mary, she Jem's woman 'n' always brought me in a sucker every year 'n' she a-mournin' Jem somethin' awful. Do her good ter git pestered 'n' take her mind off'n Jem. Got me Miz Macklin's Dora, too: she mulatto 'n' ought ter bring in a nice light-skin. Then there's ol' Liza. Mayhap she too old ter whelp but don' do no harm ter try. That six. Tell yo' what. Yo' studs 'em 'n' I'll give yo' one o' the pups.

49

Yo' takes yore choice, all 'ceptin' Dora's 'n' Miz Macklin won' part with it. Any other'n yo' wants yo' kin take it 'n' leave it here till it weaned."

Ransom considered the matter. The last thing in the world he wanted was a squalling black baby without anyone to take care of it, but to admit to Macklin that the Lightfoot family was so impoverished that it did not own even one female slave to act as mother to a child would have been to admit his poverty and his inferior status. After all, his mother could look out for it. He had antici- pated cash but, as he considered the matter, the prestige of having a slave of his own which in thirteen or four- teen years would be able to provide him with a regular source of satisfaction even though she would be his own daughter rather pleased him.

"Take one, if'n it a girl," he answered, "but ain' wantin' no buck."

"Then yo'd better come up ter the house, seein' as how yo' goin' ter stay a spell. 'N' yo' too, Mista Allen. Shore want yo' ter stay fer supper. Jes' one word o' caution tho'. Miz Macklin she temp'rance 'n' strict, too. Won' 'low no drinkin' in the house. Takes my corn out 'n the barn 'n' yo' welcome ter ride up 'n' have a drink."

Allen declined the invitation, stating that he had left the work on his farm to come over with the skull, hav- ing felt it his duty to apprise Macklin of the discovery of Jem's skeleton. The men parted, each realizing that Al- len had done his neighborly duty. Macklin gave orders to his driver to carry on the work and, with Ransom riding beside him, they departed for the barn.

"Shore hatin' to lose that Jem," Macklin said as they walked their horses toward the big house which had once been painted white but had deteriorated to a dirty gray. "He were a thousand-dollar nigger o' 'bout that. Would have bin, if'n it weren't for them whales on his back. Couldn' keep the bastard from runnin'. That all that ail him. He a good worker; do more'n any three bucks but jes' had his mind on screwin' 'n' nothin' else. Al'ays wantin' a different wench. Al'ays came back tho' even if'n he knew he goin' ter git stripped down onct he git back. Would 'a' come back this time if'n that painter

50

hadn't a-got him. Right hard on me a-losin' one so strong's him. Wished now I'd a-taken that eight hundred dollars that dealer offered me." He sighed with resignation and started coughing again. When he had conquered the paroxysm, he strained to talk, but his words were scarcely above a whisper.

"Had bad luck all my life. Guess I cain' 'spect it ter change now." Another fit of coughing shook him and he did not speak again until they reached the barn.

Chapter V

THE NEWS OF THE finding of Jem's skeleton got around. By the time it reached Marysburg, the only town in that vicinity which boasted a weekly newspaper, it was too late to get in that week's edition. But two weeks later, the *Marysburg Sentinel* carried a story about it on its front page:

RUNAWAY NEGRO FOUND DEAD

The mystery of the runaway servant of Mr. E. J. Macklin of Elm Grove was cleared up by the discovery of his body on the banks of Sour Apple Creek, about thirty-three miles east of Marysburg, by Mr. Albert W. Allen and Mr. Ransom Lightfoot some two weeks ago. Mr. Allen saw some of his colored children playing with a skull on his plantation and they told him where they had obtained it, leading him and Mr. Lightfoot to the site beside the creek where they found the skeleton of a body. On delivery of the skull to Mr. Macklin at Elm Grove, Mr. Macklin identified it, by the teeth, as that of his servant Jem.

Jem was a habitual runaway but, prior to this occasion, had always returned of his own will. After his long absence on this occasion, an absence of some nine months, it was thought that he might have gone North or to Canada. It was quite definitely established that he had been killed by a cougar, for the body had been dismembered and parts were missing.

Residents of the neighborhood where the body was found remember hearing the cries of a cougar around that time and several residents recall seeing tracks.

Jem was a vigorous boy of about thirty years of age, a prime hand, and a good worker when it was possible to keep him in. His owner says that his back was much scarred with the whip, which it was necessary to employ on him because of his habitual running away and for no other cause. The loss of such a servant is a considerable one, for Mr. Macklin had refused a large offer for him only a year ago and prices are constantly rising. The death of Jem hits Mr. Macklin harder because he had dropped all insurance on his slaves after the failure of so many insurance writers in the year before last.

Jem's end should serve as a salutary warning to any Negro in the neighborhood who might have an itch to escape. Mr. Macklin has placed the skull on a pole in the quarters at Elm Grove as a caveat and reminder to all his hands.

Talk was still strong on the subject when, a week or so later, Ransom and Macklin both felt that Ransom had accomplished his work sufficiently well. Ransom was glad of the chance to return home. Living with the Macklins had been confining and onerous. On his way, he stopped at Bannion's store. The first thing that greeted him was Fronie, sitting under the big elm tree, her baby wrapped in a rag of old sheeting. She was nursing it and looked up as Ransom stopped.

"Well, my Gawd a-mighty, yo' done whelped it already?" Ransom got down off his horse and waited for Fronie to disengage the baby's hungry mouth. She held the child up. Its whiteness was striking, though not surprising. Netty, Fronie's mother, was half white; Fronie, with a white father, was three-quarters white; and this child with another white father was seven-eighths white. The colored blood had been so attenuated that it was no longer in evidence. Its minuscule features showed no Negroid traces.

Ransom, convinced that he had fathered it, examined it closely as Fronie held it up.

"Goddam white, ain' he?"

Fronie nodded, pleased with Ransom's praise.

Ransom, through some unconscious sense of fatherhood, which he surely would have impugned had he recognized it as such, reached down and poked his thick, dirt-encrusted finger into the tiny fist. The little white fingers encircled it, but suddenly Ransom shook them loose.

"Goddam li'l bastard." He spat on Fronie and the child. "He got six fingers on his hand. He that goddam Tommy Verder's whelp, that what he is. He nothin' but a monstrosity—nothing but a goddam nigger cullion, a goddam-it-to-hell whelp o' a goddam mongrel bastard, that what he is, 'n' that son-o'-a-bitch Verder done sired him." He jammed his hand into his pocket as if afraid the baby would reach out and clutch it again. "Tol' yo' the son-o'-a-bitch never a-comin' back, didn' I? Well, he never come back, no never. But I'se a-comin' back. Yo'd better heist yore ass over behind the blacksmith's shop tomorrow. Too tired ter give it ter yo' tonight but yo'd better be ready tomorrow. Nex' one a-goin' ter be mine 'n' ain' goin' ter sire no six-fingered scum o' the earth like'n this one neither. Yo' hears what I a-tellin' yo', Fronie? Yo' be ready tomorrow 'n' don' tote this pup 'long with yo'. Might drown'd it if'n I see it. Yo' hear me?"

"Yes, masta suh. Jes' as yo' say, masta suh." She clutched the baby a little tighter to her breast and watched Ransom dismount and go into the store. Cradling the baby in her arms, she sang it a little song without words and without tune but filled with an inexplicable love which she did not know how to express.

DOVE COTE PLANTATION

Chapter I

NO MORE SIMILAR to the calla lily for which she had been named than her daughter Dovie was to a dove, Callie Verder, wife of Thomas Verder of Dove Cote Plantation, rather than being willowy and graceful, was short and obese. Yet, in spite of her huge bulk, she managed to be kittenish and coquettish and, as she fondly imagined, despite her thirty-two years, cute. This mid-morning she was sitting in her low-backed rocking chair, having her long hair brushed for her by her Negro slave, Congo. The autumn light streamed through the small panes of the window, making a splash of orange light on the wide polished pine boards of the floor. Luxuriating in this spot of warmth, the house dog, Pluto, dozed, waking at intervals to snap at a fly and then close his eyes again. There was no sound in the room but the tick of the wag-on-the-wall clock, the breathing of the dog, and the shuffle of the slave's bare feet as he retreated step by step from Callie's head, extending her hair to its full length, and then advanced again. While he brushed, he examined the dark-golden tresses for any gray or white hairs, which he had been instructed to pull out. He discovered one, traced it carefully to her scalp, and then yanked. Without turning in her chair, she gave him a backhand slap that barely brushed his thigh.

"Yo' be careful, Congo. Ain' yo' a-knowin' that I got

a miz'ble headache this mornin'? This hair o' mine a
burden—jes' a burden. It so heavy ter carry 'roun'. Jes'
a-pullin' my scalp out alla time. Thinkin' some day I
goin' ter have it cut off 'n' rid myself o' its burden."

"Yas'm, Miz Callie, ma'am, yas'm," Congo answered,
agreeing automatically. He knew that nothing in the
world would ever persuade Callie to have her hair cut off,
for it was her greatest pride and her chief claim to distinction. "Sweep the floor, it do," she was always saying proudly. "Trip up on it, if'n I walk with it down."
And, truth to tell, Congo was as proud of this crown
of glory as Callie herself was. He had been entrusted with
the daily task of brushing it since childhood, and that
luxuriant growth always kindled his pride and what
aesthetic sense he possessed. That hair had become his
passion; he was especially excited by its odor, which he
identified as his mistress' own. The nostrils in his large
flat face were wide and expansive, and his sense of smell
was inferior only to that of the hound which lay in the
patch of sunlight. Congo was always reluctant when the
time came for him to bathe Miz Callie and to wash her
hair, because the shampoo always reduced the effluvia
that so delighted him.

Congo was merely an arbitrary name—really a mis-
nomer, for he was not of Congo stock or ancestry. His
features proclaimed him to be Iwo or perhaps Hausa
with some Angola mixture. A year or so older than Callie herself, he might have been a fine-looking man were
it not for the obesity which now claimed him.

Callie's father at her birth had wanted to give her a
girl child as a companion, but of the children born that
year, there was a preponderance of males, and the girls
all had some objectionable feature. One was blind, another had a shriveled hand, and a third was crippled at
birth and was drowned. The boys, on the other hand,
were sound and vigorous, particularly the one who had
been named Congo. To give his daughter a male for a
play-child, a constant and intimate companion, was unthinkable, but Callie needed a playmate of her own age.
As his daughter, she was, of course, unique; therefore,

he decided, her play-child would be different from that of the other girls in the neighborhood.

Callie's father had summoned to the barn the old slave who always gelded his hogs for him, an expert and an artist in his craft. To him, Tom Verder submitted the squalling Congo, now just weaned. The old Negro had never before castrated a human being but was anxious to prove his ability. There was little worry about the death of the infant, for at that time slaves were low in price and newly born children were not considered any particular asset. The cost of rearing them was considered greater than their worth. Indeed the difficulty in those days was in preventing the women from bearing children rather than inducing them to breed, as was later the problem. Consequently infants were often given away like mongrel puppies, and it would have been a simple matter for Callie's father to acquire a girl child, but he had decided on something more exotic for his daughter. Let the other girls have their Negro play-girls; only Callie would have a eunuch and if this one died in the attempt it mattered little because there would be another to experiment upon.

Congo had served his Miz Callie intimately all her life. No sex or recognition of it intervened in their relations, for Congo had neither sex nor sexual impulses. Callie's comfort, the grooming of her progressively rounding body, and especially of her luxuriant hair, were his only care. Their relations were amicable from the beginning, for Congo was early made to understand his utter subservience to the white girl's will, and Callie required no instruction to realize her complete dominance over the slave. From the time she was a small child she had punched and pinched and pummeled him and continuously threatened him with the lash, although Callie, kind by nature, had never used it on him. Not only Callie but her father and later her husband had authority over him, yet it was understood that only Callie could order him whipped. Although he feared the whip himself, his greatest delight was to watch other slaves flogged. Except for his attendance on his mistress it was his only pleasure and Callie, sensing this, allowed him to observe every flogging on the plantation in order, as she explained "that he might have the fear of the lash in his heart." He did.

Now, at about the same age as Callie, he was black, fat, and flabby and, despite his height and enormous weight, he had little strength. His emasculation accounted for his flaccidity which was aggravated by his sedentary existence and his gluttony. Callie believed in *embonpoint*. To her plumpness was a mark of beauty, richness, and prosperity whether in man, woman, or Negro slave. It betokened wealth—the outward proof that one was waited upon and that one set a good table. Her one great regret was that despite the rich food she served, her husband remained muscular instead of growing obese.

Callie herself had never been slender, but after she had borne Dovie some sixteen years before, she had begun to accumulate even more flesh. Her appetite never failed her and in her desire to gain more and more weight, she never curbed it. There were no wrinkles in her alabaster-white face, and her deep violet-blue eyes and mass of golden hair were comely indeed. Her husband objectively appreciated Callie's beauty, sympathized volubly with her smallest indisposition, and catered to her every whim, but he preferred to spend his time in the arms of his young slave wenches rather than in Callie's.

Dovie had inherited neither her mother's hair nor her stoutness. She was taller than her mother by about three inches, and firmer of flesh. Her eyes were the same color but her hair, instead of being gold, was a deep chestnut. She did, however, have the same heart-shaped face, the same finely penciled brows, the same pouting red lips and slightly *retroussé* nose, and promised to be a far handsomer woman than her mother had ever been. Yet Dovie's beauty was not apparent this morning as she entered the room where Congo was brushing her mother's hair. Her face was ravaged by a recent fit of crying; her eyes red and swollen, her hair uncombed, and, instead of her usual tight-waisted dress with its bell-shaped skirt, she wore a shapeless calico wrapper. She was followed by an amber-colored girl of about her own age who served as her servant and who reflected her mistress' moods, at least to the extent of a long-faced solemnity on this bright morning. Dolly, the servant, had no concept of what might have caused Miz Dovie to weep but she knew it her duty to look unhappy if her mistress did.

"Why, what's the matter with my sweetheart? Why yo' been a-sobbin', Dovie?" Callie exclaimed solicitously as she rose with some difficulty from her chair, her hair cascading around her. She parted it with her hands, holding up its mass as she hobbled across the room on tiny awkward feet to embrace her daughter. "Yo' cryin' 'bout that Tommy? Jes' bet yo' are. Don' yo' fret no more 'bout him, jes' 'cause he ain' back here on time. Jes' cain' trust no man, never."

Dovie bit her lower lip, trying to control the tears which welled up in her eyes in spite of her efforts, but finally she gave way to a paroxysm of sobbing. "He ain' a-comin' never, he ain'," she sobbed, releasing herself from Callie's embrace and dropping into a chair where she sat, her shoulders hunched dejectedly, her hands hiding her face. Purely out of sympathy, Dolly started to howl.

"Hush yore mouth," Callie commanded, "what-all yo' got ter mourn 'bout? Git yo' self out to the spring house 'n' fetch Miz Dovie a nice glass o' cold water. Now, git!" She waited until the girl had left, then leaned down to console Dovie with myriad pettings and strokings.

"Don' let it bother yo', Dovie. That Tommy he ain' such a much. They's lots better'n him."

"But not so purty," Dovie wailed.

" 'Course they is. Purtier! Jes' don' know what got inter that boy. Yore Uncle Charlie say in his letter he ain' seen hide nor hair o' him. Ain' never come home ter Natchez. Bet he jes' went on ter N'Orleans ter sow his wild oats afore he marries. Men like ter have a fling afore they settles down. Now don' yo' fret. He'll come."

"It five months, 'mos' that." Dovie reckoned on her fingers. "Mos' that long."

"Jes' yo' wait, he'll come," Callie assured her, with a confidence she didn't feel. "Now don' yo' worry yo'self inter a dee-cline. Yo' don' want ter come down with the green sickness 'n' get yo'self all scrawny 'n' looking like a picked chicken jes' when I startin' ter get a little fat on yore bones. I do declare since yo' started ter fatten up a little, yo' looks right nice 'n' purty."

Dovie went into another spell of weeping. "Ain' fat, it ain', Mama." She stood up reluctantly. "That ain' fat, Mama, that's a baby. Jes' cain' hide it no longer, Mama. Cain' lace it in no more. What I a-goin' ter do, Mama?" The words which she had so dreaded to say were finally out and Dovie bowed her head, expecting the wrath of the world and more particularly of her mother to fall upon her.

But Callie was speechless. She opened and closed her mouth like a fish out of water, but no words came. Dovie thought her mother was going to faint but she felt powerless to support her. At the end of a moment which seemed long enough for Dovie to die in, Callie recovered her speech.

"A baby? Where yo' git such foolishness? Takes a man ter have a baby 'n' yo' ain' had no man."

"Had one. Tommy," Dovie confessed.

"Tommy?" Callie exclaimed. "No, it ain' him. It cain' be him."

"It him all right," Congo interjected, forgetting himself in his anxiety to corroborate the news. "Smelled him in Miz Dovie's bed when I a-reddin' it up. Smelled Mista Tommy's man-smell on the sheets."

Callie turned and slapped the slave across the face. "Yo' keeps your big mouth shet, less'n yo' wants ter git whaled. White folks ain' got no smell yo' kin smell. Only niggers got smell."

"He right, Mama, Congo right. Tommy was in my bed."

"Oh, Lord in heaven, what we a-goin' ter do? Him not a-comin' back 'n' yo' swellin' up. But we'll fix him. Yore papa'll fix him. He'll make him come back 'n' marry up with yo'. He right hono'ble, your papa is."

"Whur-at he a-goin' ter fin' him? How he goin' ter make him marry up with me 'n' him not a-knowin' whur-at he is?" Dovie had had ample time to consider the disappearance of her lover.

"Yore pappy'll go to N'Orleans 'n' hunt that viper

down. He'll kill him, jes' like the snake he is. Jes' ter think how good yore pappy was to that Tommy 'n' how much he loved him. Yore papa wanted yo' ter be a boy 'n' when yo' come a girl, he jes' latched onto that Tommy 'n' acted like he his own boy; kept him here 'n' learned him to ride 'n' read. Tommy stay more here at Dove Cote'n with his own papa. Yore papa always reckon on yo' a-marryin' up wid Tommy. Cain' believe it Tommy, him so purty 'n' so strong 'n' straight 'n' so lovin' 'n' all. But he jus' like yore papa, six-fingered hand 'n' all. All he think 'bout is wenchin', but yore papa never did no wenchin' here in my house. 'N' that Tommy did, right here under my own roof." She turned and grabbed the hairbrush from Congo's hand and, as he was the nearest object on which she could vent her spleen, she whacked him with it until he burst into a fit of weeping that matched that of Dovie's. "Git out," Callie screamed at him, "git out 'n' leave me 'n' my Dovie sweetheart here 'lone. This a time a daughter need her lovin' mama 'thout any great black baboon a-listenin' 'n' a-spyin' on her. Git out 'n' tell that foolish Dolly not ter come back either."

Congo did not hesitate, waddling across the room as fast as his huge bulk would permit. Once he had gone, Callie sat down in her rocker and pointed to a small hassock. "Git that hassock, Dovie, 'n' come over here 'n' sit aside me. Yo' kin trust yore mama what loves yo'. Yo' tell me all 'bout it 'n' we make plans, we do. Shore glad yore pappy he over to The Patch 'n' won' be back till mornin'. Got time ter plan, we have. Now yo' jes' wipe them tears off'n yore pretty face 'n' tell yore mama all 'bout it." Callie rocked impatiently back and forth, her pudgy hand on Dovie's shoulder. "Come now, tell yore mama," she cajoled.

Dovie's sobs gradually subsided. The worst was over. Her mother knew. She looked up and managed a wan smile. "Yo' think yo' kin fix it up with papa?"

Her mother nodded with confidence, although she had as yet formed no idea of what she might do. "Jes' go right ahead 'n' make a clean breast o' it. Yo'll feel better, darlin', when yo've told yore mama."

61

Now that she had broken the ice, Dovie was only too willing to confess.

"Tommy al'ays talkin' 'bout when we gits married up. He say it goin' ter be a lot o' fun, him 'n' me. He makin' big plans ter take me ter Natchez 'n' down ter N'Orleans 'n' everywhere. But he always a-sayin' it too bad we cain' sleep together jes' once afore he leave ter go ter Natchez, but I tellin' him no, 'tain' right 'n' seemly. Then, 'bout two weeks afore he left, we went ridin' 'n' that Tommy he want ter head fer that little copse o' pecan trees what down by the brook. Onct we git there, he say he not a-feelin' good 'n' he want ter rest afore ridin' back, so we git off'n the horses 'n sit down under the trees. Right purty there it was; sun a-comin' through the leaves, brook a-makin' a little noise, 'n' birds a-singin'. But Tommy say he tooken sick 'n' he lay down 'n' put his head in my lap. Then he pullin' me down 'n' makin' me bend over 'n' kiss him, sayin' as how mayhap that make him feel better. We kissin' a lot —real kissin' with him a-puttin' his tongue in my mouth 'n' he a-puttin' his hand up under my skirts 'n' a-feelin' while we keepin' on a-kissin' 'n' a-kissin' 'n' a-kissin'."

"Jes' a snake, that Tommy. How any boy so purty as he kin be such a devil I don' know. Wish't I had him here right now. Big's he is, I'd trounce him plenty."

"Then Tommy he stop kissin' 'n' he groan 'n' take on somethin' awful," Dovie continued, paying no attention to her mother's words, her mind on that dappled grove and the man whose head was in her lap. "Sayin' he a-goin' ter die right there quick. He a-howlin' 'n' a-takin' on jes' like he a-goin' ter die that minute. I was right scared, him so sick 'n' all 'n' not knowin' what ailin' him 'n' when I ask him what ailin' him, he took my hand 'n' put it down on his britches. He all hard 'n' rigid like, feelin' jes' like the iron pump handle only bigger. Then I git scared too 'cause I know somethin' awful wrong 'cause he never like that afore. Ain' natural. Tol' him I'd ride home 'n' git help but he tell me it won' do no good 'cause he be dead afore I git back. He say I the only one what kin help him 'n' keep him from dyin'."

"Stinkin', lyin' polecat, takin' 'vantage o' yore sweet innercence." Callie dipped her chewed twig into her box of snuff and rubbed her teeth with it. "Go on, Dovie sweetheart," she said, "Mama a-listenin' 'n' a-grievin' with yo'. What happened then?"

"Then he stand up 'n' his britches just a-stickin' out in front o' him, like'n he have a stick o' wood in 'em, 'n' he lookin' unnatural-like, a-breathin' hard 'n' pantin' and I asked him what ailed him. Then he undo his britches 'n' show me how he all swoll'd up 'n' he make me feel how hard he was. Make me put my hands on it, he did, for to see how feverish 'n' swoll'd he was. He say if'n it don' stop swellin' it a-goin' ter burst 'n' he die 'n' shore look like'n he a-goin' ter burst, him all swolled 'n' throbbin' 'n' purple-like. He say only one way ter stop the swellin' 'n' save his life 'n' I got ter help him less'n he die right off. He say if'n he kin put it in me, it stop the swellin' 'n' he won't bust. I tol' him no 'cause it ain' right 'n' I a-knowin' it ain' right 'n' he hadn't ought ter do it to me, we gittin' married 'n' all, but he say less'n we kin, we ain' never goin' ter git married 'cause he goin' ter keep on swellin' 'n' swellin' 'n' gittin' harder 'n' harder till he bust 'n' bleed ter death 'n' it will be all my fault 'n' he don' care 'cause he know I don' love him, me jes' a-sittin' there 'n' seein' him suffer 'n' not carin' if'n he die or not."

"Jes' a-lyin' faster'n a horse kin trot." Callie shook her head in disbelief at such diabolical guile. "Oh, my poor innercent little dove! What he do next?" she asked impatiently.

"Then he lie down beside me 'n' put his finger in me 'n' nearly drive me crazy 'n' then he done it. He jes' pushed me back 'n' done it. Hurt me somethin' awful it did 'n' they a lot of blood, but he say it his'n 'n' he say I just save his life in the nick o' time 'cause it almost ready ter bust 'n' the blood prove it. But it cured him, it did. When he take it out, he no longer hard 'n' stiff but just limp 'n' small like. He say he so grateful ter me fer saving his life. He say men git like that 'n' that why men have ter have nigger wenches 'roun' all the time 'cause if'n they get tooken that way, they swell up 'n' die. He

63

say when he feel it comin' on him al'ays run to the quarters o' the Romp Pasture 'n' take the first wench he kin find less'n he swell up 'n' bust 'n' die. This time he say he didn't have time ter git back to the quarters 'n' that why I had ter save him 'n' he kiss me a lot 'cause he so grateful.''

"Jes' that once he did it ter yo', jes' that once?" Callie leaned forward, waiting upon Dovie's words.

"No, we keep a-kissin' 'n' a-kissin' 'n' he start ter swell 'gain jes' like it was afore 'n' he say he got ter do it 'gain, so's he did 'n' mos' every night after that, he come a-tippy-toe ter my room when everybody a-sleepin' 'n' he git inter bed with me so's I kin kindly save his life. One night I not wantin' to 'cause I hurtin' 'n' I tell him he better do it ter Dolly, so's he say he sufferin' some-thin' awful 'n' Dolly kin 'commodate him. She cure him 'cause once he go limp the danger past." Dovie looked up at her mother, her eyes wide with wonderment. "That why, Mama, Papa he al'ays a-goin' ter the quarters 'n' over ter The Patch?"

"Men is vile creatures, Dovie sweetheart," Callie ad-monished, " 'n' they lyin' polecats, too. That Tommy he jes' a-lyin' ter yo', jes' takin' 'vantage o' your love 'n' good nature. He not a-dyin'. Men git swoll'd up like that all the time. Ain' nothin' dangerous. Jes' nature, tha's all, 'n' they ain' a-goin' ter burst 'n' die, they'd all be daid ten times over if'n it were true but 'tain'." She sighed deeply. "Well, what's done's done 'n' cain' be un-done. That's what comes from yore papa lettin' Tommy go to the cabins when he jes' a young squirt 'n' havin' the run o' the wenches in the Romp Pasture. Tol' yore papa Tommy too young 'n' it stunt him but yore papa jes' laughed. He point to Tommy a-growin' like a weed 'n' he say it make him grow ter pester the wenches 'stead o' stuntin' him. Never tho't tho' he'd do anything ter my innercent child what we have perteckted 'n' kept from all evil knowledge."

It was true. Despite the fact that she had been born and raised on a plantation where not only the mating of animals but the mating of Negroes had been an everyday occurrence, Dovie had been shielded from all knowledge of sex or human anatomy. She had yielded to Tommy, it was true, partly because he had aroused her with his amatory play, but mainly because she had believed him and felt he was in imminent danger of dying. But, in the two weeks following his initial assault on her, she had come to realize that she had been taken in by his deceit. It had not, however, dampened her love for him, but in her present emergency that love was receding into the background of her thoughts.

"What Papa a-goin' ter say when he fin' out?" she asked anxiously.

"He a-comin' in the mornin'. Better not ter say nothin' till he eats good. He always better spirited after he eat. I'll git Ruthie ter make him a good break'fus 'n' then I tells him, tho' I don' rightly know what I'm a-goin' ter tell him. But we got ter git yo' married off. Ain' havin' me no woods-colt fer a gran'child. Don' know what we a-goin' ter do." She rocked silently for a few minutes, patting Dovie's head in time with her rocking. Finally she stopped and made a pronouncement.

"Tommy's daid," she said.

Dovie burst into another fit of weeping. "Oh, he ain', my dear, sweet, lovin' Tommy ain' dead, he ain'."

"Yes, he is," Callie said, anxious to dispose of any vestige of Tommy. "I recollect now. Had me a dream the other night. Dreamed o' my mama in her casket 'n' that a sign o' death. Her spirit come jes' ter tell me that Tommy's daid. Know it now. My mama always a-warnin' me in my dreams. My dear mama she a-comin' 'specially ter tell me." She waited for the deluge of Dovie's tears to subside, pondering her next step, uncertain of what she should say or do now that she had disposed of Tommy. More to herself than to Dovie she said, "Cain' have no baby thout'n a pappy."

Dovie agreed between sobs and sniffles.

"We jes' got ter marry yo' up ter somebody so's people not a-pointin' the finger o' scorn at yo'."

"Ain' nobody but Tommy—ain' nobody but him I'm wantin'."

"He daid. They's got ter be somebody 'n' we got ter make folks think there is."

"Who?"

"Jes' anybody what ain' already gotten a wife. Who bin here 'bout that time?"

"Anybody we say, he a-goin' ter know he never had me. He a-goin' ter know."

"Let him! Ain' nobody else a-knowin', yo' a-sayin' so 'n' yore papa a-seein' that he marry yo'. They's bin shotgun weddin's afore this."

"Papa ain' a-goin' ter tell no lies."

"He ain' a-goin' ter know he a-tellin' lies. Men ain' very smart. He thinks yo're honest 'n' he thinks I'm honest. He goin' ter believe our say. He'll make whoever yo' say marry up with yo'. Jes' thank God yo' ain' been raped by no nigger. Tommy's bad enough but at least his chil' goin' ter be white."

Dovie was weakening in her refusal to accept her mother's stratagem. She was half convinced now, with the awful evidence of her mother's dream, that Tommy really was dead, and she realized she had to have a husband. Her mind darted back to the days before Tommy had left.

Callie said, "What 'bout that Mista Jackson who was here a-buyin' niggers? He stayed two nights."

"He nothin' but a pipsqueak 'n' he older'n Papa. Anyway he's married. 'Sides, he a speculator. Wouldn't want me married ter a speculator, would yo'?"

"He's a man. Tha's all we need's a man 'n' don' make no neverminds what he is long's he's white 'n' ain' already married up. Recollects now that Jackson he say he married to a wife up 'n Memphis."

Dovie brushed her hair back from her eyes and sat up straight. For the first time there was a trace of animation in her words. "Why'n't we think about it afore? That cousin o' papa's was here. He ain' married 'n' he right good-looking 'n' 'he young 'n' I think well set up too tho' he awful pious. He was here for a week a-makin' calf's eyes at me when Tommy he not a-lookin'." Although she had paid no attention to the young man while he was there, having eyes only for Tommy, she remembered that the other man was young and handsome in an overgrown country-bumpkin way.

Callie took a long breath and expelled it slowly in an immense sigh of relief.

"He the one, that Rev'nd Boggs, he the very one! He's a second cousin o' yore papa's. His grandmaw 'n' yore papa's mama they sisters. His mama a right nice woman but she marry that good-fer-nothin' Boggs. Handsome as all gitout he was, but wuthless. Runned with another woman 'n' never seen hide nor hair o' him 'gain. Yo're right, the Rev'nd Boggs's well set up 'n' handsome 'n' he ain' married neither."

"But it ain' right ter say the baby's his'n."

" 'N' tain' right fer yo' to go the rest o' yore life with no man lookin' at yo' 'n' every woman pointin' the finger o' scorn at yo' 'n' yo with a woods-colt on yur hands. Yo' jes' leave it ter me; yore papa'll make him marry yo', don' yo' fret."

"But the Rev'nd himself he knows he never bedded with me."

" 'N' who cares what he knows o' what he don' know. Ought ter jump at the chance ter git two good plantations like Dove Cote 'n' The Patch, with all these niggers 'n' a pretty girl like yo' thrown in."

"But supposin' Tommy come back?" Dovie was reluctant to give up hope.

"He jes' too late, tha's all. Serve him right, he a-runnin' 'way 'n' fergittin' he most prob'ly knocked yo' up. Serve him right if'n he comes back 'n' sees yo' married up to a fine, handsome man like Bartholomew Boggs."

"Well," Dovie said with a tearful sigh, "if'n you say it Boggs, it got ter be Boggs." Now that she considered it the prospect was not too unpleasant. She wanted Tommy, she loved Tommy, but if she couldn't have Tommy, Boggs would certainly be her second choice. Although he lacked the urbanity and polish of Tommy Verder, he did have a certain flashy good looks combined with a huge body, broad shoulders, and a two-fisted virility which was somewhat negated by his pious affectations. "If'n I say

67

it Boggs, don' make no neverminds whether he say so o' not?"

"Not a bit. Men always deny it, always. But if we both say it Boggs 'n' yore papa believe it Boggs, it shore going to be Boggs. After all ain' so much dif'rence. Tommy yore papa's nephew, Boggs yore papa's cousin. But don' yo' say nothin' 'tall. I knows how ter handle your papa."

There was a faint scratching at the door. Callie looked up. "Who thur?" she called.

The door opened slowly and Congo appeared, his face wreathed in smiles. He was carrying a big black japanned waiter with a plate piled high with hot gingerbread and two glasses of cold milk.

"Miz Dovie she needin' some 'freshment," he giggled. "She got ter eat fer two now."

"Yo' shet yore big mouth," Callie yelled at him, " 'n' yo' bring in that food 'n' set it down here. If'n I cotch yo' a-sayin' one word to the servants 'bout Miz Dovie 'n' her condition, I'll have Nero take his whip to yo'. Means it this time, I do. I'll have him raise such whales on yore back as no nigger ever had afore. I'll have him strip all that fatback off'n yore bones. I'll have him . . ."

"Ain' goin' ter say a word, Miz Callie, ma'am. Love yo' 'n' Miz Dovie, I do. Ain' sayin' a word, not a word, Miz Callie, ma'am." He drew up a small table and placed the tray on it.

Callie reached for the gingerbread, sniffing at its spiciness.

" 'Course yo' won', Congo. Knows yo' loves Miz Dovie 'n' me. We trusts yo', we do." Her voice dropped and she smiled indulgently at Congo. "Yore nose ain' so good at smellin' as yo' think. It wan't Tommy what were in Miz Dovie's bed at all. Was that Rev'nd Boggs what was visitin' here. 'Member that. It Rev'nd Boggs what yo' smelled in Miz Dovie's sheets."

"If'n yo' say so, Miz Callie, ma'am, if'n yo' say so. Recollects now it was Rev'nd Boggs 'n' not Masta Tommy. Recollects now." Congo grinned at his mistress; if she wanted it to be Boggs it would be Boggs.

"Tha's right." Callie nodded her head. " 'N' now,

Congo, git me ready fer bed, 'n' call that Dolly. Miz Dovie a-goin' ter nap 'n' so's I. We's plumb tuckered out, both of us, 'n' see that the house keep quiet. Don' wan' no clatter 'roun' here while Miz Dovie 'n' me a-nappin'."

Chapter II

FROM CONGO THE word went forth, "Mist'ess a-sleepin'"
and the whole domain of Dove Cote settled down to a
fitful hush. The birds continued to sing, the cattle to low,
the horses to whinny, and the hens to cackle, but otherwise there was no sound except an occasional banging of
pans in the kitchen where old Aunt Ruthie held sway;
the high-pitched adolescent laughter of the boys and girls
in the faraway Romp Pasture; and the faint echoes of
song from the hands in the cotton fields. Callie, plopped
like a pile of suet on her high-posted bed in the big bedroom, snored like a grenadier, alternating her snorts and
raspings with those of Congo who slept on a pallet beside her bed. Down the hall in a smaller bedroom, Dovie
slept from emotional exhaustion, but Dollie, once her
mistress had gone to sleep, tiptoed out to seek the company of a fifteen-year-old youth in the Romp Pasture
with whom she was, for the nonce, enamored. Separated
by the high fence, they could indulge themselves only in
a limited manner, but it was far more exciting to Dolly
to gaze into his bovine brown eyes than to stare at the
ceiling of Dovie's room. To be sure, it was forbidden for
her to leave her mistress and for her to go to the Romp
Pasture, but the interdict only made the forbidden fruit
sweeter to her taste.

Dove Cote was the home and headquarters of Thomas

Verder. It comprised some fifteen hundred acres of land, the larger part of it cleared for cotton but with some hundred and fifty acres still wooded and uncleared with trees so noble that the owner lacked the resolution to cut them down. The land was high for that section of the country and fertile, watered by two rapidly flowing streams, neither of which, however, was large enough to merit a name. Cotton had been grown on it for so many successive years that its yield was by no means as bountiful as the earlier one that Verder's father, also named Tom, had taken from it. Old Tom Verder had acquired the land by preemption in the last decade of the eighteenth century, choosing his location carefully and bringing his slaves there from his father's home in Georgia. The slaves of Dove Cote now numbered about seventy-five adults. Despite the fact that more were born than died, the number was kept more or less at that figure because many were sent to The Patch, Verder's other plantation. The slave population at The Patch was nearly double that at Dove Cote. The Patch absorbed those that were incorrigible, disagreeable, or unsound. Consequently the Patch slaves were not as handsome a lot as those at Dove Cote. Verder treated his slaves humanely, almost with affection. He kept all his older slaves, a few of which he had inherited from his father, and sinecures were found for them where they passed their declining years in comfort and with some little sense of responsibility.

In addition to the children born on Dove Cote were those brought over from The Patch as babies, to be reared in the healthier environment of the home plantation. These were turned into what Verder, for want of a better name, designated as the "Romp Pasture," a few acres of sparsely wooded land, some three furlongs from the house and equipped with cabins solely for the rearing of the slave children born at The Patch. It was so named because it was set aside for these children—a realm of their own where they could romp and cavort and grow, naked and unashamed, until they reached adolescence and became serviceable as laborers. Those born at Dove Cote were permitted to remain with their mothers,

71

but those from The Patch were brought over at weaning to give them the benefit of its greater salubrity and its freedom from the miasma with which the low-lying Patch was cursed.

Despite the mother's tears when her baby was taken away, Verder saw no cruelty in such a removal of the young, for he knew from experience that children left with their parents at The Patch developed into puny, frail, or sickly youths or died in infancy. Those taken to Dove Cote where they were adequately if coarsely fed usually developed vigorous lusty bodies under the care of Uncle Georgie, a crippled superannuate, and Aunt Nervy, an old crone whose name had long since been shortened from Minerva. Ol' Georgie had once been Nervy's spouse, but they had quarreled so much that, once Nervy had ceased to breed, Verder had separated them, putting Nervy in charge of the infants until the male children were old enough to be lifted over the fence to go with George, while the girls remained with Aunt Nervy. Here they all continued to stay until they were fourteen or fifteen years of age. At that time they were old enough to do productive work and were either retained at Dove Cote if they showed exceptional promise or sent over to The Patch, where the girls were assigned to families and the boys lived together in a big shedlike dormitory until such a time as they chose their own mates and their choice was confirmed by Verder.

Ol' Georgie, and those older boys whom he chose to accompany him, had the task of supplying both the big house at Dove Cote and the Romp Pasture with game. George was the only Negro entrusted with a gun and with it he provided most of the fresh meat served on the plantation. Quail, grouse, snipe, wild ducks, geese, and turkeys, along with passenger pigeons, were welcome additions to the Big House menus, while rabbits, opossums, deer and an occasional bear provided a change of meat. Only the best were delivered to Aunt Ruthie, the rest were all boiled in the big cauldron at the Romp Pasture until the flesh fell apart, after which the broth was thickened with corn meal and whatever vegetables happened to be handy. When it was all cooked, the great kettle was emptied into long, waist-high wooden troughs. This stew or porridge, along with an occasional mug of clabbered milk, was the sole diet of the growing children. Such as it was, it was supplied plentifully and the children were permitted all they could consume. They lined up at the troughs like so many hungry calves, eating with their hands and fighting among themselves for the chunks of meat and marrow bones which were considered rare delicacies. They were, all in all, a healthy lot of little animals. They were as sportive as young colts, as cute as puppies, as affectionate as kittens, and as unspoiled as lambs.

As they grew up, the boys could see the girls between the rails of the fence, although they showed very little curiosity about each other's sex. The boys, more precocious in sex matters than the girls, quickly learned from the older boys (by sleeping four or five under one blanket on a pallet) various methods of sex gratification which served them sufficiently to retard their interest in the opposite sex. The nocturnal pastimes of the boys were known to Verder. He neither condoned nor discouraged them, because he realized they were a necessary outlet. Those boys who were occasionally discovered by Ol' Georgie were punished merely by a scolding or a threat to curtail their rations, neither of which deterred them in the least. By the time they reached their early teens and took to hanging around the fence, they were weeded out and transferred from the Romp Pasture, the handsomer ones remaining at Dove Cote where Verder could admire them himself and show them off to his friends. Verder was proud of his fine slaves and they were a part of the glory of Dove Cote—his home; his family's habitation; his headquarters, and his showplace. He had built his house of logs and it was a sound house, well constructed of squared timbers. It contained seven spacious rooms, all on one floor. These opened off a central hall which ran the length of the house with a door at each end. A roofed veranda with a row of homemade, rush-seated chairs, whose only communicating door led into a room Verder used as an office, ran along one side of the house.

The original house in which old Tom Verder had lived and where Tom had been born had consisted of only two rooms, separated by an open dogtrot between. This had served as the basis of the new house, the original kitchen still remaining, with the dogtrot separating it from the rest of the house. The other room of the old house now served as a dining room. By means of the open-air but roofed breezeway between, the inmates of the new house were spared the heat and odors that emanated from the kitchen.

Verder had built his house of logs because he preferred them over clapboard or brick, although he was affluent enough to have afforded the more expensive materials. The logs had been felled from the trees on his own plantation and seemed to fit into the landscape better than other materials might have done. They had been smoothly sawed and each year were treated to a "painting" of mixed linseed oil and turpentine. The result was a solid house, plain and forthright, for Tom Verder was a plain and forthright man as well as a man of pride. Once the house was finished, its substantial and unembellished plainness seemed somehow unfitting to his position. It needed something to lift it out of the commonplace—something the plain craftsmen of the neighborhood could not construct. It was then that he and Callie, with the infant Dovie, took the first and only trip of their lives—to Mobile. Here Verder purchased a simple, white-pillared doorway with leaded side lights and a fan window above it. The massive mahogany door which it boasted had a knocker in the shape of a brass eagle and the key that turned the lock was an intricate piece of wrought iron. While in Mobile, he gave Callie *carte blanche* in the furniture shops and she bought carpets, beds, and other furniture, mostly in the heavy Empire style then in vogue. The crowning glory, however, of her purchases was an immense rosewood piano. Although she could not play it herself, it was an ornament to be proud of.

All this furniture and the doorway were transported by ox carts, along rutted and narrow roads, back to Dove Cote. Strangely enough, when the Georgian doorway was installed in the front of the house and the carpets and furniture arranged inside, the result was far from incongruous. Callie was a fine housekeeper, despite her indolence, and the furniture shone from constant beeswaxing. She, with Congo as an assistant, reigned quite as supreme inside the house as Tom Verder did outside. A few years after the house was built, Verder purchased, from an itinerant peddler, a copper weathervane which might have been intended to be an eagle but which Verder imagined to be a dove. This was placed at the peak of the hip roof where it was a constant source of admiration and wonder to the slaves.

Behind the house and entirely separate from it was another building that appeared to be a tower or fortress, protecting the main house. This, although only two stories high, reached far above the main house, the ceilings in the tower being higher than those in the house itself. The first floor of this structure was fitted up as a bedroom with cast-off furniture from the big house, but was seldom used except by Tommy Verder, who had enjoyed the freedom of access it gave him when returning from his nightly visits to the quarters. The formal guest room was in the house, next door to Dovie's room and separated from the nuptial chamber of Tom and Callie by Tom's office.

Above the single room of the tower was an unused attic which had been intended as a dove cote, although no dove or pigeon had ever deigned to nest there. This tower was, however, the most salient feature of the countryside and from it the plantation took its name "Dove Cote." It was, perhaps, more of a tribute to Verder's daughter Dovie than anything else, and its use as a dove cote was never questioned despite the fact that no dove had ever investigated its interior.

The big double parlors of the main house were furnished with the heavy, ormolu-mounted Empire pieces of massive mahogany, upholstered in green and red velvets which Callie had purchased in Mobile. These were placed at set and formal intervals on red Turkish carpets. Heavy brocades draped the small-paned windows, shutting out most of the light. The dining room departed from the heavy Empire of the other rooms and was furnished in a style that approximated Chippendale, with a long mahogany table, an equally long sideboard, chairs with lacy-carved ribbon backs and, in the center of the table, the piece which was Callie's pride and joy and a marvel to the entire countryside. It was a centerpiece, evidently inspired by Napoleon's campaign in Egypt, called the "Well in the Desert." On a massive silver plateau, silver palm trees surrounded the oasis of a crystal bowl, usually filled with fruit or flowers, while at one side, proud on his Arabian charger, a silver sheik of the desert lifted his lance in a shout of victory. It had been an extravagance on Verder's part, but it had paid off over the years in the wonder and admiration it had excited from guests passing through.

The barns were clustered around the main house— the stables, dairy barn, harness shed, smokehouse, toolhouse, corncribs, blacksmith shop, and various sheds and lean-tos, making a little community of itself. At some little distance from the house and shielded from it by a grove of sycamores were the slave quarters where the Dove Cote slaves lived. Their cabins faced each other across a dusty street, each in its own plot of about an acre of ground, which was used as a garden by the occupants and to tether the cow or pig which was allotted to them. The slave cabins too were solidly built of logs with puncheon floors. Each consisted of but a single room with a loft overhead. They were windowless but well chinked, with sound, waterproof roofs, and although each had a wattled chimney, the fireplace was used mostly for heating in the winter months, as practically all the cooking was done out of doors in fair weather, which usually prevailed.

The slaves at Dove Cote were well fed, well treated and, for the most part, well behaved. They knew that for bad conduct they would be sent to The Patch, a punishment which all of them dreaded, for it was common gossip among the slaves that those at The Patch worked harder for longer hours and were punished more frequently by the transient white overseers. It was an honor to be a Dove Cote slave, for Verder's finest Negroes were kept at the home plantation. Here were the soundest, the most vigorous, the sleekest, and the comeliest. Those at The Patch, with the exception of the quadroon and lighter girls which served Tom Verder and Nero, were the uglier, the less able, and the less manageable.

In fact, in nearly all respects The Patch was different from Dove Cote. Although its commonplace name implied a smaller and less extensive area, it was ten times as big as Dove Cote, embracing more than twenty square miles—a vast, low-lying tract of meadow, swamp, and forest which was being drained and cleared as rapidly as the Verder slaves could do it. The soil was rich and fertile—black loam that grew twice the cotton that Dove Cote did. But The Patch was so unhealthful, pestilential, and miasmic that Verder had never considered building a house there; in addition to the miserable climate the place was alive with snakes and swarming with insects, especially mosquitoes—millions of them. It was so malarial that, although its name was mentioned daily by Callie and Dovie, neither of them had ever seen it, and Tommy Verder had only been allowed to accompany his uncle there a year or so before his departure. Whether it was his continuous dosage of quinine or the fact that his bed was screened with a mosquito net, Tom Verder had never suffered from malaria. As to Nero, it was felt that the Negro blood in his veins kept him from the disease, for it was a well-grounded superstition that Negroes were immune to the ague.

The Patch was situated about fifteen miles from Dove Cote but the tortuous roads, narrow and rutted and in places low and swampy, made the distance seem longer. Although Verder spent at least half his time at The Patch, it was necessary for him to have a white overseer there, in accordance with the law which required that each plantation have a white man over the slaves. These overseers were a poor lot—the ragtag and bobtail of the white population of the south. they were mostly itinerant bachelors of a low degree of mentality and morals who drifted from one plantation to another, either fired by the owner after a year of service or leaving of their own accord to seek something that might be better. They fell into two patterns, and it was difficult to decide which of the two was the worse. One type worked the slaves with sadistic lashings to get the most out of them and thus increase their own percentage of the crop; the other type was so lazy and inept and so wedded to the bottle that they got little or no work done. There never seemed to be any happy medium. Tom Verder would much have preferred to have his own body servant, Nero, as overseer at The Patch, but this was impossible because Nero was only part white and a slave.

Nero was a handsome, tall, vigorous light-yellow man—probably octoroon if his genealogy could have been traced. He was actually Tom's half-brother, sired by Tom's father on a quadroon wench, Peaches, who was still living at Dove Cote. Nero had served as play-boy to his master during their childhood and had grown into his body servant, accompanying him wherever he went and sleeping on a pallet outside his bedroom door or beside his bed on the floor. Indeed, until they had reached late adolescence, they had occupied the same bed.

Old Tom Verder had given Nero to his son when both were babies and the relationship between them was rather that of boon companions than of master and slave, although Nero never forgot (and was never permitted to forget) his subservience. However, at times, the relationship of master and slave slipped into that of two friends and they even argued with each other about matters of plantation policy. Nero was the only person that Verder would listen to, for Verder recognized, although it was never openly acknowledged, that Nero knew as much about the management of the plantations as he did. Nero, however, in spite of his knowledge, realized his position and never pressed the point in any argument. But Tom was fair enough, when he had disregarded some advice of Nero's to his own detriment, to admit that possibly—only possibly—he might have been better off had he followed Nero's opinion.

There were no secrets between Tom Verder and Nero. They were companions, friends, and brothers, in that order. Their blood relationship was never mentioned between them, never acknowledged, and never affirmed, but both of them were always conscious of it. This consanguinity was apparent to even the most casual observer for, although Nero was taller, stronger, and several pounds heavier than Tom, with kinky instead of straight hair, the resemblance between them left no doubt as to their common sire. From their father they had inherited the same facial lineaments; from their mothers they had inherited their physiques—Nero's tall, muscular, and African, Tom's shorter and wiry.

Together they had shared nearly every experience of their lives. Their burgeoning sexual desires were first satisfied together with various experimentations, in the confines of the double bed they shared in the loft. When these desires demanded the more complete satisfaction of the opposite sex, they had both been initiated at the same time by the same person. After that, Tom and Nero preyed on any available wench they could find until Tom's father, discovering them one day in the lower room of the Dove Cote, recognized that the time had come for his acknowledgment and gave them the run of the quarters and the Romp Pasture. "My papa started me in younger'n yo' boys," he said, " 'n' never did me no harm. Jes' don' overdo it, tha's all."

It was their habit to share, and after a while Tom relinquished his prerogative of preceding Nero, when he realized he grew more excited watching Nero perform first. The only person they had never shared was Callie who, of course, as a white woman was beyond the touch of Nero, although he often saw her in bed with only a sheet pulled over her when he undressed Tom for the night. On Tom's wedding night, Nero had moved from his master's room to take up his place on a pallet outside the door. The sounds inside came to him and he was jealous of the neuter Congo who was permitted to stay in the room.

Tom was a good husband to Callie. He thought he was in love with her and probably he was, but it was doubtful that he worshiped her as much as Nero did. To Nero she was a goddess from another world.

Tom would have been shocked had anyone suggested that he did not love Callie. Probably he loved her as

79

much as most Southern men loved their wives. They were women—a symbol of virtue, home, and religion. These wives were the mothers of their children and altogether sacrosanct. Such was the way Tom regarded Callie. She managed his home and provided all the creature comforts he desired. She mothered his daughter. She gave him such companionship as her rather limited education and intelligence could provide. She shared his bed with him on those nights when he stayed at Dove Cote. On those nights he performed his duty, if he could not beg off with an excuse of being too tired, but he executed the act mechanically without any degree of pleasure. For a real romp in the hay, for all-out pleasure, he preferred a young Negro wench who could enjoy what she was doing and admit it rather than submit in frigid silence because she had been brought up to consider her husband's attentions too vulgar and too coarse for her to enjoy. Callie, although she always made the proper gestures of distaste, enjoyed him far more than she was willing to admit even to herself.

When they were first married, Tom had found her roundness appealing and exciting, for this was how both he and Nero liked their women. When her plumpness changed to obesity, however, he lost what ardor he had had. Now he preferred the musky confines of his cabin at The Patch, with his choice of his harem sharing his bed and his most recent cast-off with Nero on his pallet on the floor.

Tom had always exercised his *droit du seigneur* on his wenches. To them, their defloration by their master was their supreme moment of honor—perhaps the only time in their lives that they would be the sole object of his attentions. This was their due. They anticipated it and accepted it, glorying in their brief hour and treasuring its memory all their lives. Through his own exploits, those of his father and brothers and Nero, and now more recently of his nephew Tommy, the overall color of the Verder slaves had gradually become lighter, although Verder had never encouraged breeding for breeding's sake. Formerly the time a female slave lost through pregnancy, birth, and lactation was more valuable than the issue she produced. But now, with the rising prices of slaves, Tom was beginning to encourage breeding. A fine male slave could be sold, at the age of twenty, for a thousand dollars. It certainly did not cost fifty dollars a year to raise him and for five of his twenty years, Tom got labor out of him. He was not necessarily raising his slaves for sale but as The Patch expanded more and more slaves were needed to work it. And, of course, the more slaves he had, the wealthier he was.

He was, however, too good a husbandman not to realize that new male blood was needed from time to time to improve the quality if not the color of his stock. For this reason, as more land was cleared at The Patch and more hands were needed, Tom, accompanied by Nero, made trips to local slave auctions where, through death or insolvency or merely for gain, slaves were being sold. He purchased only the healthy, the handsome, the vigorous, and the strong, concentrating on males to add new strength and vigor to his herd, and for this purpose he bought Africans rather than the lighter colored hybrids. Although the influx of white blood produced handsomer, more valuable slaves, it did not produce the strength and endurance needed for hard work in the fields. For this Tom preferred those with recognizable Iwo, Fanti, Hausa, Kru, or Mandingo ancestry. These were the men whose strong backs could till his soil, drain his swamps, cut his trees, and still have the energy to beget more strong hands to serve him at The Patch and Dove Cote.

Tom Verder was a man of just and gentle disposition, except when he was angered and became the victim of a violent and uncontrollable rage. He was so certain of his own omnipotence that he never questioned his own actions. Occasionally his decisions were tempered by the diplomatic words of Nero, softly spoken when Tom was angry. This advice was never acknowledged by any expression of gratitude on Tom's part, but as evidence of his respect for his bondsman half-brother, Tom had raised him to the highest position of authority which a slave could hold—that of his own body servant and whipper for the two plantations.

At first Nero had not relished the job. He had not

enjoyed inflicting pain, but as time went on he perfected his technique until he became a master with the cowhide. He was so expert that he could lay an exact pattern on a slave's back—an almost mathematically exact cross-hatching or an equally spaced ladder that reached from his ankles to his shoulders. His talents were recognized throughout the county. Like all other products of Tom Verder's two plantations, Nero was the best in his line.

Tom Verder was a respected man, the owner of two fine plantations and many slaves. He was the richest man in the community, although he never vaunted his wealth. At home he was a strict disciplinarian. He was obeyed and at the same time loved not only by his family but by his Negroes. It was not unusual, when a Negro had been whipped by Nero, for him to crawl on his belly, of his own volition, and kiss Tom Verder's boots. "Never do it 'gain, masta Tom suh. Ain' never a-goin' ter be bad no mo'." And Tom, the punishment over, would look down on the groveling body and say, "Know yo' won', Tiger" (or Willie or Scratch or even Maggie). And Tom was also loved by his family—his wife Callie, his beloved daughter Dovie, and his half-brother Nero. At one time he had been loved and respected by his nephew Tommy, and this love had been returned. But Tommy had gone and when he went a little of Tom Verder's heart went with him. It had never returned because Tommy had not come back. Verder had never had a son, but he had hoped to make Tommy his son by marrying him to his daughter.

But Tommy—the gay, the handsome, the witty, the son Tom Verder had always wanted—had gone, and nobody knew where.

Chapter III

IT WAS LATE in the afternoon when Callie awoke and the length of the shadows on the floor told her it must be nearly dinner time. Congo was still snoring on his pallet and Callie, with considerable difficulty, hoisted her huge bulk into an upright position on the bed. Her calls to awaken him brought no response, for he was a heavy sleeper, so she maneuvered her body around until she could grasp one pillow and heaved it at him. It struck him full in the face and the impact awoke him. He sat up, staring at her on the bed.

"Git up, yo' lazy barrow, 'n' git me dressed." She had not intended to sleep so long. "Time we was a-eatin' 'n' I'm hungry's a bear. Ain' had nothin' since brekkus 'cept that li'l scimmage o' gingerbread. Stir yore stumps!"

Congo was on his feet in a moment, and with his help Callie inched her massive legs over the side of the bed and got her tiny feet onto the floor. Her dressing was not a complicated process. Congo washed her face in cool water and braided her hair in long braids which he tied with sprigged taffeta ribbons and draped pendant over her shoulders. He helped her into a clean, starched pink wrapper whose ruffled furbelows made her look even rounder. Neither corsets nor petticoats restricted her waist or her pendulous breasts, but the high-necked, long-sleeved wrapper covered her completely and mod-

83

estly from head to toe, and its pinkness was reflected in a roseate glow in her cheeks. Despite her rotundity, she was attractive in a clear-skinned, golden-haired way. When she stood up, after Congo's ministrations, she slipped her feet into large worn carpet slippers and scuffed along in them out of the door of her room, down the narrow hall and into the back parlor where she lowered her weight, with Congo's help, into a massive mahogany chair. Congo handed her a big palmetto fan with which she fanned herself but, finding the exertion too much, she handed it back to him with a command to continue.

Callie had no plans—at least nothing definite beyond naming the Reverend Bartholomew Boggs as the father of Dovie's child. That was a beginning and she was thankful that his visit at Dove Cote had been timed to coincide with Dovie's pregnancy. Even with his sanctimonious mouthings he was better than some itinerant slave trader. At least he was a Verder kin, as well as being young and, in spite of his uncouthness, good-looking. So much for that! Now for the next step. She was quite prepared to sacrifice anything to preserve her daughter's good name and the standing of the Verder name as the wealthiest and most respected in the community. Callie was playing for high stakes—her daughter's honor and happiness. Therefore she felt she was entitled to use any weapon she could to gain her ends. Dovie must get married. The disgrace of having her own daughter the mother of a bastard was more than she could bear and she also knew that, regardless of how much Tom Verder loved his daughter, he would never forgive Dovie unless things were presented to him in the most favorable light. Now it only remained to get Tom into some sort of good humor and try to prevent one of his blind rages when he heard the news that his cousin Bart Boggs was the father of Dovie's child. It was a problem but Callie felt she could solve it. She must solve it before Tom arrived the next morning.

Callie too would have preferred Tommy as a son-in-law. She had always been fond of him, looking on him almost as a son. Callie had a feeling, even though she had lied to Dovie about the dream warning her that he was dead, that Tommy really was dead. Either that or he had gone away to New Orleans and become enamored of some white girl whom he had married or, more probably, some octoroon who had so completely bewitched him that he was unable to leave. Drat those nigger wenches! They stole a woman's husband right out from her very bed, and she had to pretend that she didn't mind because as a white woman she was not supposed to enjoy pleasuring. Bah! What woman, white or black, didn't? And what with those wenches at The Patch a-dreanin' Tom, what did she get? Nothing! No, nothing, because she knew that more often than not Tom's final convulsive panting and release were only feigned so that he might have an excuse to go to sleep. Well, at least he had the decency to keep his wenches at The Patch. He'd never brought them into the house. And now Dovie had been raped in their own house, right under their noses.

A sound of horses' hooves on the graveled drive cut short her planning and announced the arrival of strangers. She managed to get out of her chair with Congo's help, across the hall, through the dark closet that contained the stairway to the loft above, and out the door of Tom's office onto the veranda. There she was greeted not by strangers but by Tom himself, with Nero behind him. They were just dismounting and Nero was handing the horses over to the stable boy. Stepping up onto the veranda, Tom walked across it, took as much of Callie as he could in his arms, and kissed her. Surprised at his early arrival, her plans as yet unformed, she had to do some quick thinking. She did. She flung her arms around him, weeping, clinging to him and closing her eyes.

"Nero," he called, as he felt Callie's weight slipping in his arms. "Come here 'n' help me. Miz Callie's done fainted. Where's that goddam Congo? What's bin a-goin' on 'roun' here? Git Miz Callie inside. Git her on her bed. Rout out that son-a-bitchin' Congo. Where's Dovie?"

Callie had not fainted, but she was doing a pretty convincing job of acting. With Nero supporting her on one side and Congo, who had been only a step behind her all the time, on the other, they managed to get her into the house and onto the bed. Congo, fussing and wailing like an old woman, held smelling salts under her nose, sprinkled her with Florida Water, chafed her hands, and called her name, while Tom and Nero looked on dumb-founded, not knowing if she were dead or alive. Callie managed one little moan.

"Tom, oh Tom, where are you, Tom?"

"Right here, Callie darlin'." Tom knelt beside the bed, convinced she was dying. At that moment he probably loved her more than at any time since the day they were married. "Yo' sick, Callie? What ailin' yo'?" He grabbed her hand from Congo and pressed it hard. "Open up yore eyes, Callie. Open yore eyes 'n' look at me. Yo' ain' dyin', are yo'?"

Slowly she opened her eyes and transfixed him with their dark blue stare. "Oh Tom, I'se so glad yo're here. Bin a-prayin' yo'd come. How'd yo' know I a-wantin' yo' so?"

"Didn't know, Callie. Got finished up over to The Patch 'n' thinkin' I'd like some o' Aunt Ruthie's cookin' tonight so I 'n' Nero rode over. Kin yo' talk? Yo' ain' had a stroke o' nothin', hev yo'?" He grasped her hand convulsively. "Yo' ain' dyin'?"

"Wish't I was, Tom, jes' wish't I was a-dyin'. Don' have no hankerin' ter live no longer. Thinkin' perhaps I'd better die 'n' go to sweet Jesus. Jes' cain' face it, Tom."

"Cain' face what, Callie?"

"Disgrace' tha's what. We'uns kin never hol' up our heads 'gain, we cain'. Thinkin' we'd best sell out 'n' go to the Texies o' somewhere's else. Cain' live 'round these parts no more."

Tom relinquished her hand and stood up. "Now what foolishness yo' a-talkin', Callie. Dove Cote's our home. We ain' a-goin' ter sell out 'n' move away, no matter what happen. What happen, anyway? Come home all petered out, jes' ter see yo' 'n' Dovie 'n' be at home 'n' find yo' this way." He stopped suddenly and stared down at Callie. "Yo' don' mean some nigger buck got in here 'n' raped yo'?" It was the most terrible thing he could think of, the worst disgrace that any woman could suffer.

"It's Dovie what been raped, not me."

Tom's face became purple; his hands shook with rage.

86

"What nigger done that ter Dovie? Jes' tell me 'n' I'll kill him with my bare hands. I'll . . ." He choked on the fearful punishments his racing mind envisaged.

Callie sighed and lost some of her tenseness. Now that Tom thought the worst, whatever she said would be better than what he imagined. But she did not intend to let him off without blame. The onus must be on him.

"It's all yore fault too, Tom Verder. All yore fault that we's disgraced the way we are. Yo' 'n' yore low-life Verder kinfolk. No, Tom Verder, yo' kin git down on yore knees 'n' thank God our pore li'l Dovie ain' been raped by no nigger but jes' 'bout as bad. By that polecat cousin o' your'n what goes 'roun' callin' himself a Rev'nd. Rev'nd? He better call hisself a son of Satan, that one. If'n I could get my hands on him, I'd strangle him myself. Choke his wind off, I would. Git him here 'n' I'll have Nero string him up 'n' strip the meat right off'n his bones even if'n he is white, low-life viper that he is." Callie's eyes closed and she had apparently fainted again.

Tom was almost as much at sea as he was before, but this time it was he who took charge of Callie instead of Congo. He poked the smelling salts directly beneath her nose. One whiff of them nearly choked poor Callie who came out of her supposed faint coughing instead of sobbing.

"Now yo' tell me what's bin a-goin' on here," Tom demanded impatiently. "What's all this whoop-de-do about us bein' disgraced; about Dovie; 'n' about my cousin Bart Boggs? Make some sense, Callie."

"Might's well tell yo' 'n' git it over with. Better prepare yo'self." She pointed a pudgy white finger at him. "Yore own cousin Boggs got our sweet li'l Callie in a family way. She knocked up."

"Good God in heaven! Yo're lyin', Callie." Tom flung the bottle of smelling salts across the room, where it shattered against the wall, filling the air with the sharp, acrid fumes of ammonia.

"Wish't I could spare yo' Tom, but it's true. Now yo' know why I a-sufferin'. My baby, my pure sweet innercent li'l Dovie a-taken in by that snake in the grass. All yore fault, too, Tom Verder, fer invitin' him here. Yo' know what happened up at Granby's Forge where that girl had a woods-colt what she say he fathered 'n' he not willin' ter marry her. Yo' know what kinda viper he was when yo' asked him ter stay here."

"Jes' asked him 'cause he kinfolk 'n' I felt sorry fer him."

" 'N' he a-bitin' the hand that fed him. Oh, pore li'l Dovie."

"Where is she?" Tom bellowed. "Whur's she at?"

"She's sick," Callie replied. "She's plumb wore out. She jes' confessed ter me this mornin'. Don' yo' talk ter her now. Might be the death o' her. She might slip it 'n' die. I beg o' yo', Tom, don' disturb that poor sufferin' child. She sufferin' the tortures o' the damned, 'fraid yo'll hold her ter blame 'n' not fergive her. But she blameless, Tom. 'Tweren't her fault, she so innercent like."

Tom stopped his pacing and stood by Callie's bed. "How it happen, that's what I want ter know? How it happen?"

"Kin tell yo' 'thout yo' a-askin' Dovie. Jes' yo' stop a-stompin' 'roun' 'n' listen ter me, 'n' stop yellin'. I ain' deef."

She related in detail all that Dovie had told her about her seduction, substituting Bart Boggs' name for Tommy's and embroidering some of the details with even more lascivious embellishments. Throughout her recitative, she stressed Dovie's purity and innocence and Boggs' diabolical cunning. How was Dovie to know that she was not required to sacrifice herself in order to save another's life, particularly when that life belonged to a kinsman of her father's—a guest in her own home? How was she to know that Boggs' goatish tumescence was not a portent of his imminent death? How could she understand that his lewd exposure of himself was not actually brought on by his fear of immediate death through the bursting of his body? How could she, ignorant even of the appearance of male anatomy, know that Boggs was in no danger?

Dovie had never, no never, Callie assured her husband, seen even a nigger boy without clothes on, let alone a mating between animals or niggers. Hadn't they guarded her carefully from even straying in the direction of the Romp Pasture? Hadn't they kept her sweet and pure and she not knowing that there was any difference in the male and female physique? It had been difficult, living on a plantation, but she, Callie, had guarded Dovie and watched her all these years. Why, just a few months ago she had had a heart-to-heart talk with her in reply to Dovie's questions about babies and told her that the sweet little darlings were found at night under a sheltering cabbage leaf. And hadn't Dovie, big girl that she was, teased her mother to let her go out in the kitchen garden at night and look under the cabbages to see if she couldn't find a dear sweet baby of her own?

Tom agreed with everything that Callie said. He had been as anxious as she to keep Dovie pure. She had been forbidden, since the time she could walk, to stray in the direction of the quarters or the Romp Pasture. This had been so ingrained in her mind that she had never thought of disobeying. Even female dogs or cats were removed from the house when there were signs that they were going to give birth. In his mind Tom absolved Dovie from all guilt. But, in absolving Dovie, his anger against Boggs mounted. He would willingly have killed the man had he been present, but when he threatened to do this, Callie pleaded with him. There was, she pointed out to him, only one way that Boggs could atone and he had to be alive to do that. Therefore, for Dovie's sake, Tom must drop all thoughts of vengeance. He'd have to bring Boggs back to Dove Cote and make him marry Dovie, and then they could live at Dove Cote because Boggs had no place of his own and no means of earning a living except for his circuit preaching which barely supplied him with necessities. Gradually, under Callie's barrage of words, the color drained from Tom's face and he stopped his pacing.

"Nero, yo' go out 'n' saddle our horses. Better yo' gits fresh horses. Ain' no tellin' how far we a-goin' o' how long we a-goin' ter be gone. Load up my shotgun 'n' put it in the holster on my saddle."

"Yo' ain' a-goin' ter shoot him, Tom?" Callie pleaded with her husband.

"Ain a-goin' ter shoot the bastard," Tom replied grimly, "but I shore as hell a-goin' ter scare the livin' shit outa him."

"Yo' be careful o' yore language, Tom Verder." Callie waggled an admonitory finger at him. "Yo' jes' remember where yo' are. Yo' ain' in the quarters now o' over to The Patch with yore yellow wenches. This yore wife yo' a-talkin' to 'n' I ain' standin' fer no language like that."

Immediately he was contrite. "Beggin' yore pardon, Callie. Jes' got excited, tha's all. Hopin' yo'll fergive me."

"Under the circumstances." Callie could be magnanimous now that she had won her point.

"Kin I see Dovie?"

"Not if'n yo' gets her disturbed. Not if'n yo' goes in there all riled up, a-stompin' 'n' a-swearin' 'n' a-usin' dirty words. But if yo' goes in sweet 'n' lovin' like her own true papa, yo' kin. Promise?"

Tom nodded his head, and Callie got off the bed with the help of Congo. Tom took her arm and led her down the long hall. Dovie's door was closed but Callie rapped on it.

"Yore papa's here, Dovie sweetheart. He wants ter talk ter his baby girl."

Dovie was as adept at acting as her mother. "Cain' face my own dear papa," she wailed through the door.

"Papa jes' a-wantin' ter tell his baby girl he loves her 'n' he a-knowin' she not ter blame." Callie lifted the latch and led Tom into the darkened room, where Dovie was stretched out on the bed.

"Don' yo' worry, Dovie darlin'," Tom said, all kindly solicitude and protectiveness. "Papa'll take care of everything. That Rev'nd Boggs he really a nice feller. Jes' got carried away with love fer yo', tha's all. We all got ter fergive him 'n' welcome him inter the bosom o' the family. Had al'ays wish't it might have been Tommy. Tho't you 'n' Tommy'd make a right nice pair. But Bart he's a right good-looking boy—'n' he's a kinsman o' mine, too."

"Yo' a-goin' ter git him fer me, Papa?" Dovie's words were scarcely audible.

"Don' yo' fret. When I come back Nero 'n' me'll have the Rev'nd Bart Boggs right 'longside us, all ready ter be wedded up with yo'. He a right handsome boy, Bart is, 'n' right pious, too. His mama jes' like a sister ter me— kindly fond o' her I was 'n' she a fine woman. Ain' too

90

proud o' the Boggs' blood but he shore was a fine-lookin' feller tho' not as good lookin' as Bart. Yo' goin' ter be happy, Dovie. 'N' don' yo' worry none. Papa'll take care o' yo'."

Dovie raised herself weakly for her father's kiss. Waving away Congo, Tom took Callie's arm and led her out of the room. Their common trouble had drawn them together again, and his embrace and kiss were tender. "Be back soon, Callie. Don' fret. It may take us a couple o' days ter fin' him but everythin's going ter be all right." He kissed her again and strode out the door. Nero was waiting on the veranda, the horses saddled.

"Come on, boy." Tom was grim-faced again. "We a-goin' ter ketch us a yellow-bellied polecat. We'd skin him alive only his hide ain' worth it. But we a-goin' ter put the fear o' damnation inter that bastard. Goin' ter scare him shitless."

"Yas suh, masta Tom." Nero was anxious to get started. He was as angry as his master, because he worshiped Dovie. "Tho't mayhap yo' might be needin' a cowhide too." He pointed to the whip coiled around the pommel. "Know yo' uses it only fer niggers but this man he lower'n a nigger."

"That's 'nuff, Nero. He a-goin' ter git his comeuppance 'n' yo' kin look on 'n' help me if'n I want. We a-goin' ter make him wish he'd never been borned. But, when we gits through, don' yo' fergit that he's my kinsman 'n' Miz Dovie's intended. Ain' no cause fer yo' ever ter remember what we did ter him. 'N' I don' want one word o' this ter get out to the other servants."

" 'Course not, masta Tom, 'course not."

" 'N' yo' rides alongside o' me this time, Nero. Need company, I do, a-feelin' this way."

The afternoon sun was setting as they rode down the long lane of live oaks which led from Dove Cote's white-pillared front door to the road.

Chapter IV

TEN MILES OF fairly good road separated Dove Cote
from the nearest village—a good-sized town by the name
of Brownsville—good-sized, that is, for that period of
Alabama history. In a purely agricultural area such as
that was, the towns were of small importance, but Brownsville was the headquarters for a store, a bank, a doctor,
a lawyer, a livery stable, a tavern, and a Methodist meeting house. Its only industry was the cotton gin; its only
residents, outside of the few professional men and the
storekeepers, were the gin hands. The well-to-do of that
time lived on the plantations; the townsmen were looked
down upon except, of course, for the banker, who was
usually the leading citizen of the settlement. Brownsville's
dusty main street, bordered by shade trees—gums, sycamores, oaks, and other hard woods—marked the transi-
tion from country to town. A few houses, white-painted
with verandas, boasted lawns and flowering shrubs, but
the majority of the dwellings were slab-sided cabins. One
substantial brick building housed the bank. It alone
boasted a second story where the town's attorney had an
office. The store, which included the groggery, was a
rambling wooden structure, one story high, with a wide
porch perenially decorated with washtubs, harness benches,
plows, and other farm implements.

Tom Verder and Nero rode abreast, exchanging few
92

words in their anger. The sun had set, birds were calling, and they passed small companies of plodding slaves, going home from the day's cotton-picking. Despite his preoccupation with Dovie's predicament, Tom was not above noticing the Negroes.

"Mighty pore lot, ain' they, Nero?"

"Scrawny critters mos' o' them," Nero agreed. "Not much like our Dove Cote hands."

"Nor Patch hands neither." Tom inventoried them each time he passed a group. "Them's Maitland's herd." He pointed to a group of older men, trudging along in the dust: "Al'ays heard he'd skin a flea ter get its taller. Don' look like them boys ever had a decent meal all their lives. Kin count their ribs. Cain' get no work outa a hand that ain' got no food a-stickin' ter his guts. Maitland he don' ever look like he had a good meal hisself 'n' his ol' woman's as skinny as a fence rail. What ter hell, if'n a man a-goin' ter keep niggers, he got ter feed 'em."

"We ain' et either, masta Tom. Beginning ter feel hungry, I do."

"Tighten up yore belt. We goin' ter eat sometime but I jes' don' know when nor where. Ain' a-goin' ter stop at the Maitland place tho'. Wind puddin' 'n' air sauce with a glass o' water ain' 'nuff fer us. Fust off, want ter see that preacher in Brownsville. He probably know whereat that bastard Boggs is. Preachers all hang together, I reckon."

It was nearly dusk when they cantered into Brownsville and through the dust of the main street to the other side of town where a group of tall oaks, hung with ragged gray streamers of moss, sheltered the little meeting house whose spire reached no higher than the tallest trees. At one time it had been painted white, but the paint was peeling, the steeple was awry, and timbers shored up one side of it. Tom dismounted, strode up the rickety steps, and opened the door. Inside there was a musty smell of closed-in air, dust, and decaying wood. Tom called out, knowing while he did so that it was useless, for there was nobody in evidence. He called several times until an answering halloo came from a cabin down the road and

93

a white cloth, waving in the dusk, attracted his attention. Leaving Nero with the horses, Tom walked toward the sound.

An old woman leaned on the fence, a corncob pipe in her mouth.

"Yo' lookin' fer someone, mista?" she asked without removing the pipe.

"Lookin' fer the Rev'nd Soper. That church his'n, ain' it?"

"It his'n all right. Only church in Brownsville 'n' he the only ordained preacher. He my husband. He comin' right now. Been workin' late, seein' as how he had a funeral this afternoon 'n' needin' ter git the corn in. That nigger runt what we got too lazy ter scratch the dead fleas off'n hisself if Rev'nd Soper ain' 'roun' with a cowhide. Tarnation lazy, these niggers. Too stupid ter know that if'n he don' git the corn in, he don' eat, come winter."

"I a-seekin' Rev'nd Boggs." Verder ignored her as he watched the slow progress of a mule cart up the road. "Yo' kindly know whereat I kin find him?"

"Not here yo' won'." The old woman collected a gob of saliva in her mouth and removed the pipe from her lips long enough to spit. Her rancor was evident. "I got me a houn' dog in the house and if'n ever that good-fer-nothin' Boggs come a-moseyin' 'roun' here, I'll sic my dog on him. What yo' a-wantin' that scallywag fer? What he done now?"

"I cravin' he should kindly marry my gal if'n yo' know where he is at."

"Bah!" The old woman belched and nearly lost her grip on her pipe. "If'n he marry her, she ain' married 'tall. He ain' ordained, he ain'. Got no right ter marry folks up. Whyn't yo' have my man marry her? Kin do it better'n Boggs." Envisioning the stipend they would receive if Verder engaged her husband, she went on, "He a real ordained rev'nd. That Boggs ain'. He jes' calling hisself one 'n' goes 'round a-preacherin' 'n' exhortin' 'n' enticin' folks ter hell. Yes suh, right down ter the blazin' brimstone o' hell."

"That ain' the kind of marryin' I thinkin' of. That ain' what I seekin' Boggs fer," Tom said. "He's plighted ter

94

my daughter. Lookin' fer him ter be a groomsman, I am. Aimin' ter have Rev'nd Soper perform the ceremony if'n I kin find Boggs."

Mrs. Soper's manner changed. She had recognized Tom and felt that a person of his affluence should be worth about five dollars for a marriage ceremony. The cart was now within hailing distance and Tom beckoned for Nero to join him. He came up the road, leading the horses, and arrived at the same time as the Reverend Soper. In a rush of words, Mrs. Soper tried to explain what Tom wanted as Soper got down painfully from his vehicle. Tom noticed that the man limped painfully.

Soper evidently had not heard his wife's words, for his greeting was far from friendly. "Ain' yo' that blasphemous freethinker what lives out at that Dove Cote?" he said immediately, oblivious to his wife's frantic motions to quiet him as she sidled out to the cart to whisper to him.

"Reckon I am," Verder chuckled. "I live at Dove Cote. Name o' Verder. I'm a-seekin' Bart Boggs. Know at where I kin fin' him o' when he a-comin' through?"

"That rapscallion! Don' know the scoundrel nor nothin' 'bout him. Hattie here says yo' wants me ter marry him up wid yore daughter. What she want o' him, he a-callin' himself a Baptist, a-goin' 'roun' preacherin' false doctrine, a-marryin' 'n' a-baptizin' 'n' a-buryin'? He ain' no real rev'nd like me. Ordained I am—a Methodist."

The slave, an undernourished boy of about thirteen, sat on the rickety wagon seat, listening. Soper turned to him, flicking him across the face with his horsewhip. "Drat yo', Cudjo, git along wid that mule out ter the crib 'n' get that corn out. Listenin', always listenin'. Tha's the best thing yo' do. Don' ever do no work." Soper turned to Verder. "Got ter be pitchforkin' a nigger every minute if'n yo' craves any work outa 'em. This one never does a lick less'n I'm proddin' him. Reckon his ass needs warmin'. Goin' ter send him down ter Brother Johnson at the smithy fer a good paddlin'. Cain' do it myself with only one hand but Brother Johnson kindly obliges me 'n' don' charge me nothin'."

Cudjo slapped the ropes on the mule's back and got him started. "Don' sen' me fer no paddlin', masta suh.

95

That Brother Johnson he awful strong. Last time he whaled me so I los' my eye."

Tom could see that the boy had a gaping red hole where one eye had been. He felt a strange sympathy for him as he creaked away in the cart. Tom professed to no religion himself but he despised this psalm-mouthing hypocrite who would so treat a mere boy.

Soper put his hand to his forehead and stared at Nero in the dusk. "Mighty fine-lookin' nigger what yo' got there, Mista Verder. Aims ter git me one like him sometime." Soper spoke as though the purchase of a thousand-dollar Negro were an everyday occurrence in his life. "Kindly admire ter see him shucked down if'n he fer sale."

Tom could not resist smiling at the thought of this scarecrow buying Nero, but courtesy to a white man, even a man he despised as much as Soper, demanded that he honor the request, regardless of how impossible it might seem. However, right now he could plead his haste and he apologized to Soper, who accepted.

Soper became more friendly. "If'n yo' finds Boggs, yo' plannin' ter have me tie the knot?" The only ready money he ever got came from marriages and funerals and, as his wife had, he saw Verder as a good prospect.

"Countin' on that if'n yo' might kindly direct me to whar I kin fin' him."

"Yo' not a-goin' ter set Boggs up agin me, build him a meetin' house 'n' everythin'?" Soper asked fearfully. "They a-sayin' yo' rich."

"Ain' that rich." Verder's laugh dismissed the idea. "When Boggs a-comin' through? Yo' a-knowin'?"

"Don' rightly know, Mista Verder, but kin tell yo' who would. That Salsman woman what lives this side o' the store. She'd know if'n anyone would," he sneered. "Boggs stays in her house when he here 'n' what's more"—he lowered his voice so his spouse would not hear—"he sleeps with her. She ain' scarcely more'n a whore. Used ter be right respectable once 'n' took in washin's 'n' 'tended my church but Boggs came along with his preacherin' 'n' she backslided 'n' now she's a-whorin' 'n' she's a-whoremongerin' fer her eldest gal, too. She'll know! She'll know all 'bout Boggs. Birds of a feather, I say."

96

Verder thanked him, arranged for the marriage service to be performed when he should locate Boggs, bade the preacher farewell, and set out to seek Mrs. Salsman, with whose reputation he was already familiar. He and Nero found the lady, sitting idly in the doorway of her cabin. The light from a tallow dip inside showed her to be wearing a loose wrapper which appeared to be her only garment. Two tow-headed youths, possibly fourteen or fifteen, were playing leapfrog in the yard, and upon seeing Verder and Nero stopped their play and came to stare, silent and open-mouthed, at them. Verder bade Mrs. Salsman a courteous good evening, and she rose to her bare feet, pulled free from her large buttocks that part of her garb which had adhered to them, adjusted the snuff stick which hung loosely from the corner of her mouth, and advanced a step to meet him.

"Evenin'," she greeted Verder. "Right warm fer this time o' year, ain' it?"

He agreed with her, remembering now that he had seen her before at the store next door. She was a florid, apple-cheeked woman of about thirty years, big-breasted, big-hipped and buxom—the kind of a figure Verder admired on a woman. A big loose bun of dull blonde hair shifted back and forth on her head as she talked, but it must have been more securely anchored than it appeared, for it did not fall down. Tom decided she might be pretty if her hair were neatly combed and she were dressed in a clean frock or, better, in none.

To his inquiry about Boggs she answered, "Rev'nd Boggs? Well, ter tell the truth I've bin a-lookin' fer him ter come 'long all day. He's due 'n' overdue. Don' know what's a-keepin' him. Miss his preacherin', I do. It's shore soul-stirrin'."

"Which way he a-comin' from, if'n yo' kindly knows?"

Mrs. Salsman looked down the road as if expecting Boggs to ride up on a white horse in shining armor. " 'Course I not sure," she said, "but most often he comes from Orion. That on his way here from Marseilles. Yo' a-knowin' whereat them towns is? They up Benson way. Not so big's Brownsville but Boggs he got a follerin' there."

Tom knew that the town of Orion was about seventeen miles along a road that twisted back and forth over a creek. It would be impossible to ride there tonight, and he considered going over to Pawlett, the Trueblood plantation, to spend the night. He thanked Mrs. Salsman and clucked to his horse, but she seemed eager to continue the conversation.

"What fur yo' a-wantin' Bart? He ain' in no trouble, is he? Ain' done nothin' bad?"

Tom shook his head. "No, I ain' the law. Boggs he's a kinsman o' mine. Family matter, tha's all."

She nodded her head with the sudden dawn of comprehension. " 'Members yo' now, I do. Yo're Mista Verder o' Dove Cote. 'Members that Bart visited yo' last spring. He a-tellin' me he's kin ter yo' but I not believin' it—yo' so rich 'n' all 'n' him so poor." She came over to stand by Tom's horse and put her hand up on his knee.

The warmth of it, through his trousers excited him. It was light enough so that he could look down the gaping front of her wrapper and see the white globes of her breasts. They were the only white ones he had ever seen in his life except Callie's, for he had never had a white woman before or after his marriage to Callie. The thought of their whiteness, their roundness, their softness aroused him. What would it be like to have white flesh under him? He realized that it was too late to travel any farther and he sought some excuse to linger.

"Wonder if'n yo' could git us some vittles," he asked. "We ain' had no supper yet 'n' reckon I craves somethin'."

She smiled up at him. "Kin do, but it'll cost yo' two bits 'n' ain' got much 'cept some eggs 'n' pone. But the nigger, he cain' eat inside. Cain' come in. He got ter eat outside. Folks talk 'nuff as it is 'thout no niggers a-comin' in. Right fine-lookin' boy tho'." She appraised Nero. " 'Mos' white, too. Ain' nigger-featured at all, he ain'. Bet yo' gits some good pups outa him."

"Eggs is fillin'," Verder said, ignoring her remarks about Nero. He recoiled from the very thought of a white woman discussing Nero. "Eggs 'nuff fer us."

Mrs. Salsman turned, her hand sliding up Tom's thigh.

"Lorie," she called. "Kindle that fire. This gen'man a-wantin' somethin' ter eat 'n' his boy too. He wantin' some fried eggs, 'n' pone, 'n' cawfee. Het it up."

Lorie came to the door and peered out to see who the gentleman might be. She was a younger version of her mother, but her hair appeared to be combed and she wore a starched white wrapper. She was about the age of Dovie but much more mature in her appearance. He remembered now that Soper had talked about the woman pimping for her daughter and any designs he might have had on the mother were routed by the sight of this younger, fairer flesh. He got down off his horse and motioned to Nero to hitch the horses to a chinaberry tree that grew in the yard.

The taller of the two boys spoke for the first time, grinning from ear to ear. "He a-goin' ter sleep wid yo' o' Lorie, maw? That mean me 'n' Robbie got ter sleep in the shed?"

"Yo' shet yore mouth, Dabney," Mrs. Salsman screamed at him. "Jes' shet yore mouth 'n' take Robbie with yo'. Yo' ain' so all-fired big but what I kin still wallop yo'. Now git out to that shed both o' yo' 'fore I takes a broom handle ter yo'. Git!" She turned apologetically to Tom. "Don' pay them no neverminds. They too young ter know what they a-talkin' 'bout. 'Commodates travelers here sometimes, bein' right next door to the store 'n' everythin'." She knew Tom would not believe her but it left her with a shred of respectability.

Tom directed Nero to sit on a bench outside the door while he went inside. The cabin was only one room and, to his amazement, appeared fairly neat. A big bed, covered with a rising-sun quilt, occupied one corner. Lorie was kneeling before the fireplace frying the eggs in a long-handled iron spider supported on a tripod.

"Right comely 'n' temptatious, ain' she?" The mother commented. "She a-fillin' out; mos' a woman now. Year 'go she didn' have no titties ter speak of, now look at 'em." She walked over to where Lorie was kneeling and unbuttoned the girl's dress, exposing one breast. It was large, milk-white, pink-nippled and well-rounded. "Ain' that purty?" She nudged Lorie with her elbow and took over the
99

cooking of the eggs herself. "Yo' go over 'n' set near the gen'man, dear. He might want ter git 'quainted with yo', seein' as how yo' so pretty 'n' sweet like. Go on."

Lorie, her dress still unbuttoned, walked over to Tom but, instead of sitting down beside him, she deposited herself on his lap. Without waiting, she flung her arms around him and nestled her head on his shoulder. Her finger traced little circles on his cheek and she smiled up at him.

"Awful late fer a nice handsome man like yo' ter be startin' out. Whyn't yo' stay here?"

"Thinkin' jes' might do that." Tom looked toward the rising-sun quilt. He had been tired and hungry, but now, with Lorie's thigh pressing into his crotch, he was thinking of something else besides eating and sleeping.

"Cost yo' two dollars," Mrs. Salsman informed him in a purely businesslike manner, spooning three of the five eggs she had fried onto a crockery plate and putting two squares of cold pone into the sizzling grease in the spider. "Two bits fer supper fer yo' 'n' your nigger, two dollars ter spend the night 'n' two bits more fer breakfast. Boggs will probably be here come mornin' 'n' yo'll save yourself a long ride ter Orion. Cheap 'nuff if'n yo' asks me." She took one square of the pone and placed it on the plate and started to carry the two eggs and the other pone, still in the spider, outside.

"That fer my boy?" Tom asked. "If'n so, would kindly ask that yo' give him t'other egg. He hongrier'n I am 'n' bigger, too. Needs more vittles 'n I do."

"How come yo' pamperin' that nigger? 'Course he right purty fer a nigger, he is. Wouldn' mind havin' me a buck like that. 'Pears yo' must set quite a store by him."

"'Nuff so I ain' a-stayin' here tonight 'cause they ain' no place fer him. Ain' havin' him sit outside all the night 'n' ketch the ager. He al'ays sleeps right 'longside my bed." Tom lifted Lorie from his lap and hitched his chair over to the table and started to eat the eggs while Mrs. Salsman went out to give Nero his food. When she returned she came to stand beside Lorie again, her arm around her daughter's shoulder, one hand cupping her breast, raising it and jiggling it.

100

"Right nice, ain' it? 'N' she all white. White all over 'n' clean. Washed all over ternight, she did, 'n' she sprinkled with Floridy Water. She jes' a-startin' in, nice 'n' tight. Jes' kindly broken in. One gen'man whose name I dasn't mention come here 'mos' every week 'n' he pay five dollars. He say Lorie the bes' screwin' he ever had 'n' wuth it."

"Thinkin' 'bout my boy." Tom jerked his thumb in the direction of the door. "Cain' have him gittin' the ager."

Mrs. Salsman stopped jiggling Lorie's breast and regarded Tom indecisively. She wanted the money badly but her reputation, poor as it might be, would suffer if it were known that she had kept a Negro in her cabin overnight. To be a whore for a white man certainly was not respectable, but she had survived thus far with that reputation, since it had never been mentioned to her face. But to have a Negro in her cabin would place her beyond the pale. She hesitated.

"Ain' yo' got a shed?" Tom asked. "Heard yo' tell yore young'uns ter go out there."

"Ain' havin' my boys sleep wid no nigger."

"He 'n' I slept in the same bed till we older'n them. Nero he's right clean, he is. He was my play-boy when I was knee-high ter a grasshopper. Set a store on him, I do."

"Kin see yo' do," Mrs. Salsman said, "the way yo' gave him yore egg. Well, if'n he a good clean nigger don't know if'n I mind, but it'll be two bits more if'n he stays." She glanced up to see if he agreed. " 'N' wuth it, too. Lorie wuth every cent o' it. But yo' gotta be gone, come daylight. Ain' havin' none o' my neighbors sayin' I had a nigger here overnight."

"Gotta go early anyway," Tom said, pushing back his plate. He went to the door. Nero had finished his supper and was still sitting on the bench. "Goin' ter bed here tonight, Nero. Aimin' ter try out that gal. Ain' got nothin' ter offer yo', tho'. She ain' got no wench. Yo' gotta sleep out'n the shed with her two boys."

"Tha's all right, masta Tom. Don' min' at all sleepin' with those two white boys."

Mrs. Salsman, standing behind Tom in the door, over-

101

heard. Cupping her hands she yelled, "Dabney, yo' come here." Almost immediately the two boys appeared, clutching their pants around their waists. "This here nigger's a-sleepin' out'n the shed with yo' boys. Let him share yore quilt."

"Ain' a-sleepin' wid no black nigger." Robbie, the younger boy, made a face at Nero.

"Yo' shet yore mouth o' I'll shet it fer yo'," Dabney said, slapping Robbie. "Ain' we bin a-wishin' we had a nigger buck? Well now we got one 'n he ain' black, he's yeller." He grinned up at Nero. "Yo' step right this way, boy, 'n don' yo' mind that Robbie. Come right 'roun' the house." He waited for Nero while Tom went over and spoke to him.

"Take the horses 'n hitch 'em 'roun' back. Don' want 'em recognized. 'N we got ter git up come daybreak. Go fin' the shed 'n crawl in with them boys."

Nero came closer to Tom and whispered, "Them women what they calls whores, Masta Tom? They do it fer money?"

"Shore do. Only white men tho'. Not niggers, won' take no niggers."

"Niggers ain' got no money nohow," Nero chuckled. "But yo' know somethin', masta Tom suh? Don' relish 'em so white like. Rather have 'em black o' yeller."

"Better yo' al'ays keep feelin' that way. See yo' in the mornin'."

"Good night, masta Tom. If'n yo' wants me yo' jes' yells. Yo' want ter take this gun with yo'?"

"Aimin' ter do some shootin' but ain' needin' no gun fer it." Tom laughed and walked back into the house, closing the door behind him. Lorie was already in bed, the rising-sun quilt pulled up around her neck. Tom looked around the single room. Mrs. Salsman was nowhere to be seen

"Whur yore maw?" he asked, fearful after her expressed admiration of Nero that she might have gone out to the shed. If she had, he would most certainly leave, Lorie or no Lorie. Even the thought of a white woman, no matter how loose she might be, with a Negro was repugnant to him.

Lorie pointed a finger to the loft above. "She up where the boys sleep when they ain' nobody here. If'n yo' wants her too, she'll kindly come down."

"If'n yo likes, suh," Mrs. Salsman's voice floated down from the loft. "Only charges yo' a dollar more 'n' wuth it, too."

"Thank yo', ma'am." Tom pulled off his boots. "Think I got 'nuff ter keep me busy ternight. Askin' yo' kindly tho', if'n yo' wakes me up in the mornin' come sunup."

"Shore will," the voice came back, " 'n' if'n yo' changes yore mind, yell 'n' I'll come down."

Tom, his clothes in a pile on the floor, cupped the candle flame with his hand, but before he could extinguish it, Lorie spoke.

"Maw says ter leave it lit. Better that way."

Tom knew that there was an eye watching him through the cracks in the loft floor. He blew out the candle. "If'n I'm a-payin', goin' ter have it the way I likes it." The dying fire in the fireplace showed Tom the way to the rising-sun quilt.

Chapter V.

THE SUN, which had not been up when Tom and Nero mounted their horses in back of Mrs. Salsman's house, now appeared, its slanting rays gilding the leaves of the trees and casting a pale light over the fields with their rail fences which zigzagged across them in dark lines, almost hidden by the canes of raspberry, elderberry bushes, and small saplings which had taken seed and grown up in the fence angles. A euphony of bird song rose from the roadside thickets, swelling into a crescendo of music and then diminishing as the passing horses stirred the birds from their coverts and sent them, with a scurrying of wings, to another copse. The air, freshly washed by an early-morning shower, seemed sweet in their nostrils after the sour smell of Mrs. Salsman's cottage and shed.

Owing to the narrowness of the road—scarcely more than two rutted tracks with grass growing between them—Tom rode ahead with Nero following but, as the road reached the top of a small knoll and straightened out over a level plateau, Tom waved to Nero to ride up beside him. Once alongside, Tom grinned rather sheepishly at Nero, and asked, "How yo' feelin' this mornin', Nero boy? Git yo'self a good rest las' night? How yo' like sleepin' 'lone?"

"Ain' got me much sleep las' night, masta Tom suh. Them two boys didn' give me much chance. If'n their sister anythin' like them two boys, don' reckon yo' got much sleep neither, masta Tom."

"Didn' stay there to sleep, Nero," Tom laughed, slapping his thigh, his memories of the past night making his thoughts of Dovie and his anger recede into the background. "Didn' pay out two dollars jes' ter sleep. That Lorie gal she may be jes' broken in like'n her mama say but she shore knows how to pleasure a man. Takes to it right well, she do, but guess she had plenty o' lessons from her mama"

"Yas suh, masta Tom suh." Nero rode on a few steps in silence. Lifting his head, he turned in Tom's direction. "Beggin' yore pardon, masta Tom suh, but wantin' ter ask yo' a question. Ain' such a question as a nigger should be asking but admires ter know somethin'.'"

"Go 'head! Since when yo' beatin' 'roun' the bush askin' questions when we alone. 'Spects yo' ter when other people 'roun' but ain' so heedful when we alone."

"But this a special question, masta Tom."

"Special o' not, go ahead!"

"Likin' ter know"—Nero hesitated, awed by the very momentousness of the question—"likin' ter know if'n they's any dif'rence 'twixt pleasuring a white woman 'n' a nigger wench. Never pleasured nothin' but a wench in my life 'n' of course never thinkin' o' doin' so but jes' curious 'bout white women."

"Well, yo'd better git that idea outa yore head." There was an edge of anger in Toms voice. "Ain' wantin' yo' ter get curious 'bout white women. Ain' fittin' fer a nigger ter even think 'bout them. They's sort of sacred, they is, even whores like that Mrs. Salsman 'n' Lorie."

"How come they charges fer it?" Nero asked.

" 'Cause that's how they makes their livin'. Not many o' 'em roun' here but plenty down in N'Orleans 'n' Mobile. Tha's all some women do in the cities. Heard say that some takes a hundred men in one night with 'em jes' lined up, one waitin' fer the other ter git off. Cain' quite understand it, I don', but there's them that says it's so."

" 'N' they white women?" Nero shook his head in bewilderment.

Tom nodded. "But they's whores. They's a low grade

of women but no matter how low they gits, they ain' takin no niggers, so jes' git it outa yore head that yo' ever goin' ter have one. 'N' 'sides"—his anger now dissipated, he smiled at Nero, wagging a finger at him—"yo' ain' missin' a hell of a lot, boy. Ain' no white woman ever made what kin give yo' a good time like a wench kin. Jes' don' seem ter put their heart in it, white women don'. They try hard but jes' cain' do it like'n a wench kin. So let me tell yo' one thing, boy, yo' ain' missin' nothin' 'n' don' yo' ever let me hear 'bout yo' thinkin' bout a white woman 'gain. If'n I ever hear o' yo' a-touchin' one, no matter even if'n she a whore, o' she a-beggin' you, I'll strip yo' down my ownself, I will."

"Yes suh, masta Tom suh, guess yo' done tol' me what I want ter know. Ain' got me no hankerin' for a white woman nohow. Jes' curious, tha's all. Satisfied with the wenches, I am."

"Yo' shore better be if'n yo' don' want ter get nutted like that goddam Congo. Don' know what Callie's papa ever wantin' to do that fer. Jes' cain' sell the bastard 'cause Miz Callie puttin' such a store by him but cain' stand the sight o' him 'n' had ter have him a-sleepin' 'longside my bed every night since Callie 'n' me got married. Wish the bastard'd take sick 'n' die but he's as strong as a horse. Eat like a pig, he do."

Nero shook his head in kindly commiseration. "Shore feel sorry fer him, I do. Ain' his fault he the way he is. If'n he hadn't been nutted, he'd of been a fine strong man. Don' seem right ter me, Miz Callie's papa doing what he did. Niggers ain' got much anyway, 'cept eatin', sleepin', 'n' screwin'."

Tom bristled. "Miz Callie's papa had the right ter if'n he wanted to. Congo his'n. If'n I want ter make a gelding outa a stallion, I does. If'n I wants a barrow o' a wether, I makes 'em. Same with a nigger. They belongs ter me jes' like a horse o' a pig o' a ram. 'Course I wouldn't do it seein' as how I never believed in it fer niggers, but it my right if'n I wants. May jes' take the notion in my head some day, I might. Seein' as how nutted nigger boys is bringing good prices fer house servants, 'specially light-skinned ones. What yo' think 'bout it, Nero? Think we should nut some fer the fancy market?"

"Yo' asked me, masta Tom suh, yo' asked me." Nero looked straight at Tom. "Now I'm a-goin' ter answer yo'. Ain' right, masta Tom, jes' ain't right. Niggers different from animals. Niggers think, masta Tom. They feel. Lived with yo' all my life, masta Tom, 'n' I knows yo'. Knows yo' won' hurt nobody. Knows yo' treats yore niggers fine, jes' fine. All Dove Cote niggers love yo' 'n' all Patch niggers too, even if'n yo' have ter whop 'em sometimes. Knows too that deep down in yore heart yo' respects a nigger too much ter change him from a man inter somethin' like that Congo. Knows that, masta Tom suh."

Tom glanced at Nero quizzically, undecided whether to lash out at him with a verbal dressing-down or to accept his words as a compliment which, he was sure, was how they were intended. For the first time in a long while, he really looked at Nero and felt a stirring of emotion which rose up in his throat, almost choking him. He knew he could not buy the love and devotion which this man had for him. And, for that one infinitesimal moment while he searched his own soul, he realized that he cared more for Nero than for any other man on earth. But this was something which he would not admit, not even to himself.

"Got a long ride ahead o' us," he said brusquely. "Never git there if'n we go on gassin' like this. Better yo' fergits about sech foolishments. Yo' a nigger, 'n' tha's that. But, yo' half human. I white, 'n' that's that, 'n' I all human. Ain' no use talkin bout it 'cause we cain' change it even if'n we wants. But"—his voice softened and he reached far out to slap Nero's knee—"I'll say this, boy. Yo' the goddamndest finest nigger I've ever seen 'n' I mean it. Yo're the salt o' the earth, Nero boy. Now, let's git goin'."

They covered the rest of the journey Indian file, owing to the narrowness of the road. Once they stopped at a rocky ledge where a spring gushed forth a stream of crystal water into a bank of ferns. They dismounted, drank their fill of the water, and splashed it on their faces.

"Must be 'mos' there," Tom observed as they started out again.

107

They were nearer than they thought. The road descended a hill to where the creek made a bend, widening out into a placid pool. Strangely enough, although there were no houses within sight, a large gathering, composed of a few men, some twenty or thirty women, and a number of scampering children were clustered on the bank. As Tom and Nero came nearer, they saw that the entire assemblage was kneeling, shouting hymns and clapping their hands. All faces were turned toward the stream and the press of bodies hid the object of their attention. At first Tom thought that someone had drowned and that those on the shore were praying for the victim's safety, but when he came nearer and looked over the heads of the kneelers, he knew that his search was over. Waist-deep in the middle of the stream, the Reverend Bartholomew Boggs, clad in a white cotton nightshirt which was wetly plastered to his body, was exhorting those on the bank while he supported a young woman in his arms. At the sight of him, and particularly of Boggs' right hand caressing the girl's breast under her wet garment, Tom's anger was rekindled. He rode up to the assemblage, shouting for them to make way for him, and they, frightened by the onrush of his horse and the grim look on his face, stood up and made a path to the water, through which Tom rode, Nero following. His horse halted for a moment at the edge of the water, but Tom urged him on and rode out to within a few feet of where Boggs was standing.

Surprised at this sudden and completely unexpected sight of his cousin, Boggs ceased his shouting, relinquished his hold on the girl, and stood her on her feet beside him. He quickly recovered his aplomb, however, and smiled sanctimoniously at Tom. The spurious piety of his expression did not sit well on Boggs face. Florid and sensual with a short broad nose, wide moist lips, and hooded green eyes, he did not easily assume an aura of sanctity. Everything about Boggs seemed too big, too coarse, too exaggerated. His unruly shock of curly black hair grew low on his forehead and far down the nape of his neck. His broad shoulders, under the thin, wet, cotton garment, strained at the seams, and his huge hands, now quiet, dangled like hams in the water. He did, however, possess some histrionic sense, which he well knew how to use. Now, as he looked up at Tom, his welcoming words were directed more to the assemblage than to his cousin.

"Why God bless yo', Cousin Tom. Yo're welcome here 'n' I right glad to see yo'. Yo' a-comin' ter be baptized in the bosom o' sweet Jesus? Glad I am, Tom, that you seen the light, the blessed light, 'n' come ter me ter be saved. Hallelujah.'"

"Hallelujah!" echoed the crowd on the bank, but Tom's voice cut through their cries. "Yo'd better save yo'self, yo' goddam, horny, screwin' bastard." Tom pulled his shotgun from his saddle holster and aimed it at Boggs. "Yore fornicatin' days're jus' 'bout over. Aimin' ter blast yo' ter hell in jes' 'bout another minute. Don' know jes' whether I'll blow off yore fool head o' shoot off yore goddam pecker. Don't yo' move a step, yo' fornicatin' deceivin' rake-hell. If'n yo' moves I'll blast yo'." Tom uncoiled the whip from the pommel of his saddle and silently handed it to Nero, who was beside him. The girl who had been in Boggs' arms screamed and splashed to the shore, her long wet garment impeding her progress.

"Jes' don' un'erstand, Cousin Tom, why yo' come here like this, a -breakin' up the Lord's work 'n' me a-baptizin' 'n' everything. Whaffor yo' a-pointin' that gun at me? If'n yo' joshin' gotta ask yo' ter stop 'cause this the Lord's work 'n' He 'pointed me ter do it."

"Suppose it the Lord's work that yo' went 'n' done what yo' done ter Dovie. Goddam yore stinkin' soul ter hell. Shootin's too good fer yo'. But I'm goin' ter teach yo' a lesson. Nero, yo' got that whip ready?"

"Yes suh, masta Tom, got it ready, but what yo' want-in' me ter do with it?"

"Wants yo' ter lay it on this water snake here. Lay it on good. Don' spare him."

"But he a white man, masta Tom. Cain' whop no white man."

"Kin whop him if'n I tells yo' 'n' I'm tellin' yo. Jes' don' hit his face. Don' wan' his face marred up 'cause Dovie she gotta look at it. 'N' don't blister his ass neither 'cause he got ter ride. 'N' if'n he try ter git 'way, I'll shoot him down."

"Dovie?" Boggs was now completely flabbergasted. "What I ever do ter Dovie?"

"Yo' know what yo' done, goddam it. Yo' know."

"Ain' done nothin' ter that child. Ain' never."

"Lay on, Nero," Tom yelled, and, despite his unwillingness to do so, Nero snapped the cowhide far out behind him and brought it down on Boggs' shoulders. Nero was adept, and the thin lash coiled around Boggs' neck, then uncoiled and dropped into the water only to be flung out behind and again fall on Boggs' shoulders. Covered by Tom's gun, he did not dare to flee, and the assembly on the stream made no attempt to help him. They seemed as baffled as Boggs. A few of them had recognized Tom, knew that he was a respectable man, and exaggerated his influence and power.

"Come ter my house yo' did." Tom's anger was now uncontrolled, and he was oblivious to the fact that he was scandalizing his own daughter before these strangers. " 'N' take advantage o' my poor sweet innercent li'l gal. Tellin' her yo' a-goin' ter die 'n' exposin' yourself t' her. Deceivin' her 'n' screwin' her 'n' knockin' her up. What kin' o' a preacher are yo'?" He half turned in his saddle to face those on shore. "Better yo' all looks out fer yore womenfolk when this snake come crawlin' outa the grass. No woman safe with this horny bastard. He jes' a-preacherin' so's he kin git his screwin' free, tha's all. Despoilin' womanhood all the way from Benson south 'n' leavin' a string o' black-headed bastards all the way."

While the lashes of Nero continued to descend, cutting the thin nightshirt to ribbons and staining its rags with blood, those on the bank reviled poor Boggs, throwing gravel and stones. Boggs sank down on one knee, his big arms waving in a futile attempt to ward off the stones and the blows of the whip. Then, completely overcome, he fell, face first, down into the water, struggled up, stumbled, and went down again.

"Tha's 'nuff, Nero." Tom's words stilled the singing of the lash. "Got ter save somethin' ter take home ter Dovie. Git down 'n' pick him up 'n' drag him up ter the bank." He waited for Nero to climb down off his horse into the hip-deep water and lug Boggs out. Boggs' huge body was slumped in a pile of white flesh and bloody nightshirt. Tom turned to the people who were already ringed around it.

"Good people," he said, the anger gone from his voice now, "go back to your homes. This man done wrong 'n' he bin punished. I'm takin' him away with me. He a-callin' hisself a reverend but he ain' one. Jes' take care from now on who-all yo' listen to what go 'round exhortin' 'n' preacherin'. I kindly bid yo-all good day 'n' asks yo' if'n yo' kindly fergive me if'n I said anythin' ter offend the ladies, but it all true. He took advantage o' my poor innercent sixteen-year-ol' daughter 'n' yo cain' blame a father's righteous anger. Now if'n yo-all will please leave us be, I'll deal with this man."

Slowly and silently they left, departing in ones and twos, on foot and on horseback, until there was nobody left but Bart, who was now sitting up, and Tom and Nero standing over him.

"Tell me what-all I done, Cousin Tom." Bart painfully managed to get to his knees and stand up.

"S'pose yo' never gulled my gal, eh? Never deflowered her 'n' ravished her 'n' raped her 'n' knocked her up?"

"Why no, Cousin Tom, I never did none o' those thin's. Never! How yo' talk 'n' come here 'n' have a nigger whop me before all my flock. I'm a preacher, yo' know, don' yo'? Now yo've disgraced me. Ain' fittin' fer a nigger to whop a white man nohow. Ain' fittin', in the eyes o' God."

"Fittin' fer yo', tho'. Yo' tryin' ter say my Dovie lie? Yo' puttin' the lie in her mouth 'n' in Callie's mouth 'n' in my own? She a-sayin' yo' done it ter her. She a-tellin' her mama. I'm jes' grateful my poor Cousin May ain' a-livin' ter see what a polecat yo' turned out ter be. It's that Boggs' blood in yo' what did it. Yore paw, he was al'ays a-sniffin' 'roun' like a dog after a bitch in heat. My Dovie she sayin' yo' did it, 'n' Dovie never lied to her papa. Never!"

"Ain' a-sayin' she lyin'," Boggs pleaded, "jes' a-sayin' I didn' do it. Never touched her, never craved her 'n' if'n I did she not even lookin' at me. She jes' havin' eyes fer that Tommy. Why, Cousin Tom, yo' knows I wouldn' despoil that fine young gal what my kin. Mayhap I looked at her a little 'n' admired her and . . ."

"Screwed her, too. Tha's what yo' done."

"Ain' true. I'se a preacher, Cousin Tom."

"Preacher, hell!" Tom scoffed. "Yo' a hell of a preacher, yo' are. Preacher's jes' as horny as common folks. Hornier I reckon, after what I hears from Miz Salsman 'n' Lorie how yo' a-takin' 'em on one right after t'other. Preachers are men too. Never knew a preacher but what had a passel o' young uns. But yo' the wust o' all. Yo're more pecker'n man. Whereat yore trogs?"

Bart pointed to a thicket of bushes.

"Git 'em on. Got ter git movin'. Got ter git yo' 'n' Dovie married up 'fore nightfall. Nero'll help yo' git yore trogs on. Yo' a bit bloodied up but guess yo' ain' hurt much."

Leaning on Nero, Bart disappeared behind the clump of elders only to reappear in a few minutes, dressed in a shabby green (once black) ministerial frock coat, so patched and mended it was almost in rags; frayed butternut trousers; and dusty boots. His wet hair was covered by an immense black slouch hat, and his dirty white shirt, damp from his skin, showed red stains at collar and chest. The horse he untied was but a pony, undersized, underfed, undershod and ill-cared-for. The animal's coat was dirty and unkempt, the saddle a bag of corn shucks, and the bridle a length of frayed rope.

Bart looked longingly at Nero's horse, a handsome and mettlesome gray mare with a fine leather saddle.

"More fittin' if'n I ride yore nigger's horse. Ain' right we be seen with him ridin' a fine horse 'n' me like this."

"Tha's his horse 'n' ain' takin' it from him. Your'n good 'nuff. Yo' ain' my son-in-law yet. Not by a damn sight! Come that time mayhap I mount yo' on something decent."

Bart mounted—a weird and woebegone spectacle astraddle his pony. His gangling legs, without stirrups, nearly reached the ground. If ever there was a picture of complete desolation it was Bart Boggs. His career as a preacher, of which he had been inordinately proud, was apparently over. No longer would he be looked up to by the

112

men and fawned over by the women. He had been humiliated as much as a white man could be by being whipped by a Negro and that in full view of his followers. Now he was being dragged off against his will to be married—a prospect he did not relish. And, to make matters worse, he was innocent of the charges against him. In many, very many, cases he could well have been guilty, but in this one instance he was innocent. But there was nothing he could say. Tom Verder would not believe him. He rode alongside Tom, who was compelled to slacken his gait so that Bart's pony might keep pace with it. Nero, whose horse followed, grinned at the sight of Boggs' discomfiture. Slowly and silently they retraced the road to Brownsville which Verder and Nero had followed earlier in the day.

They had gone nearly two miles in silence when Bart decided to make one last appeal. "Why yo' a-doin' this ter me, Cousin Tom? Why yo' breakin' up my baptizin' meetin' 'n' all? Them folks a-thinkin' I done yo' wrong. I'll never git 'em back."

"Might's well make up yore mind. Yore preacherin' days are over. Ain' havin' no preacherin' son-in-law a-gallivantin' 'roun' the country a-screwin' all the women. Yo're comin' home with me. Yo' done Dovie wrong 'n' yo're goin' ter marry up with her 'n' make her honest 'n' give yore child a name. Little I thought las' spring when I a-keepin' yo' at Dove Cote durin' the rains jes' 'cause yo' my Cousin May's boy, yo'd be pesterin' my gal 'n' ruinin' my good name. But the way yo' did it! So sneaky 'n' sly like, pertendin' yo' a-goin' ter swell up 'n' die jes' cause yo' needed a woman. Tellin' her you'd die if'n she didn' let yo'. Tha's the part I cain' fergive."

"What'd I do yo' cain' fergive? Don' know what in tarnation yo' talkin' 'bout." Bart was as much at sea as ever, completely ignorant of what he was supposed to have done.

"Yo' a-goin' inter her room 'n' exposin' yourself 'n' tellin' her yo' taken sick 'n' swellin' 'n' goin' ter bust less'n she let yo'. Knowin' she so innercent 'n' so good she thinkin' she goin' ter save yore life."

"But I never done it, I'm a-tellin' yo'. Never! If'n yore
113

gal have a woods-colt, I say, 'n' if'n she have a bastard, I say, I ain' the sire o' it 'n' tha's all. 'N' I ain' a-goin' ter marry her."

"We'll damn well see if'n yo' ain'. If'n yo ain' wedded 'fore supper time this evenin', yo're goin' ter be dead, tha's all. Deader'n a goddam doornail 'n' tha's final. Kin talk till doomsday that yo' never done it 'n' won' believe yo'. Won' believe yo' if'n yo swear on a stack o' Bibles. Might have listened ter yo' once but after hearin' what yo' did ter that Lorie Salsman, know yo'd do the same thing to any gal."

Bart saw that it was inevitable and there was no escape, but he felt he had to make one more attempt to vindicate himself.

"Bet it was that boy o' Charlie's—that Tommy. Could've been him, couldn't it? He right there at Dove Cote too 'n' yo' know that boy, he right horny, a-pesterin' yore wenches every night 'n' a-braggin' ter me 'bout it every mornin'.'"

Verder was shocked at the suggestion—hurt and offended. "That's why I know he didn' do it. Tommy have all the screwin' he wanted. Those wenches jes' drean him dry every night. Didn' need ter rape Dovie ter get it. 'N now I know jes' what happened. Kin see it clear. Dovie tol' him what yo' did. Tha's why he lef' 'n' gone where nobody ever see him again. Broke his pore heart, it did, 'n' he wandered away. Didn' even go home ter Natchez. Probably went ter Mexico o' the Texies 'n' got hisself kilt by the Indians. O' he dead from a broken heart 'n' yo' did it all. Yo' drove pore Tommy 'way, ruint my daughter, brang tears ter her mama's eyes 'n' sent me traipsin' all over the county fer yo'. But I foun' yo' 'n' if'n I ever hear yo' deny it again, I'll string yo' up 'n' have Nero really slice the meat off'n yo. Dovie a-sayin' yo' did it 'n' that 'nuff. Should've killed yo', Bart, but cain' have Dovie 'thout a husband."

The utter finality of Tom's words convinced Bart that his case was hopeless, and he trailed along in silence. There was no alternative, no escape. His career as a preacher was over, for the gossip would spread from Orion to all the surrounding hamlets where he rode circuit. True, he had never cared a whit for the morals, ethics, or the immortal souls of those to whom he preached his hellfire-and-damnation sermons. Poor and illiterate as he was, there had been no other way in which he could attain any status at all. His ego had fed upon the importance he had achieved as a preacher— a reverend—on the attention that had been paid to his words, the fuss that was made over him when he arrived in a town, the women who had literally thrown themselves at his feet. And he had used them, for he was unmarried and the "Thou Shalt Not" of adultery did not apply to him. If the woman with whom he bedded was married, the sin was hers, not his, and he had always prayed with her afterwards, asking forgiveness for the sin she had committed. He had always had plenty of women—white ones—so he had never needed the wenches. He had no taste for colored flesh.

Carefully now, he reviewed the situation he was in. Dovie was a handsome girl—perhaps not as much to his taste as the more full-blown Lorie Salsman, but a beautiful girl nevertheless. He remembered how he had admired her during his week's stay at Dove Cote the past spring. Yes, he would willingly have seduced her if he could have, but she had had eyes only for Tommy. And now, if he married her she would be his. Although the child she bore would be another's, she would be his after that, and the prospect was far from unpleasing. And then there was the almost palatial luxury of the house, the fine clean beds, the sumptuous meals, the magnificent furniture, the host of servants. He recalled the elaborate silver centerpiece in the middle of the table which probably cost more than he would make in twenty years of circuit preaching.

He had never had a home since his mother died and now he would have a home of his own, far better than he had ever envisaged. Cousin Tom was a rich man. Why, that yellow son-of-a-bitch on the gray horse behind him was worth a thousand dollars or more on the slave block, and Tom had more of them—perhaps a hundred, two hundred, three hundred. Tom kept that yellow nigger back there just to take his boots off at night. He, himself, had managed to get his own boots off every night of his life. He wouldn't want a black buck around to do that. Niggers were niggers and their place was out in the field breaking their backs to get the work done or up on the auction block turning their black flesh into ready cash.

But far more important than all the rest was the fact that he'd be the heir to Dove Cote once Tom Verder died. Dovie was an only child and, according to the custom, indeed according to the law of the time, a wife's property belonged to and was at the disposal of her husband. Of course Callie's dower right would intervene while she was alive but eventually Dove Cote and all its wealth would be his. These circumstances were slow to strike Bart's awareness, the more so because he had never envisioned himself as a man of property. A pair of new britches, a decent horse to ride, a meal in his belly, and a bed to sleep in (preferably with a woman alongside) had been his only ambitions. Now, the very prospect of the untold wealth of Dove Cote electrified him. It was a small price to pay for the paternity of another man's child, although that, in itself, was a bitter pill for Boggs to swallow. It would be difficult also for him to give up his sexual promiscuity for one of the things that had appealed to him in the circuit preacher's life was the fact that there was always a different bed awaiting him in every community he called at, a bed he had never felt any pangs of guilt about accepting.

He was a passionate, sensuous man and he knew it would be difficult to confine his attentions to one woman, but once he was married, any dalliance with another man's wife or even an unmarried woman would be adultery, and he would not risk the eternal damnation of his soul and an eternity of hellfire for one brief moment of satisfaction. However, he could still take wenches, because, since they were not human, it would be no sin. Bart did not necessarily believe in his own sermons but he had preached hellfire and brimstone so much he had become afraid of them himself. Yes, there would still be nigger wenches around if he could bring himself to stomach them. Other men seemed to like them; that Tommy Verder had. He could still hear him bragging at the breakfast table when Callie and Dovie had left. "Come on out to the quarters with me tonight, Bart, 'n' I'll git yo' dreaned. Ain' healthy fer a big man like yo' ter go a whole week 'thout it. Took on three myself las' night. Easy ter git one fer yo' if'n yo' wants it." But Bart had always shaken his head in refusal.

Yet, he argued with himself, giving up white women, like assuming the paternity of Dovie's child, would be a small price to pay for what he would receive. Dovie's child would be considered his—would bear his name. As far as he knew, despite his sexual prowess, he had never fathered a child. The one which the girl at Granby's Forge had tried to lay at his doorstep had not been his, and he had proved it was not by producing the rightful father, a young man who had been frightened by Bart's sermon of everlasting punishment into confessing. It was strange, Bart thought, that a man of his size, strength, and undoubted virility had never fathered a child. He wanted one—a son—passionately.

He was entirely aware that he was a handsome figure of a man with his tall, muscular body, his hirsute chest, his clean-cut, even features, fine teeth, green eyes, and shock of curly black hair. He could scarcely have avoided being aware of his good looks, since the women of his flock reminded him of them, even those who refused his embraces. He had been compared to the Archangel Michael and one female, more erudite than the rest, had written a poem about him in which she compared him to Apollo—whoever he was. Yet with all his puissance he had never begotten a child, at least not one he was aware of. Was there something wrong with him? Was he barren? How could his sap be worthless when it was so plentiful?

Of course in marrying Dovie he would have to overlook her one misstep. He wondered who it had been and he envied him. It must have been Tommy. It couldn't have been anyone else unless—and the very thought made him shudder—she had been raped by a Negro buck and that was why they were forcing him to marry her. Tommy's child would be difficult enough to accept, but Tommy was his cousin after all, and the child

117

would be of the same blood as his own. But a nigger child! Well, if it was a nigger there was only one solution; they'd have to drown it. No, he argued with himself, it couldn't be that; Dovie was too carefully guarded. And yet, such things had happened; he had heard about them. But that was a bridge he did not have to cross until he came to it.

Now only one thing remained to be ascertained. How would he be treated at Dove Cote? Would Tom's hatred toward him continue, making his life miserable, or would he be given some position of prestige as Tom's son-in-law? Remembering Callie, he felt she would treat him kindly once he was married, but he was unsure about Tom. It was something he must know. He kicked his horse and managed to enliven it sufficiently so that it drew abreast of Tom.

"I'll be marryin' up with Dovie like'n yo' say, Cousin Tom, 'n' I'll be a good husban' to her, treat her good 'n' everythin'. Won' go tomcattin' 'roun'. But hopin' after I marries her, yo' ain' a-goin' ter hold no grudge agin me 'n' hate me 'n' revenge yo'self on me 'n' put me down with yore anger 'n' spite towards me. Ain' Christian that yo' goes on a-hatin' me. Ain' godly, it ain'."

Tom had had time to cool off. He had accomplished his purpose. He had located Bart and he had punished him. The red fog of temper had disappeared from his brain and he now turned and beheld Bart as though for the first time. He regarded him dispassionately. He was his own Cousin May's boy. He was not a stranger but part of his own family. And he was a strong, handsome fellow to boot. Of course he was not Tommy—gay, handsome, insouciant Tommy who was always laughing, joking, and wenching. But next to Tommy, given a choice, Tom would have chosen Bart. Bart was all man, all six feet-two of him, and Tom was wise enough to know that the sanctimonious attitude which Bart had adopted was only superficial. Once having lost that, he'd be a real man instead of a psalm-singing, gospel-spouting hypocrite. For the first time he relaxed the grim lines of his face and almost smiled at poor Bart.

"Ain' holdin' no grudges once yo' does what yo' have

118

ter do. Once yo' my son-in-law, upholds yo', I do. Yo' the father o' my grandson. Yo' my family—been jes' a kinfolk before but onct yo' married ter Dovie, yo' my family. I'll be fair 'n' square with yo' if'n yo' willing ter go ter work 'n' fergit this preacherin'. Ain' goin' ter have it said that I feel 'bove yo' o' mistreat yo'. Yo' comin' inter the bosom o' my family. Yo' goin' ter be my son."

"Thank yo' kindly, Cousin Tom." Bart fell behind Tom Verder, his thoughts already envisioning the church he would get Tom to build for him. Certainly Tom was not serious about his giving up preaching. The family should be only too glad to have the added prestige which a reverend would give it, and once Bart had a church he'd be a real reverend. He wanted a church with a white steeple, and pointed Gothic windows, preferably of colored glass. He could see the congregation coming in the door, filing down the center aisle, and taking their seats. He heard the notes of the organ, for certainly there would be an organ, and he saw Dovie sitting in the front pew with a line of small Boggses—all boys—beside her, all with his own green eyes and black hair. Somehow his mind was unable to picture the eldest—the one Dovie was now carrying—that would not be his own. There would be a hush and he would stride up on the platform, all in shiny black broadcloth, and stand at a pulpit with a big, gilt-edged Bible open before him. He'd have to learn to read better. As it was he could barely spell out some simple passages in the Bible.

His congregation would be spellbound by his words, interspersing them with "Amens" and "Hallelujahs," and there would be a steady stream coming to the mourning bench to be saved. Now, in looking out over the congregation, he could catch the eye of a pretty girl, glancing up at him from under the edge of her rose-trimmed straw bonnet. Her eyes devoured him and he knew what she wanted. He stepped to one side of the pulpit so her eyes would go down to the bulge in his britches which he was unable to hide. Of course, he couldn't touch her, no matter how much she begged him. He'd be a married man and that would be adultery. But would it?

Technically yes, but he must remember that he was pastor of his flock, a father to them all, a counselor, a guide, a loving mentor. Then wouldn't it be better for him to initiate this tender loving young girl? Of course! He'd do it easily and gently and how much better it would be for her than the frantic thrusting of some hot-peckered young Lucifer who'd bust her ruthlessly in the high grass on her way home from church or out behind the barn some night at a play-party. All he would be seeking would be her body, while Bart would be trying to save her immortal soul. After he had finished with her, he'd get down on his knees and pray with her so that she would know that what she had done had been sacred and not a sin because she had done it with her own dear reverend. Yes, it would be his duty, his bounden duty, to keep this poor girl from the lewd ways of sin.

Then, with Tom and Callie dead, he'd be the Reverend Bartholomew Boggs of Dove Cote Plantation. "Pleased ter meet yo' sir 'n' madam and we would be honored if'n yo'd stop by Dove Cote 'n' partake o' our vittles this Sunday after church. 'Course we ain' 'spectin' company, jes' a picked-up meal 'cause Miz Boggs don' 'low no cookin' in the house of a Sunday, but guess she kin hassle up a ham 'n' a turkey 'n' one o' two chickens 'long with some collard greens 'n' poun' cake 'n' sech so reckon yo' won' go hungry."

It was an ecstatic vision, and poor Bart forgot his aching body and his utter humiliation at the hands of Nero. He scratched his head, dislodging his hat, and it fell to the ground. He pulled at the frayed rope to halt his horse and then thought better of it. Turning on his corn-shuck saddle, he called to Nero, "Pick up my hat, boy."

He was dumbfounded to see Nero dismount, pick up his hat, wipe the dust from its brim with the sleeve of his shirt, then ride up and hand it to him.

"Here's yore hat, masta suh."

Bart placed it on his head, straightened his sore shoulders, and jogged his horse up beside Tom's as they rode into Brownsville. He passed Mrs. Salsman, sitting in her doorway, soaking her feet in a tub of water, but when she waved at him gaily, he bowed formally to her, lifted his hat with a studied gesture, and greeted her mellifluously, "Evenin', sister, evenin', 'n' God bless yo'."

She stared at him open-mouthed as he rode along beside Tom. Calling to Lorie, who was inside, she exploded, "Why that high-falutin' son-o'-a-bitch. One'd think we nothin' but the dirt under his feet. Got big-headed already 'n' him as poor as Job's turkey 'thout a pot ter piss in o' a window ter throw it out of."

Lorie and the boys appeared in the doorway. "Shore glad that ol' man Verder ain' a-stayin' here ternight," Lorie said. "He ain' no fun 'tall. Jes' one shot 'n' he done. Now Bart, he a solid-gol' repeater, he is."

"Wisht that nigger a-stayin', tho'," Dabney whispered to his brother. "Don' yo', Robbie?"

Robbie nodded his head and they all four watched the three horsemen riding under the shade of Brownsville's Main Street.

Chapter VI

By THE TIME they had collected the Reverend Soper, waited for him to change into his rusty black suit, and partially satisfied their hunger with Mrs. Soper's leaden biscuits and weak coffee, it was nearly dark. Tom had wondered just how the two reverends would hit it off but strangely enough, despite his vituperations against Bart earlier that morning, Soper now treated him with respect and even camaraderie. Of course, he envisioned the fee he was to receive from Tom, and it would hardly be exercising good judgment to disparage the prospective bridegroom.

After they had set out, Soper mounted a horse nearly as decrepit as Bart's, and the two reverends rode along together, followed by Tom and Nero. From bits of their conversation which drifted back, Tom could hear that it was a friendly theological discussion, centered mainly around the prescribed manner of baptism. Boggs contended that the entire body must be immersed under water; Soper argued that a mere sprinkling was sufficient. Neither seemed able to convince the other, and the argument continued until they arrived at Dove Cote.

As they rode up the avenue of trees which led off the main road to the big house, Tom felt a rush of gratitude for his home. It seemed so secure, so firmly established, so homely with the candlelight streaming from the windows. His conscience did hurt him a little when he recalled Lorie Salsman, and he resolved in his own heart never to visit her again. He had Callie—dear sweet loving Callie! Perhaps he had never appreciated her enough, but he'd make it up to her, he would. And he had Dovie and now Dovie was to be married and he was not too regretful that she was marrying Bart. Bart would turn out all right and now that Tommy was gone, Bart would be his son just as he was his Cousin May's son.

Now, within hailing distance of the house, he hallooed. In answer to his voice, the front door opened and Callie appeared in the light, almost blocking the doorway. Supported by Congo, she came out onto the steps, her arms outstretched, welcoming him. It took a little squinting in the darkness for her to recognize Bart and Soper but when she did, she knew that all their problems were solved. When they had dismounted and entered the house, Nero accompanying them, Callie greeted them with her great-lady manner. She had evidently anticipated their return, for she had dressed for the occasion in a gown of cerise grosgrain silk which had, like all her clothes been continuously let out at the waist and gusseted with other materials, none of which exactly matched the original cloth. Her heavy hair was wound high on her head in an enormous chignon, bolstered up by a tortoise-shell comb, and for this special occasion she wore the only jewels she possessed—a parure of amethysts which had belonged to Tom's mother and a string of corals which had been Tom's wedding present to her.

Bart was given a chance to freshen up in the spare room, but there was little he could do to make his clothes more presentable. When he came out, Dovie was waiting for him, wearing one of her mother's dresses whose voluminous girth hid her condition. Bart thought he had never seen anything lovelier. The dress of sprigged dimity which alternated tiny pink rosebuds with pale-blue forget-me-nots was the most elaborate toilette he had seen. Dovie's eyes showed no signs of tears and matched the blue of the forget-me-nots; her cheeks were flushed, as pink as the roses; and her chestnut hair was bound with a blue ribbon, sweeping back from her

123

forehead and falling in a cascade of curls behind.

Callie pressed a thin gold band into Bart's hand—another heirloom from Tom's mother—and called the house servants into the front parlor, where they clustered in a group by the door. Congo, who had an ear for music, had often amused Callie by strumming nameless songs on the piano, and now she motioned for him to take his place on the stool, where he drummed a soft accompaniment to Soper's words.

The ceremony itself took only a few minutes. Soper recited the marriage service of his creed. He knew it by heart, word for word, and it was impressive as he intoned it. Even Tom was moved. The woman being married was his own daughter, his beloved Dovie, and although she had been wronged by this man, it was now being righted. Tom took little stock in ceremony and ritual; the sex urge had been all he had felt at his own wedding. But this moved him, whether to joy or sorrow he did not know.

Callie wept abundantly—as behooved the mother of a bride. Copious tears trickled down her cheeks and she sobbed audibly, leading the Negro women, headed by old Aunt Ruthie, to add their lamentations to hers. Callie had not consciously forced the moisture from her eyes, but she knew it was expected of her and her sobbing was partially motivated by this expectation.

If the marriage ceremony itself was short, the prayers which followed it were lengthy. The whole company, Negroes and all, including Tom the agnostic, got down on their knees. Tom had no faith in the efficacy of prayer, but this was Dovie's wedding and he listened with patience to the wise advice that Soper gave to the Deity and to the solicitations from Him of not unreasonable boons in exchange for his counsel. Tom was not critical; if Soper had asked for the sun, moon, and stars in behalf of Dovie, he would have believed that she merited them. At length, when Soper had run out of breath and ideas and concluded his prayer with a hoarse "Amen," Bart, not to be outdone, started a prayer of his own which was even longer than Soper's. He prayed for everybody in the room, especially Dovie, that she might be freed from all taint of sin. Tom waited, kneeling, his hands tightly clenched, for Bart to exculpate himself before the Lord for Dovie's condition, but although he skirted the topic several times, he wisely avoided mentioning it directly. Had he done so, Tom would have jumped on him. But Bart was beginning to realize on which side his bread was buttered. His pleadings for blessings on Callie and Tom and on Dove Cote itself somewhat mollified Tom, so that by the time the long-anticipated "Amen" was uttered, Tom was unable to think of anything except his aching knees.

Callie had had Aunt Ruthie prepare a collation, and the long table, with its silver candlesticks and wax candles, its opulent centerpiece filled with fall chrysanthemums, and its white damask cloth overawed Soper and Bart. This then, Bart thought, was the luxury which was to be his from now on. It was hardly credible, when he remembered the miserable meals of fatback and greens, served on tin plates, which he had eaten in so many of his parishioners' cabins. After they had eaten, Soper took his leave, beaming over Tom's unexpected gift of a gold eagle—worth more than anything he had ever received in his life—and Tom, tired from a sleepless night and a long day of riding, suggested that they all go to bed. Callie took her husband's arm and beckoned, with her pudgy fingers, for Bart to come over to her.

"Gotta kiss my own dear son-in-law good night," she trilled, "jes' gotta see that he 'n' my Dovie happy their weddin' night. 'Members mine, I do"—she glanced coyly at Tom—"but Dovie already broke in, I guess, so she won't have it so hard as me. Now yo 'be careful o' my Dovie, Bart. She 'bout five months 'long so yo' take care." She turned to Tom. "Puttin' 'em out in the dove cote, I am. More private like fer them. Had it all redded up today 'n' Dovie's furniture moved out there, jes' like a li'l home o' their own. They got ter have things nice, Tom, 'n' that reminds me. Them trogs o' Bart's ain' fittin' fer a son-on-law o' Tom Verder. He right poverty-stricken lookin'. 'Cain' have people comin' here 'n' seein' him like that. Fust thin' tomorrow yo' gotta go ter

Brownsville 'n' have Bart measured fer a new suit 'n' git him some boots."

"Due back ter the Patch tomorrow. We a-pickin' over there." Tom had already missed one day and had no desire to miss another.

"Kin go directly there after yo' finishes in Brownsville," Callie said. "Aimin' ter have the Truebloods 'n' the Maitlands 'n' the Ketchells 'n' the Skaggses fer a swah-ray jes' as soon's I kin, 'n' want Bart dressed up fine. Cain' have Dovie's husband looking like a scarecrow what bin out in the rain. Now yo' promise, Tom. Yo' promise me yo' will."

Tom nodded. He was too tired to argue. All he wanted to do was sleep. Bidding the newlyweds good night, he wearily propelled Callie toward their room. Dovie, standing beside her new husband, smiled up at him. Discounting his miserable clothes, he was more than she had hoped for, and she envisioned him, clad in fine raiment, as a husband to be proud of. At least he was a man, and after her experience with Tommy she longed for a man—almost any man. Even while mourning for Tommy, memories of Bart's good looks had often been present in her thoughts, and she had hoped that he might return for another visit. Now he was here and what's more, he was her husband. She cuddled up to him, taking his arm. "Time we was a -leavin', Bart." She smiled up at him. "Mama's got our room all ready out 'n the cote. Won' be exactly like'n the first time we together here in my room but now we married up, so it's better. Ain' 'fraid yo' goin' ter die no more. Mama's bin tellin' me 'bout thin's."

Bart squeezed her hand and smiled down at her. He knew that she was lying, she knew that she was lying, and she knew that he knew it, but he could scarcely accuse her of that now that he had married her. For better or for worse! Those were the words he had said and promised. So now, for better or for worse, he was the acknowledged father of her child. He snuffed out the candle and with Dovie on his arm, walked out the dining-room door into the breezeway and down the steps. In the little area of darkness which separated the main house from the dove cote, he leaned down, bringing his face on a level with hers.

"Guess yo' don' know what yo' got comin' ter yo', Dovie."

"Thinkin' mayhap I do." She clung a little closer to him.

"Yo' shore?" He stopped and pulled her to him. "Men not all 'like, Dovie. Some of them's big; others are little. Cain' never tell 'bout a man till yo' beds with him. Mayhap yo' goin' ter fin' me diff'rent from Tommy."

"Don't know nothin' 'bout Tommy nor no other man, Mista Reverend Bart Boggs," Dovie said, skillfully avoiding the trap.

"Must of been some other man yo' was with before—him what planted his seed in yo' 'n' knocked yo' up."

She stood on tiptoe, forcing his head down so that his lips met hers. For a long moment they stood there in the darkness, frantically clutching each other, and then she released him. "Mighty poor memory yo' got, Bart darlin', if'n yo' cain' remember what we done. Ain' never forgotten yo', I ain'. Bin a-hopin' yo'd come back yo'self but had ter send Papa ter fetch yo'. Reckon yo' didn' love me much like yo' said yo' did. But don' make no neverminds now. We married up." She urged him toward the candlelit open door of the dove cote where Dolly was awaiting them. Poor Bart followed along, more bewildered now than ever. For the first time he had doubts about his innocence. Could he have walked in his sleep and ravished Dovie without remembering anything about it? Had he, in some moment of mental aberration, done this thing which Dovie, her father and mother were all so certain that he had done? He just didn't know and, moreover, at that particular moment he didn't care. Pulling Dovie close to him, he entered the lower room of the dove cote, inventoried its new and to him elegant furnishings, and closed the door. He glanced at Dolly.

"Ain' she goin'?" he asked.

"Why mercy no, Bart. How'm I goin' ter git undressed 'thout Dolly. Cain' undo all these buttons myself. She goin' ter stay here 'n' sleep on a pallet like'n

127

she always do. Later 'n yo' git a body servant, him 'n' Dolly kin sleep in the room upstairs."

" 'Thout marryin'? That's a sin."

"Niggers don' marry. They jes' jump the broom, tha's all. Ain' never no niggers here at Dove Cote bin married up. Ain' necessary."

Bart sat in a chair and watched while Dolly removed Dovie's dress, let down her hair, and got her ready for bed. He himself did not undress until Dolly had finished her ministrations, but when she was through, he blew out the candle and shucked off his own clothes. Groping in the darkness, he found the edge of the bed and eased himself down onto it. Stretching his arm over the sheet, he pulled Dovie to him. When she accepted him without the usual little gasp of surprise he had always elicited from his other companions, he grew more unsure than ever, but he did not allow his puzzlement to spoil his happiness. He found Dovie as avid and as responsive as Lorie Salsman—even more so, for whereas Lorie had often flattered him on his being a "solid-gold repeater," Dovie seemed to find him inadequate. He laid the blame for it on the welts on his back and shoulders and, having reached his limit, he turned over on his side and went to sleep.

But not Dovie! During the long hours of the night, she sorted out her emotions. This man beside her had pleasured her more expertly and more passionately than Tommy ever had. But he was not Tommy and it was Tommy that she loved. She preferred Tommy's lighthearted gaiety to Bart's ponderous solemnity. But . . . Tommy was gone and Bart was here beside her. He'd go a long way toward making up for the loss of Tommy, and if Tommy ever did come back . . . well, she'd cross that bridge when she came to it.

Her hand reached across, feeling the muscles of Bart's back, then wandering down over the rounded musculature of his chest to his flat belly. Where Tommy had been smooth and glabrous, Bart was heavliy hirsute, but she decided she liked his hairiness. He stirred in his sleep and rolled over on her back, and she found her explorations easier. But, instead of the rigidity which

128

she had anticipated, she discovered only an inert member which, try as she could, she was unable to bring to life. Drat it! Men were strange creatures. At one moment they were rampant with desire, and when it was expended they were limp and useless. It wasn't that way with her. Now that she had discovered this strange fever of excitement, she knew she would never be satiated. Never! She snuggled up into the curve of Bart's arm, pleased as a child with a new toy, almost too happy to sleep, but sleep she finally did until she heard a knocking on the door and Congo's voice. "Brekkus ready, Miz Dovie, ma'am". This morning she dismissed Dolly and she and Bart dressed together. With a new feeling of tenderness she surveyed the welts on his back and pitied him. He had suffered this for her and she resolved to make it up to him. His new clothes would help. She realized how much it would mean to him to be well-dressed.

After breakfast, Tom gave orders to Nero to saddle the horses. He designated a fine roan mare for Bart, with one of his best saddles. It was the finest horse Bart had ever mounted and, despite his shabby clothes, he felt like a superior being, especially compared to what he had been yesterday. Even his manner changed. He was no longer sanctimoniously meek—a mere seeker after the crumbs of the table. He sat his horse with arrogance, riding beside Tom with Nero following behind. He surveyed Dove Cote with a proprietary air, feeling that it was all his now—well, almost his, anyway. Even if he wasn't a reverend any more, at least he was Bartholomew Boggs of Dove Cote Plantation, son-in-law of Thomas Verder. He, Bart Boggs was all that and mayhap he'd be a reverend, too.

At the dusty little tailor shop in Brownsville, Tom passed over the homespuns and the shoddy blacks and picked out a rich bottle-green broadcloth for Bart, although Bart would have preferred the ministerial black. He was measured and the suit was promised in another week. Boots were ordered, black ones of the finest leather, and, as a final generous gesture, Tom took Bart into the general store, and, from a catalog profusely

129

illustrated with woodcuts, chose and ordered a gold watch and chain for him. Bart, quite overwhelmed, wished that all these things might be his immediately. The clothes he had been wearing now seemed shabbier than ever, but he consoled himself with the thought that, until the new ones were ready, he would stay in seclusion at Dove Cote, and then, dressed in his new clothes and mounted on his new horse, he would ride through Brownsville, pontifically greeting those who had been his old parishioners. "Mornin', brother." He inclined his head unconsciously. "Mornin', sister." But that would be all. It was scarcely fitting that he, Mister Bartholomew Boggs of Dove Cote, should associate with people of the level of Mrs. Salsman. "Mornin', Miz Salsman, 'n' how're yo' 'n' Lorie 'n' the boys doin' out?" That would be enough.

"I'm a-goin' ter ride on over ter The Patch from here," Tom stated after their errands were done. "Nero a-comin' with me 'n' yo' might's well come along, too. Ain' suggestin' that you' stay there but yo'll be jes' making a circle on yore way home. Straight road 'n' yo' won't git lost." Tom then went on to explain about The Patch, which Bart had heard mentioned during his visit in the spring, though not enough to give him a true idea of its scope and riches. Now he felt even wealthier than before. He was not only "of Dove Cote" but also "of The Patch." Few men had the distinction of owning two plantations, especially two such prosperous ones as these. He sat his horse a little more arrogantly. But there was still one final generosity on Tom's part in store for him.

"Yore goin' back ter Dove Cote 'lone reminds me that yo' ought ter have a nigger o' yore own. Only fittin' that yo' have one. Got ter pick one out fer yo' o', if'n yo' wants, yo' kin look 'round Dove Cote 'n' see if'n any one there appeals ter yo'. Dove Cote got the best niggers. Better if yo' gits a young buck, 'cause yo'll need ter housebreak him. Cain' have no niggers a-pissin' in the house, but they learns fast. Mos' Dove Cote niggers housebroken anyway, livin' in cabins like they do. Those over ter The Patch more beastly like. Might be a good idea ter git one what mates up good with that Dolly what serves Dovie."

"She mentioned it already."

Tom merely nodded his head and continued. "'N' now 'bout the wenches. Ain' got no objection if'n yo' picks out some nice wench fer pleasurin'. Cain' 'spect a white woman ter accommodate yo' all the time. They delicate 'n' high-strung 'n' don't take ter pleasurin'. Hard fer them it is. But don' ever take no wench inter the house or inter the cote neither. Callie dead set against it. Pester her out 'n the quarters if'n yo' wants but leave them young uns in the Romp Pasture 'lone. They pretty small fer a big man like yo'. Ain' puttin' no restrictions in your way. Yo' behaves yo'self 'n' we ain' goin' ter never have no dif'rences. . . ."

His admonitions were cut short by the sudden rearing of his horse. Bart's roan also started sidestepping in the road. It was scarcely surprising for suddenly, as though he had been dropped down from the sky, an immense Negro, entirely naked, had appeared in the dusty path. It was as though Caliban had suddenly materialized out of thin air. He was the most horrendous sight Bart had ever seen and, tall as he was, Bart felt dwarfed by comparison with this giant.

Standing well nigh seven feet tall, spraddle-legged in the middle of the road, he appeared like a savagely heroic statue carved of black marble which someone had patiently striped with white lines of paint. A head, seemingly too small for the powerful body, topped a columnar neck. Close black wool, almost indistinguishable from the back skin, grew far down on the forehead, which jutted out to shadow two eyes, so dark that they seemed to be all black pupils faintly rimmed by yellowish whites. The nose, flat, broad, and short, descended straight from the forehead, spreading out to encompass the large nostrils. Lips, purple-black and broad, parted to show strong white teeth. Each cheek was scarified by a series of diagonal lines running from nose to ear and chin—small washboard corrugations which extended down over the shoulders onto the massive chest, curling around the black discs of the nipples.

131

These cicatrices had been made with almost mathematical accuracy and, to accentuate their decorative pattern, stripes of white had been painted between them which brought out their curving pattern. Running through them at random like a bramble patch were the thicker corrugations of welts made by a whip which continued down the entire body, even around the massive legs. No attempt, however, had been made to decorate these.

The belly was flat and firmly muscled, with a slightly protruding navel, and entirely glabrous except for the thick patch of pubic hair, a black mat against the shining black skin, from which depended the smooth, semierect virile member, pendulous and broad, completely hiding the other genitalia. Through the long pierced prepuce a length of wire had been inserted which in turn was threaded through a piece of smooth black polished stone about the size of an egg. The weight of this had further stretched the skin.

A broad grin appeared across the rough-hewn face, and with it the savage threat disappeared and what had seemed a menace now seemed only friendly. But not to Bart's skittish horse. Bart tried to calm him with his whip, which only caused the animal to rear. Bart, unused to such activity in the horses he rode, was unable to control it, and slid off the cantle of the saddle down over the horse's rump to the ground. Nero, jumping down, calmed the horse, lifted Bart up from the ground, and brushed the dust from his tattered clothes. Bart was uninjured, but he had been so suddenly brought to earth from his daydreaming that he was angry. He regarded the giant in the road and then looked up at Tom. His anger completely dissipated his superficial piety.

"What that goddam nigger a-doin' here, buck-assed nekkid, a-scarin' people ter death? Ain' yo' goin' ter have him whopped?" Bart shook his fist at the man, who, despite Bart's six feet-two, towered over him by nearly a head. The grin disappeared from the man's face and he attempted to sidle past Bart, now showing the basket, made of plaited green osiers, which he had concealed behind his back. Bart glowered at him and, as he passed, slashed at him with his whip. The fellow turned, once again a savage, his upraised hand poised at Bart's throat. For an instant he stood there, then dropping his hand he ran to Tom. Once beside Tom, he lowered his head, placing it affectionately on Tom's knee, rubbing his cheek back and forth along Tom's thigh. Tom placed his hand on the black wool reassuringly, patting the man as if he were a favorite dog.

"Don' whop Big Kru." Tom was serious. "He ain' done nothin', have yo', Big Kru?"

"Masta suh, masta suh." The big fellow had difficulty in mouthing the syllables. "See, masta suh." He held up the shallow basket, showing two speckled trout bedded on ferns. "See, masta suh."

"He ain' done nothin?" Bart saw his role of authority disappearing. "Ain' done nothin'? Could of been killed, I could. 'N' why ain' he dressed.? What he doin' runnin' roun' like a goddam savage, 'n' what that thingumabob on his pecker? He jes' like a savage."

"Tha's what he is." Tom continued to pat the kinky head. "He nothin' but a savage, Big Kru is, but he a good boy. Ain' yo', Big Kru? He's the goddamndest worker I got. Hoes two rows o' cotton whilst the others hoe one. Stronger'n an ox. Gentle's a lamb, too, ain' yo', Big Kru?"

"Masta suh, masta suh." Kru leaned down and kissed the toe of Tom's boot.

"He jes' knowin' that I like trout 'n' they hard ter git 'round here. Must of bin out 'n' caught 'em fer me. Al'ays bringin' me something mos' every day in a basket he make himself. Sometimes fish, sometimes game, sometimes jes' a bunch o' flowers. His way of showin' his love. 'Fectionate he is, jes' like'n a big puppy."

"Then whaffor the big bozal got them whales all over him? Must of whopped him pretty hard ter git them."

"Ain' never whopped him 'tall. Tha's from his other mastas. He did something on'y he ain' knowin' what he did was wrong but tha's why he got whopped. Nearly killed the poor bugger, they did, and tha's when I bought him. Poor Big Kru! He looked like a hunk o' meat what

133

the buzzards bin a-pickin' at." Tom reached into his pocket and drew out a small paper sack, extracted one peppermint ball therefrom, and popped it into Big Kru's open mouth.

The fellow grinned again. "Masta suh, masta suh!" He rolled the candy around on his tongue and closed his eyes in ecstasy. It was his greatest delight.

"Now get down to the fields 'n' git to work, Big Kru. See how much lint yo' kin pick today. Picks more'n the rest, yo' gits 'nother peppermint come night." He watched Big Kru lope away into the roadside bushes. "We 'mos' ter the Patch," he said to Bart while he handed the basket to Nero. "Git back on 'n' while yo' rides alongside, I'll tell you 'bout Big Kru. Quite a story, it is. Quite a boy too. He suffered 'nuff during his life —ain' aimin' ter whop him no more."

While their horses walked along under the plentiful shade, Tom told Bart, who had not entirely regained his composure, the story of Big Kru.

" 'Course I don' know too much 'bout him 'cause Big Kru he ain' never learned to talk English. Seems ter understand 'mos' everythin' I says but never talks hisself. Ain' that he cain' talk but he got a langwidge all his'n. Gabbles away 'mos' o' the time when he a-workin'. Ain' none o' the other niggers what kin understan' him, 'cept ol' Uncle Zekiel what spoke the same langwidge 'n' he dead now. Mos' I know 'bout Big Kru's early days come from what Uncle Zekiel tol' me.

"Seems that Big Kru was taken when he 'bout four-teen, fifteen years ol' from Africky. He a Kru nigger 'n' Uncle Zekiel he say Big Kru's papa a chief in Africky. Bringin' him ter Havana they were, 'n' Jean Lafitte captured the ship 'n' brought the slave cargo ter N'Orleans. Ol' Dan'l Harrison what lived over on Argyll Plantation happen ter be in N'Orleans at that time, a-lookin' fer ter buy some likely hands. Went ter LaFitte's blacksmithin' shop 'n' saw this big bozal what LaFitte say a Kru boy jes' 'rived from Africky. That was Big Kru 'n' La-Fitte say he'll sell him fer a dollar a pound, him being but a bozal 'n' not talkin' nor nothin'. Kru weighed in at two hundred 'n' eighty-five pounds. He a real bozal;

134

never wore no trogs in his life 'n' Ol' Dan'l had an awful time keepin' britches on him while he fetch him from N'Orleans. Once back at Argyll, Kru tear the britches off jes' so soon's Dan'l put em on so Ol' Dan'l, not havin' any womenfolk at his place, seein' as how his wife dead 'n' none of his three sons married up, he let Kru go buff-nekkid 'n' now Kru used to wearin' nothin'. Tha's why I keep him over ter The Patch."

"Jes' a savage, ain' he?" Bart interrupted. "Ain' never bin baptized, ain' never been saved? Mayhap a good baptizin'—clean under—do him good."

"He baptized all right," Tom laughed, picturing Bart, as big as he was, trying to immerse Big Kru. "He the washingest nigger I ever saw. Washes himself all over two, three times a day in the creek, winter o' summer. 'N' he the workingest too! Picks more lint'n any other three hands I got, 'n' chops more trees. Kin tote a bale in his own two hands. If'n Kru live long 'nuff, goin' ter have The Patch all cleared. Don' cost me no keep neither."

"Don' eat no vittles? How he stay 'live?" Bart demanded.

"Don' 'zackly know. Leastwise he don' never come ter git nothin' less'n it be a little salt now 'n' then. Lives on things like grasshoppers 'n' grubs 'n' lizards, 'n' birds 'n' fish what he catches himself. Eats 'em raw, he do. Has hisself a li'l hut out 'n the woods where he sleeps. He took'n me there onct 'n' right neat it was, all snug 'n' tight from the weather 'n' lined with grass inside."

"Should get some good pups outa him. Suckers outa a big bozal like that ought ter be good strong ones. Bring a good price." Bart, now that he had a proprietary interest in all that took place on the Verder plantations, had an eye out to increase their productivity.

Tom shook his head. "Funny thing, jes' cain' mate up that boy. Tried ter mate him a dozen times but Kru cain' do nothin'. Jes' goes limp when I put him to a wench. Thinkin' he never had a wench in his life."

"Could be that doodad he a-wearin' on his pecker. Cain' do nothin' with that on."

"No, Kru kin slip that on 'n' off in a minute. Come ter me every few months a-beggin' some wire 'cause the ol' one worn out. Ain' that. Jes' seems skeert ter death o' all wenches. Ol' Uncle Zekiel he say it 'cause Kru not had his foreskin cut off like'n all them Kru boys do. He thinkin' he cain' do nothin' ter a wench 'thout bein' cut first seein' as how that how his people believe. Shies 'way from all the wenches, but he al'ays has two o' three o' the young bucks what I takes over ter The Patch from the Romp Pasture a-taggin' 'long after him. Big Kru he right fond o' them boys. Takes 'em to the creek 'n' teaches 'em how ter swim 'n' how to hunt. Sometimes takes 'em out to his hut ter stay with him. Usually has three o' four young squirts a-tailin' roun' after him, but when I put them ter wenches they leave him 'n' he gits some new ones."

"Ain yo' got no whip? Little touch o' the leather 'n' he'd have ter mount a wench," Bart suggested.

"Big Kru whopped 'nuff during his life, I reckon. Ain' never goin' ter whop him no more. Never does no wrong 'n' tamer'n a kitten. Them stripes he a-wearin' I never laid on. The Harrison boys did it ter him.".

"What he done ter warrant all them whales?" Boggs asked. "He run?"

"No, he never run." Verder shook his head in negation, clearing his throat and spitting. He knew full well that the explanation he was about to give would cause astonishment to Bart, and he hesitated just long enough to produce the full dramatic effect for his story. "He got them whales from eatin' Ol' Dan'l Harrison's liver."

Bart's face showed that he was properly shocked. "He a cannibal?"

"No, not hardly a real one. Ol' Dan'l dead when Kru ate his liver. Ol' Dan'l died 'n' they buried him 'n' Big Kru a-takin' on somethin' awful 'cause he loved Ol' Dan'l like'n a houn' dog love his masta. Jes' worshiped him he did, 'cause Ol' Dan'l a big strong man. Well, that night, Big Kru went out to the buryin' ground 'n' he dug up Ol' Dan'l's corpse, cut open the belly, and et the liver. Was a-chewin' on the las' o' it when Ol' Daniel's three boys caught him a-doin' it. Uncle Zekiel he 'splain it ter me later. Seems like them niggers 'n Africky believe that if'n a man eat another man's liver, it make him like the dead man—he gits all the dead man's grit 'n' everythin'. Big Kru jes' worshiped Ol' Dan'l 'n' his boys too 'n' he not thinkin' it anything evil 'cause he wanted ter be like Ol' Dan'l.

"Daniel's boys, howsomever, talked it over 'n' decided not ter shoot Big Kru, 'cause he worth money and they settin' a store by him too. But they felt they had ter punish him somehow. Decided ter give him a good lacin', not jes' 'n ordinary whoppin' but a real one. Sent a hand over from Argyll ter invite me over 'n' asked mos' o' the other planters too. Made a big day outa it. Had a barbecued hog 'n' everythin'. After we et, they dragged Big Kru out 'n' strung him up by his feet. Them three Harrison boys all took turns a-whoppin' Big Kru. They all big fellers, them Harrison boys, 'n' each one whopped till his arm ached. Kru never cried out onct, not even whimpered. Then when they couldn't whop him no more, they asked if'n any o' the men there wanted ter add a fer more larrups 'n' three o' four o' them did. Finally they cut him down 'n' rubbed pimentade inter the whales 'n' when they got all through, yo' know what that Big Kru did?"

"Ain' got no notion," Bart answered.

"He jes' crawled on his belly up ter them Harrison boys 'n' kissed their hands. Guess it must of been Ol' Dan'l's liver already a-workin' on him what made him so spunky."

"Should of burned him, leastwise shot him o' whopped him ter death," Bart commented. "Tha's what I'd of done."

"Them Harrison boys ain' killin' a nigger what worth somethin'. 'N' besides, they set quite a store by Big Kru, him sort o' growin' up with 'em 'n' everythin'. But they wanted ter get shet o' him after he whopped. They say any man what wanted could buy him. Mostly the planters skeered o' him, him having et Ol' Dan'l's liver, so only two, three bid on him. I offered a hundred 'n' Maitland raised me ten, another bid twenty-five 'n' then I raised him 'nother ten 'n' got the bugger fer one hundred 'n' thirty-five. Bes' bargain I ever got. Nero 'n' I run him home 'tween us 'n' him runnin' 'long with the blood a-streamin' down his back. Lef' him here at The Patch 'n' he disappeared fer 'bout a week. Tho't he'd runned fer sure but he jes' out'n the woods a-lickin' his wounds. Came back, he did, 'n' come up ter me 'n' kissed my boots. Since that time I let him do as he likes. Ain' never caused me no trouble 'n' he workin' like a Trojan all the time. Al'ays a-bringin' me something fer a present like them fish there. Sometimes a raccoon, sometimes a basket o' persimmons—he always make a basket fer whatsomever he bring—sometimes jes' a bunch o' flowers, but always somethin'. 'N' yo should see him choppin' trees 'n' pickin' lint."

Verder finished his talk and pointed through an opening in the trees to a cluster of barns and cabins. "That there's The Patch." He encompassed the entire landscape with a wide gesture. "Bes' land for miles 'round. Grow more cotton here on one acre than we kin grow at Dove Cote on two. Aimin' ter git it all cleaned 'n' drained sometime but ain' no fit habitation fer white folks. Niggers don' seem ter git the ager but it shore kills off white folks. Tha's why I don' want yo' ter stay. Cain' have Dovie a widder jes' soon's she a bride. Yo' ride on back ter Dove Cote. Cain' miss it; ain' no turns off'n the road. Tell Callie I'll be here fer two o' three days." Tom turned in the saddle and stretched out a hand to Bart. "No hard feelin's, son?" He smiled.

Bart took his hand and shook it. Things were working out better than he had thought possible. He anticipated his ride home on a fine horse and the prospect of Dovie awaiting him along with a good meal and a fine bed to sleep in. He'd even have a nigger of his own. Parting from Tom and Nero, he cantered down the road to Dove Cote, singing psalms at the top of his voice. He'd been riding for about a quarter of an hour when he saw, for the second time that morning, the figure of Big Kru standing in the road, spraddle-legged as he was before. Bart geed his horse to one side to pass the menacing figure, but as he went by, Big Kru's huge hand shot out and grasped the bridle, halting the horse.

"Let go o' my horse!" Bart raised his whip to bring it down on Big Kru's shoulder, but felt it torn from his grasp. Kru broke it in one hand as easily as a match and threw the pieces down on the road. There was no grin on his face now. It was set in grim lines. He came close to Bart but instead of laying his head on Bart's knee as he had on Tom's, he glared up at him, meeting and holding his eyes. The black eyes bored into Bart.

"No masta suh," he mumbled. "No masta suh." He shook his head vigorously. "No masta suh." He released his hold on the bridle, struck the horse a sharp blow on the rump, then cleared the road in one gigantic leap. Bart, frightened, had difficulty in keeping his seat on the galloping horse. There had been something fearful in Big Kru's malevolent stare and he wanted to get away. He would have shot the son of Satan if he belonged to him. Well, perhaps someday he would. Someday everything would belong to him. He'd only to wait, but, when that day came and he was master, they're'd be no boot-kissing and lollygagging around with these niggers. Not by a damn sight!

Chapter VII

THE FOLLOWING MORNING Bart arose, later than usual, and even then contrary to Dovie's pleas to remain a little longer. They had gone to bed, as was the custom on most plantations, soon after daylight faded. Staying up, there was nothing to discuss, nowhere to go, and certainly nothing as entertaining to do as going to bed. Candlelight was poor at its best and expensive. Tallow candles were used as a rule and these gave off an even dimmer light than the more expensive wax. After the long day's work, bed was welcome to white and black alike. Certainly none, black or white, looked forward to it more than Bart and Dovie.

During the day, with Tom over at the Patch, there was really nobody for Bart to talk with except the womenfolk. He was the only white man on the plantation and although he was at home with women—most of his followers had been women—he found few topics of conversation either with Callie or Dovie. His usual subject—the saving of one's immortal soul through the avoidance of eternal damnation—was lost on Callie, who plainly showed her indifference. He had formerly employed his role as a reverend as a method of seduction on those women he desired but he had no desire for Callie and he certainly did not need to use words to get Dovie to do his bidding. Nor could he preach repentance to her during the daytime when he cohabited and co-indulged with her at night. Dovie was indeed a puzzle to Bart. Brought up, as he knew she had been, under the strictest conditions, she displayed an inventiveness and a knowledge of carnality which shocked him. He found her to be insatiable, and it was he who always called it quits, while she was always willing to continue. He rebelled at some of her innovations, castigating her for her unbridled lust but yielding to it in the end. Verily, his spirit was willing but his flesh weak, for he always succumbed. Bart was actually a puritan when it came to venery. He enjoyed it, true, but he insisted there was only one method of satisfying the flesh and all others were sinful. Not so Dovie! What Tommy Verder had not taught her (and Tommy had been a resourceful tutor) she had discovered through instinct and forced upon the—at first—unwilling Bart. After two nights with her, he felt he had married a woman far more wanton than either Lorie Salsman or her mother could ever be. Yet despite his verbal unwillingness, he was beginning to discover that there were other ways to kill a cat than by choking it to death with butter, and that some of these circumnavigations around what he had always considered the only acceptable and normal *modus operandi* were even more lickerish. Consequently Dovie drained him as no other woman ever had, and he realized in view of her innovations that, even as her pregnancy increased, he would not be free from her demands.

Today was considerably less lively than the previous night. He watched Congo brush Callie's hair. He listened boredly to Callie discuss with Aunt Ruthie the meals for the day, and to Dovie's instructions to Reba, the plantation seamstress, as to how she wanted a dress altered. He came to life only when Reba, a ponderous black wench, measured him for a half-dozen shirts of fine nainsook, of which Callie had sufficient yardage. These would be suitable accessories with his new suit. After the fitting, his hints for a lengthy session of morning prayers having been ignored, he wandered out onto the gallery and settled in a rush-bottom chair. He would have ordinarily composed a new and even more frightening hellfire-and-damnation sermon in these idle moments, but that now seemed rather futile, as he had been forbidden any more circuit-riding and had no permanent church to preach in. There remained nothing to do but sit and look off into space which, after half an hour, became boring.

At length he arose, stretched his big frame, snapped his galluses, and determined to make a survey of his new domain. He had no particular desire to learn any of the details of plantation management, being naturally lazy, but he felt he might at least familiarize himself with what he felt would someday belong to him. Since the stables were nearest to the house, he visited them first. As he entered the dim coolness with its ammoniacal pungency, he saw a Negro sitting in the open doorway of a small room. He walked over and discovered that it was the tack room, where saddles and bridles were kept along with the harness for the chaise which Callie used. The man, who was repairing a bridle, got to his feet. He was an elderly Negro, grizzle-headed and toothless with a humped back that forced him into a perpetual genuflection.

"Yo' de new masta, suh? Ain' jes' a-knowin' what ter call yo'. I'se 'Thuselah, suh, servant ter masta Tom's pappy I was. Whatsomever I call yo', masta suh?"

"Kin call me masta Bart, seein's how yo' one of the house servants o' nearly so."

"Ya'as suh, masta Bart, 'n' thinkin' yo' wantin' yo're drap o' corn like'n masta Tom 'n' his pappy afore him. Miz Callie, she like'n Miz Martha what was masta Tom's mammy, don' hol' wid havin' no corn in the house. Masta Tom he keepin' it out here." He shuffled over to a cupboard on the wall and drew out a jug and a tin cup. "Give yo' masta Tom's cup. T'other for Nero 'cause sometime masta Tom he give a drap ter Nero too." He poured the cup over half full and extended it to Bart.

Bart made no effort to take it and shook his head. "Bein' as how I'm a reverend, I'm temp'rance. Don' never touch no hard likker. Strong drink is ragin'. It the temptataion o' Satan."

" 'Course 'tis, 'course." The aged man had learned he should always agree with a white man. " 'Course 'tis, but

142

settles the stomach jes' fine. Masta Tom say he a'needin' his drap every mornin'. Jes' medicine 'tis. Masta Tom he knows. He guv it ter Nero too 'n' ter young Tommy whilst he here. Tha's why he 'n' Nero so healthy-like 'n' strong." He placed the cup in Bart's unwilling fingers. "Good fer what ails yo'." He grinned, stretching the slack lips over his toothless gums.

Bart glanced at the cup of liquid in his hands. He had no hidebound principles against liquor except that his position as a reverend had always caused him to denounce it. Now that he was temporarily no longer a reverend, there were no prohibitions. And it *was* good for the stomach. Just now he felt the need of something. There was no necessity for him to excuse himself before a slave, but he felt some explanation was in order.

"Stomach not feelin' too good this mornin'," he said, attempting to placate his own conscience rather than offering an explanation to the old man. "Think mayhap I'll try it." He sipped the drink. He choked on the fiery liquid, but it felt comfortably warm in his stomach. When he handed the cup back, the old man, instead of taking it, filled it again.

"Stomach bad, yo'd better have 'nuther." He nodded wisely.

Bart found it easier to down the second cup. He handed it back empty, then straightened his shoulders and walked out of the barn into the sunshine. Although the liquor burned in his throat and stomach, he suddenly felt much better, and as he walked along aimlessly, sauntering among the scattered oaks that stood near the house, he felt his worries and frustrations disappear. A glow of well-being possessed him. By God, this was all his. When the time came for Tom to die, he'd be master of it all. To hell with Dovie's bastard! It was a small price to pay. And to hell with Dovie, too! He'd give her all she wanted. By God, he would. He'd never had to cry quits with any woman and he wouldn't with Dovie. Whatever she wanted of him, he'd go her one better. By God he would! He'd show her and he'd show Mrs. Salsman and Lorie, too. He felt the strength of a Samson as he wandered out from the trees and reached the vast expanse of untimbered land which, at that time of the year, was stippled with the white of the ripe cotton. Feeling a slight dizziness, he stopped to wipe his brow and admire this domain which his marriage to Dovie had vouchsafed him. He was aware of a plaintive but not unhappy song, and soon found himself in the midst of a drove of slaves, dragging their sacks behind them up and down the rows while they filled them with the bolls of cotton which they nipped from the browning plants.

When a slave became aware of the presence of a white man, his singing stopped and the quiet spread from row to row until the silence was general. Even between rows so far apart that the Negroes were unaware of the stranger, they no longer sang. Those who caught a glimpse of him grew fearful of something, they knew not what. A strange white man among them augured almost anything, and chances were that it would mean something bad for them. The pickers hastened their work; the drivers were more aggressive in their efforts to demonstrate their efficiency and that of their gangs. As Bart came closer the work accelerated. The Negroes were like a flock of sheep, fearful of an encircling wolf, acutely aware of the presence of this white stranger.

The drivers, even more nervous than the workers, shouted peremptory orders, punctuated by flicks of the whip.

"Hurry up, thar, Pearl."

"Yo' lazy no-good Bijah, yo' missin' mo' bolls'n yo' pickin'."

"Whaffor yo' draggin' yore sack through the puddles, Minta. Does it onct more 'n' I'll have Nero whop yo' good."

A sense of power overwhelmed Bart as he stood watching the slaves. These were his. He was the only white man around and these people, old and young, male and female, adult and children belonged to him. It was a heady sensation—one which he had never experienced before.

"Look like a lazy bunch ter me," he said to the driver nearest him. "Cain' yo' poke 'em up a bit. Jes' crawlin' 'long they be. Ain' never a-goin' ter get no pickin' done if'n they don' step lively." He reached for the whip in

144

the driver's hand. Circling it about his head, he brought it down indiscriminately on anyone who came within reach of it. Although the driver had put plenty of strength into his efforts, Bart's were far more vicious.

"Ya'as suh, masta suh. Workin' fas' 's I kin."

"Don' whop me, masta suh. I'se workin'."

"Don' whop me! Don' whop me! Don' whop me!"

But Bart, drunk with authority, continued to swing the whip. As it made contact with black flesh it gave him the feeling of absolute power and mastery. This black flesh would some day be his and when that day came, he was determined that he would turn it all into good hard cash. Then, in his own magnificent church, he would be a real reverend, entirely independent of the niggardly alms of his parishioners.

Among the workers was a well-built, light-colored buck who had discarded his shirt, and his broad back made an excellent target for Bart's whip. It was so inviting that Bart concentrated on it, bringing it down again and again on the rippling muscles until red welts appeared on the yellow skin. This fellow, unlike the others, did not beg for mercy, and, although he speeded up his work, he bore his punishment without flinching. Once he straightened up and stared back at Bart and in that brief moment, when their eyes met, Bart thought he detected some resemblance between the fellow and someone whom he had once known. The resemblance penetrated his whisky-inflamed mind, but he could not identify it. It was, however, sufficient for him to lower his whip. There was something he was trying to remember. What was it? Then it came to him. Tom had said that he could pick out a slave for himself, for his own body servant. Something about this defiant young buck who looked so familiar appealed to him. Coming a step closer he inventoried the fellow.

He stood, stiff legs wide apart, with only his soiled osnaburg trousers covering him. The look of defiance which had flashed in his eyes had now disappeared and there was a suggestion of fright, although he was no coward. His hair, instead of being kinky, was long and straight, reaching nearly to his shoulders; his eyes were long and narrow, his cheek bones high; his forehead was higher than most colorèd men's and his nose thinner, and his lips were not Negroid.

"Yo' got a name, boy?" Bart spoke thickly, the whisky slowing his words.

"Ya'as suh, masta suh," the boy answered. "My name Sippi."

"Who-all yore pappy? Got one?" Bart inquired, even more conscious of the resemblance now but unable to place it.

The boy shrugged and dropped his eyes. "Don' know, suh. Reckon I got one but not knowin' what his name be." He pointed to a woman ahead of him. "That my mammy tho'. She 'Smeralda."

Bart glanced at the woman ahead, possibly a mulatto. "Yo' must of been sired by a white man, I reckon," he speculated. "She right dark 'n' not more'n half-blooded, 'n' yo' right yeller."

Sippi looked at his hands. "Yas suh, masta suh, I'se yeller."

"How old are yo'?"

The boy hesitated, anxious to give the right answer but entirely unacquainted with either his age or the number which might express it. His face lit up with the memory of a number. "Reckon I'se ten." He nodded his head vigorously.

The estimate was preposterous. Bart's guess was eighteen or nineteen. "Ever bin whopped? Got any whales on yore back?" Bart stepped closer and ran exploring fingers over the sweaty skin.

"Not 'ceptin' what yo' jes' whopped me, masta suh. Ain' never needed no larrupin'. I good. If'n masta he got ter larrup a nigger, he sen' him down ter The Patch fer Nero ter larrup there. Don' keep no wuthless niggers at Dove Cote, he don'." The mere fact that he was a Dove Cote boy exculpated him from all guilt.

"I'll larrup yo' if'n I wants any time I wants. Yo' jes' been lazy now, draggin' yore ass 'n' not workin'. Tha's why I larrup yo'. Ain' havin' no lazy niggers here no more." He raised the whip as if to bring it down again. This time the boy cringed but did not take his eyes off

146

Bart. Bart lowered the whip. "Yo' pesters the wenches a lot, I reckon. Yo' look strong and full o' sap."

Sippi denied the charge so wholeheartedly that Bart knew he was not lying. "Naw suh, masta suh, naw suh!" He placed particular emphasis on the "suh." "Masta Tom ain' said I could yet. Naw suh, not 'till Masta Tom say I kin. That Nero he know everythin' 'n' if'n I pester a wench, he a-goin' ter know it nex'-day 'n' he take down my britches 'n' horsewhop me wid his whip. Ain' like'n a real larrupin' over ter The Patch but Nero he right strong 'n' he hurt."

Sippi looked up hopefully and said, "Masta Tom goin' ter give me a wench soon. He say soon's a nice light one come ripe in the Romp Pasture I kin have her. He say he a-lookin' fer one fer me."

"How yo' like ter be my nigger—my body servant?" Bart said. "Reckon yo' could learn? Got ter keep clean, learn ter be polite 'n' sech 'n' help me git dressed."

"Gotta leave my mammy?" Sippi dreaded changing the known for the unknown.

"Jes' go yonder to the big house. Reckon yo' could?"

" 'N' live in the big house like Nero?"

Bart nodded.

" 'N' have trogs like Nero?"

Bart was not so sure of the answer to that question but he assumed that any body servant of his would not wear the rough osnaburg pants and shirt that a field hand wore. Again he nodded.

" 'N' have a horse ter ride on?"

Again Boggs nodded, although he was even more uncertain about the horse than the clothes.

Sippi leaped high into the air, clapping his hands and grinning. He had just had the highest honor that it was possible for any slave to have conferred upon him, and, strangely enough, it had come from a man who only a few moments before had been laying a whip on his back. But that didn't matter now! To be a servant to a white man, to dress in fine clothes, to ride a horse and live in the big house and be a part of the family would raise him to the zenith of slave aristocracy. He'd rank second only to Nero. He was not sure who this white man was, but the mere fact that he was white, that he lived at the big house, and wielded a whip with authority was enough for Sippi. He imagined that he might be someone like that young masta Tommy who used to be around. However, his identity made little difference. He was white, that was all that mattered.

"Shore like it, masta suh, 'n' shore likin' ter serve yo' too, masta suh. I a good boy. Work hard, I do. I housebroke too. Ain' never doin' nothin' in the house. My mammy strict, she is."

"Well, go back to yore pickin 'n' step lively. Wasted 'nuff time. We'll see does I need yo'."

The interruption had thrown Sippi behind his fellows, and the fact that he had to run up and tell his mother about the momentous happening caused him to lag even further behind. Bart watched him, and feeling that Sippi lingered too long in conversation with his mother, he stalked up, whirled the cowhide, and brought it down again on Sippi's back, flicking its tip a second time on the woman.

"Ya'as suh," Sippie cried out, more to protect his mother than himself. "I'se hurryin', masta suh, I'se hurryin'."

Bart handed the whip to the driver who took it readily, anxious once more to have his badge of authority. "He a lazy son-o'-a-bitch, that Sippi. Got ter git this pickin' finished. Look like rain."

"Tickle him up, boy, tickle him up," Bart urged. "Cain' have no sluggards in the race. All yo' boys gotta be up 'n' doin'. If'n that Sippi lazy give him a taste o' the cowhide. 'N' if'n I find yo' lazy, I'll give yo' a taste o' it too." He nodded in approval as the driver flicked at Sippi again, then, spying a cotton wagon coming which was slowly proceeding toward the house, he hailed it and climbed on.

The black man driving the mules hazarded a statement that the weather was fine, with which Bart concurred. At length the black's curiosity got the better of him. "Yo' a-visitin' here?" he ventured. "Leastwise ain' never seen yo' 'roun' here 'fore now."

"Live here," Bart replied. "This my place." He spread

148

his arms in an all-encompassing gesture. "Belongs ter me."

" 'N' the niggers, suh, all the niggers?"

"Every black varmint on the place. Jes' 's good as ownin' them, that is. I married up ter Miz Dovie."

"So it yo', eh?" the driver said. "I seen Miz Dovie t'other day. She stickin' out 'n' I reckoned it that masta Tommy."

The statement stung Bart. Even though a white man was supposed to pay no attention to what a Negro might say, Bart resented the driver's assumption that Tommy was the sire of the child his wife carried, resented it almost as much as he resented Tom's insistence that he was the father. The slave's remark implied that Bart was unable to sire a child of his own. Yet Tom's allegation that it was his was unjust. Indeed, Bart was torn between his desire to name the real father and his avarice. But his avarice conquered. Even that Sippi, if nothing more, would be rich payment for claiming Dovie's brat. Why, that one nigger was worth a thousand dollars! The possession of Sippi which had, at first, been only a matter of indifference, had become of paramount importance. He halted the wagon before the stables and climbed down. Another drink of corn would be tasty after his walk in the hot sun. It certainly had helped his stomach. He'd have to take it often, purely as a medicine, of course. But, when old 'Thuselah poured out a generous cup for him, Bart cautioned him, "This jes' medicine, yo' know. Ain' fer nothing else. Yo' knows that I'se a rev'nd 'n' don' hold with no strong drink. Ain' wantin' yo' ter say nothin' 'bout this ter nobody. Understand? Yo' pretty ol' 'n' feeble like 'n' don' know how yo' stand up under a real good larrupin'."

"Ya'as suh, masta, ya'as suh." The old man's face betrayed his fright.

Bart waited impatiently till Tom had returned to Dove Cote and, as soon as he had an opportunity, he broached the subject, identifying Sippi as his choice for a body servant.

"He the one I a-thinkin' he is?" Tom looked to Nero for corroboration. "Kinda good-lookin' yeller buck what look like his pappy 'cept that he kinda Indian-lookin'?"

Nero nodded. "He my git, he is. His mother, she got some Indian blood."

"He a good boy, tho'. All yore young uns biddable. Do as they told but lazy like, jes' like yo', Nero." Tom slapped Nero on the shoulder with affection.

It was a joke and intended as such, for Nero was one of the hardest workers on the place, and was acknowledged with hearty laughter on Nero's part. Bart, however, saw nothing funny in it. To him all Negroes were lazy.

"If'n Nero lazy, he ought ter get whopped, too. Cain' stan' no lazy nigger 'bout."

" 'N' who a-goin' ter whop him?" Tom grinned at Nero. "He do all the whoppin' hisself." He suddenly remembered that Nero had laid the whip on Bart and sought to change the subject.

"Ride out 'n' bring that Sippi in, Nero. Shuck him down 'n' see if'n he all right, 'cause I'm a-goin ter mate him up with Miz Dovie's Dollie. Promised him a wench fer some time I have, 'n' Dolly right likely fer him."

"He kinda small-peckered if'n I 'member." Nero took off his hat and scratched his head. "Al'ays said it the Indian comin' out in him."

"Don' make no neverminds if'n he got sap in him. Ain' the size what counts. Go fetch him 'n' tell him ter scrub all over in the creek with some of that new batch o' soft soap. Seems stronger'n usual. Git the musk off'n him 'cause cain' stand no musky niggers 'roun' the house. Git Aunt Ruthie ter give yo' some new trogs fer him 'till we kin order him some real ones when we go ter git Bart's. 'N' he'll have ter have some boots, too." He looked down at Nero's feet. " 'Pears like'n yo' need some, too. Want yo' should al'ays look spruce 'n' chipper 'cause yo're my boy. Take that Sippi in hand 'n' teach him ter serve Bart here. He kin wait on table, too. 'N' while yo' 'bout it, fetch Fanny 'n' Jasmine over from the quarters 'n' tell 'em I want that upper room o' the cote washed out 'n' whitewashed. Git a corn-shuck mattress up there 'n' git the place cleaned out fer Dolly 'n' Sippi. Might's well be gittin' some pups outa them." He watched Nero depart and turned to Bart.

"Sippi's yourn," he said, "but ain' goin' ter deed him ter yo'. Ain' necessary."

"Shore would like him in my name, tho'." Bart desired the full legal ownership of Sippi. It would inflate his ego to know that he was the actual and lawful owner of a slave.

Tom disregarded the remark. "Le's git washed up fer eatin'. Right hungry I am fer some o' Aunt Ruthie's cookin'. That wench I got over ter The Patch kin fry ham 'n' eggs 'n' make pone 'n' that 'bout all."

Bart walked beside him crestfallen. But he consoled himself with thinking that some day things would be different. By God Almighty, they would be! And when that day came! Oh, when that day came!

Chapter VIII

THOUGH HIS DRINKING in the stables had not yet become a habit, Bart continued to imbibe regularly. He managed, however, to avoid taking it during the time that Tom was at Dove Cote. At the height of the picking season, this was not often, and then only for a day or so. The plantation of Dove Cote practically ran itself, and although Tom employed a white overseer at The Patch—a worthless and inept creature by the name of Laudermilk—the man merely filled the demands of the law and was entirely incompetent without Tom and Nero there to direct him. Tom had, in order to make Bart feel more at home, assigned certain duties and responsibilities to him at Dove Cote. These assignments were merely nominal, designed to give Bart something to occupy his time, and Bart carried them out indifferently and perfunctorily. The only part he enjoyed was his mastery over the slaves. It gave him a sense of power to command them and see them obey him and he assumed his authority with such an arrogant and peremptory manner that they all feared him and, although such an expression of emotion was not to be manifested, hated him. His whip, for he had now acquired one of his own, was always seeking a victim, and the fact that his punishments were seldom deserved only added to the slaves' resentment.

Bart's new clothes had arrived; his new boots, glossy

black although somewhat tight, were now on his feet; and his gold watch reposed in his pocket, the chain draped across his waistcoat. Tom had neglected to order him a new hat, but repeated brushings by Sippi had somewhat restored the appearance of his big black slouch hat, and it did not detract from his well-dressed look. Sippi, now accoutered in a short blue jacket with brass buttons and trousers to match, looked quite as spruce as his master. His long black hair and light coloring, along with his high cheekbones and narrow eyes, gave him an Indian appearance which set him apart from the other servants. Sippi's training under Nero—which perhaps would have been less rigorous had Nero not felt a great responsibility for his offspring—had been strenuous and accompanied by frequent blows of Nero's whip, but Sippi was beginning to learn. His new position was far from the bed of roses he had imagined it to be. Bart, never having had a servant before, was overbearing and difficult to please while Nero, more masterful even than Bart, was determined that Sippi should be a very model of perfection. Poor Sippi, buffeted by one and chastised by the other, often longed for the carefree days in the field when his only responsibility was manual labor. People in the big house, it seemed to him, set a powerful store on a multitude of useless and unimportant things. Like, for instance, polishing the big silver centerpiece, which took many hours and had to be done once a week. Polish it as he might, Callie always found some fault with his efforts. But Sippi was naturally intelligent and each day he learned a little more. And in spite of the hardship of his days, he found solace with Dolly at night on the corn-shuck mattress in the upper room of the dove cote. They had little in common except the contact of flesh with flesh, but that was enough for Sippi if not for Dolly. After Tommy and her paramour in the Romp Pasture, she found Sippi rather disappointing.

Bart, despite Dovie's continuing demands, was becoming bored and discontented. He had adapted himself to his new affluence and now took being well fed and waited on for granted. He missed the change of both scenery and venery which his wanderings as a circuit preacher had brought him. He desired the position of power and prestige which the title conferred, and he resented the fact that with all his father-in-law's wealth, Tom did not offer to build him a church. Didn't Tom know that as the Reverend Bartholomew Boggs, he would bring more honor to the family than he ever would as a mere overseer? Didn't Tom realize that Dovie too would profit? She'd be the wife of a gospel preacher. And for that matter, even her unborn bastard would profit. Why, the brat would be acknowledged as a preacher's son. What bastard could ever hope to achieve such a position?

Bart's hints and innuendoes fell on deaf ears, however. Tom did not rise to the bait and always dismissed the matter. Nor did Bart's lengthy prayers meet with any popularity in the household. Callie was willing to listen, fidgeting the while, for a few minutes only, after which she always found some pressing duty in another room. Dovie refused to listen at all, particularly at bedside prayers, when she would silence Bart with a "For heaven's sake, get into bed." He had tried holding prayer meetings in the quarters and, although the slaves were obedient listeners, regarding his rantings as an entertaining novelty, Tom had forbidden him to pray, preach, or exhort them. "Takin' too much time 'way from their work o' 'way from their sleep which they a-needin'." Sippi, however, a captive audience, was forced to endure long sessions of prayer and exhortation in the stables where Bart, fortified by more and more liberal dosages of corn, forced him to his knees for an hour at a time.

Bart loved to advise the Deity, and the sonorous sound of his own powerful voice hypnotized him. He was able to continue for hours at a time and, although his prayers were mainly repetitious, he never tired of them. The fact that he believed little of what he was bellowing about was immaterial. He became an actor, occupying the center of the stage with all eyes focused on him, and that was what he loved. The fact that his audience consisted only of Sippi did not deter Bart. His mellifluous words, however, seemed wasted on Sippi and Bart longed for a wider, more appreciative audience—one which would not only appreciate his prayers but his new affluence. It served little purpose to be so richly attired and to have no opportunity to display this elegance except to the Verder family and their Negro servants.

But, while the Verders denied him an opportunity to exercise his talents fully, he knew where he could. Yes, suh! Mrs. Salsman appreciated him! And Lorie too! Mrs. Salsman was a fine woman, and her buxom body had been even more exciting than her willingness to listen to him. She certainly appreciated a strapping young fellow who was about ten years her junior. And so did Lorie. He'd enjoy being a "solid-gold repeater" once again. It would be a welcome relief after Dovie's constant importuning. A man wanted to be master of the woman he was with, not her servant. That's all he was to Dovie—just someone to do her bidding, and he was getting tired of it, damned tired of it. A man wanted his screwing when *he* wanted it, not when some goddamned woman forced him into it. He'd show them. By God he would!

Consequently, that coming Sunday with Tom still at The Patch, Bart, with Sippi's assistance, dressed himself meticulously—clean drawers and a clean shirt, a carefully tied black satin cravat, and an extra polish on his boots. He had Sippi dress in his own best clothes and cautioned 'Thuselah to have his and Sippi's horses carefully brushed and curried. After a plentiful Sunday dinner, he pushed back his chair and rose from the table.

"Ain' Christian, not havin' no services nor no prayers on the Lord's day," he announced. "If'n I cain' hold 'em here, reckon I kin go in ter Brownsville 'n' listen ter that idiot Soper. He ain' no true believer but he better'n nothin'. Don' suppose any o' yo'-all wan' ter go?" he was certain they would not. Dovie's advanced pregnancy prohibited her from being seen in public, and he could not imagine Callie hoisting her bulk into the chaise just to go to service. Nevertheless he breathed more freely when they both declined and offered no objction to his going.

He and Sippi rode into town but, instead of proceeding through the town to the meeting house (where he hadn't had the least intention of going anyway), he stopped to greet Mrs. Salsman. She was, as usual, sitting on the bench outside the door, strangely closed now, of her cabin. Bart was somewhat surprised to see her hair combed, her calico dress clean, and worn-down and shapeless black slippers on her feet. In the process of greeting her, he pulled out his watch and ostentatiously glanced at the time. Dismounting and turning his horse over to Sippi to hold for him, he was greeted, although not so warmly as he had expected, by Mrs. Salsman, who cautioned him in an elaborate pantomime to be quiet. Finger on the lips, a shaking head, and a meaningful nod toward the closed door of the cabin warned him of something, he did not know what, taking place within. She did not invite him in and motioned to him to be seated on the bench beside her. All this took place without her usual effusive cordiality. She passed the time of day with him perfunctorily, quite heedless of his new apparel or the watch which he extracted from his pocket and consulted every alternate minute. She seemed to be listening to what was going on inside the cabin and, as Bart strained his ears, he could hear noises—the creaking of the rope bedstead and strangled gaspings. These ceased suddenly and were replaced by the cries of a man and a woman. The woman's voice he recognized as Lorie's. Mrs. Salsman suddenly stopped listening at the door and turned her whole attention on him. Almost immediately the door was opened and a handsome, red-haired youth, a few years younger than Bart, and even more handsomely dressed, emerged, smiling and happy, followed by an adoring Lorie who stood in the doorway, clutching a pink wrapper about her middle.

"Had yore fill? I reckon she real good?" Mrs. Salsman put it as a question. "She young yet."

The boy grinned back at her. "Right buxom; right temtatious and downright purty. She better'n any wench my papa got on the whole plantation. 'N' she smell right sweet 'n' flowery too." He reached in his pocket and drew out a silver dollar, but Mrs. Salsman frowned and shook her head, waving him back inside the cabin and beckoning for Bart to follow. Once inside she cautioned, "Don' never go offerin' me money outside fer all these nosy neighbors ter see. Might think Lorie's a whore o' somethin'. 'N' me 'n' Rev'nd Boggs just a-talkin' as to how

156

everythin' goin' up in price. Goin' ter have ter require two dollars out'n yo' this time." Her quick look at Bart included him in her falsehood.

"A rev'nd?" The young fellow stared at Boggs in surprise. "Never reckoned I'd see a rev'nd here."

" 'N' why not," Mrs. Salsman bristled. "We decent people, Lorie 'n' me. We ain' heathen. Jes' 'cause we pore ain' meanin' we trash. Mayhap yo' thinkin' 'cause yo're Johnny O'Neal whose papa got that big plantation over Orion way 'n' a passel o' niggers, yo're better'n us. Well, yo' ain'. Rev'nd Boggs here, he from Dove Cote Plantation 'n' he ain' too good ter come here 'n' pray with us."

Johnny did not forget his manners. "Pleased ter meet yer, Rev'nd Boggs." He was an engaging chap with a ready smile and a likable manner.

Bart bowed with dignity in acknowledgment of the greeting. Although he was not much older than the O'Neal boy, he accepted the other's deference as his due.

"He a-comin' regular like ter see Lorie, he is." Mrs. Salsman laid a proprietary hand on Johnny's shoulder. "Lorie she ain' a-caperin' with none other. No suh, she keepin' pure jes' fer this fine boy here. 'N' that reminds me, Johnny, think it 'bout time yo' 'n' me havin' a little talk. Rev'nd here comin' 'long jes' 'the right time. Wantin' fer him ter listen ter what I got ter say." She glanced at Bart for approval as she gently forced Johnny down into a chair and pulled Lorie over beside him. "Mayhap the Rev'nd will start us off with a word o' prayer."

"Got ter be goin', Miz Salsman." Johnny shifted uneasily on the chair. "Mama's 'spectin' me home fer supper 'n' if'n I don' come my pappy'll git awful mad."

"Thinkin' perhaps yo'd better stay, son, if'n Miz Salsman so kindly request it," Bart said in a fatherly, benign manner. " 'N' now, we'll pray." He got down on his knees and Mrs. Salsman followed, but Johnny continued to sit in the chair, unabashedly drawing Lorie down on his lap, and teasing, caressing, and kissing her. Lorie offered no objection. Nor did her mother.

Bart's prayer was based on the theme of fornication, and painted a vivid portrait of the scarlet woman, her temptations, and the punishment of those who surrendered to the enticements of the flash. As the flames of hell circled around the poor victims of their own lusts, writhing in untold agonies, Bart abandoned them to ascertain what business Mrs. Salsman might have with Johnny O'Neal. Although he had never seen the fellow before, he knew that the O'Neals were nearly as prosperous as the Verders, and he wondered what, besides the purely commercial transaction he had witnessed, Mrs. Salsman might want with Johnny. Johnny's appearance was so striking and so debonair that he seemed out of place in Mrs. Salsman's cabin. Bart did not have long to wait after his "Amen." As soon as he had got up from his knees and seated himself, Mrs. Salsman pointed a finger at Johnny and Lorie.

"When yo' two a-goin' ter wed?" she demanded. "Reckon yo' kin have the Rev'nd here say the lines right now. He kin do it, yo' know, Mista O'Neal."

Johnny O'Neal was so startled at the suggestion of a marriage with Lorie that he tried to push her from his lap, but she clung all the more tightly to him. "I reckon we ain' goin' ter wed," he gasped.

" 'N' I reckon yo' are. She knocked up. Missed her monthly las' time," Mrs. Salsman lied glibly. She had grown impatient and the sudden advent of Bart with his ministerial power had decided her on this precipitate action.

"But I paid yo'. Paid yo' fer her every time. She jes' a whore. 'N' 'sides, I not choosin' ter marry yet awhile," Johnny stammered. "Not 'specially ter no whore."

"Careful now there, son," Bart said pompously, not only pleased to see someone else caught in the same web that had entrapped him but scenting a fat marriage fee from this wealthy young man. "Yo' jes' be careful who-all yo're callin' a whore. Miz Salsman's a fine upstandin' Christian woman 'n' Lorie a sweet young gal. If'n yo' paid Miz Salsman a dollar ter be here that right 'n' good, yo' bein' rich 'n' all. Jes' a gift o' 'preciation, tha's what it is, 'n' that don' make Lorie no whore neither. 'Sides, yo' gotta think o' yore soul 'n' if'n yo' goin' ter hell fer despoilin' a sweet young gal like Lorie. If'n yo' done her wrong, yo' got ter right it, 'n' I'm a-thinkin' yo' shore done her wrong. Yo' must of known her carnally 'cause I bin a-settin' out in front 'n' I heard the squealin's 'n' the rampagin's goin' on in here. Them bed cords ain' a-squeakin' by theyselves." Bart stopped suddenly, his hand clutching at his stomach, his eyes rolling back in his head.

"Yo' all right, Rev'nd?" Mrs. Salsman was alarmed to see a man as big and healthy-looking as Bart in such apparently acute distress.

"Got them cramps in my stomach again," Bart gasped. "Jes' one thin' kin cure 'em but don' reckon yo' got a drop o' corn here."

"Never do have." Mrs. Salsman shook her head, as if to deny the suggestion of such a preposterous thing. "We's temperance. But Mista Remick what has the store next door, he askin' me if'n I kin store a jug fer him. Ain' got no right ter open it but seein' as how yo're so poorly guess he won' hold it 'gainst me fer savin' yore life." She reached under the rumpled bed and drew out a jug, twisted out the corncob stopper, and poured a liberal portion into a cup, which she handed to Bart.

He hesitated before drinking it. "Seems more sociable like if'n yo' offer Mista O'Neal a drink too." Bart nodded in Johnny's direction.

Mrs. Salsman took down another cup and filled it and passed it to Johnny, then reached for a third and filled it for herself. She neglected to pour one for Lorie.

"Ain' that I look on drinkin' as right"—Bart shook his head—"but it medicine ter me. Yet seems right yo' should have some if'n I do." He tossed off the drink and watched Johnny down his. Mrs. Salsman finished hers and refilled the cups.

"If'n yo' marries up with Lorie, it'll save yo' money, too." Mrs. Salsman pointed her finger at Johnny. "Yo' kin have her every night 'stead o' jes' once a week 'n' it won' cost yo' nothin'. She a right pretty piece, Lorie is, 'n' yo' ought ter be glad ter git her even if'n yo' has ter pay two dollars from now on 'n' mayhap five. Yas suh, goin' ter have ter charge yo' five dollars every time, but of course if'n yo' marries up with her won' cost yo' a penny."

"Lorie wuth it all right," Johnny admitted, then stared into space for a full minute, his eyes glazed. When he spoke again his words were thick. "She right purty 'n' she the hottest piece I ever had, only she a whore. My mama goin' ter be awful rageful, me weddin' up with a whore."

"Lorie ain' no regular whore, she ain', least not more'n most females her age." Mrs. Salsman was emphatic. " 'N' she ain' no bastard neither 'cause I was married up to Salsman—rest his soul. No, Lorie bin keepin' herself pure fer yo'. She knows yo're the paw o' that brat she's a-carryin'. She knowin' that yo' are 'n' I knowin' it, too. She'll swear to it 'fore a Justice 'n' I'll witness it 'n' now I got the Rev'nd here ter witness it, too. He jes' saw yo' a-comin' out 'n' he knows yo' bin beddin' with her." She pointed to the rumpled bed and then filled Johnny's cup again, purposefully neglecting Bart who, nevertheless, pushed his cup forward to be replenished. She was aware that Johnny O'Neal would never come back if he were permitted to escape today. At hazard was a son-in-law with a wealthy father. She began to fear that she had been premature and that she should have waited until Johnny had really got Lorie pregnant. But it was too late now—it was now or never.

Bart got down on his knees again and with loud prayers urged upon Providence the desirability of the union. His words, somewhat confused by the whisky he had taken, poured forth in a never-ending torrent, calling down the vengeance of Heaven upon this fair maid's despoiler, painting in vivid colors the soaring flames of hell which were kindled especially for the snatchers of young girls' maidenheads. None of these exhortations were lost on poor Johnny.

The boy sat, running the fingers of one hand through his mop of red curls, clutching at Lorie with the other, and gazing at he knew not what. He was too callow, naïve, and inexperienced to seek to controvert the reasons for the marriage, and too accommodating by nature to deny anybody anything. Bart's sonorous invectives frightened him, and for want of something better to say, he fell back on his father.

"What yo' reckon my pappy's goin' ter say if'n I marry me up with a whore? Cain' marry 'thout my pappy's say-so."

"He'll be right proud o' such a pretty gal as Lorie.

Right proud! Ain' many so pretty's her." Lorie, in Johnny's lap, had begun to reciprocate Johnny's fondling. Between Bart's rantings on the floor, Mrs. Salsman's urging, Lorie's stimulating caresses, and the muddling effect of the whisky, poor Johnny was beset from all sides.

Bart stopped his praying and looked up at Johnny. "How come yo' got ter ask yore pappy? Ain' yo' a man yet? Ain' yo' twenty-one? 'Pears like'n yo' are. If'n yo're man 'nuff ter git a girl knocked up, should be man 'nuff ter marry up with her."

"I twenty-two, goin' on twenty-three," Johnny belligerently asserted. "I do what I craves ter do 'n' ain' nobody goin' ter stop me."

Lorie pressed her lips to his, twisting her face the better to accommodate her mouth to his. For a long moment they kissed, and when she took her lips away, she murmured, "Ain' yo' cravin' ter stay the night with me? 'Pears like'n yo' ready 'gain. If'n we married we kin spend every night tergether, yo' 'n' me. Don' yo' want ter marry up with me?"

"He got ter! He a-goin' ter make yo' honest," Bart said, interrupting his prayer. It was impossible for him to watch Lorie's manipulations of Johnny and pray, too. "His pappy a right honorable man 'n' he ain' a-goin' ter tell him no." It seemed right and fitting to Bart that this fellow should be forced to marry as he had been. And at least Johnny O'Neal could be fairly sure that Lorie's progeny belonged to him.

"Reckon he scairt," Mrs. Salsman said in childish mockery. "He jes' tied ter his mama's apron strings. Ain' got no gumption 'tall. He jes' a weaklin' what ain' outa his didies yet. Callin' hisself a man!" She stood up as though to end the matter once and for all. "Lorie, git down off'n that bantlin's lap less'n yo' soil his swaddlin' clothes, 'n' as fer yo', Johnny O'Neal, git outa this house 'n' don' yo' never come back. If'n Lorie births yore brat I'll have the law on yo' 'n' make yore high 'n' mighty pappy pay through his nose, but I don' wan' no weaklin' fer a son-in-law."

Lorie started to weep and clung closer to Johnny, but

he pushed her off his lap and stood up, oblivious of his tumescence.

"I ain' a-goin' ter leave 'n' yo' cain' make me. Lorie's mine. I'm a man I am 'n' if'n I want ter marry up with her I will. 'N' I'm a-goin' ter. Ain' no one kin stop me. Preacher right here now. I'll show yo'"—he stuck his chin out toward Mrs. Salsman"—if'n I a-wearin' didies o' not. Goin' ter stay here tonight with my sweet Lorie 'n' yo' cain' gainsay me neither. Nobody kin stop me onct I make up my mind." He reached behind him and pulled the weeping Lorie up. "Stand up!"

Lorie's weeping ceased suddenly and she twined her arm in Johnny's. Bart stood up before them while Mrs. Salsman sidled over to Lorie's side. The ceremony was short, but Bart's prayer which followed was long. When it was over, Johnny appeared half hysterical at what he had done, his laughter interspersed with tears. He showered kisses on Mrs. Salsman as well as on his bride, and shook hands repeatedly with Bart. The remainder of the jug of whisky was poured out, this time Lorie participating along with the rest.

Bart was reluctant to depart for Dove Cote and would have preferred to stay with Mrs. Salsman and the newlyweds, but he knew he was expected back and he could think of no alibi which might excuse his absence. He hinted at the marriage fee and Johnny, in his euphoria, emptied his pockets. But there was only a dollar and eighty-five cents, rather poor pickings for a lad of his wealth. Bart accepted it, albeit glumly.

Mrs. Salsman accompanied him out the door. "If'n yo' wants ter stay with me, Rev'nd, it only cost yo' a dollar. We kin go out 'n the shed 'n' leave the young folks in the house."

Bart was tempted, but he resisted. He knew if he yielded to Mrs. Salsman now, he would not be able to accommodate Dovie tonight and besides, it would cost him a dollar to stay with Mrs. Salsman and nothing to be with Dovie. He declined, saying that his stomach was still cramped and he had to get home.

Sippi had tied the horses to a tree and was sound asleep, his back propped up against the side of the house.

Bart kicked him awake and they rode home together through the gathering dusk. Bart's plans for Mrs. Salsman had not turned out as he had hoped, but he still had Dovie to anticipate and, after all, he had nearly two dollars, which was better than a half-hour in bed with Mrs. Salsman. There would be a good supper awaiting him at Dove Cote and Sippi to serve him. It might be boring at Dove Cote but it certainly had its advantages. He turned to Sippi who was riding behind him.

"Cain' yo' keep up with me?" he shouted. "Yo' gittin' lazier every day. Got a mind ter give yo' a taste o' leather once we git home. Yo' a-gittin' so lazy yo' cain' even shake the dead lice off'n yo'."

"Yas suh, masta Bart suh." Sippi trotted his horse nearly up to Bart's. "Yas suh. I'se awful lazy, masta Bart suh, but I a-thinkin' if'n 'Thuselah he not in the barn when we git there, seein' as how it gittin' dark 'n' he gone to his cabin, mayhap yo'd like me ter pour yo' a cup o' corn jes' ter settle yore stomach 'fore supper."

"Good idea, boy, good idea!" Bart exclaimed, his thoughts diverted. "My stomach's a-crampin' me somethin' awful. Best medicine they is."

Sippi slipped back several paces behind Bart. He had successfully evaded the promised whipping. It wasn't too hard to handle these white folks, he thought. Sippi was learning fast.

Chapter IX

THE LONG, PLEASANT AUTUMN was followed by a spell
of inclement winter. Days followed days of cold, rain,
and drizzle. Each morning the fields were gray with hoar-
frost, and a thin veneer of brittle, glassy ice covered the
black puddles that had been left by the rain. There had
even been a powdering of snow one night—the first time
many had ever seen snow. For a succession of days, the
sun, hidden behind leaden clouds, gave neither warmth
nor comfort, and everyone hovered about the fireplaces,
toasting on one side and shivering on the other. Nero,
Sippi, and Congo carried in armfuls of oaken knots to
stoke the fires that scorched the inmates of the big house
rather than warmed them.

There was little work, either at Dove Cote or The
Patch, except the clearing of the virgin land done at
that time of the year. The wood, although green, kept
the fires in the cabin fireplaces roaring. Tom Verder knew
that the slaves at Dove Cote were warm and comfortable,
but he worried about those at The Patch even while he
consoled himself with the thought that the intense cold
destroyed the malarial miasma there and made it a more
healthful place. Aunt Nervy and Uncle George provided
the children and the adolescents at the Romp Pasture
with a varied assortment of garments—mere sacklike cov-
erings which served equally well for both sexes and pro-

vided a modicum of warmth. Most of the boys and girls were content, however, to remain in their cabins, snuggled down in tattered patchwork quilts and straw, cuddled closely together, warming each other with their bodies.

Tom made frequent trips to The Patch, despite the fact that he was suffering from a bad cold. He was aware that Laudermilk, his white overseer, was trifling, lazy, drunken, and altogether worthless, and he had decided, when spring came and it was time for planting, that he would dispense with the man and try to find another. The situation was next to hopeless. White overseers were a shiftless lot.

Most days Callie sat before the fireplace in the kitchen, which was the largest in the house, ensconced on a high-backed settle which conserved some of the heat and kept her back warm. She suffered from chilblains, and to keep her feet warm she had Congo lie down on the floor, placed her feet on his bare belly, and then covered her legs with a knitted afghan. He, stupefied by the heat from the fireplace and the heavy covering over him, slept for hours at a time, quite content, although it would have done him no good had he complained. Bart, drawn more and more to the demijohns of corn in the barn, experimented with several ailments for which he hoped Tom would prescribe whisky, but it was not until he hit upon a particularly hacking cough that Tom suggested the corn, whereupon Bart's coughing fits increased in frequency, intensity, and duration.

Dovie, now far advanced in her pregnancy, moped about from room to room, chafing at the rigorous weather that confined her indoors except when she crossed the areaway to the dove cote. There was no provision for fire in the dove cote and she and Bart made short shrift of dressing and undressing in order to get under the piled-up quilts. Dolly, above, sought the warmth of Sippi's body with a greater degree of desire than ever before, and poor Sippi attributed her closeness to an increase of affection on her part rather than a wish to avoid the chill.

It seemed as though the sun was never going to shine again but one day, after weeks of cold, rain, and scudding clouds, it surprised them all and appeared, making the day almost summer-like. The Dove Cote slaves emerged from their cabins, stretching in the warm sunshine. The nesting adolescents of the Romp Pasture crawled out from their tattered rags and gamboled, naked once more, on the winter-sere grass. Nero laid the whip on Sippi's legs with more enthusiasm, and Callie released poor Congo from his task as foot-warmer.

It had been a practice of Dovie's from childhood to wander and play in the oak groves behind Dove Cote that Verder had saved from the primeval forest. He had cut out the smaller trees and undergrowth, leaving the large, spreading, moss-draped oaks to which he was reluctant to lay an axe. Uncleared land such as this had little value, and Tom deemed it an extravagance to devote this irregularly shaped expanse of so many acres to an uncultivated, wooded park, but its beauty impressed him and he had been loath to sacrifice it. A small brook trickled through this wilderness, fed by several springs. There were a variety of other trees besides oaks—hickory, elm, tupelo, and gum—but the majority were majestic oaks, scattered sufficiently so as not to interfere with one another's spreading growth. One monster among them shielded almost an acre of ground beneath its outspreading branches. The woods were the home of wildflowers in the springtime—purple and white violets, mayapples, Dutchman's-breeches, bluebells, dogtooth violets, and a tangle of thorns of single pink wild roses.

Dovie, despite the difficulty in walking posed by her burgeoning pregnancy, decided, on this suddenly spring day, to seek her old haunts in the woods. She had no idea how advanced her pregnancy was or just when she might expect her child, but in her utter ignorance, she was unworried, and although her cumbersome belly was awkward, she did not allow it to hamper her. The warmth and brilliance of the day, after the gloom and chill of the past weeks, begot in her a euphoria such as she had seldom felt. She had no intention of wandering far and did not insist that Dolly go with her. After all, there was nothing to fear. The grove harbored a few deer and some rabbits and skunks, but they would scurry away at a human approach. Black snakes and garter snakes might be sunning themselves on such a day, but they were harmless. No rattlers or copperheads had ever been seen in the grove.

She ambled along at random, picking clumps of snowdrops, the only flowers out at that time of year. She got deeper and deeper into the forest but she was so familiar with the terrain that she went on unafraid, enjoying herself completely. The years slipped away; she forgot about her pregnancy; once again she was a small girl.

Suddenly she was seized with a sharp pain, so cutting and demanding that she stopped and gasped for breath. It was followed by another violent stab, and, unable to stand, she sank down on a convenient rock. The pains increased in intensity and she screamed. Clammy sweat covered her face and she became panicky. Then, as suddenly as they had come, the pains subsided and left her completely. But she still felt weak. She had been sitting in the sun and now she longed for the leafy shade of the oaks. She hurried to a spring which she knew bubbled up out of a wall of limestone under one of the big trees. Reaching it, she drank deeply of the cold water, and then sank down on the dry leaves which formed a carpet under the big tree.

Her thoughts wandered to Bart and she wished he were here beside her. Somehow she could never get enough of his maleness. When she felt him throbbing in her hands, it was the only time she felt close to him. For those few moments, she knew she had the power to make him utterly subservient to her. He even spoke her name when he was consumed by the force of her caresses, pleading with her not to cease. It was the only time he would display any feeling toward her. She could not understand why these moments of closeness between them were of such short duration. Why, after he had acquitted himself, did he turn from her? Why did he have no further desire for her to continue touching him? Why did he either rave and rant at her for being a scarlet woman or else turn his back to her and go to sleep? She could not understand. But then, perhaps it was the cross she had to bear.

At first he had seemed to want her, but never the way she had desired him. They had had nothing in common but the desire for contact of flesh with flesh, and lately she had found it more and more difficult to rouse any desire in him. Perhaps it was because her body was so ugly now—so stretched and swollen and misshapen. He still responded to her touches, but unwillingly and mechanically, without any ardor or enthusiasm, and he was soon satiated, turning over and going to sleep without even a "good-night" or a kiss.

How unlike Tommy he was! To be sure, in some ways he was better than Tommy—his huge frame, his coarse good looks, his strength, and his youthful virility exceeded those of Tommy, but his superiority ended there. Tommy had been gay, vivacious, companionable. They were always laughing together and they had a thousand little jokes between them. With Bart there was never any conversation at all. All he wanted to do was pray. Even before he got into bed he wanted to pray and she, for one, was sick of it. She'd heard enough about the wages of sin! Bah! Everything according to Bart with a sin. Tommy had been unconcerned about sin, while Bart continually ranted about it even while he was squirming under her. Oh well, she consoled herself, Bart was better than nothing. He was a man and she needed a man. Oh, how she needed one! Somehow it seemed to her that she craved a man more than any other woman ever had. She could not imagine her mother needing her father in that way. Surely if she did, she would not allow him to spend his nights over at The Patch and be content to sleep with that *it*—that Congo—in her room. How could her mother share her father with some quadroon wench? She'd never share Bart. Never! If he as much as looked at another woman, she'd . . .

Without warning the pains started again, so severe now that she could not sit upright. She crouched on the ground, kneeling and wailing like an animal in pain. It seemed as if they would never stop, and when they passed, after an eternity of suffering, she felt a blessed relief. She finally managed to raise herself to her feet, and it was then that she saw It. Even after she had recovered, she could not exactly describe what had happened, except that suddenly, out of thin air, the most horrendous black giant appeared, slipping out from behind a tree. She wondered afterward if she had not dreamed it, because surely nothing in real life could have appeared so frightening. He was stark naked. The ebony black of his skin glistened in the light and the whorls of white that covered his body shone with a ghostly phosphorescence. Around his neck he wore a plaited garland of red berries, and in one hand he carried a small basket of withes while in the other he held an axe. He advanced, smiling and showing his white teeth in his scarified black face while she, transfixed with horror, could only stare at him and utter voiceless exclamations of terror. With a scream which was frozen before it was ever uttered, she sank to the ground, writhing in pain. In her agony she saw him lay down the axe and the basket and come toward her, and she could remember the relief she felt when she realized she was not going to be decapitated.

From that moment on, she realized little of what happened to her. She was consumed by pain and terror, yet she recalled strong, gentle hands lifting her as she struggled in her travail, clutching at the skin of this horrible black form whose strength seemed to flow into her and give her courage. The black and white mask lost some of its grotesqueness and she forgot her fear in her pain. Hands gently and soothingly massaged her belly. Those same hands held her upright on her knees while shooting pains that seemed impossible to bear tore at her vitals. She remembered no words except "masta suh" and "no masta suh," and then after what seemed hours of torture there was a final paroxysm of pain that made all the others seem as nothing, and then a quietness—a blessed relief—that was punctuated by the wail of an infant at her breast. Following that, cold water wiped away the sweat from her face and she felt herself and the child picked up and carried. In those huge black arms, she was able to steal a look at the child nestled against her, and she moved it enough to see its tiny wormlike male sex. She glanced up at the savage face of the black that carried her and, although the grotesque mask was ugly, it was no longer fearful. The sounds that came from the mouth were soothing ones, giving her an assurance of safety.

Then a merciful blackness overwhelmed her and she remembered nothing more until Congo was bending over her on the veranda of the big house, screaming for her mother to come. Then it was Bart who was carrying her and she was in bed in the dove cote and her mother and Dolly were fussing over her. All she wanted was to sleep and sleep forever.

There was utter confusion at Dove Cote. Sippi was dispatched by horseback to The Patch to fetch Tom and together Bart and Callie tried to make sense of Dovie's ravings. All they knew was that Congo had found her unconscious on the veranda with a child in her arms, her skirts decently straightened out and a wreath of red berries in her hair. There was a basket of six speckled brook trout on the floor beside her. Surely it was a mystery which they could not understand and Dovie could not coherently explain.

Verder was stunned when he arrived back at Dove Cote and learned what had occurred. His first concern was for his daughter's comfort and welfare. When he was reassured and had gone to her bedside and talked to her, his attention centered on the baby, which he took in his arms, cuddling and cooing to it. He pulled back the length of sheet which covered the child and ascertained its sex. That it was a male child pleased him, and he decided immediately that it should be named Tommy after himself and his departed nephew. As he went to cover the child before returning it to Dovie, he noticed the infant's right hand. He stared fascinated, counting the fingers audibly, even counting them a second time to prove that the hand had six digits. He was so excited he almost dropped the precious bundle.

"Hey, Callie, come here!" Verder shouted. "Come quick. It's a Verder, a shore 'nuff Verder. What do yo' reckon to that?"

Callie, frightened by the outburst, toddled across the areaway from the main house. "What's wrong?" she called. "Tol' yo ' not ter lift it. Knowed yo'd let it fall."

"Cain' yo' hear?" Tom bellowed. "It's a Verder, a genuine six-fingered Verder jest like me 'n' my pappy 'n' my grandpappy 'n' like young Tommy, too." For an instant the possibility that Tommy might have fathered the child crossed his mind, but he dismissed it. The baby had received the malformation from him.

Bart, who followed Callie, was unimpressed by the discovery. He had accepted the child's birth, knowing that none of his own blood flowed in its veins. If he had any feeling at all it was that now, the child being born, he could return to normal sex relations with Dovie rather than endure the perversions she had forced upon him. He had no affection for the baby—in fact, he despised it—but he did not allow his feelings to show beyond a lack of exuberance over its birth.

Verder had not expected the arrival of the child so soon and had made no provisions for a wet nurse for it. There were, as a rule, always women either at The Patch or at Dove Cote who had recently given birth to children, but, as he reviewed the nursing mothers in his mind, he decided that all of them were too black, too crude, too fat, old, ugly, or undesirable to take a place in his home in the heart of his family. He remembered one, however, at Dove Cote, who was gravid with child, an octoroon, about seventeen years old. But how far along she was he did not know. Although he was reluctant to have Dovie nurse her own son lest it might result in pendant breasts (a thing of horrow to the white women of the South) there seemed to be no way out of the situation until the Dove Cote slave gave birth to her child. It was certainly unworthy for a white woman of any degree of affluence to suckle a child but, for the present, at least, there was no other alternative for Dovie. However, she would not have too long to wait for the termination of the wench's pregnancy.

Boggs was unable to understand Tom's and Callie's anxiety. All his parishioners had suckled their children, even his own mother had suckled him, so why should his wife be too good to suckle her brat?

Although Bart was uninterested in Dovie's child and the matter of a wet nurse, he was extremely interested in the manner of the child's birth. Dovie described the man over and over again, blaming the birth of her child on the fright he had occasioned, quite forgetting that the

171

pains had commenced before she had seen him. However, she remembered the gentleness of the big hands. He had evidently severed the umbilical cord with his teeth and had disposed of the afterbirth, then carried both Dovie and the child to the house and placed them on the gallery where they were sure to be found.

"Must 'a' been that Kru." Verder nodded his head wisely at Bart. "Guess I better tell Dovie 'bout him 'n' set her mind at rest. Jes' can't rightly tell tho', but that basket o' trout tells me it's him. Kru supposed ter be over ter The Patch 'n' that 'bout twelve o' fifteen miles cross-country. He must 'a' been comin' over here, thinkin' I was here, jes' ter fetch me them trout. Cain' figure out how he smart 'nuff ter help birth Dovie's child 'n' yet have been him. Dovie a-sayin' it some black monster, nekkid as a jaybird 'n' white stripes on his face. Must 'a' been him."

" 'Course yo' a-goin' ter kill him, ain' yo'? Him a-skeerin' 'n' a-touchin' Dovie 'n' all?" Bart demanded.

Tom shook his head in denial, staring at Bart in amazement.

"Whaffor I goin' ter kill pore Kru? If'n it not fer him, Dovie mayhap died out there in the woods 'lone. Cain' see why not yo' didn' go with her. Yo' her husband. How come 'yo' lettin' her wander off 'lone like that?"

"Didn' know she a-goin'," Bart protested lamely.

"Up ter yo' ter fin' out whereat she a-goin'. Looks ter me the blame more your'n than poor Kru's. No suh, ain' a-goin' ter kill poor Kru. He not very bright but he shore saved Dovie's life."

" 'N' skeert her 'mos' ter death." Bart persisted in making his point. "Ought ter be strung up 'n' whipped—stripped right down. Ought ter take all the meat off'n his bones. Ought ter whop him till he near dead 'n' then shoot him."

"Whoa, there." Tom raised a warning hand. "Mighty fond o' Kru, I am. 'N' Kru mighty fond o' me. Always a-doin' something fer me like'n them there trout. 'N' he works harder'n any four men. He did the best he could fer Dovie. If'n not fer him, she'd 'a' died out there. No suh, ain' a-killin' Kru 'n' ain' a-whoppin' him nuther. Goin' ter tell Dovie she owes her life 'n' little Tommy's ter him.

Wishin' I had ten more jes' like him. Yo' jes' don' like him 'cause he don' cotton ter yo', tha's all. Don' reckon he fergit that time yo' slashed at him when he wan't doin' nothin'."

Bart grumbled and walked away, certain of one thing. He would have strung the savage up and punished him for touching a white woman. That he had undoubtedly saved Dovie's life he did not take into consideration. Any male Negro who had done what Kru did, even with the best of intentions, should be killed. He had gazed on Dovie's private parts and that was enough to sentence him to death. Bart started a fit of violent coughing and headed for the barn. Tom watched him go. He was beginning to be more than a little disappointed in his son-in-law.

For the prescribed three weeks, Dovie lay in the bed in the dove cote with Tommy beside her, while Bart slept in the guest room of the big house. Each morning when Dolly and Sippi crawled down the ladder to open the front door of the cote, they found a nosegay of flowers on the threshold—first snowdrops, then later as the days passed, the first spring violets and branches of dogwood and redbud.

Callie accepted the child with a certain amount of cooing and grandmotherly pride, but it was plain to see she was not as enamored of it as Tom was. Whenever he was at Dove Cote he managed to spend most of his time with it. That Tommy was the son of his beloved Dovie accounted for a large part of his devotion; that his tiny, six-digited hand denoted his Verder blood endeared him even more. His baby strength and vigor fired Tom's pride. Never entertaining again the thought that the Tommy Verder who had so mysteriously disappeared might be the baby's sire, he yet imagined a resemblance to that handsome boy which he attributed to the relationship to himself or rather to their common descent from his father.

Dovie adored the child and played with it as with a doll, but she soon tired of it. She was anxious for the three weeks (which was the allotted time for a white woman's confinement) to be up so that Bart might replace Tommy in her bed. Bart ignored the child as much

173

as possible, paying little attention to it and never speaking to it or about it unless necessary. He realized its link to his present position, and felt that he had done enough to give it his name and that was all he would ever do. It was Tom and strangely enough Sippi who gave the baby the most love and attention, and, of course, the savage Kru who left woodland offerings daily at the door.

Chapter X

NERO RETURNED one morning a few weeks after Dovie was up and around with a wagonload of staples from the store in Brownsville. He ran into the house, waving a letter for Tom, who was just sitting down to his midday meal. The arrival of a letter at Dove Cote was such an unusual happening that when one did arrive, the whole family took an avid interest in it. Callie, immediately apprehensive, felt that it betokened ill news from her family—her father and mother were still living. Dovie, who had never received a letter in her life, knew that it could not possibly be for her, and Bart realized by the address that it was not for him, but they all sat expectantly at table with Nero peering over Tom's shoulder, while Tom deliberately slit the wax seal with his knife and unfolded the paper.

" 'Tain' nothin' but a handbill." Tom studied the printed sheet with its big block letters and its small print carefully. "Seems that Mista Edmund J. Macklin o' Elm Grove Plantation, what is over Marysburg way, died a spell back 'n' his widder a-sellin' off his stock by auction. Looks like'n he might have some prime hands." Tom read on, squinting over the fine print. "Le's see. Forty-two male Negroes, ranging in age from fourteen ter sixty-five. Twenty-eight wenches from sixteen to thirty-five or thereabouts—two nursin' mothers 'n' three with child. Might pick up a likely wench what could nurse young Tommy. Assorted lot of younger Negroes, male 'n' female from two ter thirteen years of age. Two fine carriage horses, one five-year-old gray stallion, eighteen mules, a herd of twelve milch cows, one bull 'n' two heifers not freshened as yit, pigs, ducks, geese, chickens, 'n' guinea fowl. Goes on ter tell 'bout furniture 'n' sech." He laid the bill down on the table and started to eat.

"Yo' a-knowin' that Mista Macklin?" Callie asked. "Marysburg a long ways from here. Ain' never knowed nobody that far away. Shore would like ter get me some more o' them moss-rose plates if'n they a-sellin' any. Broken two o' 'em 'n' ain' got 'nuff ter set the table if'n we have more'n ten."

Tom held up a hand to silence her. "Ain' knowin' Macklin. Met him. Jes' met him once or twice at sales 'round the country." He swallowed a mouthful of fried ham and washed it down with a gulp of coffee. " 'N' ain' buyin' no moss-rose plates if'n I go, but think I might jes' go 'though ain' particularly needin' any stock myself. Might pick up one or two bucks 'n' a wench fer Tommy if'n they a-goin' cheap. Need new blood once in a while ter keep 'em from inbreedin'. Got so mos' every buck 'n' wench in the Romp Pasture lookin' like one o' Nero's git." He turned and winked at Nero, who was still standing behind his chair. Tom did not actually need any new stock, but a sale meant a get-together of all the planters in the surrounding country. It was a place to meet people, talk man-talk with the other plantation owners, get a little drunk, finger the stock to be sold and, although Tom would be the last to admit it, show off a little. As the owner of Dove Cote and The Patch, Tom Verder was a man who was looked up to and respected throughout that whole section of the country as a man of affluence. He rather enjoyed his position and an auction like this when the planters all came together was one of the few times he was able to strut a little.

Although he might have made the trip easily in one day by horseback, he deemed it wise to drive there in the big farm wagon. If he did purchase any slaves, it would be easier to transport them back in the wagon than to have them walk and have to pace his horses accordingly. Consequently he decided to take two days to get there, spend one day at the sale, and take two days to come back, a total of five days in all.

He hated to be gone five days. Fields both at Dove Cote and The Patch were being plowed in preparation for spring planting and Laudermilk, his overseer at The Patch, was absolutely incapable of handling matters there. Bart could well look after affairs at Dove Cote, which practically ran themselves anyway, owing to the efficiency of Tom's Negro drivers, but The Patch presented a problem. He decided to solve it by having Nero go over to oversee the overseer and taking Sippi with him instead. He would miss Nero's companionship but Sippi was a bright, good-looking boy who would be a credit to him. Unthinkingly Tom did not bother to ask Bart's permission to take Sippi, merely remarking to his son-in-law, "Guess yo' kin git yore trogs off 'n' on fer a few days 'thout Sippi. Takin' him with me 'stead of Nero, I am." Tom's high-handed attitude with Sippi made Bart resentful—Sippi was supposed to be his boy; Tom had given him to him. But he did not demur.

As a matter of fact, he was only too glad to see Tom depart. Any authority which Bart possessed at Dove Cote had turned out to be purely nominal. At first he had been really interested in the workings of the plantation and had made one or two suggestions which, if carried out, might have proved profitable. But Tom, seconded by Nero, had negated the suggestions. Tom Verder was far too accustomed to making his own decisions to accept those of others. As a result, any real interest which Bart might have had had been dissipated, and what he did now was purely routine and entirely without inspiration. Tom had taken away his calling and he had nothing left. He was no longer a reverend and he certainly was not a planter. Outside of being Dovie's husband, he was nothing at all. However, with Nero at The Patch and with Tom away for five days, he would be able to do exactly as he wanted, which meant drinking, tickling the ass of any Negro he wished to with a bullwhip, possibly going into Brownsville to hold a prayer meeting at Mrs. Salsman's house, or just sleeping off the effects of the liquor he planned to consume.

Any journey which involved five days' absence from home was regarded as a major adventure. Callie, whose parents lived only some forty miles away, had never visited them since she was married, nor had they visited her. Outside of an occasional trip to Brownsville to buy dress goods or trimmings with her mother, Dovie had never been anywhere, and although Bart had been on the road most of the time before he married, his travels had all been within a twenty-mile radius. Consequently it was with some fear and trepidation that Callie and Dovie bid good-bye to Tom, who was setting out with Sippi even before daybreak. There was a multitude of last-minute instructions which Tom felt necessary to give to Nero, all of which Bart resented because he felt that as a white man and the logical next in command at Dove Cote, they should have been given to him. He sulked in the background of the group that surrounded the long farm wagon with its team of four mules. Sippi, on the seat beside Tom, was primed for the great adventure. He was dressed in his best suit, clothes carefully pressed, shoes polished, and a change of linen in his bundle under the seat. His appearance was important, that the position of his master might be readily ascertained. The mules had been brushed and curried, the wagon repainted, and, although it was by no means a fashionable turnout, it did reflect the prosperity of the owner of Dove Cote.

Their spruce smartness, however, was not so readily apparent after the dusty miles they had traveled, stopping only briefly overnight at a small plantation whose owner was an acquaintance of Tom's. He had departed for the sale himself, but Tom accepted his wife's hospitality for the night, staying with perfect propriety, as her father was there. They were up again early in the morning and arrived at the small hamlet of Emporia, which was the nearest town to the Macklin plantation, early in the afternoon. The tavern was crowded with planters, for a sale of this kind drew patronage from a wide area. Tom was unable to find any accommodations for himself and Sippi there. The owner informed him that he was already sleeping four men to a bed and that all the beds were taken and there remained not even room enough to make up an extra pallet on the floor. It appeared to Tom that he and Sippi would have to sleep in the wagon until a young man approached him, holding out his hand by way of greeting and introduction.

"Man inside a-sayin' that yo' Mista Verder o' Dove Cote Plantation," the young man said with an affable smile. "Ain' never had the pleasure o' meetin' up with yo,' but heard tell 'bout yo'. My name's Warren Maxwell o' Falconhurst Plantation down Benson way."

"Pleased ter meet yo'." Tom offered his hand, which was heartily shaken by the other. "Wished I could say that I'd heard 'bout yo', Mr. Maxwell, but jes' cain' say it honestly 'cause I never have. Howsomever, mayhap you'll tell me how come yo' heard o' me."

Maxwell laughed. "Heard 'bout a full-blooded Kru boy what yo' bought from the Harrisons over on Argyll Plantation. Was a-wantin' a boy like that myself. Always like ter breed full-blooded niggers when I kin, 'n' Kru blood's good blood. Writ to the Harrisons but they said yo'd a-bought him. Was a-goin' ter write yo' but jes' never did git 'round ter it." He grinned an apology.

It was now Tom's turn to grin. "Jes' as well yo' didn'." He released Maxwell's hand. "That Kru he a damn good boy. Do more work'n ten others but he ain' a damn bit o' good fer breedin'. Jes' cain't git him ter cover a wench. Tried it, 'cause I'd like ter git some pups outa him, but poor Kru, he jes' go limp 'n' tha's all. 'N' then he starts tremblin' all over. Jes' cain' do it. Plenty o' sap in him but jes' don' cotton ter the wenches n' don' know why. First nigger I ever had what wouldn't."

Maxwell smiled knowingly. "Thinkin' mayhap I know the reason. Had a boy like that once myself—a big Gullah. Some o' them bozals that come over from Africky been brought up ter think they cain' cover a wench till they been cut. This boy probably sold 'fore he got cut 'n' jes' thinkin' he cain' do it. Ain' his fault but makes him no damn good as a breeder."

"Glad yo' told me." Tom was beginning to like the knowledgeable young fellow. "Shore has been a puzzle ter

179

me. Say, how 'bout joinin' me fer a drink? Tavern's mighty crowded but think we might edge in sideways fer a drink o' corn."

Maxwell gestured toward the tavern and shook his head. "Every planter fer fifty miles 'round got the same notion. Ain' room fer a fly ter crawl in there. Tell yo' what we'll do. Got me a jug o' corn in my wagon 'n' could go up ter yore room 'n' drink it."

It was Tom's turn to shake his head. " 'Preciate it, Mista Maxwell, kindly appreciate your hospitality, but ain' got no room. Me 'n' my boy here planning ter sleep out 'n our wagon. Tavern filled up, a-sleepin' four to a bed, so thinking we'll have ter bed down 'n the wagon."

"Oh, no, yo' ain'! Ain' necessary! I'm a-stayin' out ter Miz Maxwell's cousin's place. She a Hammond, yo' know," he added proudly, " 'n Courteney Hammond what's her cousin, he has a place, Courteney House, 'bout five miles south. Plenty o' room fer yo' ter bed down there. Kin accommodate yore servant too. Insist yo' go, Mista Verder, I insist."

"Don' have ter insist, Mista Maxwell. Takin' yo' up on it 'n' kindly 'preciate it. Heard tell 'bout the Hammond place. Fust-rate quality, I guess. Don' pretend ter be quality myself so hopin' they won' mind me."

"Ain' so much quality myself, Mista Verder," Maxwell acknowledged, "but married inter it. Miz Maxwell she's a Hammond 'n' don' never let me fergit it. Our son, birthed 'bout six months ago, he named Hammond." He pointed to a spring wagon hitched under the trees. "If'n yo' kindly wait till my boy 'n' I git started, yo' kin follow us, 'n' by the way, name's Warren."

" 'N' mine's Tom." He waited until the Maxwell wagon started down the road, then followed its dust. Both he and Sippi presented a sorry sight when they turned into the wrought-iron gates that marked the entrance to Courteney House. Its splendor of brick and soaring white pillars quite overwhelmed Tom, and he could see that even Warren Maxwell was somewhat ill at ease when the liveried footman came out on the steps and two stable boys appeared to take their mules. But once inside, despite the ornate elegance of the house, all Tom's nervousness disappeared in the cordial welcome of Courteney Hammond and his gracious wife. He and Sippi were led upstairs to a commodious room with a high-testered bed and a trundle bed under it for Sippi. Warm water was brought and poured into a tin tub for Tom to bathe, after which Sippi used the same water. Dressed in clean linen with freshly brushed clothes, both Tom and Sippi looked presentable. Even before they had finished dressing, Warren knocked on the door, followed by a servant with a tray of drinks.

Sipping their drinks in the hour before dinner, young Warren Maxwell and Tom Verder found they had much in common. Warren propounded some interesting theories which Tom had had in the back of his mind but had never formulated to himself. Cotton, according to Warren, was a losing game. It destroyed the land, eating it up in a few years so that each successive year brought smaller and smaller crops. Eventually the land became so worn out that it was worthless and the only thing to do was to abandon it and move west to fresh lands. But, Warren assured Tom, there was one crop which most of the planters did not recognize and that was niggers. With no slaves being imported into the country from Africa— except those which were smuggled in from Cuba and the Indies—niggers were a cash crop which never failed. He himself, he assured Tom, was going in for niggers. To be sure, it took them some time to mature—eighteen to twenty years as compared to one year for cotton—but once the cycle was started it would be a yearly crop, with some coming up for sale each year, and it would be a far more valuable crop than cotton.

With the price of slaves going up each year it was just a matter of simple arithmetic. Say one had ten slaves ready for market each year. Ten slaves at a thousand dollars a head would be a ten-thousand-dollar cash crop. Twenty slaves would be twenty thousand dollars. And that money would be practically clear because the cost of raising a slave was small. No work, either. Figure out how much time, effort, and labor was required to produce a thousand dollars worth of cotton. Plowing, sowing, hoeing, harvesting! To raise a thousand-dollar slave all one had to do was feed him and house him and give him a few clothes. Before he was sold at the age of twenty, he would already have seeded two or three wenches, leaving a future profit behind him. Yes suh, set the niggers to breeding and at the same time pick up young niggers cheap. Eight-, ten-, and twelve-year-old boys were selling for little or nothing, and that gave one an advantage because they would reach selling age more quickly than those one raised oneself.

But, and here Warren was most emphatic, it was necessary to pick and choose carefully. Get to know niggers, just the same way a horseman knew horses. Train one's fingers to go over those black bodies and judge them by their bone structure and their flesh. Never mate them indiscriminately. Mate the strong, healthy bucks to strong, healthy wenches. Buy only those which showed promise of good strong bodies. Pick the good-looking ones; choose the intelligent ones; get good blood lines whenever possible. Be on the lookout for Dahomeys, Hausas, Krus, Fantis, Ibos, and—here Maxwell sighed—Mandingoes. He'd never had a Mandingo, that is, a full-blooded one, but he was always hoping. Handsomest breed of niggers in the world! Big, strong, gentle as kittens, faithful as dogs. He hoped he'd have a chance to get one full-blooded Mandingo sometime.

Choose the bucks and the wenches well and sow the seed carefully. That was the easiest part of it. If there was one thing a nigger knew how to do and do well it was how to cover a wench. Goddamndest animals for screwing there ever was. A strong buck had more sap in him than a bull or a stallion and he was always ready to let it go. A good buck nigger could cover a wench three, four times in one night.

Feed them well, work them enough to drain off their surplus energy, keep them dry and warm during the winter, and give them wenches to knock up and that's all there was to it. Change the wenches often so there would be no permanent attachment and no excess of sentiment. Take the suckers away from the wenches and raise them separately so there'd be no weeping and wailing when they were sold. Forget about all this foolishness of niggers marrying and having families. Don't try to make human beings out of them. Breed them like animals because after all that's what they were—fine animals. Treat them well. Be kind and good to them. Pet them as one would a favorite dog. But keep the whip handy to keep them in line.

It seemed like a good idea the way Warren explained it, but somehow, to Tom's way of thinking, it didn't seem right, even though he himself had considered it. After all, land was for raising cotton. He'd look into it, but in the meantime, Tom decided, he'd continue to raise cotton. There was still a lot of land at The Patch to be cleared, and Tom was of the opinion that if land worn out by successive crops of cotton, were allowed to lie fallow for several years it would replenish itself. With all the land he had at Dove Cote and The Patch, he could afford to alternate his fields. However, there'd be no harm in raising and selling a few niggers, too. He'd consider the matter.

A muted bell rang downstairs and they went down to a sumptuous dinner, although Tom had to admit the cooking was no better than he enjoyed at Dove Cote. It was served in an array of fine napery, crystal, and silver which attested to the hospitality of Courteney House. Tom was pleased to note that there was nothing on the table which compared with the big silver centerpiece at Dove Cote. Not even the Hammonds had anything as ornate and elaborate as that. Dinner finished, he and Warren and their host retired to the gallery, where the conversation once again centered around slaves.

Courteney Hammond ridiculed Warren's plans for slave-breeding. "Make you nothing more than a slave trader, Cousin Warren," he admonished. "That's about the lowest breed of polecat there is. You might just as well start out in a buckboard leading a caffle of slaves behind you." He dismissed the entire operation as far beneath the dignity of a white planter. At Courteney House, he boasted, no slave was ever sold. He purchased, yes, but he never sold. Warren, Tom could see, listened attentively, but did not put much stock in his kinsman's advice. It would take a lot to turn aside Warren Maxwell, once his mind was made up. Tom could see that in the determined set of his jaw.

The Hammond hospitality extended beyond mere board and lodging. When Tom reached his room, he found a light-skinned girl sitting in a chair beside the bed. She greeted him smilingly, helped him off with his clothes, turned down the sheets, plumped up the pillows and then, waiting for him to nod his head, slid into bed beside him. Poor Sippi, in his low trundle bed, was not accorded like attention, nor did Tom, as he might have done with Nero after he had finished, offer to share his companion with Sippi, who found it hard to sleep, picturing in fantasy the movements so near him in the darkness.

The next morning, Tom and Sippi, in their own wagon, accompanied by Maxwell and his servant Agamemnon, traveled the few miles to the Macklin plantation and, once there, were caught up in the excitement of the sale, which started soon after they arrived. Prices were higher than Tom had expected and, although he bid several times, he purchased only one buck—a tall black fellow by the name of Djoubo, whom Warren insisted he buy because, he said, he looked like a full-blooded Ibo. Warren refrained from bidding, and Tom got the boy for eight hundred dollars, which, Warren informed him, was a good buy. He appeared to be about twenty, was tall, strong, and well-muscled, had an intelligent face and a friendly grin, and spoke fluent English. Warren assured Tom that he had fingered the boy the day before and that he would make a good breeder. Warren made several purchases for himself. He bought four boys ranging in age from about eight to fourteen and three wenches in the same age range. He also, after spirited bidding, purchased a strapping young female, tall, straight, full-breasted, and striking, by the unusual name of Lucretia Borgia, whom the auctioneer guaranteed to be a first-rate cook. Tom would have preferred her to his boy, Djoubo, but he was loath to bid against Warren. When she had at last been knocked down to Maxwell, he handed her over to his boy Agamemnon, saying, "Bought yo' a fust-class wench, 'Memnon. Needin' a good cook we are

184

with Mercy getting along in years, 'n' she kin bed down with yo' in the kitchen." He turned to the girl. "Yo' thinkin' yo' like this boy?" he asked. "What's that yore name is, anyway?"

"Loo-cree-sha Bor-jah, masta suh," she replied proudly. "Old masta afore Mista Macklin he done named me. He sayin' if'n I'm a cook, mayhap I won' pizen him if'n I named that. 'N' as fer this buck here"—she darted an appraising glance at 'Memnon—"he a right likely-lookin' boy, but he don' 'pear like he las' very long with Lucretia Borgia, suh. Shore dreans 'em out, I do, but already gave Mista Macklin two good suckers 'n' got lots more a-comin', that is if'n this boy know how ter do a good job."

Instead of rebuking her for her familiarity, Warren laughed and slapped her on the rump, and put her in 'Memnon's charge. Soon after that, the sale was over, at least as far as the slaves were concerned, and neither Tom nor Warren had any interest in cattle or household furnishings, Tom having completely forgotten about the moss-rose plates that Callie wanted. Tom, owing to the early hour, decided not to accompany Warren back to Courteney House. He was heading north and would have to travel five miles this afternoon and an additional five miles on his journey the next morning. He hated to bid good-bye to Warren Maxwell; he liked him and was sorry to part from him, but his way was to the north and Warren's to the south. They promised, however, to meet at the next sale, and both extended sincere invitations for their families to visit each other.

As he was leaving the Macklin plantation, Tom happened to glance up and see a human skull impaled on a tall pole. It was such an unusual sight, so different from anything he had ever seen before, that he turned to the slave he had just purchased.

"What's that thing a-doin' up there? Lookin' like'n it belong to a man."

"Shore did," Djoubo answered, "shore did, masta suh. That there head onct belonged to Jem what was a hand here. Runned he did 'n' painter gotten him 'n' et him. Tha's all what's left o' him 'n' Mister Macklin done put

185

pore Jem's haid up tha'r jes' so we-uns'd know what happen if'n we run."

Tom stopped and gazed up at the bleached skull. He pointed up to it, admonishing both Sippi and Djoubo, "Mista Macklin shore was right. Hope that be a lesson ter yo' boys. Look at it good, Sippi. See what happens ter boys what run. 'N' yo', Djoubo, don' yo' ever fergit it. 'Member it."

"Ain' never had no mind ter run, masta Tom suh," Sippi said, gazing up at the skull. "No suh, masta Tom suh, ain' never a-goin' ter leave Dove Cote."

"Me neither, Masta suh," Djoubo said, shaking his head dolefully. "Don' wan' ter be like pore old Jem tha'r."

They started out on their way home, Tom and Sippi sitting on the seat and the new boy in the back of the wagon. Djoubo seemed amenable and willing to go with them, so instead of spanceling him Tom let him ride free. It was still early in the afternoon and Tom figured that, come nightfall, there would be some plantation or tavern where they might spend the night. He was anxious to get home now. He'd had enough of traveling. He'd enjoyed meeting Warren Maxwell, staying with the Hammonds, and going to the auction, but it would be good to be back at Dove Cote again.

Chapter XI

THE LONG, HOT, dusty afternoon was drawing to a close with the sinking of the sun. It was slipping down behind the trees in a hot blaze of scarlet, casting long shadows on the ground, elongating the trailing shadows of the wagon wheels into strangely distorted ovals. For the last hour, Tom had been looking for a place to spend the night or, failing that, a place where they could get food. If worst came to worst, they could pull up alongside the road and sleep in the wagon, for the redness of the setting sun betokened good weather for the night. But neither Tom nor Sippi had had anything since breakfast and Sippi had been fretting.

"Ain' we a-goin' ter eat nothin', masta Tom suh? Feelin' awful ga'nt in my stomick. Reckon I'se gittin' powerful hungry, masta Tom suh, 'n' this yere Djoubo, he jes' 'bout starvin', ain' yo' Djoubo?"

"Shore am, masta suh. Feelin' like'n I could eat a nice mess o' grits 'n' gravy right now."

" 'N' some ham 'n' some aigs 'n' some watermelon 'n' some o' that there poun' cake 'n' some collard greens 'n' some clabber 'n' some fried fish 'n' some . . ." Sippi was almost in a trance, his eyes half-closed, a spun-hair of saliva drooling from the corner of his lip.

"Whoa there, boy." Tom cuffed at him without really touching him. "Jes' yo' keep yore big mouth shet. Mayhap all yo' a-goin' ter get tonight's a big dish o' wind puddin' with air sauce."

"Ain' never et that," Sippi said interestedly. "That taste good, masta Tom suh?"

" 'Pears like'n yo' goin' ter find out. Goddamndest poverty-stricken country I ever did see. Ain' passed a place what looked like they could spare a hunk o' pone. Mostly poor white trash 'round this here part—rednecks a-lookin' like they never had a decent meal. Even yo' niggers better off'n them. Leastwise yo' eats." He paused to shield his eyes from the setting sun and stared down the road to where a couple of swaybacked log cabins squatted at the crossroads. "Looks like we a-comin' ter somethin'." He clucked to the mules and slapped them idly with the reins without effect.

As they drew nearer they could see a weather-beaten sign over the door which read STORE. A young light-skinned girl, whose skin might have been several shades whiter if she had had a bath, sat nursing a white child on the lower step. On the step above her, a loutishly handsome young man with a shock of yellow curls sat idly whittling on a pitch pine stick. In the doorway a white man, gross of belly, unshaven, and unkempt, his dirty shirt ripped in several places to disclose lardy flesh, lounged against one side of the door, chewing on a piece of grass. They all looked up at the sound of the wagon, following its progress down the road until it stopped before the store. Tom cramped the front wheels and jumped out, stretching.

"This here a store?" he asked.

"Reckon it be." The man in the door shifted his weight and removed the piece of timothy from his mouth. "Says so over the door, don' it?" The girl removed her breast from the infant and stared up at the strangers, her gaze resting on Sippi, then shifting to Djoubo and back to Sippi again. The towheaded fellow stared dully, his knife poised over the stick.

"Lookin' fer a place ter bed down fer the night." Tom continued to stamp the kinks out of his legs. "Willin' ter pay fer it, 'n' food fer me 'n' my boys. Any place 'round here or further down the road?"

"Nope," the man answered with finality. "Ain' nothin' 'tween here 'n' Tupelo Creek 'n' ain' much there. Tavern o' sorts but yo' wouldn't hanker ter bed down there. Bedbugs carry yo' 'way by mornin'. Et there onct 'n' puked fer three days afterwards. Kin mayhap put yo' up here if'n yo' willin' ter pay. Figure 'bout a dollar fer lodgin' 'n' another dollar fer vittles fer yo' 'n' the niggers. Name's Bannion," he added as an afterthought, " 'n' this yere's Ransom Lightfoot." He jerked his thumb in the direction of the whittling fellow.

"Verder," Tom replied, "Tom Verder o' Dove Cote Plantation up Brownsville way. Bin over ter Macklin's sale 'n' bought me this buck here." He nodded toward the wagon. "On my way home 'n' lookin' fer a place ter eat 'n' bed down. Me 'n' the boys are hungry 'n' ain' fond o' stayin' out all night in this part of the country. Painters 'round here."

"Shore are." Bannion sensed a chance to augment his income. He had remembered Tommy's name of Verder and recognized this man from Dove Cote as Tommy's uncle. It was as much to his advantage as to Ransom's to keep Tommy's visit to the store a secret. Tommy's deposit on Fronie had long since been spent and he had no desire to return it. "Lots o' them varmints. Et up a nigger 'bout a year 'go. Belonged to that there Macklin where yo' been to the sale. Didn' leave nothin' but his bones."

Tom nodded as Bannion continued. The storekeeper allowed as he could, if properly recompensed, make up a pallet on the floor of the store after it had closed for the evening. His wife would be able to give them a meal of sorts—fried salt pork (which he called sowbelly) and corn pone with coffee and sweetening. If Tom desired a more elaborate supper for himself, say ham and eggs, it would cost him another two bits. He figured on closing the store in about an hour, so Tom would be able to bed down early, and he'd see to it that they had a breakfast before an early departure. Of course, if Tom didn't want to sleep in the same room with his niggers, they could stay out in the wagon, but Bannion went on, it wouldn't be any cheaper if they did. He again mentioned the "painters," by which he probably meant bobcats or lynxes, as a real panther or mountain lion would have been a rarity in that locality.

Tom decided to stay. The surroundings, to say the least, were unsavory and uncomfortable and he didn't care for the whining, avaricious Bannion, but it would mean something to eat and a warm place to stay with the added protection of four walls around him. He did not relish salt pork and expressed a desire for the more expensive meal, not only for himself but for his servants. Bannion seemed shocked at his willingness to give his slaves as good as himself, but, as it increased his income, he offered no objection. He nonetheless formed a poor opinion of Tom as a nigger-lover and a man who spoiled his slaves. Ham and eggs were white man's food and were far too good for varmints like them. Treating them like humans, it was. He advanced a step out of the doorway as a gesture for Tom to step inside and addressed the girl who had resumed nursing her child.

"Yo', Fronie, take yore tit outa that sucker's mouth 'n' h'ist yore ass over ter the cabin 'n' tell yore mistress ter fix up ham 'n' eggs 'n' pone fer three, seein' as how this gentleman a-thinkin' his niggers 're as good as him." He could not refrain from expressing his opinion of such an outlandish action. " 'N' when it's ready, tote it back over here. Tell that lazy Netty ter stir her stumps 'n' git thin's started."

Tom, still standing at the foot of the steps that led to the store, idly observed the girl stand up, speculating in his own mind as to whether the baby was hers or whether she was nursing a child of Bannion's. The conjecture reminded him of his need to procure a wet nurse for Dovie, and he made a quick appraisal of the girl, noting her good looks and light color through the dirt that covered her. She was about the same age as Dovie, he judged, and whiter than any slave on either of his plantations. Washed and dressed in something better than the shapeless osnaburg sack that covered her, she would be actually pretty. He stepped nearer, more to satisfy his own curiosity as to the child than anything else. She, noting his interest, held the baby up for him to see, letting the cloth that covered it fall, and displaying its

190

full length. It was a boy, but although his head, arms, and lower legs were white—the pinkish white of a white man—his body was spotted like a calico pony with large irregular brown areas. The demarcation between white and brown was clearly marked. The colors did not blend, the pigmentation changing immediately from dark to light. It gave the child's body a curious appearance, something that Tom had never noticed in a hybrid before, and he beckoned to the girl to bring the baby closer.

"Calls him Calico, we do," Bannion jeered. "Now ain' he the goddamndest sight? Never saw such a pinto afore. 'N' he's this yere Ransom's git, too. This boy Ransom he's studded mos' o' the wenches on the plantations round about 'n' this the first one he ever had what pinto-like, ain' it, Ransom?"

"Shore is." Ransom nodded. "I'd 'a' drowned it if'n it had been mine. Cain' ever sell a spotted brat like'n that. Who'd want it? Ain' wuth raisin'."

Fronie protectively lowered the child to her breast, reaching for the cloth to cover it, but Tom stopped her. He reached over and examined the baby more closely, lifting its small right hand to examine it, his own hand trembling in its urgency. Suddenly he felt a sharp stab of pain in his chest, cutting off his breath. The pain passed, leaving him weak.

"Goddam brat got six fingers, too. Jes' a freak, tha's all," Ransom guffawed. He tossed away the stick he had been whittling. "Every time I look at it, 'n' think it my git, makes me madder'n a turkentined cat. Feared it might happen 'gain sometime. If'n it do happen to a planter what hired me ter stud his wenches, he ain' goin' ter pay me no more money. No suh! Goin' ter be outa business, I am. Shamed o' this one, I am. Pinto skin 'n' six fingers."

As if to answer him, Tom stretched out his own right hand. Both Ransom and Bannion stared at it.

"Well I'll be goddamned," Bannion exclaimed, "if'n yo' ain' got six fingers, too." He shook his head in wonderment. "Ain' never seen it but once before in my whole life 'n' . . ."

"That were on that fellow yo' a-tellin' me 'bout yo'

onct saw in Mobile," Lightfoot finished Bannion's sentence. "The one yo' a-tellin' me yo' saw which had six fingers what yo' saw a-takin' a drink."

"That the one," Bannion said quickly, conscious of the nudge of Ransom's boot against his own.

Tom looked from the baby to his own right hand and then at Ransom and finally at Bannion. "Yo' say yo' saw a feller in Mobile with six fingers on his hand? How long ago that yo' saw him?"

Bannion seemed to be trying hard to recollect. " 'Bout six months ago, reckon it were. Had ter go down there ter see 'bout some goods, I did. Went into a tavern 'cept that they calls it a bar down there 'n' was standin' 'side o' a young feller what was drinkin'. His hand looked mighty peculiar 'n' could see he were six-fingered. Never saw it before so 'membered it. Tol' Ransom here 'bout it when this sucker came. Seemed maybe somehow my havin' see that feller might 'a' marked this un but cain' see how, seein' it's Ransom's git 'n' not mine. Damn shore it ain' mine 'cause though this wench's mine, ain' never pestered her."

" 'Bout how old was that fellow?" Tom persisted in his questioning. " 'N' what he look like?"

" 'Bout Ransom's age, I reckon, give or take a year or so, 'n' right nice-lookin' feller, too. Not so tall's Ransom here 'n' not towheaded like'n him. Well-dressed, too."

It must have been Tommy, Tom decided. Couldn't have been anyone else but Tommy, but what could he have been doing in Mobile when he was supposed to be home in Natchez? The thought occurred to him that Tommy must have heard of Dovie's pregnancy and sought to lose himself in his grief. But at least he was alive, Tom comforted himself. He might come back some day. The thought made him feel easier in his mind. He turned his attention to Fronie and her child. Without asking Bannion's permission, he took the child from her and held it up, examining it carefully. With the exception of its pied skin, it was a perfect man-child in every way. He handed it back to Fronie, who comforted the wailing infant.

"This girl your'n?" Tom asked Bannion.

"She mine all right. Her dam's Netty what's over to the house 'n' Ransom's older brother sired her. Older'n Ransom by a lot he was. She 'mos' human 'cause her maw got a lot o' human blood. Right smart gal too, Fronie is. Ain' never had no man till I let Ransom cover her, thinkin' I'd get me a nice bright-skin sucker ter sell. But this un turned out all spotted 'n' ain' wuth much."

"She housebroken?"

"Always lived in the house with me 'n' my wife." Bannion nodded his head slowly in approval of his own tender solicitude for Froni.

"Yo' ever tho't o' sellin' her?"

"Ain't never considered it, seein' as how my wife set such a store by her 'n' she so purty 'n' smart like," Bannion lied glibly. " 'Course"—he cleared his throat judiciously, appraising Fronie and the child from under shuttered lids—"if'n I had a good 'nuff offer jes' might consider it. Ought ter bring a good price, she being a fancy 'n' all 'n' willin' ter throw the sucker in. Even if'n he's spotted, he's worth somethin'. Right curious him havin' six fingers like yo'. Suppose if'n someone offered me a thousand dollars fer her, I'd consider it. Jes' supposin', tho'."

Tom shook his head. "Ain' worth that, she ain'. Better wenches'n her sold today fer less money'n that. I'd say seven hundred 'bout a right price fer her 'n' the sucker to boot. 'Course I ain' never seen her shucked down 'n' ain' buyin' no pig in a poke, but seven hundred a likely price."

"Shuck yo'self down, Fronie," Bannion said peremptorily, " 'n' let the gentleman finger yo' if'n he wants." He regarded Tom studiously to see if there was any chance of dickering. "But won' do him much good 'cause seven hundred ain' 'nuff."

"Y'o a-goin' ter sell me, masta Bannion suh?" Fronie laid the child down on the ground and pulled off her dress.

"Shet yore goddamned mouth 'n' don' ask me no questions. Sellin' yo' if'n I gets my price. Ain' sellin' yo' if'n I don'. Look her over, Mista Verder, 'n' see

193

fer yo'self if'n she ain' wuth more'n seven hundred. Right likely piece she is, 'n' good breeder too. She caught 'mos' the first time Ransom pestered her, didn' she, Ransom?"

"Shore did, Mista Verder. I the fust man she ever had. Right tight she was too, 'specially fer me." He could not resist boasting a little of his extraordinary endowment before this man.

Tom called her to him and gently went over her body with his hands. Her rank odor was nauseating but he knew that could be remedied by a good application of water and soft soap. She was well-formed, with high round breasts, good bones, ample hips, and an intelligent face. Her whiteness and lack of Negroid features appealed to him.

"My daughter's got a baby 'bout the same age as your'n," Tom told her. "Lookin' fer a gal what kin nurse her baby. Yo' got plenty o' milk, gal?"

"Got lots." Fronie lowered her head modestly. "That is, I would have if'n Ransom there didn't steal it. He a-suckin' at me every chance he gits."

"Yo' aimin' ter git stripped down?" Bannion advanced threateningly. "Yo' keep yore mouth shet. Yo' know I don' 'low no sech goin's on 'round here."

Tom held up a warning hand. "She ain' a-meanin' nothin' bad, Mista Bannion. Ain' fittin' ter punish her fer that. Tell yo' what I'll do. I say seven hundred. Yo' a-sayin' a thousand. Split the difference, I will. Give yo' eight hundred 'n' fifty 'n' that's more'n she 'n' the sucker's wuth but sort o' taken a notion to that sucker, seein' as how it's six-fingered like me."

It was a hundred more than Bannion had ever hoped to get for Fronie, and the worth of the baby was negligible. However, he did not want to appear too anxious. He stroked his bristly chin, pondered the matter and, finally, as though he were making a great concession, he spoke. "She'll have a good home with yo'? Yo'll treat her good?" Not that he cared a whit but it sounded good to express some interest in her future.

"Live right in the big house with us."

"Have ter talk it over with my wife. Netty's her'n 'n'

194

so's Fronie, so should kindly ask her. Yo', Fronie, git inter yore trogs 'n' come along with me. Be right back, Mista Verder. Yo' 'n' Ransom kin pass the time o' day."

They departed along the dusty path to the cabin, and Tom was left alone with young Lightfoot. For all his coarse good looks and his air of bravado, Ransom seemed somewhat bashful now that he was alone with Tom, and a period of silence ensued. Tom was not a little surprised when Ramson commenced the conversation.

"Yo' got a big place, Mista Verder?"

"Got me two o' 'em. Live at one called Dove Cote 'n' the other 'bout fifteen, twenty mile away, called The Patch. Patch's bigger'n Dove Cote."

"Lookin' fer a job I am. Likin' ter be an overseer some day but ain' had no experience. Cain' git none 'round here. Mos' places here right small 'n' don' need no overseer. My maw got a place o' her own but ain' big 'nuff ter make a livin' on. 'Course I pick up some money now 'n' then a-studdin' wenches for them planters what likes ter git good bright-skinned suckers. But reckon if'n word gits around that my git a-goin' ter be pinto 'n' six-fingered, ain' goin' ter want me fer studdin'. Do a good job tho'. They gits caught right soon when I covers 'em."

An idea suddenly occurred to Tom which might solve his problems at The Patch. "Wantin' ter learn, huh?"

"Kindly do, Mista Verder."

"Don' suppose yo' bein' a young squirt yo'd be willin' ter take orders from a nigger tho'?"

"Ain' rightly thought 'bout such a thing, Mista Verder, me bein' white 'n' all. Cain' see takin' no orders from a nigger howsomever. Ain' fittin'. How come yo' askin' me that?"

"Jes' thinkin' I might use yo', tha's all. Lettin' go my overseer at The Patch. Ain' worth a damn, he ain'. Lookin' fer a new one. Now my man Nero, what's my own body servant, he bin brought up there 'n' he knows more about runnin' the place'n any white man. Right good head on his shoulders, 'n' I respects his judgment. If'n yo' willin' ter let him tell yo' what ter do, jes' might consider hirin' yo' fer The Patch. Nero knows his place. He ain' goin' ter give orders, jes' kindly suggest 'em but 'spect yo' ter follow them. Could call yo'self overseer if'n yo' wants. Don' make me no neverminds what yo' call yo'self, but Nero'd have ter show yo' what ter do when I ain' there. Could learn a lot from Nero, yo' could, 'n' he right easy ter git along with. Pay yo' twelve dollars a month; give yo' a good cabin; furnish yo' yore vittles 'n' a wench ter cook them. Pick yore own wench if'n yo' wants. Warn yo' tho', ain' standin' fer no foolishness. No drinkin'! Drinkin' man ain' no damn good. No smokin' neither. Might set the place on fire. Ain' standin' fer no wenchin' neither less'n I say so. Yo has yore own wench 'n' that's that."

" 'N' if'n she gits knocked up? Ain' no good ter a man then."

"Let yo' have another. Got plenty over ter The Patch but I team 'em up with bucks 'n' don' want 'em broken up. Come nine months from now 'n' I see any light-skinned suckers 'ceptin' from yore own wench, I'll know who ter blame 'n' yo'll git yore walkin' papers. Well, what do yo' think?"

"Twelve dollars?" Ransom hoped to do a little dickering like Bannion had done.

"Take it or leave it. 'Thout experience yo' ain' wuth that."

"Be needin' a horse too 'n' a saddle. Cain' take this un; my maw a-needin' it."

Tom nodded. "Horse 'n' saddle too."

" 'N' 'nother wench what I kin pick out soon's I git the first un knocked up?"

Tom nodded.

"Reckon as how I'll take it, Mista Verder. Don' never smoke 'n' ain' much o' a drinker 'ceptin when someone treats me." He eyed Tom hopefully. " 'N' won' charge yo' no extry fer gittin' yo some nice bright-skins neither. Mos' o' the planters 'round here pays me ten dollars. Right powerful I am at covering wenches. Catches 'em the first time, like'n that Fronie. Cain' figure out how her sucker got six fingers tho'. 'Pears like'n yo' 'n' me might be kinfolk. My maw she was a Smith."

"My papa had an a'nt what was married ter a man named Smith. Could be. Right common name tho'."

"Jes' bet we kinfolk, Mista Verder." Ransom felt a claim to kinship might be to his advantage. "I'll ask my maw if'n they's any Verders in her family. Kin I go 'long with yo' in the wagon tomorrow? Don' mind having that nigger o' your'n show me how to do things if'n he don' order me, 'n' him mindin' that he a nigger 'n' I a white man. Right anxious ter learn from him if'n he know his place."

"He knows," Tom agreed, "I taught him." He wondered now if he had done the right thing in hiring this stranger. But then, he was a cut above the average overseer—young and strong and not bad-looking. With no experience he'd not assert himself too strongly, and just having a white man in residence at The Patch with the title of overseer would fill the legal requirement. He'd be there himself most of the time, and he'd leave Nero there when he came back to Dove Cote. Although he would not admit it, even in his own thoughts, he set quite a store by Nero's knowledge. He offered his hand to Ransom and they shook hands to bind the bargain. As they were doing so, Bannion reappeared with Fronie, now dressed in a cleaner shift, still toting her child.

"Miz Bannion says it's all right with her 'n' she's a-cookin' supper fer yo' 'n' yore niggers. She's sendin' over some quilts fer a pallet. Yo' a-goin' ter pay me cash?"

"Got jes' nuff.' Tom' pulled his poke out of his pocket and loosened the string. He slowly counted out the notes and the double eagles into Bannion's hand. When he had finished he had only a handful of silver left, barely enough to pay for his food and lodging. He noticed both Bannion and Ransom eyeing the gold as he counted it and he was glad he had no more.

"I'm a-goin' 'long with Mista Verder," Ransom announced proudly, and told Bannion the details of the contract between him and Tom. Bannion was loud in his congratulations.

"Good boy, this Ransom Lightfoot, Mista Verder. Goin' ter miss him, I is. Jes' like'n my own son, Ransom

197

is. Glad yo're going ter give him a chance. Planters 'round here a-goin' ter miss Ransom tho'. Shore got a reputation he has. First white fellow I ever knowed what could satisfy a wench better'n a buck. 'Fore yo' knows it, yo'll have a passel o' towheaded mustees a-runnin' over yore place onct Ransom gits there."

"We got an agreement 'bout that, Mista Bannion, me 'n' Ransom has. He'll keep his britches buttoned less'n I tells him 'n' if'n he don't, he'll be back here sure's God made little green apples." He turned to the wagon. "Hey yo' there, Sippi 'n' Djoubo. Git yo'selves down ter the crick there 'n' wash yo'selves. If'n I got ter sleep in the same room don' wan' yo' boys a-smellin' musky. 'N' when they gits through"—he turned to Fronie—"yo' asks yore mist'ess if'n she kindly let yo' have some soft soap, 'n' yo' scrub yo'self, too. A musky buck stinks bad 'nuff but al'ays seems ter me a musky wench stinks worse."

Chapter XII

THE DEVELOPMENT of Tommy Boggs and of Calico seemed normal through their infancy. While the brown areas on Calico spread until they reached his chest and shoulders, it seemed that they faded in intensity, so that they blended with the white instead of being distinct patches. Both squalled and cried or laughed and cooed side by side. They were nursed alternately at Fronie's breasts. Tommy was the first to walk and by ten months was able to crawl across the floor and, by clinging to Verder's trouser legs, raise himself up on his feet, a feat that the grandfather deemed precocious and worthy of wonder and commendation. The comparative backwardness of the bigger, lustier Calico discouraged Fronie but augmented Tom's satisfaction. It was interesting to observe the differences in development of two children of the same age, and brought up together in the same environment. Verder was unable to be objective in his estimates of the progress the boys were making, always praising Tommy for a more rapid approach to maturity than the pie-bald Calico. This he attributed to race and superior blood.

However, it was noticed very early that Tommy was indifferent to sounds. To talk to Calico elicited a coo or a smile, while Tommy quite ignored a similar attempt to win his attention. Tom insisted that this was not backwardness but only a disregard of being spoken to—a mere gravity begotten of sagacity.

At eleven months, however, Calico was speaking intelligible words while Tommy emitted only amorphous cries, screams, calls, and whimpers, unlinked to any ideas or concepts. As time went on, Calico accumulated a vocabulary and finally came to string words together to formulate simple sentences. Boggs, ever resentful of Tommy's very existence, ignored his failure to speak; Dovie was undisturbed, assuming that her son would talk eventually; Fronie was silently triumphant about Calico's greater precocity, urging him to repeat for the members of the family his every new utterance. To Tom Verder, however, it was a tragedy that his beloved grandson could not utter a word.

It was not until the two boys were well past three years and Calico was speaking volubly that Tom conceded that Tommy was mute. He had come to recognize much earlier that the child was deaf, but it never occurred to him that a person's congenital inability to hear might result in his inability to articulate words. Tom affixed the appellation "The Dummy" to his grandson, a term which was in no manner derogatory. It was merely a reluctant acknowledgment of the fact of the boy's inability to speak. Deaf-mutes were known as dummies and Tommy was one of them. That was all. The term did not imply any lack of intelligence, but only that the person so denominated was unable to express himself. Tommy was indeed not stupid. Within his limits to understand and communicate, so far as Tom could surmise, he was of normal intellect. But his disability was partially compensated for by his unusual beauty. Both his father and mother were handsome young people, yet it seemed that Tommy's beauty far exceeded either of theirs. Perhaps it was somewhat due to the fact that Dovie refused to have his hair cut and his long curls, the color of dark amber, gave him a girlish look. The pinafores he wore as a child, the long curls, the fair skin, the unusually clear, lash-rimmed hazel eyes, and a certain languid grace and daintiness of movement made him look more like a girl than a boy. This was perhaps accentuated by contrast with Calico's close-cropped head, his lustier, more boyish attitude, and his strong body. When dressed in his little tow-linen shirt and breeches, which Fronie insisted that he always wear, he did not show his piebald coloring, and, although his skin was not the creamy white of Tommy's, there was no hint of any Negro blood in his face, neck, arms, or hands. Of approximately the same age, with the same facial characteristics and coloring, they gave the appearance of a twin brother and sister. Calico was larger, stronger, taller, and distinctly boyish; Tommy was more finely boned, more delicate, finer-featured, and somewhat effeminate.

Tommy was unaware of the silence in which he existed. As he grew older, he realized that others had a means of communicating which was not vouchsafed to him. He saw lips move and he noticed that people paid attention to those moving lips but when he moved his own, nobody paid any attention to him. The manual alphabet for deaf-mutes had been formulated in the previous century, but its use had not penetrated into what was then Mississippi territory. Even if Tommy had had such a means of conveying his thoughts, there would have been nobody to read his fingers. He could have been taught to read and write but neither Dovie nor Callie (although both had some slight book learning) were capable of teaching him. Tom was far too busy and not too learned himself. Bart was nearly illiterate and was entirely too uninterested to waste a moment's time on Tommy, whom he hated and whose presence he resented. The boy existed and functioned in an absolute and complete silence.

But, without hearing, he was able to observe and acquire a sense of the atmosphere in which he lived. Among the matters he absorbed was an awareness of the hierarchy within the family. At its head stood his grandfather, followed by Callie and Dovie, then Bart Boggs and, on the rare occasions when he saw him, Ransom Lightfoot. These people were all white and Tommy grew to understand that they had authority over

201

Nero, Fronie, Sippi, and the household servants, all of whom were colored. As he grew older, and went about the plantation, he saw that all the other people there were black. He came to realize that they all treated him with deference and a certain amount of decorum. However, he had difficulty in figuring out Calico's place in the overall scheme of things. Calico was not black. Calico slept with him, played with him, was in constant attendance on him, yet if he hit him before any of the white people, Calico would not hit back. When he and Calico were alone, however, Calico often pummeled him. At first, Calico did not eat at the table with him and the rest of the family, but crouched under it. This had not suited Tommy and he'd raised such a howl, refusing to eat, that a place was made at the table for Calico beside Tommy, where he ate the same food that Tommy ate. It bothered Callie and Dovie that a slave should sit at their table, even when guests were present, but the fact that Calico's origin did not show, and that everybody who visited them took it for granted that he was a white boy, possibly a cousin of Tommy's, made it easier for them to accept it.

Indeed, Tommy was yielded priority in everything. As the presumptive heir of his grandfather, and a deaf-mute at that, he was denied nothing. "Let him have it," or "let him do it," Tom would say. "Poor boy, he doesn't have what others do." He was the apple of Tom's eye, and everybody was forced to conform to Tommy's wishes in so far as Tommy, by means of cries and gestures and grimaces, was able to make those wishes known. Here again, his beauty was a ready tool. Nobody wanted to refuse such a handsome little fellow anything he desired.

Calico and Calico alone was able to understand Tommy, and what he didn't understand he was clever enough to pretend he did. The two boys had a system of communication which baffled the others. Tommy's grunts and gurglings, his exaggerated facial contortions, and his gestures were answered by Calico with gestures of his own. Sticking his finger in his mouth and chewing indicated eating; eyes closed and hands against cheek indicated sleep; pointing called Tommy's attention to something; and a multiplicity of other gestures made up a language between them. Calico learned very early to attribute his own desires to Tommy. The adults believed him and granted him whatever he alleged that Tommy longed for. As the boys grew older, this knack of Calico's improved to the extent that he was able almost entirely to dominate the policy of the household.

Tommy possessed no concept of slavery or what it implied; no notion of ownership, whether of things or of persons. But he came to recognize that Negroes were considered inferior to whites, and that they served whatever purpose the superior whites wished them to. Gradually he came to identify Calico as one of the inferior breed. Since Calico was part white, he could be his constant companion. But since Calico also had dark spots on his body, he was his to treat as he pleased. He had no idea that he actually owned the Negro boy; they were merely together, and Calico was for his use and service.

He thrilled at the spectacle of Fronie's spanking Calico. He enjoyed brushing Fronie's hand away and slapping Calico himself on his round and mottled buttocks. Although he was deaf to his cries and yelps, he was aware that this chastisement was painful to Calico. Yet he exulted in seeing his contortions and his tears. Then, after the spanking was over he would comfort the wailing Calico by taking him in his arms and kissing him, the one gesture of endearment he had learned. When they were playing alone and he attempted to take down Calico's pants and chastise him, Calico fought back and by his superior strength kept Tommy from inflicting punishment upon him.

Tommy himself was never punished. In view of the boy's infirmity, Tom had given orders he was to be spared. And who would punish him? Certainly not his adoring grandfather. Boggs was too indifferent, Dovie too forbearing, Callie too fat, and Fronie too frightened to reprimand him. When, in Fronie's opinion, Tommy's misbehavior warranted discipline and he was too difficult to control, she diverted his attention when there were no white people about by that well-known device employed by nursemaids on little boys the world over. She captured him, held him in her lap, and massaged him, at the same time covering his face with kisses. He would stop his screaming, respond, then nestling, sleepy and content, in her arms. Calico also used this method of pacifying Tommy and keeping him under control.

Calico, who knew he was a slave, early was made aware that it was a crime for him to strike his master, and was taught it was the right of the white boy to humor or abuse him as he saw fit. Fronie was at pains to make this fact clear to her son. Calico might sulk or pout, even complain to his mother at the ill treatment that he was forced to undergo at Tommy's hands, but as he grew older he knew better than to retaliate, at least when anyone else was around. When they were alone, he often struck back, knowing that Tommy would not be able to tell on him. But generally the two played amicably together. Tommy was good, generous, and affectionate, if he could have his own way, but demanding and subject to wild tantrums when he could not. Then he vented his wrath on poor Calico. He ruthlessly pinched, bit, struck, or kicked. The boys slept in the same bed, and if Calico repulsed Tommy's advances, Tommy would kick him out of bed. Calico would curl up on the floor until his master, missing the warmth and proximity of Calico's body, would get up, smother him with kisses, and pull him back into bed.

As he grew older and entered his teens, horses began to fascinate Tommy, but, despite his pleadings, echoed by Calico, Tom did not permit him to ride, apprehensive that his lack of hearing might lead to an accident. Seeing others mount their horses and ride away, Tommy conceived the idea of using Calico for a horse. He would force him to the ground and ride him, sitting astride his back as Calico cavorted on all fours. Calico at first joined in the play gladly and would shy and rear and buck in an effort to unseat his rider. Tommy conceived of using a short twig of oak as a bit and, after tying strings to each end to serve as reins, forced the bit into Calico's mouth, using the reins to guide his steed. This was uncomfortable if not actually painful to Calico but he, while often reluctant to carry his rider, was never recalcitrant. Fronie, whose duty it was to supervise the play, saw to it that neither of the boys would be injured, although she knew that the white child was supreme and if Tommy's amusement necessitated more distress but no real injury to Calico, she dared not interfere with their game. Later Tommy hit on the idea of using a switch—a sucker from an apple tree—as a whip to control his mount, but he soon learned that larger whips produced a greater smart. One day he found a discarded rein which he discovered to be even more effective.

Although the adults never suspected, it was more than merely a childish game. Tommy, a-straddle Calico's back, found pleasure in the contact of his groin with the warm back of the boy underneath. As a result, he spent most of his time riding Calico.

Calico trotted Tommy about while Tommy lashed him with the strap from time to time, though never abrading Calico's flesh. Tommy particularly enjoyed their excursions into the oak grove. Here, where one of the small streams widened into a pool, they conceived the idea of damming the stream with stones and clods of dirt until its level rose to their middles. They enjoyed taking off their clothes and splashing in the water. Tommy soon discovered that riding Calico in the nude increased his pleasure. Calico agreed to this play, for he had learned by experience that ultimately Tommy would cease to ride him and the two boys could play normally at the things Calico enjoyed—working on the dam; building a hut which he was continuously improving; making bows and arrows; setting traps for birds; and catching frogs, which he tried to keep as pets in small pools that he constructed in the brook.

One afternoon, when Calico was in the midst of his prancings, both boys were surprised by the sudden apparition of Kru. The sight of the huge black giant, appearing suddenly from the underbrush, as naked as they were except for a wreath of tawny field lilies around his head, frightened both boys, and Calico froze in his tracks with Tommy still on his shoulders. Kru's broad grin, however, reassured them, and Calico remained still as Kru advanced slowly, his hands held out before him in a gesture of friendliness. He came to within a foot of the boys, then dropped down to his knees, took Tommy's hand in his and laid it on his head. "Masta suh," he said, and although Tommy did not hear, he recognized the gesture of obeisance and patted Kru's head.

"Cain' talk, he cain'," Calico, whose face was on a level with Kru's, explained. " 'N' cain' hear nuthin' neither." His words were wasted on Kru, who did not understand. Instead he gently lifted Tommy from Calico's shoulders and placed him on his own. Tommy gurgled with delight as Kru ran with him through the clearing, leaping high in the air, ducking, turning, and jumping. Then Kru put him down and lifted Calico, giving him a wild ride until he was breathless, whereupon he lowered Calico, stretched out on the grass, and, taking one boy in the hollow of each arm, pillowed their heads on his chest and slept. His body smelled pleasantly of the mint and bergamot with which he had rubbed it. His powerful arms were protecting and secure. His huge body was a warm thing of wonder and excitement. Eventually the boys slept alongside him until, waking, Kru awoke them knelt before Tommy again, and then sped off into the bushes.

When they returned home, Tommy put his fingers on Calico's lips to signify that he was not to tell about their episode. What they had done did not seem wrong to either Tommy or Calico, but it was a part of their life they wished to keep secret, like the hut in the woods or the dam they had built. Thereafter, nearly every afternoon, they met Kru at the same spot, where Kru cavorted with them like another child, after which, stretched out beside Kru, they played with him until, exhausted, they slept. Tommy in particular was entranced with Kru.

He did, however, have a vague and wordless fear of discovery; of someone putting an end to this delightful play. He knew that neither Callie nor Dovie would venture out in the woods (Dovie had avoided them since

206

the day Tommy was born). He did not particularly fear discovery by his grandfather, whom he was accustomed to wind around his finger by the simple process of squeezing out a few tears. He was completely indifferent about being discovered by any of the slaves, but he did fear Bart, for he had long been aware of Bart's dislike.

Tommy as a child had scarcely merited Bart's attention, but Tommy at fourteen could no longer be entirely ignored. Tommy, with the perversity of a spoiled child who knew he would not be punished, delighted in plaguing Bart. Whenever he and Calico were around him, Tommy giggled and gabbled, pointing his finger at Bart and setting Calico off into gales of laughter. Bart knew that he was the object of their ridicule. Tommy, denied the expression of speech, had become an adroit and expert mimic. He could imitate another person to perfection and delighted in aping Bart's every movement, exaggerating his slowness and clumsiness into a ludicrous burlesque.

Bart had always insisted on saying grace at meals. The rest of the family put up with it resignedly if impatiently, but to Tommy, to whom it was a meaningless delay when he was hungry, it was anathema. To annoy Bart and to discourage this time-consuming and, to him, empty ritual, he would mimic him, pressing his hands together, closing his eyes, and pontificating mutely. Tom decided he was trying to pray and forbade the others to stop him, but at times even he found Tommy to be so comical in his apery that he could not keep from laughing. This would set Dovie and Callie off, and even the servants were unable to hide their amusement.

During the fourteen years of his marriage with Dovie, Bart had become embittered. His cherished dreams of ever having a church of his own and becoming a real reverend had long since vanished. He wanted to be admired and respected and looked up to, but in this backwater of Dove Cote, he saw almost nobody and his position was dubious—he was a mere hanger-on without real authority. His ability to satisfy Dovie's voracious appetite was waning, and gratifying her had become a dreaded chore. Merely tolerated by Tom, almost completely ignored by Callie, suffered by Dovie because he was the only white

207

man available to satisfy her hunger, even despised and sometimes openly sneered at by Nero, he sought solace in drink. But he was a cautious drinker. He never became actually drunk, though he was never completely sober. He drank only a little at a time, but it was a continuous process. Denied the authority he desired over the plantation slaves, he became a martinet in regard to Tommy, and not even Tom could gainsay him. "I'm his father, ain' I? Ain' I got the right ter tell him what ter do 'n' how ter behave hisself?" It was difficult to deny that authority, particularly when it did not take the form of physical chastisement. Consequently Bart's somewhat erratic disciplinary measures were the only reprimands that Tommy ever received, deepening the hatred between the two.

As afternoon followed afternoon and Bart, sitting on the gallery, watched Tommy depart astride Calico into the woods about the same time every day, he finally became suspicious. He could see by Tommy's fluttering hands and excited manner that this particular departure was something Tommy had been eagerly anticipating. Calico too seemed anxious to leave. For several days, after he had first begun to notice them, Bart timed them and confirmed that they always left right after the noonday meal and always headed in the same direction. Remembering his own burgeoning appetites during adolescence, he suspected that they were keeping a rendezvous in the grove with some of the girls from the Romp Pasture, and he felt certain that if he could surprise Tommy in the act of pleasuring one of the girls, he could inflict a severe punishment which even Tom would not attempt to mitigate. He wanted nothing more than a valid opportunity to tickle Tommy's bare bottom with a horse-whip and, if he were fortunate enough to discover what he was sure was the reason for their departure, he would have the excuse he craved. He knew how strict Tom was with the Romp Pasture girls, Nobody was to touch them, and any slave who dared to do so was severely punished. What he did not know, however, was that Tom had been planning to turn one of the girls over to Tommy, feeling that he was now old enough

to have one. He had done so with his beloved nephew Tommy and he intended to do the same with his grandson.

One day, with Tom and Nero absent at the Patch, Bart finished his noonday meal earlier than the rest. Tommy and Calico appeared. "Where yo' boys a-goin'?" Bart inquired of Calico as he knelt to take Tommy on his shoulders.

Tommy's thrust-out chin and air of defiance plainly told Bart that it was none of his business, for Tommy sensed the hostility behind Bart's question.

"We jes' a-goin' down in the grove ter play, tha's all," Calico answered, shifting Tommy's weight more comfortably. "Jes' ter play," he repeated. "Tommy a-wantin' ter go. He like it there."

Bart grunted. It was neither a denial of their right to go nor an acceptance of it. They departed, Tommy slapping his strap against Calico. Bart roused himself, waited till they had rounded the corner of the stables, and then followed them. He passed through the stables and out through the back door just as they were disappearing into the woods. When they arrived at the clearing in the woods, they stopped, and he hid himself behind some bushes, hoping to see one or two of the Romp Pasture wenches already there. But much to his surprise when the bushes parted Kru leaped out, and both boys ran up to him, embracing him and nuzzling against him. Kru seemed as happy to see them as they were to welcome him. Bart was disappointed. He had hoped to find some valid excuse for punishing Tommy and now all that had happened was that the boys had met Kru. He began to feel that his trip in the hot sun was in vain, but when he saw the boys shucking off their clothes, he remained. Again he waited hopefully, but all they did was go into the pool and splash around, Kru seemingly as young and sportive as the boys. When they came out of the water, Kru lifted Tommy onto his shoulders, running and leaping with him. There was absolutely nothing wrong in what Bart saw, yet he was so chagrined that his plans had gone awry that he decided to find something wrong. He had seen Kru but seldom but he had never forgotten the animosity Kru had displayed toward him.

Well, one thing certainly was wrong. Kru had no right to be there. That was certain. He was a Patch slave and had no business leaving it and coming over to Dove Cote. Shirking his work was an offense worthy of punishment. That sufficed for Kru. As for Tommy, he had been absolutely forbidden to play with any of the other slaves except Calico. Tom had made that clear several times. Certainly Kru was a slave and Tommy was playing with him. Good and sufficient grounds for punishing Tommy. Calico was an eager accessory to Tommy's disobedience, and that was reason enough for punishing him. So, Bart decided, all three could be punished legitimately and without fear of reprisal from Tom. Nobody could deny him the right to punish his own son. He broke off a branch from one of the bushes, stripped it of leaves, and crashed out from the underbrush, taking the three by surprise.

"What yo' boys a-doin', playing with that black savage?" he demanded. He looked from one to the other until his gaze rested on Calico, the only one able to answer him.

"We jes' playin', tha's all. Masta Tommy he like to ride big Kru. Kru's his horse. He's a stallion 'cause he's bigger'n me. I jes' a pony, tha's all, 'n' masta Tommy he likin' ter ride a stallion."

" 'N' lookin' like a stallion." Bart pointed to Kru. Somethin' a-goin' on 'roun' here what ain' right." He advanced toward Tommy, astride Kru's shoulders, and raised his arm. The stick swished through the air and landed on Tommy's rump.

Tommy squealed and slipped down from Kru's back. Undeterred by the flailing stick in Bart's hand, he rushed at his father, pummeling him with his fists, screaming and hollering in his unintelligible jargon. Bart, with Tommy so close to him, was unable to get in any very telling licks, but he managed one or two which made Tommy howl the louder. Suddenly Kru reached over, wrenched the stick from Bart's hand and broke it, throwing it on the ground. He did not raise his hand to Bart but the expression on his face was menacing. Tommy flew to the protection of Kru's arms.

210

"Yo'-all come back ter the big house with me, hear me?" He pointed to Kru. " 'N' yo come 'long 'n' don' make no trouble. Ain' no nigger son-o'-a-bitch goin' ter defy me."

Calico, who was the only one who could understand what Bart was saying, was frightened. He knew that when a white man spoke, he must be obeyed, and that direct disobedience only called down a more severe punishment. Calico was aware that Bart could have seen nothing today, but he knew that what had been happening between Tommy and Kru and himself was wrong. Nobody had ever told him that it was wrong, but he sensed that it was. He was relieved that Bart had appeared as early in their play as he had, but he was fearful lest Bart had been spying on them for several days and had seen enough to justify chastisement of all three. Moreover, he knew that if Kru were to run now, he would be hunted down and even more severely punished. Calico worshiped the big black with the idealistic hero-worship of a young boy for an older man who treated him as an equal. Hoping to save Kru, he took the big fellow's hand in his.

"Masta Bart say yo' come with us. Better yo' come, Kru." He nodded his head vigorously and pulled Kru a step or two. Kru seemed to sense the urgency behind Calico's words and stood still, looking from Bart to Tommy to Calico. Tommy, expressing himself in the only way he knew how, slipped from under Kru's arm, stamping his feet and waving his hand, but Bart, secure now in his authority, slapped Tommy across the face, changing his screams once more into tearful howls.

"Yo' hurtin' masta Tommy, masta Bart suh." Calico was in a panic. Nobody had ever laid hands on Tommy before.

" 'N' if'n yo' tell anyone I hit him, I'll whop yo' so's yore ass'll be blistered fer a week. Might jes' whop yo' anyway 'n' take some o' that bezom outa yo'. 'N' Tommy, too! Needin' a dressin'-down, he does. But I'm a-goin' ter whop that goddam black bozal till his hide falls off. Tell him ter git started 'n' if'n yo' kin tell The Dummy, tell him too. Now git, all of yo', ter the horse barn."

211

Kru seemed to understand. He squatted down and signaled to Tommy to hop on his shoulders. He glared defiance at Bart, but followed Bart's pointing finger to the path that led to the big house. Bart picked up Calico's shirt that was on the ground and handed it to him. "Tie that roun' that black savage. Cain' have him traipsin' roun' the big house, nekkid as a jaybird."

He waited until the three of them preceded him and then followed in the rear. Kru stalked along angrily. Tommy, weeping audibly, leaned over and kissed Kru's face, which further sickened Bart. Calico, frightened out of his wits, stumbled along the path, his eyes so filled with tears that he could hardly see where he was going. He was certain that Bart had witnessed some of the things that had happened on previous days and he knew that his punishment would be much more severe than Tommy's, if less than Kru's.

When they reached the vicinity of the big house, Bart herded all three of them into the stables, sending Djoubo posthaste to fetch Honey, the plantation blacksmith, and to bring Sippi, Duke, Ramrod, Shushan, and any other of the hands he could find.

" 'N' tell that Honey ter bring spancels with him," he hollered at the running Djoubo. "Better tell him ter bring two sets. We'll be a-needin' 'em ter hol' this goddam black ox."

Chapter XIII

SIPPI, HIS ARMS WAVING WILDLY, his breath coming in great heaves, was scarcely distinguishable in the darkness, and it was not until Tom and Nero were nearly upon him that they saw him, about a mile down the road from Dove Cote. Tom, riding a few paces ahead, pulled up his horse, peering into the blackness, which was illuminated only by the row of Sippi's white teeth.

"That yo', Sippi? Wha's a matter, boy?" Tom sensed immediately that something was wrong; only something of vital importance would have sent Sippi running along the road to intercept him. All sorts of tragedies flashed through his mind. Dove Cote was afire; Callie had been stricken; something had happened to The Dummy. He felt his own heart racing and tried to draw a long breath but could only gasp.

"Oh, masta Tom, masta Tom suh." Sippi materialized out of the darkness to clasp Tom's knee. "Masta Bart, he's a-killin' masta Tommy, suh. Wantin' me ter whop him, masta Tom, 'n' I runned. Was a-goin' ter run ter The Patch ter fetch yo'. Masta Bart he a-sayin' he a-goin' ter wallop me 'cause I wouldn' whop masta Tommy. Honey a-whoppin' that Kru boy. Djoubo he a-whoppin' Calico 'n' masta Bart hisself, he a-whoppin' masta Tommy."

"He a-whoppin' him?" Tom could not believe Sippi's words. "Wha' for he a-whoppin' The Dummy?"

"Don' rightly know, masta Tom suh, but he sure a-layin' it on with the horsewhip. 'N' so's Djoubo 'n' so's Honey, 'ceptin' Honey he a-usin' the paddle on Kru. He shore a-strippin' down that Kru."

Nero, beside Tom, was equally incredulous. He reached down a hand and pulled Sippi up behind him. Momentarily, in this emergency, he forgot his relationship to his master.

"Better ride, Tom. No tellin' what that fool Bart a-doin' if'n he lickered up. He always a-hatin' Kru 'n' don' think he like Calico much neither. Cain' see him a-whoppin' The Dummy tho'."

Tom did not answer. Apprehension filled him, but the fierce pounding of his heart told him to conserve his strength. He slapped his horse, leaned low over the animal's neck, and whipped his canter into a gallop. The horse, running wildly, barely made the turn into the lane that led up to the big house, but slacked his pace as he drew near the barn. Tom was off the horse and into the barn before Nero and Sippi had turned into the driveway. Screams and groans from the barn hastened his steps. The light from two glass hurricane lanterns had been augmented by two of the iron hog-scraper candlesticks from the kitchen. Apparently nobody had heard Tom arrive—with such a caterwauling it would have been impossible. Kru was yelping like a wounded animal. Calico was screaming for his mother, for Dovie, and for Callie, and in the same breath pleading with Bart, who stood over The Dummy, spraddle-legged over the boy's prone body on the floor, while The Dummy howled maniacally. With two wrists spanceled to a rafter, his feet about six inches from the floor, Kru swung slowly back and forth. His back and rump were red and glistening in the candlelight and Honey, the powerful blacksmith, was waiting for Kru's body to cease swinging before aiming the heavy, perforated ox-hide paddle again.

"Had 'bout all he kin take, masta Bart suh," Honey said, shaking his head doubtfully.

"Keep yore goddam trap shut 'n' give him ten more," Bart growled. He reached down and got his hand in The Dummy's long hair and yanked his head up, turning it to stare malevolently into the boy's eyes. " 'N' yo' shut yore trap too." Bart slapped him and let his head fall. He turned to where Djoubo, his eyes rolling in his head until only the whites were visible, brought the horsewhip down onto the squirming naked body of Calico, who was tied by his wrists to the stanchion of a horse stall. "What ter hell yo' slowin' up fer, Djoubo? Yo'll stop when I tell yo' but not less'n yo' wants ter git it yo'self. Goddam niggers 'round here a-gittin' out o' hand. Every goddam one o' yo' needin' strippin' down. Pour it on! We a-goin' ter teach that pinto who's masta 'roun' here." He raised his own light horsewhip to bring it down on The Dummy's lacerated back but Tom, behind him, snatched the whip from his hand.

"Wha's goin' on 'roun' here? What the hell does all this mean? Who said ter whop these boys 'n' what yo' a-doin', whoppin' The Dummy?"

"My son, ain' he?" Bart backed up, stepping over Tommy. "Whop him if'n I wants. Whop him till he knows he's a-goin' ter mind me. Cavortin' out in them woods with this naked savage. How come yo' don' know wha's a-goin' on 'roun' here?"

"Touch him once more 'n' I'll have yo' nigger-whipped. Nero whopped yo' once 'n' he'll do it again if'n I tell him. Don' know what these boys done. Don' know what The Dummy done neither, but ain' goin' ter be no whoppin' here less'n I say so." Tom staggered, held onto the side of the stall, and then reached down and pulled Tommy up. Tommy sobbed against his grandfather's chest. Tom, looking beyond the frightened Honey and the trembling Djoubo, saw Nero and Sippi at the edge of the candlelight. He motioned to them to come over.

Sippi sidled up next to him. "Yo' ain' a-goin' ter whop me, masta Tom suh?"

" 'Course he ain'." Nero pushed Sippi aside and stood before Tom.

"Git that there Kru down. Untie Calico 'n' yo', Sippi, carry him inter the house. Come here, Honey. Yo' take masta Tommy 'n' carry him in 'n' put him on his bed. Put Calico alongside him. Tell Aunt Ruthie ter het up some water. Make a bed out here on the straw fer Kru 'n' I'll tend ter him later." He turned to Nero, who was three rungs up the ladder against the beam from where Kru was suspended. "Let Djoubo do that," he ordered, " 'n' yo' come with me. Bring this Bart inter the house. Ain' takin' no chances with him."

"Cain' git in, masta Tom suh," Sippi said. "Masta Bart done locked the house with the wimmenfolk in it. Miz Dovie she a-screamin' 'n' a-yellin' 'n' Miz Callie she done fainted 'way. Masta Bart a-sayin' it don' make no never-minds. He a-goin' ter punish masta Tommy anyway 'n' he a-tellin' me ter whop him. Ain' fittin' that I whop masta Tommy. Tha's why I runned ter fetch yo'."

Tom held out his hand toward Bart, and silently Bart dropped the key to the door in it. Reluctantly releasing the still-sobbing Tommy to Honey, Tom turned and walked slowly out of the barn toward the house. Once, across the short distance that separated the stables from the house, he was forced to stop to catch his breath, and the whole procession halted behind him. Then he went on, slowly and painfully, as though each step were a painful chore. Up on the gallery, he fumbled with the big key, inserted it in the lock, and turned it. Dovie was waiting just inside the door. She flung herself into his arms, sobbing.

"Bart's gone crazy"—she pointed an accusing finger at Bart—"he's outa his head. Rampagin' 'roun' here like'n a wild man. Cain' do nothin' with him. Oh, Papa, I'm glad yo're home."

"Where's Callie?" Tom had to assure himself of the safety of all his family.

"She on her bed. Congo 'n' Fronie with her."

Tom stood aside to let the procession enter the house, first Honey with Tommy in his arms, then Sippi with Calico, then Bart and Nero close behind him, ready to grab him if he tried to run. Dovie, set off into a fit of weeping at the sight of The Dummy's bleeding back, supported his head as Honey carried him. Fronie, called to the door by the commotion, keened and wailed when she saw Calico's condition, which was far worse than Tommy's. Tom, gesturing for Sippi who was acquainted with the house, pointed to Tommy's bedroom, and Honey, who had never been in the house before, followed him.

They went to the boys' bedroom where they laid Tommy and Calico down on the bed, Dovie and Fronie each standing beside her son. Bart, sullen and defiant now, stood at the foot of the bed. Dovie pulled the sheet up over the boys' bleeding backs. Aunt Ruthie poked her head in the door, threw up her hands in horror, and shuffled off to the kitchen, to return with a basin of warm water and an armful of clean linen rags.

Tom waved them all out of the room except Fronie and, with his own hands, carefully washed the body of his grandson, letting the tenderness of his fingers convey to the boy the love and protection he felt for him. When he had washed the blood off, he found that Tommy's back was not badly scarred. Calico, however, was much worse, and while Tom worked on The Dummy, Fronie, watching him to see exactly what he did, followed suit on Calico. Tom spoke to the boy when his hysterical sobs had quieted, for he was the only one of the three who had been punished who could give any logical account of the happenings.

"Wha' for masta Bart punish Tommy 'n' Kru 'n' yo'?"

Calico's reply was gasped out between sobs, but eventually Tom got the whole story, at least the version that Calico wanted him to hear, for Calico also realized that he was the only witness who could be questioned.

"Jes' don' know, masta Tom suh, wha' for masta Bart he whop us. Ain' don' nothin' bad, me 'n' masta Tommy. Ain' done nothin' more'n we ever done what is masta Tommy he a-ridin' me horseback. We a-ridin' out'n the grove 'n' Kru come 'long. We been a-splashin' 'n' a-playin' in the pool what we dammed up in the crick. Kru he take masta Tommy up 'n' put him on his shoulders like'n he see me do 'n' he ride masta Tommy 'cept that Kru he do it much better'n me 'cause he big 'n' strong. He run 'n' jump 'n' gallop 'n' masta Tommy he like it. Then Kru give me a ride too 'n' masta Tommy he run ahind Kru, hittin' him with the strap ter make him go fast but Kru he don' min' 'cause masta Tommy he not whoppin' Kru hard. 'N' then, masta Bart, he come bustin' through the bushes awful mad 'n' he say we all three got ter git whopped 'cause he ain' havin' masta Tommy a-

217

playin' with no black buck like Kru what runned from the Patch. Tha's all we do, masta Tom suh. Cross my heart 'n' die, masta Tom suh. Ain' a-lyin' ter yo', I ain'. Masta Bart he a-sayin' we got wenches from the Romp Pasture out there 'n' Kru a-teachin' us ter pester them gals but ain' true, masta Tom. Ain' never had no wenches from the Romp Pasture out n' the grove 'n' Kru ain' doin' nothin' ter no wenches like'n masta Bart say. Masta Bart he tryin' ter make me say we a-doin' things like that but cain' say it if'n we ain' doin' it."

Tom nodded his head wisely, Calico had indeed vindicated himself, because Tom well knew that Kru would not be bringing out any wenches for Tommy and Calico. He did, however, have one lingering suspicion.

" 'N' yo' two boys ain' a-doin' nothing vicious with that Kru? Ain' a-lettin' him do nothin' ter you'?"

Calico's face was the very image of innocence as he lied glibly. "We jes' a ridin' Kru, that's all, masta Tom suh, 'n' if'n masta Bart say we ain't he lyin'."

Tom realized now that Bart's punishment had been purely vindictive, brought on by his long-standing hatred of Kru and his resentment of Tommy and Calico. He finished sponging Tommy's back and sent Fronie for a jar of mutton tallow and a bottle of laudanum. He smoothed the soothing grease on Tommy's back and bade Fronie do the same with Calico, then gave each boy a dose of laudanum and sat with them until they quieted.

Although his first violent rage had subsided, his anger now burned more fiercely within him. It was quiet but ominous. That Bart had abused Tommy as he would a Negro and in the company of Negroes was bad enough. That he had tried to delegate the whipping of Tommy to Sippi was even worse. But what angered Tom the most was that a strong man like Bart would wreak his vengeance on a physically handicapped boy who could not even plead his own innocence. Nor could he forgive him for meting out punishment to Kru and Calico. Tom was the sole judge and arbiter of his domain. It was he who designated those to be punished and the exact extent of their punishment, and this he never did in the heat of anger.

218

Tommy was now sleeping, and Tom bent over, lightly kissed the boy's hair, patted Calico on the shoulder, and motioned to Fronie to sit with them. With some difficulty he arose from the bed and walked out into the parlor, where Dovie and Bart sat stiffly at opposite ends of the room. Callie had joined them and sat halfway between them with Congo fanning her and holding a bottle of smelling salts before her. Nero stood rigidly behind Bart's chair.

Tom's entrance was the cue for Bart to break into a violent fit of coughing, but Tom ignored it; he had long ago seen through the ruse. He turned to Dovie.

"This man's yore husband, Dovie, 'n' he's the father o' your son." Tom spoke slowly, grimly, weighing each word. "Since the day he first came, he brought us trouble. He broke up yo' 'n' Tommy. Tommy ran away brokenhearted 'n' ain' seen hide nor hair o' him since he went. Had ter lambaste this nogood bastard ter git him ter marry yo'. Tommy born deaf 'n' dumb. I'm askin' yo' now, Dovie, 'n' I want that yo' tell me the truth. Yo' love this man Bart what yo' married up with?"

Dovie looked at her father and then at the man sitting in the other chair. She saw how Bart's youthful good looks had disappeared under the florid jowls and wattled chin. His once trim belly now sagged over the waistline of his breeches. His tousled hair, his rumpled, greasy clothes, his stinking breath, the rank odor of unwashed sweat which she knew always existed under his armits, the coarseness of his skin, black-pored and dirty, repelled her. Even the virility which had once appealed to her had been weakened by alcohol until she found it more and more difficult to arouse him. But her knowledge of the man penetrated further, beyond the outer grossness, to the hypocrisy of this mealy-mouthed, psalm-singing backwoods Tartuffe. She remembered his laziness, his selfishness, and his complete indifference to her. She recalled the nights when he had denied himself to her; his long lectures on what he considered her whorish perversions; and his unwilling submission to them in the end. She remembered his indifference to her deaf-mute son and, in some strange way, she blamed Tommy's affliction on

219

this man who had never fathered him, even believing that perhaps he had, in some manner unknown to her, marked him while still in her womb to revenge himself on her. And now her father stood before her asking her if she loved Bart. Love him? She hated him. As she continued to stare at him she compared him with the hard-muscled, still-handsome Ransom Lightfoot whose lips and hands had sought hers in the tool house that same afternoon.

Her eyes shifted from the crumpled, gross Bart to her father who was standing over her. For the first time, in the flickering candlelight, she saw that her father looked old. He had suddenly aged, and it frightened her. If he were to die, she would be left alone with Bart. Her father seemed to waver a little and she sprang from her chair to a steady him.

"Yo' askin' me if'n I love that? Yo' know better'n to ask me. Yo' know what he did ter me, a-gittin' me in a family way 'n' drivin' Tommy off. Tommy the only one I ever loved. But I married up with this one 'n' I've lived with him fer fifteen years. He ain' even a man. Cain' sire no more young uns. Drunk all the time 'n' stinkin' like a goat 'cause he never wash himself. Prayin' 'n' exhortin' 'n' takin' on all the time. Yo' askin' me if'n I love him? If'n he be struck dead this minute, couldn' shed nary a tear."

"Then he's a-gittin' out. Ain' havin' him 'roun' here no more. Sick o' him I am, great big lazy hog that he is. Ain' never done a day's work since he came here. Livin' off'n the fat o' the land 'n' all he kin do is drink corn 'n' set." He turned to Bart. "Yo're gittin' off'n this place. Understand? Yo' pack what trogs yo' got 'n' git. I'll give yo' a horse 'n' tha's a damn sight more'n yo' had when yo' came here. 'N' I'll give yo' a saddle so's yo' won' have ter ride on a shock o' corn husks. 'N' then I'll give yo' one hour ter git yore things together 'n' git t'hell off'n my land. 'N' if'n yo' don', by God, I'll trounce yo' with my own hands." He advanced to Bart, his fists clenched, his hands raised. Suddenly, about two steps from Bart, who sat slumped down in the chair, staring up at Tom, he stopped, wavered for a long moment, and then fell to the floor.

220

With a scream, Dovie was at her father's side. Callie rolled from her chair onto the floor beside him as Nero abandoned his post as sentinel behind Bart's chair to kneel beside him. He lifted his master's head and cradled it in his arms. Tom's eyes were open, staring, expressionless. Nero ripped open his shirt and with a frightened glance at Dovie, he jerked his head. Understanding him, Dovie pressed her ear to Tom's chest, but there was no answering heartbeat to reassure her.

"He's daid! My Tom's daid." Callie looked for denial in Nero's eyes, but he shook his head.

Bart's big hands, resting on the arms of the chair, pushed him up into a standing position, and he took a step toward the group on the floor.

"He's daid." He stared down at Tom. "He's daid 'n' he ain' shootin' off his mouth no more 'roun' here. It's God's justice. He a-tellin' me ter git off'n the place 'n' God punished him. Yo' a-tellin' me yo' won' shed no tear fer me if'n I die so God tooken him 'stead o' me. He's the one what had ter go 'n' not me. Ain' no one kin make me go now. No one! I'm masta here now. All this's mine. I'm Mista Bartholomew Boggs, masta o' Dove Cote Plantation 'n' masta o' The Patch Plantation too." He stared down again and nudged Nero with the toe of his boot. "Git him up off'n the floor. Git Honey ter make a box fer him 'n' git the niggers ter dig his grave 'n' then fetch old Aunt Nervy ter come 'n' lay him out. We'll bury him come mornin' 'n' I'll preach his funeral service. Ain' no use payin' out money fer a rev'nd when I'm one." He walked toward the door but stopped and turned around, pointing his finger at Nero. " 'N' after yo' finish all what I tol' yo' ter do, tell that Honey I want him ter whop Sippi. Ten strokes with the paddle 'n' pimentade after it. Tol' him that if'n he didn' do like I tol' him, he'd git whopped. Goin' ter be discipline 'roun' here from now on. I'm the masta now." He stalked out and slammed the door behind him.

Chapter XIV

THE FUNERAL of Thomas Verder, Esquire, of Dove Cote and The Patch, was a hasty and shoddy affair. Dressed in his best black suit, he was placed in a box hurriedly nailed together out of oak planking, with a pillow under his head and a nosegay of Callie's fuchsias in his hand. The family burying plot had not had a new occupant since the death of Tom's father and mother, both of whom occupied unmarked graves (there had once been wooden crosses to mark them but these had long since rotted away). The burial plot was in a crudely fenced section of the cow pasture, some little distance from the house, overgrown with nettles and bindweed, except around the edges of the rail fence where some cow had twisted her head through the bars to graze on the ranker vegetation which flourished inside. A grave had been dug there during the night and early the next morning, Tom was interred in the presence of Callie and Dovie, while Bart delivered a grudging prayer. It was, perhaps, the shortest prayer he had ever uttered, being merely a catalog of Tom's sins, a reminder to the Deity of his father-in-law's shortcomings. There was a wailing mass of black humanity around the grave, but these did not count. No other white person from the community had been notified of Tom's passing and, except for his slaves, his wife, and his daughter, nobody witnessed his burial except his son-in-law. It had seemed unnecessary to wake either The Dummy or Calico from their drugged sleep.

Bart had not slept the night before. But it was not sorrow which disturbed his sleep as it did that of Callie and Dovie. The howling of the slaves who had gathered around the big house prevented any thought of sleep, but even had he desired rest, Bart would not have taken it. He was far too interested in his plans for the future. In one short moment he had been transformed from a barely tolerated hanger-on to a man of affluence and authority. From having been ordered off the plantation, he was now in complete charge and, to his way of thinking, in complete ownership. He knew nothing of law but he did know that what belonged to a wife belonged to her husband, and that a woman had no authority to hold property as long as there was a male member of the family to inherit it. Callie, to be sure, had a dower right in the plantations, but Bart was ignorant of this, and as to Tommy's rights, well, Bart was nominally his father and Tommy was still a minor.

After the brief prayer was over, Bart took advantage of the slaves all being assembled to speak to them. He mounted the rickety stile which climbed over the fence into the burying ground where the mound of raw red earth marked Tom's last resting place. The weeping slaves were starting back to their quarters, turning their backs on Bart, when he yelled out at them.

"Hol' yore horses, there, yo' niggers! Pay 'tention to what I'm a-goin' ter say. Yore ol' masta he's daid 'n' buried 'n' he ain' yore masta no more. Yo' gotta new masta 'n' I'm him. Understand that! I'm yore masta now 'n' ain' puttin' up with no foolishments like'n yore masta Verder done. Now on yo' works, 'n' when I say yo' works, I means yo' gits out in them there fields come sunup 'n' yo' works till sundown, 'n' if'n it ain' all done what needs ter be done, yo' keeps on workin' till it is. He"—Bart pointed to the raw dirt—"bin too soft with yo'all. He a-coddlin' 'n' a-pettin' 'n' a-feedin' yo' till yo' got ter thinkin' yo' jes' as good's white folks. Well, yo' ain'. Yo' ain' nothin' but a bunch o' thick-skulled joltheads. Yo're niggers, tha's what yo' are—goddam ignorant niggers what ain' no better'n polecats. 'N' I ain' makin' no 'ceptions neither." He pointed a warning finger at Nero. "Ain' no one o' yo' better'n any o' the rest, not even if'n some o' yo' got a smidgin o' human blood. Ain' takin' no sass nor no back talk from none o' yo'. Yo' here ter work 'n' don' fergit it. I got me whops over 'n the barn, 'n' I got me paddles that'll take the meat right off'n yore bones 'n' I'm a-goin' ter use 'em. I got me whoppers who kin lay it on 'n' I goin' ter see that they does it. I got spancels 'n' I got leg irons 'n' I kin use 'em, too. 'N' if'n the whoppin' don' work, I'll sell yo' off. Sell yo' down South ter one o' them cane fields in Lou'siana. Yo'll wish yo' were back here 'cause they knows how ter handle niggers down there. So 'member! Ain' no more runnin' up 'n' sayin', 'Masta Tom suh, I wantin' ter do that,' o' 'Masta Tom suh, I'se got a miz'ry this mornin' 'n' cain' work.' Not by a damn sight! Ain' goin' ter be no more chitterlin' fries, 'n' huskin' bees, 'n' chivarees. No more jumpin' the stick neither. Yo' may be nothin' but a bunch of ignorant niggers but yo're goin' ter be Christian niggers from now on. We a-holdin' Wednesday-night prayer meetin's 'n' we a-holdin' Sunday services 'n' ain' nobody a-goin' ter get 'scused from them. Ain' goin' ter be no more screwin' less'n a man gits hisself married up with a wench afore me. Catch any man o' any wench neither a-screwin' 'roun', he goin' ter git it 'n' her, too. Whops a wench jes' as quick's I whops a buck. Now, git! Back ter work! 'N' each one o' yo' 'members what I'm a-sayin' if'n yo' wants ter keep the skin on yore ass."

He dusted his hands on his pants and followed Callie and Dovie, who were making their way toward the house. He reached it before them, passing them on the way without a word, and once in the house, he went into Tom's office, slammed the door, and bolted it. He had previously brought in a supply of corn and had had a bed moved into the office. Except at meals, the family saw little of him for five days, but Bart was not idle, nor was his brain addled by liquor. He was involved in making plans which included only himself.

Meanwhile life at Dove Cote proceeded almost as usual. Nero took over the duties of overseer there, following along in Tom's footsteps. The Patch was fairly well managed by Ransom Lightfoot, who was now thirty and a man. Much to Tom's surprise, he had turned out to be the most efficient overseer he had ever had. Ransom, granted an opportunity to learn, had applied himself, and had accepted both Tom's and Nero's instructions. Isolated as he was on The Patch, he had given up drinking, and with a continuous round of mulatto and black mistresses—which he impregnated with unerring regularity—he had derived both pleasure and satisfaction from his work there, as well as a steady increase in financial rewards. Tom and Nero had instructed him well and Ransom had been an apt pupil. He turned out to be an industrious worker, perhaps a mite hard on the slaves, but one who produced results in cash crops. His hard work and abstinence from liquor had kept him strong and youthful in looks and he had become a better-looking man than he had been a boy. Ransom was well aware of Dovie's interest in him, which he reciprocated only to the extent that a white woman was a novelty to him. He was curious about them, and now that Dovie had displayed an interest in him, he hoped to progress eventually beyond the few hurried and mainly one-sided gropings and experiments which Dovie had instigated with his cooperation. He was almost convinced, from what little he had known of Dovie, that there was no truth in the common belief that white women didn't like loving. Dovie sure did. She had surprised him by her actions. He wanted to find out more, and, for that matter, so did Dovie.

Dovie and Callie, during the days that Bart had sequestered himself in his room, had occupied themselves with the formalities of mourning. All the shades in the house were drawn, the shutters closed, and the piano draped with sheets. Callie, governed not only by her sorrow but her understanding of what was fitting and customary, cried almost continuously, breaking into hysterical and uncontrolled fits of weeping whenever neighbors and friends came to pay their calls of condolence. Dovie's grief equaled that of Callie's, but custom did not dictate that she demonstrate it so profusely, and besides, there was a restrained streak in Dovie's nature—an inheritance from her father—that forestalled such dramatic displays of her emotions.

Callie had all her garments, even the most intimate of her clothes, dyed a dark brown, as nearly an approximation of black as she was able to attain with the walnut hulls she was forced to use for the purpose. It was required to dip and dry the pieces of white underwear three times to bring them to the shade of rusty black that satisfied Callie. She had been embarrassed to attend Tom's funeral wearing colored clothes, even though she and Dovie were the only mourners, but she expiated her disrespect to Tom as soon as her clothes were dyed. She fashioned a small bonnet of black crepe to wear on her head, the flowing veils of which covered the still-golden glory of her hair, and once having become accustomed to the black costume, she adhered to it for the remainder of her life. Dovie too went into mourning dress, but only in her outer garments. As a daughter, she was not constrained by the local mores to mourn with the degree of lamentation imposed upon her mother.

The Dummy failed to comprehend the death of his grandfather. When he awoke, the morning after Tom's death, he recalled his grandfather's ministrations, but not having seen Tom in death, in the wooden box or being placed in the ground, he did not know that his grandfather was dead and gone forever, nor was it possible to explain the matter to him. He merely took it for granted that Tom was at The Patch. Calico realized what had happened but, for once, he was unable to communicate his knowledge to The Dummy. Consequently Tommy resumed his play as usual, although neither he nor Calico dared go to the grove to meet Kru. As for Kru, he had disappeared completely. A bed had been made for him in the hay after he had been taken down from his punishment, but the next morning he was gone and the tattered quilts on the hay had not been disturbed. Bart, remembering Tom's story of what Kru had done to his former master, had Dioubo watch over Tom's grave for two nights, fortified by a lighted lantern, but Kru did not appear. Nobody saw nor heard from him either at The Patch or at Dove Cote.

At the end of five days of comparative solitude, Bart emerged from Tom's office, demanding that his suit be sponged and pressed, his white shirt be washed, starched, and ironed, and his boots polished. He also gave instructions that Tom's horse should be brushed and curried, his saddle oiled and the hardware on it polished. He had a tub of hot water carried to the dove cote, shaved, washed himself, and dressed. Immediately after the midday meal, he mounted his horse and rode off to Brownsville, his objective the bank where he had done business.

The golden sun that shone down on him as he rode along was no more glorious than his thoughts or his plans. He had achieved far more than he had ever hoped for, and he was about to attain the great object of his hitherto thwarted ambitions—his church. For the last five days he had been building it in his dreams. He could see it now, standing white-spired and gem-windowed at the corner of the two intersecting streets in Brownsville. There was a small dwelling house now on the corner he had in mind, with a millinery shop on the ground floor, but he anticipated no difficulty in purchasing it from the widow who owned it. Nothing, no nothing, could stand in the way of his church! Everything had been worked out in his mind to the last infinitesimal detail—the pews, the pulpit, the organ, the communion service, the collection boxes, and the hymnals. He could close his eyes and picture the tripartite, Gothic-arched glass window which he planned behind the pulpit and, even more important, he could see its multicolored lights reflected on himself as he stood there, resplendent in glossy black broadcloth and white linen, facing a congregation of filled pews— because, of course, people would come from miles around to listen to his inspired words. And now it was possible! It would take a little time, of course, but what were a few months of watching his church being built compared to the futile years he had waited.

When he arrived in Brownsville, he rode directly to the bank, a false-fronted brick cube with heavily barred windows. Upon dismounting and trying the door, he found it locked. His watch told him that it was only four o'clock, and he had expected that a banker, like a plantation

227

owner, would continue his work until sundown. He rattled the doorknob enough to shake the door from its hinges and stopped only when he saw it open from the inside, but the white-haired Negro who poked his head out certainly was not banker Norsmith.

"Bank's closed, masta suh." The elderly Negro bobbed his head. "Ain' nobody here 'ceptin' me. Bank kindly closes at half-pas' three, masta suh, 'n' ain' open 'gain till eight o'clock come tomorrow mornin'."

"What the hell's the use o' a bank if'n it close up in the middle o' the afternoon? Ain' no way ter run a bank." Bart was disgruntled. His plans were formulated and he needed banker Norsmith's advice before he could proceed.

"Cain' say, masta suh." The aged Negro closed the door and Bart mounted his horse. It seemed too long a ride all the way back to Dove Cote only to return in time for the bank's opening on the morrow. Bart decided to call on Mrs. Salsman, whom he had seen only infrequently over the years, and see if he could wangle an invitation to stay overnight. As he passed her house, he was nearly deterred from stopping by the smart new chaise and the liveried coachman in front of her door. Recalling, however, that he was now the peer of any person in the neighborhood, he decided to stop anyway. He could at least knock on the door, and if Mrs. Salsman were occupied, he'd go back to Dove Cote. Much to his surprise, his knock was answered by an extremely fashionable young woman, whose modish garb of emerald-green bombazine was lavishly embellished with jet passementerie. It took him a while to realize it was Lorie. She stared at him blankly for a moment, then smiled in recognition.

"Well, I do declare! If'n it ain' the Rev'nd Boggs what married me. Kindly ter step in, Rev'nd. Maw 'n' I jes' talkin' 'bout yo' 'n' how yo' now masta o' Dove Cote." She stood aside to let him pass into the house, adding perfunctorily, "Please ter accept our sympathy on yore loss. If'n my husban' 'n' me had a-knowed, we'd of come ter the funeral."

Bart stepped inside, surprised first at the tawdry opulence of the interior, but even more by the heavy figure of Mrs. Salsman, ensconced in a big chair by the fire-place. Over the years she had put on considerabele weight. Her hair was streaked with gray, but it was enriched by a high tortoiseshell comb. A sprinkling of rice powder gave her face a ghostly whiteness which was accentuated by the twin circles of red on her cheeks.

"Ain' seen much o' yo', Rev'nd, 'roun' these parts lately." She seemed glad to see him after his long absence. "Like'n Lorie say, we sympathize with yo' folks over yore loss. Trust that Miz Verder 'n' Miz Boggs bearing up well under their heavy sorrow." She sighed lugubriously in observance of the conventions.

Bart thanked them both for their sympathy, pulling a long face and rolling his eyes back in what he considered a properly pious attitude.

"The Lord giveth 'n' the Lord He taketh away," he muttered. "Jes' in town ter see banker Norsmith but the bank it closed. Needin' me 'bout five thousand dollars." Bart had no real conception of what five thousand dollars was but it sounded sufficiently impressive to awe his listeners. "Thinkin o' buildin' me a church 'n' needin' some money ter git started on. 'S matter o' fact, that what I called here 'bout 'n' right glad that yore daughter here too. Wantin' the both o' yo' ter be members. Ain' askin' no contributions fer the buildin', less'n o' course yo' wants ter make them, but hopin' tho' that yo'll both 'tend onct the church's raised."

"New church, heh? 'N' right in town here?" Mrs. Sals-man was intersted. It would be an opportunity for her to display in public the new gowns which Lorie had given her. "Yo' ter be the rev'nd, of course?"

Bart nodded. "Ain' had no time fer preachin', what with runnin' two plantations," he admitted modestly, "but time come now when I kin devote myself ter my callin'. Called by the Lord I am ter rescue his sheep 'n' lead 'em ter the Promised Land. Cain' put off my callin' no longer. Lord's word gotta be obeyed. Cain' wait now ter git started. Goin' ter have the finest church outside o' Mobile. Steeple with a bell 'n' glass winders 'n' organ 'n' everything. Aimin' ter start meetin's 'fore it's finished so's we kin git ter baptizin' 'n' savin' souls. Tho't mayhap

I'd talk the matter over with yo', seein' as how yo' use ter be a member o' my congregation. Thinkin' perhaps if'n yo' could accommodate me, could stay the night here 'n' save me the trip back ter Dove Cote 'n' comin' back in the morning. 'Spects ter pay yo' o' course, but cain' till I gits ter see banker Norsmith come tomorrow" He turned to regard Lorie. "Wishin' yo' might stay fer a while too." Lorie's stylish figure had made an impression on him, and for the first time in years, he felt excited over the thought of a woman.

"Love ter, Rev'nd, but jes' cain'." Lorie said, affecting an air of extreme gentility. "Me 'n' my husban', we entertainin' at dinner tonight fer supper fer ten. Tha's how come I had Pip drive me in my new high-steppin' horse 'n' chaise what my husban' jes bo't fer me. Ordered me a new damask cloth 'n' a dozen napkins from Mobile but ain' come yet. Jes' have ter use the old ones what my mother-in-law heired me." She spread her hands in a gesture of affected despair. "But we'll be a-comin' ter yore new church, Rev'nd, me 'n' my husban' both. Thinkin' I'd better be gettin' me some new Sunday-go-ter-meetin' gowns made up jes' special. 'Bye, Mama. 'Bye, Rev'nd." She gathered up her voluminous skirts and swept out in a rustle of taffeta petticoats.

"Figures that if'n yo' stay all night, Rev'nd, 'n' has yore supper 'n' breakfast here 'n' what all"—Mrs. Salsman glanced archly at Bart—"a-goin' ter set yo' back five dollars, 'n' I a-makin' it less coun' o' yo' being a rev'nd."

"Like I a-sayin', cain' pay today."

"Credit's good, I reckon," Mrs. Salsman replied, stepping closer to Bart so that the overpowering odor of bay rum mixed with stale sweat reached him. "Boys ain' here no more. Both of 'em up 'n' married. Thinkin' mayhap yo craves a little lovin' afore we eat."

"Thinkin' mayhap we should do some prayin' fust." Bart did not want to step out of his role too quickly.

"Thinkin' prayin' kin wait." Mrs. Salsman came a step nearer, and Bart succumbed. After all these years of Dovie, another woman was a welcome change, and his flagging desires found new impetus in this woman's tired

230

but professional ministrations. She was not like Dovie—she let a man do what he wanted to do and did not force herself on him. Mrs. Salsman knew how to satisfy a man and make him feel like a man. He did not bother to put on his clothes again until next morning when he, dressed and fed but with a full day's growth of beard on his face, presented himself to the bank.

Inquiring from the same aged Negro who had spoken with him the day before, he was ushered into the small back room where Norsmith sat behind a green baize table, peering over his tiny, steel-rimmed spectacles at this lumbering figure of a man who seemed to fill the little room. He looked up, his watery blue eyes catching those of Bart's.

"Mista Boggs?" His voice was reedy—a quavering falsetto which seemed to deny any request before it was made.

"Rev'nd Boggs," Bart corrected him.

"What jes' now heired Tom Verder's Dove Cote 'n' The Patch?"

Bart nodded in acknowledgment.

"Sympathy." The single word emerged from Norsmith's thin lips as a gratuity that he begrudged. "What kin I do fer yo', Mista—that is I mean Rev'nd—Boggs?"

Bart was awed by this little man. "Kindly like ter know, that is, if'n yo' kin tell me, jes' how things stand here with Tom Verder's affairs. Seein' as how I heired his place, rightful far as I know."

Norsmith inclined his head slightly in acknowledgment of Bart's enquiry, thereby giving it his approval. "Jes' what yo' wantin' ter know, Rev'nd?"

"To know kin I git some money. Needin' me 'bout five thousand dollars," he said pompously. "Thinkin' that might be 'nuff but not 'xactly sure. Mayhap be needin' more."

Mr. Norsmith put his fingers together, meticulously matching tip with tip while he peered at Bart. "Tom Verder made a will," he pronounced, "willin' everythin' he had ter his daughter 'n' his grandson with a dower right fer his wife which in the event o 'her demise reverts ter his grandson. Know 'bout it 'cause I drew it up fer

231

him. So, he ain' heired yo' nothin' directly, nor legally yo' might say, yet so far's I kin see yo' heired it all in a way, 'ceptin' that which belong ter Miz Callie Verder. Yo' bein' his daughter's husban' 'n' father o' his grandson 'n' him bein' yet a minor, yo' in charge o' all Tom's estate 'n' if'n Miz Callie given yo' permission, yo' kin handle her part, seein' as how she a woman 'n' cain' rightly handle it herself. Up till yore son 'rives at his majority, which being ter say when he reach twenty-one, yo' handles everythin', 'ceptin' yo' must make an 'countin' ter take care o' Miz Verder's dower right 'n' have a separate 'countin' fer yore son come the time he attains his majority. That ain' so's ter say, howsomever, that yo' ain' got the right ter use the money's yo' sees fit, provided"—he underlined the word with a horizontal gesture of his index finger—"yo' has the consent 'n' approval o' Miz Verder 'n' yore wife in which yo' as guardian fer yore minor son must approve 'n' concur. Now, if'n Miz Verder she say yo' kin have the money 'n' Miz Boggs agree 'n' yo', speaking fer yore son, give yore consent, which I suppose yo' already have, ain' no reason why yo' cain' have Tom Verder's money 'ceptin' one."

Bart had become hopelessly entangled in Norsmith's verbiage, but he did understand the last few words. There was only one reason why he could not have the money. " 'N' what might that be?" he inquired anxiously.

"There ain' none." Norsmith pronounced momentously. "Now I ain' a-meanin' that Tom Verder wan't a man what I consider well-off. He were. Two fine plantations, stocked with slaves 'n' nary one o' the slaves blistered nor the plantations neither. Talkin' 'bout ready cash I am. Tom he got 'bout eight thousand here on deposit in this bank."

"Thought yo' sayin' there ain' no money."

"But Tom he owin' me a note come three years now, what he borrowed. Five thousand dollars he borrowed with interest at 12 per centum per annum. If'n yo' want ter figure that out, yo'll see there ain' no five thousand dollars left fer yo' ter draw. 'Course cotton ain' in yet 'n' when cotton sold yo' kin pay the note 'n' use the money what on deposit here. Howsomever, now that Tom

232

passed on, note gotta be settled, 'n' I'm feelin' it necessary ter take that money which here ter settle the note, so they ain' no way o' yo' gittin' yore hands on any ready cash till cotton's in 'n' sold. Kin talk 'bout it then."

"Cain' wait till then." Bart was willing to brook no delay in starting his church. "Tom tol' me fifteen years 'go when I wedded his daughter that come the day he pass on, he'd see to it I could build my church what I bin sacrificin' fer all these years. Fifteen years I bin workin' fer Tom Verder 'n' ain' a-wishin' he die neither, but his time's come 'n' I want my church. Want ter git started on it now. Cain' wait till cotton's in 'n' sold."

"A church?" Norsmith sucked at his teeth, nodded his head, and again placed his fingers together, this time making a steeple out of his index fingers. "Where?" he inquired.

It was Bart's turn to make a pronouncement. "Right here in Brownsville. Was thinkin' mayhap I could buy the widder Stimson's house. Good location, right in the center o' town. Goin' ter build me a right fine meetin' house, steeple 'n' all. Whole town a-goin' ter benefit. Be a fine buildin'."

Norsmith, who held a mortgage on the Stimson property on which he was finding it increasingly difficult to collect the interest, saw an opportunity to make some money. He'd foreclose on the property, get it for a mere fraction of its worth, then sell it to Boggs at a handsome profit. For the first time he smiled—merely a parting of his thin lips, but a smile nonetheless.

"Well now, Rev'nd Boggs, that's a laudable ambition, mighty laudable. This town a-needin' a fine meetin' house 'n' yo're right. That corner where the widder is is jes' the right place. Thinkin' I kin get that property fer yo' cheap, if'n yo' kindly 'low me to negotiate it fer yo'. Now as fer cash, Rev'nd. No need fer yo' ter worry 'bout that. Yo' got it. Tom Verder loaded down with niggers what he didn't need. Niggers as good as cash 'n' what with prices like'n they are now, if'n yo' sell off a few bucks 'n' wenches what yo' don' really need, yo' kin build yo'self the finest meetin' house in the Mississippi Territory. Good bucks a-bringin' roun' seven hundred 'n'

233

fifty 'n' house servants even more. Even saplin's a-sellin' well. Yo' sell off ten o' fifteen bucks 'n' a few saplin's, yo've got yore money. That is"—he allowed a slight frown to crease his forehead—"if'n of course, Miz Verder 'n' Miz Boggs a-willin'."

"They a-willin'," Bart said, "but jes' don' know how a body goes 'bout sellin' off niggers. Ain' no traders ever come 'roun' ter Dove Cote 'cause Tom he 'mos' never sold none. 'Sides, traders ain' payin' prices like'n yo' say."

Norsmith pursed his lips and shook his head vigorously. "Trader ain' no good. Better if'n yo' has a sale. Auction sale the best way ter get rid o' niggers. Got us one of the best auctioneers in the country right here in Brownsville. Mista Jedidiah Brookins. 'Course he mighty particular who he sells fer but if'n I speak a word fer yo', jes' likely he'll take on the sale fer yo' as a favor ter me." Norsmith scented another commission which he could later negotiate with the auctioneer. "Mista Brookins, what lives 'bout five miles out on the other side o' town is shore the one ter talk ter. Tell yo' what I'll do. Write yo' out a letter of introduction ter him 'n' ask him ter kindly help yo' in any way he kin. Seein' as how he's beholden ter me, he'll be glad ter. He'll get the highest prices fer yo'. Yo' kin advertise the sale all over the county. 'S a matter of fact, if'n yo' have a sale I'll come too. Miz Norsmith she bin lookin' fer a right likely boy fer to work in the stables 'n' take care o' her garden. Our old Jules he a-gittin' crippled with rheumatiz."

"Thank you kindly, Mista Norsmith." Bart was quite overwhelmed with the banker's helpful consideration of his problem.

"Ain' nothin', Rev'nd." Norsmith waved any obligation aside with an airy gesture. "We all got ter help a man o' God, 'n' help him bring the Word. Yes, suh, Rev'nd, yo' go to see Jed Brookins 'n' arrange ter sell off some of them niggers what's eatin' their fool heads off out there at Dove Cote. Been tellin' Tom for years he ought ter sell 'em off. I'll git the widder Stimson's house fer yo' cheap, 'n' I'll arrange with Mista Jenkins what has the sawmill over Orion way ter sell yo' the lumber cheap, seein' as how it's fer a place o' worship. Then, if'n yo' wants, I'll talk ter Clem Bigelow what's the best carpenter in the country ter build it fer yo'. I'll git yo' rock-bottom prices fer everythin' right down ter the last keg o' nails. That's my contribution ter yore meetin' house seein' as how it'll benefit the whole community 'n' put the fear o' God inter some people's hearts 'n' make 'em more honest 'n' upright. Yes suh, Rev'nd, yo' shore came to the right man."

Norsmith dipped a molting goose-quill into an inkwell and scratched off a few words on a piece of stationery with an elaborate letterhead, sprinkled sand on it from a pewter shaker, folded it carefully, and handed it to Bart. "Now, yo' jes' give this ter Jed Brookins, 'n' yo' let me know if'n he don' treat yo' right." He rose in a gesture of dismissal. " 'N' jes' ter show yo' that I'm behind yo' all the way, I'll put up one o' yore sale broadsides right here in the bank." Norsmith considered that he had done a good morning's work. He'd make a handsome profit on the Stimson house; he'd get a fat commission on the sale from Brookins, and he'd get commissions from the sawmill, the carpenter, and whatever other material Bart would order.

Bart tried to express his thanks. He wondered if he should favor Norsmith with a prayer but decided against it. Mumbling, "God bless yo', Mista Norsmith," he backed out of the room. Walking through the public section of the bank, he saw one or two men waiting at the teller's cage, and he straightened his shoulders and swaggered out the door. He, the Reverend Bart Boggs, had just had a conference with his banker. The cherished dream of his church was nearer reality now than it had ever been before. He was indeed a man of substance now. Life was changing. He'd had his night with Mrs. Salsman, his interview with Norsmith, and now he was on his way to Brookins, armed with the paper which would open the door for him. He clucked to his horse and set off down the road, singing a gospel hymn, timing the notes to the hoofbeats of Tom's horse.

Chapter XV

BART DEPARTED FROM the bank feeling that he had been most astute and successful in his dealings with Norsmith and that he had outsmarted the banker. He had more than achieved his purpose. Money would shortly be forthcoming to build his church, and if it meant the sacrifice of a few niggers, particularly those who were not productive, it would matter little. There were too many of the black varmints now, eating and sleeping and screwing without a care in the world.

As he turned out from the town onto the road that led to Brookins' place, he mentally reviewed those whom he would dispose of first. And what a pleasure that was! First on his list was Nero. There had always existed a certain antagonism, well-concealed though it was, between Nero and him. Bart had been jealous of him from the very first days he had seen him, when Nero had been riding on a fine horse with a good saddle while Bart had to make the journey to Dove Cote on his broken-down nag and corn-shuck saddle. Nor had he ever forgiven Nero the beating he had received, even though Nero had wielded the whip at the command of Tom. Much to Bart's digust, Tom had always favored Nero, treating him often like an equal, even going so far as to share his wenches with him. Bart had once overheard Tom and Nero comparing the merits of certain wenches whom they had both used at The Patch. Yes, he'd sell Nero! He'd be glad to see the last of that uppity nigger who thought himself as good as a white man. Damn his yellow rind!

Then there was that *it*—that Congo! Just the sight of him had always turned Bart's stomach. Fat, smooth and glossy like a brown slug under an upturned stone, he was enough to cause a body to puke. And the way he hung around Callie, combing her hair, washing her, and sleeping on the floor beside her bed. Wasn't even Christian to have an *it* like that around the house. What good was a man if he couldn't beget children? That thought made Bart himself ponder why he had never been able to sire a child himself. Dovie's fault, he decided. She'd weakened him so much with her unnatural practices that he had lost the ability to father a child. Dreaned the good seed right out of him and spilled it on the ground like that bastard in the Bible. Onan, was that his name? Well, God had punished Onan and now it was Bart's turn to punish Dovie. He'd show her: He'd put her in her place! Damned if he'd sleep with her anymore! He'd ride into Brownsville once a week and sleep with Mrs. Salsman, who knew how to please a man by letting him be a man and doing the things a man should do without all this nuzzling and kissing and fingering.

Too bad he couldn't get shet of Dovie and Callie as easily as he could dispose of slaves. For a few minutes he indulged in the fantasy of seeing Dovie and Callie up on the auction block. Dovie'd bring a good price; she was a handsome woman until you got to know that animal craving that she had. Nobody'd bid on poor old fat Callie, even if she did have long hair. Well, by God, there was one thing certain! He wasn't going to be run by two women. It occurred to him that Norsmith had said something about his having to get their permission to sell the slaves. Permission! He'd tell them and that would be it. Neither of them had ever seen Norsmith or ever would. Suppose he told them that Tom had owed money at the bank—and that was no damn lie either because he had —and that now he had to sell some of the slaves to pay the debt. That would hold them. They'd have to give their permission if they thought that Dove Cote and The Patch might be taken away from them. By jumping Jehosophat, it would be easy to pull the wool over their eyes. Women were stupid creatures anyway.

Now, whom else would he sell? Well, certainly that dagnab pinto Calico. Another nigger what was being treated like a white person, eating at the same table, off the same dishes, and of the same food. Sleeping with the Dummy too, and no telling what was going on between them. Anyway, The Dummy was old enough so's he didn't need a play-boy, and that Calico with his light face, housebroken as he was, would fetch a high price. There'd be no more snickering and fooling around between those two brats. No more mimicking him and making fun of him. From now on The Dummy would have to toe the mark. Yes suh! He'd make him come to service and sit through it. No matter if he didn't hear a word, and if he so much as contorted his face once in mimicry, Bart would give him the flat of his hand. By God! He was master now, and he'd not stand any interference from Dovie or Callie in regard to Dovie's bastard. He wished he knew who had fathered the whelp. He'd tried to get it out of Dovie, but she had never told.

And then that Kru, when they found him. Bart hoped that whoever bought him would work the hell out of him and whop him until he realized he had to wear clothes. Tom certainly was slack, letting that big bozal tramp the country as naked as a jaybird with his black pecker hanging down to his knees. He only worked when he felt like it and horsed around like a ten-year-old kid when he didn't. He wished now that he had waited a little longer that day and had actually caught Kru in some flagrant misdeed with The Dummy and Calico. He was sure that he had grounds for suspicion. Something had certainly been going on but he had jumped the gun. Well, with Kru out of the way he'd never have to look at that ugly face again.

Then there was Sippi! He didn't do a damn thing anymore and he was getting fatter and lazier every year. Might as well get rid of that Dolly, too. Either Sippi or some other buck had kept her swollen up over all the years. She'd foaled almost every year since he had been at Dove Cote and he was sick of looking at her bulging belly. But he'd keep Fronie. Old Aunt Ruthie was getting pretty feeble but she had taught Fronie how to cook, and Bart loved his victuals too well to deprive himself of a cook.

And there was Nate, who had charge of the dairy barn and some twenty cows. No use in keeping a herd of cows just to provide milk and clabber for niggers. Two cows would be enough for the household, and he could sell Nate and the cows too. Then that Oniontop who had been taken from the Romp Pasture to help Nate could go along too. Nate would probably set up a howl because he had been living with Marjory in one of the best of the cabins and they had a brood of young ones. But what the hell! Niggers weren't humans. He'd give Djoubo to Marjory and that would keep her quiet. Plug, who was in charge of cutting firewood for the house and for the cabins, could be dispensed with too. Let the bastards cut their own firewood when they got through work in the fields, and while they were cutting it they could cut enough for the big house, too. No sense in keeping all those pigs, either. Niggers could get along without fatback for their grits. That would release Judgment Day and Hoarhound. From now on, Bart was determined, the niggers were going to have their rations cut. Tom had fed them too well—more than necessary. They had hog meat and eggs and fresh vegetables and clabber and molasses and just about everything else. That was going to change.

Then there were some young bucks and wenches in the Romp Pasture who were just eating their heads off doing nothing. Turn them into hard cash and hymnbooks. Weed out some of the saplings and they'd pay for the organ. Then he'd go over to The Patch and pick out some of the niggers there. The Patch made him think about Ransom Lightfoot. What would he do about him? Better keep him. He had to have a white overseer at The Patch and Lightfoot seemed to know his business, even though he was a damned truckling son-of-a-bitch, always sucking Tom's ass and that Nero's, too. Well, they'd all know who was boss now.

He let his thoughts wander farther afield. After he'd built his church, he'd sell some more niggers. No use in living in a log house like Dove Cote. He'd tear it down and build himself a brick house and have a coach and four. The Reverend Bartholomew Boggs, Pastor of the First Church of Christian Holiness and True Faith of Brownsville, couldn't live in a log house. Not by a damn sight. Hell, he wished he had a good swig of corn. Riding made him thirsty.

A weed-grown driveway led up to an unpainted house whose only claim to distinction was the two-story gallery which sagged along the front. Bart decided that it was Brookins' place. An obese man sat on the lower gallery, whom Bart took to be Brookins himself. A thatch of brick-red hair covered his head, and his beard was so thick and bushy it was difficult to figure out just how he ever found the way to his mouth. He was attired in a pair of stained and soiled butternut trousers, and what might have once been a white shirt over whose front a profusion of gravy, egg, and grease stains testified to the man's taste in food. Two slate-colored bunioned feet were propped against the broken rail of the gallery. Beside the tilted-back chair a Negro wench was sprawled on the floor. Brookins was playfully tickling her belly with a thin switch upon which a tuft of leaves had been left at the end. He neither moved nor stopped his play as Bart rode up, looped his horse's reins over the hitching rail, and negotiated the rickety steps which led to the gallery.

"Yo' Mista Brookins what sells niggers?" he asked.

The man nodded in affirmation.

"Rev'nd Bartholomew Boggs o' Dove Cote Plantation 'n' The Patch Plantation what were Tom Verder's 'til he died."

Again the man nodded, and this time he dropped his feet from the rail and nudged the wench with a dirt-encrusted toenail. "Git t' hell outa here, Venus, 'n' pin up yore dress. Look like this gen'lemun 'n' I a-goin' ter talk bizness. He a-wantin' ter sell some niggers, I reckon. Bring out that jug o' corn."

"I'm temp'rance, I am"—Bart smiled wanly—"seein'

240

as how I'm a rev'nd, but mouth got mighty dry 'n' dusty a-ridin' out here. Thinkin' perhaps I'd 'cept a drink even if'n it's corn."

"Don' have ter be." Brookins shrugged his shoulders. "Kin have spring water if'n yo' wants but never knew a rev'nd yet but didn't like a snort o' corn when none of the old chick-a-biddies o' his congregation wan't snoopin' 'roun'." He pointed to another chair on the gallery— a straight chair with a cowhide seat. "Set."

Venus reappeared, her finger hooked through the handle of a jug which she handed to Brookins, who drank long and deep. He wiped the jug with the palm of his hand and offered it to Bart who drank even longer and deeper, welcoming the whisky as it made a comfortable ball of warmth in his stomach.

"Now we kin talk." Brookins accepted the jug back from Bart and set it down midway between them. He took the letter from Norsmith which Bart handed to him, unfolded it, pored over it for several moments, then lifted his head to stare at Bart.

"Mista Norsmith a-sayin' as how yo' got niggers ter sell. Ain' rightly doin' business with no man I don' know but Mr. Norsmith he a-vouchin' fer yo' so guess it all right." He pointed to the jug, "Help yo'self if'n yo' wants. If'n yo' got some niggers ter sell yo' come ter the right man. Git yo' a higher price'n any other. Ain' never had a sale yet but what I got higher prices fer niggers'n anyone else. Ain' nary a one like me what kin git the men in a good mood. Jes' got ter tell 'em some dirty stories 'n' git em laffin', tha's all. Keep 'em entertained. Git 'em in a good humor 'n' keep 'em that way. Man a-laffin' his fool head off ain' a-thinkin' o' his poke. When'd Tom Verder die?" he asked abruptly.

" 'Bout a week 'go. I his daughter's husband 'n' I heired both places," Bart boasted. "Tom he had too big a herd. Got ter cut it down. Never scarcely sold a nigger in the fifteen years I bin there 'n' they jes' increasin' till we got more'n we needs, 'specially house servants 'n' trained hands."

"Bring the best price, that kind do. Got any nice yaller wenches? Big demand fer 'em." Brookins' little eyes sparkled in anticipation. "Shore likes ter have some toothsome wenches fer the men ter finger. Puts 'em in a good mood. Git a man horny 'n' he ain' thinkin' how much he a-apayin' fer a fancy wench till he gits her home 'n' his old woman starts givin' him hell."

"Kin put in five o' six light ones, I guess. Mos' o' Tom's stock at Dove Cote run ter the light side. That at The Patch blacker but got a white overseer there now what a-sirin' light ones."

"Strong black bucks 'n' light-colored wenches is what sells today. How many head yo' got all told yo' wantin' ter sell?"

"Ain' sure 'xactly. Might be some twenty-five o' thirty."

" 'Tain' 'nuff. Got me some fifteen o' so here what I picked up cheap at other sales. Kin put 'em in but need 'bout fifty 'n all. We kin advertise it as the biggest sale o' the year in the county. People come from all over if'n they know fifty head a-goin' ter be sold. Verder had a good reputation 'n' everyone a-knowin' he got prime niggers. Now . . . le's git down ter bizness."

Bart's euphoria evaporated as he discovered that it was going to cost him money to sell his stock. Brookins enumerated item after item which could cut down the net amount received. To each separate item, Bart hemmed and hawed, but conceded in the end. The sale must be advertised for several weeks in the weekly *Courant,* the newspaper that was published in Brownsville. Handbills would have to be printed and posted in all the surrounding towns. Important purchasers like, for instance, Warren Maxwell of Falconhurst Plantation in the next county, would have to be notified by mail. Decent clothing would have to be supplied for the slaves to be sold: nobody would believe he was buying prime stock if they appeared on the block clad in dirty osnaburg shifts and work-stained trousers. A platform and slave block would have to be built at Dove Cote, and Brookins cautioned that it should be built at some distance from the house so that the womenfolk would not be able to hear the prurient anecdotes with which he planned to enliven the sale. Then there was the necessity of hiring a

242

clerk—someone who could read, write, and figure. And on the day of the sale, Bart would have to barbecue an ox or a couple of hogs. A barrel of corn was indispensable in order to get the buyers in a frame of mind for bidding. The more Brookins talked, the more Bart saw his money evaporate and then, most discouraging of all, Brookins informed him that he would expect a ten-percent commission on all sales.

Bart had no conception of what ten percent might be until Brookins explained that out of every dollar taken in, he would expect to receive one dime. The receipts of the sale, Brookins informed him, would be turned over to Mr. Norsmith at the bank, who would pay him his ten percent, deduct two percent for a handling charge, and credit the rest to Bart in the bank. This, Brookins assured him, would guarantee Bart fair and honest treatment, as neither he nor Brookins would handle the money, leaving it all in the hands of good, honest Mr. Norsmith. Thus Brookins managed his own straight ten percent and took care of Norsmith for his recommendation of himself to Bart.

Brookins suggested that he ride into Brownsville with Bart and that together they stop at the *Courant* office to place the ads and contract for the printing of the handbills. They reached the place and found that they could get the ads in the *Courant* of that week; the paper was scheduled to appear on Thursday but was usually a day late. Bart demurred at the price of the full page and reading notice he wanted, and the publisher, in order to induce him to use a full page at the regular price for three weeks, agreed to print one hundred broad-sides at no additional cost, using the same copy and the same type. After considerable argument between the publisher and Brookins on one side and Bart on the other, Bart agreed to pay the excessive price of sixty dollars for the three full-page advertisements, but not until after the sale. Bart considered advertising a waste of money, but Brookins threatened his withdrawal from the auction unless Bart consented to give it publicity, and Bart tempered his extravagance by deciding to put one more sapling in the sale.

After a good deal of discussion among the three, the copy for the advertisement was written. An old woodcut, used in most of the advertisements for slave auctions during the previous decade and showing the grinning face of a young Negro, was unearthed and again utilized in the center at the top of the page. Then followed, in elaborately fancy type, the stereotyped message:

AUCTION! AUCTION! AUCTION!

NEGROES! NEGROES! NEGROES!

Saturday, July 26

at

DOVE COTE PLANTATION
East of Brownsville

To Close the Estate of Thomas Verder, Esq., deceased, will be offered for sale at auction to the highest bidder fifty or more servants, carefully chosen for health and soundness and sold for no fault. MEN and WOMEN, BOYS and GIRLS. Trained house servants and artisans. Vigorous field hands. Anybody desiring good Negroes can obtain same at their own price by attending this big sale.

FREE BARBECUE
FREE DRINKS

Largest Auction Sale of
Negroes in the County this
Year!

Sale starts at ten o'clock rain or shine and lasts till all are sold. All the servants offered are

guaranteed unencumbered and free from vice.
Terms cash!

Jedidiah Q. Brookins
Auctioneer

The pubisher promised personally to set the advertisement and guaranteed that the third insertion of the ad would be distributed on the 24th, just two days before the auction. Brookins promised to call for the broadsides and to tack them in public places throughout the county. The publisher, by way of parting, said that he intended to attend the auction and that he would carry a story about its results in the *Courant*.

Boggs was triumphant as he left Brookins and galloped toward home after a day of successful planning. His visionary church would cost him only a few slaves, some of whom he would be glad to be rid of. After all these years of mere toleration he was about to achieve his life's ambition—to be a real reverend, preaching in his own church, with the fawning respect of the whole countryside. Now nothing could stand in his way. Nothing!

Chapter XVI

WHEN BART ARRIVED back at Dove Cote, he was met by a sullen Sippi who, although his back was partially healed from the ten strokes his master had imposed upon him, nevertheless complained whenever he had to exert himself. His slow movements, his constant mumbling under his breath, and his surliness provoked Bart who was, in fact, now that the sale was decided upon, disturbed over breaking the news to Dovie and Callie. He found in the luckless Sippi an object on which to wreak his ill-humor, and when Sippi came up to take his horse, he slashed at him violently with his riding whip. That Sippi, ducking to avoid the blow, evaded the full brunt of it only angered Bart the more. He dismounted, throwing the reins at Sippi.

"Wipe that look off'n yore ugly face, boy. Ain' havin' no stubborn niggers 'roun' here. Better yo' grin 'stead o' scowl o' yo' goin' ter git ten more."

"Please, masta Bart suh," Sippi said, in deadly terror of another whipping. "Ain' stubborn. Back jes' hurtin', tha's all. Cain' smile when my back's achin', kin I, masta Bart suh. Yo' knows I am a good boy, masta Bart suh. Ain' never caused yo' no trouble, never." Sippi essayed an ingratiating grin.

" 'N' ain' never done a lick o' work in yore life neither. Lazy luggard, that what yo' are. But yore a-goin' ter fin'

246

out. Goin' ter sell yo', I am. Goin' ter put yo' up fer sale 'n' goin' ter sell yo' to a masta what looking fer a hard-workin' fiel' hand. He'll work yore goddam ass off'n yo' 'n' mayhap yo'll 'member how easy yo' had it here."

The threat of another lashing had frightened Sippi much more than the threat of being sold. He'd heard Tom threaten more than once to sell one of the hands. Callie threatened almost daily to sell Congo to some master who would put him to work out in the fields. During his lifetime, Sippi could count on the fingers of one hand those slaves whom he had known who had been sold. To him it was inconceivable that he would ever be any other place besides Dove Cote, though he was reminded of the trip he had taken with Tom when Djoubo had been purchased. He remembered the procession of slaves who had stood on the auction block and been sold. Yes, the thought had occurred to him that he too might one day be sold, but it was such a remote possibility that it never had any reality for him. He was a Dove Cote boy and Dove Cote servants were never sold.

Bart followed Sippi and the horse into the barn, and while there fortified himself with a quick swig of corn before going into the house. On his way from the barn to the house he saw Dovie's face briefly at the window, but it vanished quickly, and when he entered through the door into Tom's office, she was there to confront him. They had barely spoken to each other since Tom died but now, with anger blazing in her eyes, she stood before him, barring his way.

"Where yo' bin?" she demanded. "Yo' didn' come home las' night. Sleepin' up with some whore, I 'magine."

"None o' yore goddam business!" Bart shouted, emboldened by whisky. "We a-goin' ter talk. Got news fer yo' that yo' not a-goin' ter like but cain' help it. Like it o' not it's the truth 'n' all yore papa's doin's. Git Callie in here 'n' tell her to leave that Congo where he is. She gotta learn ter walk by herself. 'N' comb her own hair, too," he added.

He seated himself before the worn deal table which

247

had served Tom as a desk, and loosened his short collar and the waistband of his trousers, grunting in relief as he did so. Callie teetered into the room and sank down onto a chair like a balloon collapsing. Dovie, her eyes still on Bart, edged cautiously back onto a chair.

"Bin ter the bank, I have." He surveyed them both. "Had a busy day what with one thing 'n' the other. Ol' Man Norsmith at the bank he have bad news fer us. Seems like'n Tom, he borryed money from the bank two, three years ago. Ain' never paid it and it a-drawin' int'rest at twelve percent." Bart congratulated himself on remembering this technicality which, although he did not understand it himself, sounded sufficiently ominous to impress a woman. "Ol' Man Norsmith he a-sayin' we got ter pay it and it more'n eight thousand dollars. Sayin' he kin sell Dove Cote ter pay it but sayin' if'n we wants we kin sell off some o' the herd 'n' do it that way. Cain' have all these useless niggers 'roun' here a-eatin' their heads off 'n' jes' standing 'roun' like that there stupid Sippi, 'n' jes combin' Callie's hair like'n that Congo, 'n' jes' playin' like'n that Calico. Cain' afford it no more. Got ter sell off a few fiel' hands too 'n' some wenches 'n' some o' the saplin's at the Romp Pasture. Got ter sell off some from The Patch too 'n' sure as hell goin' ter sell that goddam Kru what don' do nothin' at all. Take a lot o' niggers ter pay that money we a-owin' at the bank but gotta pay it 'cause if'n we don', Norsmith he a-sayin' he a-goin' ter sell Dove Cote ter pay it. Better if'n we sell a few niggers than losin' this place. Ain' no fittin' place ter live at The Patch."

Neither Dovie nor Callie had ever been to The Patch so they had no conception of what it was like, but they had heard enough from Tom to fear it. Dove Cote was their home and as their home they loved it. The mere thought of having to leave its familiar protection terrified them. Callie's attitude toward Bart underwent a slight change. At least he was a man and competent to cope with such a complicated business matter, which was more than she could do. But Dovie was not so easily impressed and considered the matter. How she wished she were a man! She had a feeling she could handle things much better than Bart.

" 'N' if'n we sell the niggers, that goin' ter pay everything?" she asked finally.

Bart nodded his head portentously. "Got ter git yore permission ter sell 'em. Not that it amount ter anythin' howsomever, but jes' got ter ask yo'. Norsmith says this place all mine now"—an all-inclusive wave of his hand denoted his ownership—"everythin' here 'n' at The Patch mine now. But Ol' Man Norsmith he a-sayin' I'd better ask yo' both seein' as how yo' Tom's wife 'n' daughter. So, what yo' say? Yo' both willin' I sell the niggers 'n' save Dove Cote o' yo' wantin' ter keep the sons-o'-bitches 'n' lose yore home?"

"We cain' sell Congo." Callie wiped her eyes with a bit of black cambric. "Cain' git 'long 'thout him. 'N' he's mine. Brung him here with me. He ain' no Dove Cote servant."

"Sure as hell got ter sell the bastard."

" 'N' Calico?" Dovie asked. "Ain' no one kin talk with The Dummy 'ceptin' him. Ain' a-goin' ter sell The Dummy's play-boy."

"Cain' keep him 'roun' jes' ter talk ter The Dummy. Better he go than yo' lose yore home."

Callie looked at her daughter and burst into tears. Dovie, as fearful as her mother, managed to keep herself under control. She had no reason to doubt Bart's statement. Although Tom had never talked business with his womenfolk, she had heard him mention the note at the bank, although he had never seemed worried about it. It was difficult for her to believe that the stability of Dove Cote might vanish and she would be left homeless.

"Ain' necessary ter sell neither Congo nor Calico," she stated emphatically. " 'N' we ain' goin' ter sell them. We got plenty o' niggers 'roun' here 'thout sellin' them two. 'N' ain' sellin' Nero neither, jes' in case yo' got it in your mind. Papa said Nero a-knowin' as much about runnin' this place as he did. We a-goin' ter need him more'n ever now."

"Mista Norsmith 'n' Mista Brookins—he the one which sell the niggers—they both say we gotta put some house servants in the sale ter bring the buyers. Nero he's a house servant, so's Congo 'n' so's Calico. What for we a-needin' Nero now? Tom' dead 'n' don' need Nero ter flunky him. Mista Brookins say we gotta put in house servants 'n' we ain' got no others. I a-puttin' Sippi in. He's mine too. Guess if'n I kin put my own boy in, yo' kin too." Bart had not anticipated this opposition on Dovie's part.

"Won't!" There was a finality in Dovie's one grim-mouthed word which precluded any argument. "Now yo' jes' look here, Bart Boggs! This my papa's place 'n' so's The Patch. My papa he worked here all his life 'n' this his'n. Now it's mine 'n' it ain' your'n. Yo' came here nothin' but a pauper 'n' yo' ain' sayin' all this your'n 'cause it ain'. If'n we got ter sell some niggers, we'll sell 'em, at least some o' 'em. But we ain' sellin' Nero nor Calico nor Congo. Reckon I got somethin' ter say 'bout what we a-sellin' 'n' I'm a-sayin' it now. Mista Norsmith ain' a-askin' yo' ter git my permission less'n it necessary." She rose from her chair, put her head out the door, and called "Fronie!"

Fronie's quick appearance betrayed the fact that she'd been eavesdropping in the hall.

"Yas'm, Miz Dovie ma'am."

"Go out 'n' ring the bell. Call all the hands in from the fields. Send Sippi out ter the quarters 'n' tell him ter bring in all the wenches. Git Uncle George 'n' A'nt Nervy to bring all the young uns from the Romp Pasture. Want 'em all lined up."

"What yo' a-goin' ter do?" Bart saw his authority slipping. "I ain' said nothin' 'bout ringin' no bell 'n' callin' the hands in." He had never been able to stand up to Dovie and he felt that once again she had gained the master hand. " 'N' 'sides," he added lamely, " 'tain' right fer a white woman ter see them young bucks from the Romp Pasture. Ain' half o' 'em got britches on. Nekkid, they are."

"Seen yo' nekkid 'n' guess a buck no dif'rent from yo'. Goin' ter pick out what ones we a-goin' ter sell 'n' don't make me no neverminds if'n yo' say so o' not."

"That's my job. Ain' no job fer wimmen, a-foolin'

'roun' with niggers. Man's work it is. I'm yore husband 'n' I'm masta 'roun' here. I forbid yo' ter go out there 'n' look at a lot o' stinkin' niggers. Yo' stay in here with Callie. Place fer wimmen is in the house."

"Shet up! I'm goin' 'n' if'n yo' want ter come along yo' kin. I pick 'em out 'n' yo' got a chance ter say whether o' not yo' likin' those that I pick out. Listen ter yo', I will. But I'm a-tellin' yo' now, Bart Boggs, ain' nothin' a-goin' ter happen 'roun' here 'cept I knows 'bout it 'n' I have a finger in the pie. Like it o' not, tha's the way it's goin' ter be. Yo 'ain' a-runnin' thin's here at Dove Cote yet."

"Mr. Norsmith, he say . . ." Bart felt he could quote the banker with authority.

"Don' give a tinker's damn what Ol' Man Norsmith say. He ain' a-runnin' me 'n' he ain' a-runnin' this place either. If we owin' him money we'll pay it. Thinkin' mayhap I'll ride inter town come mornin' 'n' tell him ter mind his own bizness 'n' I'll mind mine."

"Now, Dovie." Bart was willing to accede to any request she might make to keep her from talking to Norsmith and uncovering his duplicity and his plans for a new church. He had expected Dovie to swallow his story hook, line, and sinker. He saw that he would have to use a certain amount of diplomacy or the jig would be up. "Ain' necessary fer yo' ter go ter all that trouble. Mista Norsmith he an honest man 'n' don' yo' rile him. Yore papa done business with him all these years 'n' yo' knowin' he's honest. 'N' he mighty good too. Could of taken Dove Cote 'thout askin' us but he tellin' me 'bout how we kin sell the servants 'n' he writ me a letter ter Mista Brookins tellin' Mista Brookins ter take care o' me. Mista Norsmith he a-sayin' he jes' cain' bear ter have his dear friend Tom Verder's widder 'n' daughter out 'n the cold 'thout no place ter lay their heads. He wan' called 'pon ter do none o' them things but jes' did 'em outa the kindness o' his heart 'n' his friendship fer yore papa. Look seemly, wouldn' it, if'n yo' go a-flouncin' in 'n' argifying with him after all he done ter help us keep Dove Cote. What he a-goin' ter think o' Tom Verder's daughter? Ain' no way fer a refined lady
251

ter act—ter go traipsin' 'roun' stickin' her nose into man's business."

"Well . . ." Dovie hesitated. She could see some wisdom in Bart's remarks. It was true, white women did not mix in men's affairs.

"Yo' helps me pick out the niggers we want ter sell if'n yo' wants. Fittin' that yo' do that if'n yo' wishes, 'n' after we gits through"—he came closer and reached around her waist with an affectionate gesture, something he had not done for years—"thinkin' mayhap we kin go out in the dove cote where we kin be alone. Bin a-thinkin' 'bout yo' all the way home 'n' wishin' I could be with yo'."

Callie sighed with relief to see harmony established between the two while she listened to the plantation bell clanging outside. The threat of losing Dove Cote had terrified her, and that of selling Congo nearly as much. She managed to get to her feet, calling for Congo to come and help her.

"Yo' ain' a-sellin' pore ol' Congo, I'm hopin' Jes' cain' live 'thout him. He the only one what helps me with my headaches."

"Ain' no one sellin' Congo, Mama," Dovie reassured, although in truth she would not have minded seeing him go. A man who was not a man disgusted her. "Cain' see tho' why yo' wantin' him. Think yo'd rather have a nice wench."

Callie shook her head. "Used ter him, I am. Need him." She gave her arm to him as he appeared in the doorway and left them. Bart, maintaining his role of affectionate husband, squeezed Dovie's waist.

"Yo' didn' come home last night. Bet yo' stayed with that Miz Salsman. Jes' bet yo' did," she said, all trace of anger gone.

Bart appeared properly shocked. "Miz Salsman! Why, Dovie, how yo' run on. What makes yo' think I stayed with her? Got yo', ain' I?"

"Where'd yo' stay then?"

"Why, Dovie, yo' jes' mistrustin' me." Bart's big hand crept up to cup her breast. "Banker Norsmith he asked me ter spend the night at his house. Stayed with him 'n' Miz Norsmith. Mus' say, howsomever, she don' set much of a table. We jes' had grits 'n' fried eggs 'n' yams 'n' mighty scarce on them, too. No wonder he got a lot o' money, that Mista Norsmith. Don' spen' none on feedin' hisself." He felt that the embroidery had substantiated the lie. At least Dovie seemed to believe it.

Actually it mattered little to her where he had stayed. In a way she hoped it might have been with Mrs. Salsman. It would have given her an advantage over him—something to reproach him with. His fumbling hand stirred her, but only because it was a man's hand, not because it was his. She wished that it might be Ransom's. Her brief encounters with him promised much. He did not have to be tempted and cajoled like Bart. Ransom's response was immediate and vigorous and necessitated no preliminary exercise of her talents and, unlike Bart and reminiscent of Tommy, Ransom had no scruples. Whatever she initiated he was only too willing for her to finish, and he did not admonish her for her carnality or pray over her, naming her Jezebel. But despite her longings for Ransom, the warmth and pressure of Bart's hand aroused her, and she felt closer to him than she had in a long time.

Together they walked out the door. The Dummy was riding Calico in the yard, and he sensed that something unusual was happening. The hands were beginning to straggle in from the field in answer to the summons of the bell. Women were coming from the direction of the quarters, and Aunt Nervy and Uncle George were approaching with their menagerie of naked and half-clad charges. Nero put in an appearance from the stables, and Dovie told him to line them all up, first the men, then the women with whatever children belonged to them, and then the adolescents and the children from the Romp Pasture.

It took some minutes for Nero to achieve order out of the milling crowd, but when he had them in the semblance of a line, Dovie and Bart walked slowly along before it. Dovie knew most of the adults by name. She had lived with them all her life and they were, in a manner of speaking, her family. She passed by those she knew the best, choosing the younger and the stronger of the hands as well as the more buxom and the younger of the women. Bart would have taken some of the older whom he knew would soon be pensioners, but Dovie would not allow it.

None of the slaves knew, of course, why they were being singled out and Dovie offered no explanation, merely asking those chosen to step out of line and join the separate group. When it came time to choose from the Romp Pasture group, she did not know how to make her selection. At Bart's insistence, she took the lighter-colored ones, for she knew, or at least so he informed her, that they would bring the better price. When they had finished with their selection, Dovie sent Bart to the house for Tom's old ledger and together they laboriously wrote down the names of the ones they had chosen, dismissing them one by one. The list totaled fourteen bucks, eight wenches, and twelve adolescents. These would be supplemented by some extras chosen from The Patch although Nero, who had been made privy to their actions, advised against depleting The Patch herd. It was a larger plantation than Dove Cote and, Nero counseled, it needed all the hands they could muster there to get the work done.

"I'm a-goin' ter ride over ter The Patch come mornin'." Dovie was not asking Bart, merely stating her intention. "Takin' Nero with me, 'n' we'll pick out 'bout ten from over there. Ain' no use 'n yore goin', too. Plenty ter oversee here if'n we a-goin' ter have that sale. Want Dove Cote lookin' fust-rate if'n everyone a-comin' here. Want the tall grass all mowed down 'n' whole place picked up neat 's a pin. Ain' goin' ter have nobody a-sayin' Tom Verden's place lookin' poverty-stricken. 'N' wantin' yo' ter ride inter Brownsville 'n' get me two bolts o' black cotton cloth, good 'n' heavy fer to make britches out of, 'n' plenty o' thread 'n' needles. Wantin' one bolt o' white muslin too, cheapest kind yo' kin git, fer shifts fer the wenches. If'n we a-sellin' Dove Cote servants they goin' ter be a credit to my papa."

"Ain' fittin' that yo' go over ter The Patch 'lone."

"Ain' goin' 'lone, Nero goin' with me."

"He nothing but a nigger. White women cain' go out ridin' 'roun' the country with a nigger. People talk."

"Let 'em. Their talk don' butter my bread. I'm a-goin' 'n' that's that. Yo' a-goin' ter Brownsville, I'm a-goin' ter The Patch. We both got work ter do."

"Well, if'n yo' say so," Bart consented, fearful lest Dovie might change her mind and send him over to The Patch and make the journey to Brownsville herself. At least there'd be no danger of her talking with Norsmith if she went to The Patch.

Dovie paid no attention to his consent. She would have gone without it. All these years, she had had no curiosity about The Patch. Now she longed to see it. She reached for Bart's hand and placed it around her waist again. And . . . Ransom Lightfoot was at The Patch. Tomorrow they could have more than a few stolen minutes in the tool house or the corn crib. Ransom Lightfoot was a handsome fellow. She pulled Bart's arm closer around her and placed his hand on her breast.

Chapter XVII

DOVIE, WHOSE INTEREST had seldom extended beyond the flummery that Aunt Ruthie was to make for dinner; seeing that The Dummy had clean shirts; engaging in small talk with Callie; and endeavoring in one way or another to elicit the favors from Bart which she demanded, embarked upon the administrative duties of the plantations. This she did over Bart's head, countermanding his orders as she saw fit and making her authority felt not only at Dove Cote but at The Patch. She had learned much over the years by listening passively to Tom and Nero discuss plantation matters, and now she was putting into practice what she knew. In this she was assisted by Nero.

Bart seemed powerless to restrain Dovie. He stormed and ranted, trying to belittle her ability because she was a woman, but his objections to her initiative amounted to little. Aided and abetted by Nero at Dove Cote and by Ransom Lightfoot at The Patch, Dovie's orders were the ones which were carried out, while Bart's were disregarded. He knew almost nothing about plantation management whereas Nero, having spent a lifetime at Tom's side, and Ransom, who had learned all he knew from Tom and Nero, were both experienced. When, as often happened, Bart tried to give orders on his own, he was informed by the drivers that "Miz Dovie done say we uns ter do it this way. Cain' stop less'n Miz Dovie she say so, masta Bart suh."

It was frustrating, but Bart reassured himself that the day of the auction was getting closer and that soon he would have the money to start on his church. That would keep him busy in Brownsville, and he didn't much care what happened at Dove Cote. He would have a far more worthy occupation than the mere picking of cotton—the saving of souls. He did, however, busy himself carrying out the preparations for the auction sale. The far barn was cleaned out, the hard-packed dirt floor swept, part of two walls knocked out to let in more light, and a platform about six feet high erected at one end on which a stand about three feet square was built to further elevate the slave for sale so that he would be plainly visible. The deal table from Tom's office was placed on the platform for the clerk, and a rough pulpit was built for Brookins, which Bart figured he could use after the auction for his Sunday sermons and prayer meetings. The barn would make a good meeting house for the slaves and the platform could well be his rostrum. Accordingly he took some pains in its construction.

A detail of field hands, swinging scythes, mowed down the high grass and weeds surrounding the barn, and a long hitching rail was built for the convenience of those attending the auction. Having finished their job, the same detail was set to digging two pits for the hogs Bart intended to barbecue. Two sawhorses were set up for the barrel of whisky which he had purchased from the tavern keeper in Brownsville. This he had been forced to pay cash for, as well as for the yards of cloth he had purchased at the store and which was now being made into shifts for the women and shirts and breeches for the boys. Fronie was supervising this work, as well as doing most of the cooking, and the kitchen was filled with six seamstresses, besides Dolly, Fronie, and Aunt Ruthie. For two days before the actual sale, the kitchen was a hive of activity with its profusion of light breads, cakes, and pies; jellies, jams, and pickles.

In the midst of all this confusion, Bart was disconcerted by the arrival of a prosperous-looking man and a young boy of about The Dummy's age. Although both were dressed in ordinary clothes such as any planter might wear, their horses and saddles were superb—a fine stallion for the man and a high-bred mare for the boy. They cantered around to the side door, dismounted, and came up onto the gallery. It was only then that Bart noticed that the boy walked with a slight limp. Seated on his horse he had displayed no evidence of being even slightly crippled.

"Warren Maxwell suh, at yore service," the man addressed Bart. " 'N' this here's my son, Hammond. We from Falconhurst Plantation, down Benson way. Sorry suh, sorry indeed ter hear o' Tom Verder's death. We good friends, Tom Verder 'n' me. Didn' see so much o' each other as might have wished, but we good friends. Understan' yo' havin' a sale o' some o' Tom's niggers, so my son 'n' me we rode over. We always a-lookin' fer likely niggers fer Falconhurst."

Maxwell had come to the sale with the expectation of buying young slaves at private treaty, thus saving at least the auctioneer's commission. Nobody could know for certain what a given Negro would bring at auction, but Maxwell watched the market and believed that he could estimate a slave's worth at auction. By buying directly from the owner he figured on saving ten per cent of the auction price. He was always on the lookout for adolescents which were well-grown for their ages, sturdy, healthy and, as he would say, "likely."

Prices for slaves had been advancing constantly ever since their importation had been forbidden by Federal law, and Maxwell anticipated that prices would continue to rise. By buying young Negroes at current prices and keeping them a few years, feeding them well and exercising them and getting out of them what work he could, then selling them just when they had achieved maturity, he could make a considerable profit. Food for slaves, which he grew at Falconhurst anyway, was of small value, and the few clothes that they wore and their rude shelter cost him practically nothing. He seldom, if ever, had contagious diseases on his plantation, and very few accidents. He had lost one or two Negro

258

wenches in difficult childbirths, but he had never had a buck die on his hands.

The profit on a boy of twelve to fifteen years might be one hundred, two hundred, or sometimes three hundred per cent just for keeping him five to eight years. Buying adolescents when he could find the kind he wanted, at prices he was willing to pay, yielded him a greater profit than breeding Negroes (although Falconhurst was a breeding farm also). By acquiring half-grown stock, he knew more about how it would turn out; he could avert childhood diseases; and he did not have to feed stock during unproductive years. Moreover, he could choose the sex he desired. Boys brought bigger prices unless a girl was especially good-looking, with some admixture of white blood. These were called "fancies," and if pretty enough and white enough, brought high prices in the markets of New Orleans, Natchez, and Mobile, where they were eagerly sought after for house servants and concubines. Girls matured earlier than boys and could be sold two or three years younger. Young men were purchased with their probable ability to reproduce in mind; girls, if they could be kept so, brought more as virgins.

Maxwell eschewed the ugly, the malformed, the stupid, and the ill-visaged. By the time a boy had reached his adolescence, Maxwell could judge fairly well how he would turn out. He sought the clean-limbed, the narrow-hipped, the wide-chested, and the tall, those whose youthful bodies betokened strength and vigor. He picked out the smooth-cheeked, the less Negroid, the clear-eyed, and the intelligent. His specifications in regard to the genitalia were that they be well-formed and free from phimosis, that they heft well in the cup of his hand, and that with a slight manipulation they form an incipient erection. With girls he studied the lines of their figure, looking for broad hips that denoted they would be good bearers of children, budding breasts that had a promise of fullness, light color, narrow lips, and fine nostrils. But in both boys and girls, he looked for something more than mere physical perfection—that clear look of intelligence, that indefinable something that established a sympathy between him and his purchase. This latter quality he did not always secure, but when he did, it made the boy or girl doubly a prize, and these few were the ones he was prone to keep at Falconhurst without selling.

This then was Warren Maxwell's mission at Dove Cote. When it was at all feasible, Maxwell always took his son along on his trips, upon which the boy was as anxious to go as his father was to have him. The serious youth was vitally interested in his father's business and mirrored the older man in his acts and speech, his manner and mannerisms. The mutual devotion of the two was intense. But Hammond, young as he was, served his father as more than merely a companion, much as Maxwell enjoyed the companionship of his beloved and pampered son. From the time he could remember Hammond had been with Negroes. He had grown up with them; been indoctrinated into the business of buying, breeding, and selling them. He had been an apt pupil and his interest in the business exceeded even that of his father. Although he had learned all he knew from his father, he had improved on that knowledge, with the result that there were few grown men in the surrounding territory that were as good a judge of black flesh as young Hammond Maxwell. Indeed, his knowledge was such that even experienced slave traders accepted his judgment. He could examine and judge a slave expertly and without offense to the slave—not that that made any difference—in half the time most buyers spent at such a task, and give a valid opinion without hesitation. Many times he would detect a fault or noteworthy attribute that his father had overlooked. Maxwell always listened to his son's advice and usually accepted it. Very occasionally there was disagreement between them as, for instance, when the boy would recommend the purchase of a boy or wench and the father would think the slave not worth the price asked for it. At such times the youth might accept the father's decision grimly, but he would accept it as better than his own.

Boggs was disturbed by the Maxwells' arrival, for he was busy giving orders and making the final arrangements for the sale. Moreover, he saw that these early comers would have to spend the night at the house, an inconvenience for the entire family, especially since Brookins and his helper were also expected before nightfall. He greeted the Maxwells with what cordiality he could muster and dispatched their horses to the stable. Then he waited for Maxwell to state his errand.

"I reckoned comin' early and a-buyin' afore the sale, you would let me have the niggers cheaper," Maxwell said. "Save the auctioneer's commission fer yo', that way."

"Cain' do it." Boggs shook his head. "Spoil the whole dingus—the sale—yo' knowin'."

"I only cravin' saplin's. Thought yo' would be glad ter sell 'em off 'thout payin' the auctioneer aught," Maxwell urged. "Money as good ter yo' as ter him."

Boggs let the idea of saving the commission percolate in his mind a minute. "But how yo' a-goin' ter know how much? Might go high on the block—higher'n yo' willin' ter pay me."

"Tha' right," Maxwell admitted. " 'N' 'gain could be they go lower'n yo' calculate. No tellin'." He shrugged his shoulders as if the matter was of small importance to him anyway. "Jes as lief wait 'n' see 'em at the sellin' tomorrow if'n yo' reckon. Only yo' a-payin' the auctioneer his ten per cent. If'n I seein' any I craves, I give a fair price fer it now an yo' don' have to fee no auctioneer. Ain' no reason fer him ter know nothin' 'bout what we do in private sellin' anyway."

"Well," Boggs replied, "reckon yo' right, Mista Maxwell. Only ain' never calculated on no one comin' today. Varmints ain' washed nor fixed none." The excuse was a kind of apology.

" 'S all right. Seen plenty o 'dirty niggers in my lifetime 'n' don' mind a little nigger musk," Maxwell said.

Just at that point The Dummy, astride Calico's back, guided his steed into the group. He could hear nothing, understand nothing of what was going on, but he could not refrain from intruding, especially as there was a white boy of his own age whom he might inveigle into play. Boggs ignored him completely except to mention to

Maxwell and his son, "He my son. Deef he is 'n' cain' talk. He a dummy."

"That a shame, Mista Boggs." Maxwell was genuinely sympathetic, thinking what a terrible cross it would be for him to bear were his own son so afflicted. " 'N' him such a handsome boy too." Hammond, who had disregarded The Dummy, now stared at him, unable to believe that this boy his own age could neither hear nor speak.

Bart, however, dismissed the matter. "Well, come along then I reckon," he said as he led the way to the Romp Pasture—that part of it where the older boys were. Maxwell followed with the three boys in his wake. Hammond, intent upon his father's deal in slaves, ignored The Dummy upon Calico's shoulders, considering in his own mind, however, that he would never treat a servant so callously and wondering why Boggs permitted it.

When they arrived, Boggs spread his arms in a wide gesture toward the field. "There they be. Take yore pick—'s many's yo' crave," he declared. "Got ter leave some fer the auctioneer tomorrow, mayhap six o' seven, but rest 's your'n if'n yo' wants 'em. Six hundred dollars, I reckon, each one," he estimated, uncertainty in his voice.

"No, I reckon not. Not at that price. No good me a-wastin' my time a-lookin' at 'em." Maxwell shook his head and turned his back on the enclosure, where the slave boys were wrestling and chasing one another or merely sitting in the shade on a bench. There were some thirty boys in the field, ranging from eleven to about sixteen years, according to Maxwell's rapid estimate. They were of all colors from jet-black to light sepia, and of all heights. Some were clothed in smocks reaching to their knees, some in tattered breeches, and some entirely naked.

Not having overheard his father's refusal, Hammond had scaled the stake-and-rider fence and begun a survey of the boys. He called one of the larger boys to him, threw his head back, and examined his mouth, while the slave youth wriggled his resistance. He then raised the boy's smock and, seeing the scrawny shanks and

262

knobby knees, dismissed him. Next he reached out and caught a light-skinned boy who was chasing another, quickly examined his teeth, lifted his smock and, liking what he saw, removed the garment and threw it on the ground. Hammond was in his element until his father called to him. He was prepared to spend the afternoon examining and comparing the young bucks.

"No good a-wastin' time. Come along, Ham," said the elder Maxwell. "The gen'lemun here what owns them askin' too much. They not a-goin' ter bring on the block how much he askin'. Better we wait till tomorrow 'n' git 'em cheaper."

Hammond reluctantly reclimbed the fence and joined his father.

Maxwell turned to address Boggs. "I reckon you know, don' yo', yo' gotta git six hundred 'n' sixty dollars on the block fer 'em ter git yore own six hundred outa 'em."

"That so, I reckon that so," Boggs was forced to admit. He did not relish losing the sale. "How much yo' willin' ter give?"

"Well, don' rightly know till I examines 'em." Maxwell surveyed the group of slave boys who had, by now, all collected at the fence and were staring over it. "But I'd say 'bout four-fifty—that about five hundred dollars on the block. Won' bring that much, I'm certain. Bin a-buyin' fifteen-and sixteen-year-old bucks 'round four hundred, more or less. Extra good one I'm willin' ter pay roun' five hundred fer." While Boggs considered the proposal, Maxwell looked at the sky and added, "Lookin' like rain; feelin' like it, too. Won' be no turnout tomorrow, I don' reckon."

The prediction so frightened Boggs that he decided immediately. "Might consider five hundred. Take yore pick 'o em—five hundred every one," he proposed.

"That mean five-fifty on the block. Yo' ain' goin' ter git it. Four-fifty I offered, take it or leave it."

Boggs hesitated and Maxwell started to walk back toward the house, Hammond following dejectedly. Boggs suddenly turned and said, "Well, if'n yo' won' give no more, then four-fifty it is. Yo' kin go ahead, I reckon."

263

He consoled himself with the fact that he would not have to pay any commission.

Maxwell turned back toward the Romp Pasture and awkwardly climbed the fence. Hammond, despite his crippled leg, went over it with agility and The Dummy, dismounting from Calico, scrambled over after him. He followed Hammond to where he was re-examining the boy he had abandoned and watched him with wide-eyed interest. Hammond felt the urchin's flesh, ran his hand over his musculature and examined his genitals, at which point The Dummy, babbling his incoherent jargon, insisted on doing the same, much to Hammond's amazement. But The Dummy's smile was so engaging and his eyes so sparkling that Hammond did not have the heart to push him away. The Dummy looked on, grimacing and making his uncouth sounds, while Hammond pushed the slave boy to his knees, spread his buttocks, and then again explored his mouth with his fingers. He picked up a stone and cast it, telling the boy to "Go fetch," which the boy did in a leisurely way. Hammond brought from his pocket his barlow knife and cut a sucker some three feet long from a handy chinaberry. Throwing the stone again, he flicked the switch smartly on the brown legs and ordered, "Fetch again, this time faster." The young buck, his legs smarting, ran off and brought the stone back, handed it to Hammond, and panted, "That fast 'nuff, young masta?" Hammond nodded his approbation.

While his son was engaged with this boy, Maxwell made a superficial examination of a half-dozen others, and dismissed them as unsuited to his purpose. Hammond called to him enthusiastically. "Here one, Papa, one I reckon goin' ter do. Come here 'n' give a look."

Uncle George appeared out of Nervy's cabin in the next field, recognized the procedure, and intruded himself modestly into the conclave. He carried a light whip, and seeing Ham's switch, offered him the whip, which Ham accepted, snapping it.

"That's right, young masta suh," the old black man said. "Whup 'em an' they not good. That one yo' jes' gotta whup a lot."

"Why? What's wrong with him?"

"Jes' rambunctious, tha's all. He spirited, that one."

Maxwell came up and took over the examination of the young slave boy. "I likes 'em with spirit," he replied to old George.

He also put the boy through his paces and discovered nothing wrong with him. Then he turned to Boggs and inquired, "How old this yere varmint?"

"Don' rightly know how old. Don' rate 'em by how old but by how big they are. Don' know nothin' 'bout them, where they come from, who their mammy, o' who sired 'em. Don' know if'n they got a name nor nothin'."

"What yore name, boy? Got one?" Maxwell asked as he continued his inspection of the boy.

"Yes suh, masta. They calls me Wash. Wash-ing-ton."

"The father of your country, huh?" Maxwell chuckled.

"I got a lot o' fine wenches fo' you to cover. How yo' like that?" Maxwell went on. "Yo' mine now. I a-buyin' yo'. Un'erstand?"

Washington did not understand what was taking place, and he hung his head, ashamed of being exposed to public view in his present condition. Maxwell had nothing with which to mark the youth as his own, so he asked Ham for his knife. With the point of the small blade, he scratched an "M" on the boy's belly. The youth flinched, but the wound was only superficial and oozed a trifling amount of blood; however, it would last a day or two and would mark the boy as his. Maxwell and Hammond walked with Bart over to another group of boys and continued their examination until they had selected the five best slaves and scratched their initials on their bellies. Then they adjourned to the next pasture where the girls were and the procedure was repeated. Hammond especially felt a stirring as he caressed the maidens and envisioned having them in his bed.

The party wended its way back to the house, well satisfied with the transaction on both sides. Maxwell delved into his saddlebags and brought out gold coin with which he paid for his six purchases, and received and pocketed the bills of sale for them, laboriously written by Bart with the stub of a pencil.

Dusk was growing when Brookins rode in with his white

clerk, Snodgrass, and two mulatto slave assistants, the latter of which were duly fed in the kitchen and sent to a cabin where two of the women who were to be sold were quartered. The women were physically somewhat gross and were scorned at first by Brookins' boys, who nevertheless bedded down with them for the night.

Brookins surveyed the setting of the sale with approval, especially the commodious platform from which he was to work. He and Bart returned to the house to see Maxwell enjoying a toddy before supper. The meal was a plenteous one, with large slices of barbecued pork and apple pie which had been prepared for the sale, along with an unlimited assortment of jellies, jams and preserves. The boys gorged themselves, and although Hammond had at first shown his disgust and disapproval at having to eat at the same board with Calico, a warning nod from his father advised him to ignore the matter, and he ate as heartily as the others. After the meal was finished they all repaired to the parlor and sat around stiffly for a short time in observance of the conventions, but all were anxious to get to bed for the difficult day on the morrow, and soon went up to their rooms.

Quartering all the guests had presented a problem. Brookins and his clerk were given Bart and Dovie's room, they having long since abandoned the inconvenience of the dove cote. Bart and Dovie moved into Callie's room and she slept on the couch in Tom's office. Warren Maxwell was given The Dummy's room, and it was decided to quarter Hammond and The Dummy, with Calico in attendance, in the dove cote. Maxwell was offended that Bart's hospitality did not extend to offering him a wench for his bed, to him an indispensable part of plantation hospitality. He was aware, however, that his host was busy and preoccupied, and that, since he claimed to be a preacher, his wife might not approve of what was a routine procedure at Falconhurst.

Hammond was compelled to share The Dummy's bed with him while Calico was relegated to a folded quilt on the floor beside the bed. The Dummy disturbed the visiting boy during the night. No such phenonomon had ever confronted Hammond before. At his father's suggestion, he had had young wenches in his bed at Falconhurst for more than a year, but when he was tired of his sexual play with them, he told them so and they let him sleep. Of course they were his slaves and were constrained to obey his orders. Hammond, despite his knowledge of slave-breeding and his intimacy with all the sexual mores of the slaves, was most naïve. He did not wish to violate the laws of hospitality, but he was tired of this mauling and slavering. At length, his patience sorely tried, he let go and struck out blindly at The Dummy. The mute boy cried out and uttered an incomprehensible string of sounds. Hammond regretted that he had done it and that he had made the deaf boy cry, but the deed was done and he extricated himself from the sheet and crawled in beside the sleeping slave.

Chapter XVIII

THE PROGNOSTICATION that Maxwell had made the previous day proved valid. It had rained during the night, with lightning and thunder and a drizzle persisted until late morning. The weather prevented many persons from attending the auction, and Boggs was desolate. However, by nine o'clock, people began to arrive, and they continued to come. The crowd was not so large as had been anticipated, but Brookins rationalized that those persons whom the weather had deterred from coming were, at best, only curiosity-seekers and not potential buyers.

By ten o'clock the area was swarming with men, the larger part of whom had ridden, athough many had come in buckboards, surreys, and democrat wagons. Some of them had their sons with them—boys ranging from ten to maturity. Before noon there must have been some fifty altogether, men and boys. They all kept at a safe distance from the house so as not to disturb the ladies who remained indoors.

The Dummy bestrode Calico's shoulders, as usual, employing his strap upon the servant. A kindly, bearded man sought to prevent his striking Calico, but, unable to make The Dummy comprehend, he was forced to cease his interference, although he complained to everyone within earshot about a slave being so mistreated.

The visitors were not long in finding the whisky barrel and helping themselves to its contents. Some were half-drunk before noon.

Those slaves who had been chosen for sale, attired in their new finery, sat on the floor before the platform, subject to examination by possible buyers. A few of them were weeping, but most of them were cheerfully excited at the prospect of a change in their lives. Some of the more knowing ones were depressed. They talked in low tones among themselves and occasionally laughed, more out of bravado than humor. The women were clean and smart in their new clothes, to which some of them had added a bit of pitiful finery discarded from the big house —a piece of ribbon or threadbare lace. The boys from the Romp Pasture had exchanged their smocks for tight, knee-length trousers which impeded their movements.

A box stall had been emptied and cleaned for stripping and intimately examining women and girls. The men and boys were stripped, examined, and put through their paces where they were. Anybody who wished was at liberty to examine and question the slaves for sale in whatever manner he might choose; to scrutinize them; to comment on their features or parts; to finger, handle, and manipulate them as much as he desired. Their members were pawed at and explored; personal inquiries were made about their health and reproductive ability, largely by young adults and smart-aleck boys. There was little reticence on the part of the white men, and the slaves dared not show any. The answers the slaves made to inquiries about themselves were often modified by their wish or fear of being purchased by the questioner.

Snodgrass, Brookins' clerk, tried futilely to keep the younger boys out of the stall where nude wenches were examined. Hammond Maxwell, however, stuck closely to his father and was not even tempted to intrude into the stall. Naked wenches were no novelty to him, and he had seen none that he wished his father to buy. He confined his attention to the male slaves and the boys, in two of whom he thought his father might be interested. Maxwell looked them over but decided against them. He had made his purchases the previous day and did not seriously consider buying any more stock at the sale. He did, however, notice and admire Calico. He was impressed with the boy's intelligence and good looks, but more especially by his patience and his forbearance under the mistreatment he suffered at the hands of The Dummy. Not that he would have condoned Calico turning on his master —that would have been unforgivable, but it was unusual to see a spirited boy submit so meekly to such continuous torment. Maxwell wished that the boy was one of those which were being offered for sale. There was good stuff in the lad.

Congo, whom Callie had permitted to come out to the barn, sidled up toward the platform, took a seat on an upturned keg, and gazed out over the milling men with wide-eyed interest. He had never before seen so many people congregated in one place, and he was enjoying it hugely. The Dummy, still larruping Calico with his strap, wove in and out of the assemblage, paying particular interest whenever any of the prospective buyers stripped and examined a male slave. He gurgled and grimaced his pleasure at seeing the men handle the Negroes, and more than once he inserted himself between the prospective buyer and the slave he was examining. Snodgrass tried his best to keep The Dummy out of the way, but he continued to make himself a nuisance to all.

It was getting on toward noon; the slaves up for sale had been looked over to the satisfaction of the customers, and the crowd drifted out to stand in a queue at the whisky barrel or to mill about the long table with sandwiches of barbecued pork in their hands. Pans of the inferior parts of the hog and slices of corn pone had been distributed among the slaves—as much as they could eat. Brookins' two husky yellow boys were moving about, light whips in hand—the symbols of their authority—busy with the preparations for the auction which was due to begin. Tables must be placed in exact positions for the auctioneer and the clerk. A pitcher of watered whisky for Brookins must be provided. The floor of the platform must be swept and sprinkled with water; the ladder to the platform must be inspected and tested.

At length Brookins ponderously mounted the stand, his gold-headed cane—his scepter—in his hand. He laid

270

it with exaggerated care on the table, making sure that the gold head was pointed to the audience for all to see. He was the hero of the occasion, the center of attraction. Men had felt complimented when he'd addressed them by name on his way to the platform, and others, who did not know him, had demonstrated their own measure of prominence by introducing themselves to him.

He carefully picked up his gavel, moved the small block of polished black walnut to the exact position where he wanted it on the rough pulpit, and struck three blows, followed by three more and then a final three. "Gather 'roun', gen'lemen, gather 'roun'. I say gen'lemen 'cause I reckon there ain' no ladies here, less'n some folks goin' ter call these here wenches what I'm a-goin ter sell ladies. Wenches such's these 'most fine 'nuff ter be called ladies; leastwise"—he nodded knowingly and winked— "mos' o' yo' gen'lemen knows that they's 'quipped with everything necessary ter be ladies." Brookins chuckled at his own joke, which was not, however, heard by many, as there was still a confusion of finding seats and getting adjusted. He banged on his gavel again, this time more peremptorily. "We a-goin' ter begin right now. No time ter waste. Got us a lot of fine niggers here ter sell 'n' know that a lot o' yo' gen'lemen want ter git home in time fer supper 'n' oversee yore chores. Got ter sell a good-sized herd while daylight lasts." Once more his gavel sought to quiet the restless assemblage. This time it was successful.

The slaves for sale were seated on the ground on either side of the platform—males on one side, females on the other. The crowd, some standing and some sitting on rude benches, became quiet, anticipating the bawdy jokes which usually opened the auction and which were always the best in the auctioneer's repertoire. Just as he was about to launch into his jocular discourse, Boggs hurried through the onlookers and climbed up the ladder to the platform. He held a brief whispered conference with Brookins, then approached the front of the rostrum, spread his arms, and proclaimed, "Let us kneel down to our knees and worship the Lord. We a-goin' ter pray."

He knelt and Brookins, shrugging at the interruption,

joined him, as did the Negroes. Four or five of the more devout of the assemblage sank to their knees. The rest bowed their heads.

Boggs' supplication opened in a low key but soon grew louder, swelled to stentorian volume, and gradually subsided to a whisper as though his concluding remarks to God were confidential. In the course of the prayer, he besought the blessing of God upon his whole audience, collectively and in part, so far as he knew the names of the individuals present. He even included the slaves to be sold and solicited divine concern in the prices they should bring. He expatiated at great lengths upon the joys of heaven as if he had been there, and contrasted them with the tortures awaiting sinners in an incredibly hot hell, threatening them with being broiled alive forever upon incandescent gridirons.

The prayer was interrupted frequently by shouts of "Amen" and "Bless God" from a kneeling man, which Boggs interpreted as a sign of applause and an invitation to prolong his harangue. He sensed that his hearers were tiring but he could not relinquish the satisfaction his oratory produced in him. After half an hour had elapsed, he brought his discourse to its final "In the name of Jesus Christ, Amen." He rose slowly to his feet, dusted off his knees, and beamed on his audience, confident that his prayer had been a personal triumph. It had at least served to reestablish him in public as a "reverend," the title he treasured. Now he advanced two steps to the edge of the platform and raised both hands, imploring silence. Brookins sighed audibly, anticipating another prayer, but this time, Boggs' words were for his audience.

"This sale a special one," he said. "Every man what buying a nigger here, givin' to God. Yes suh! Every penny what these servants bring goin' ter God. Ain' nothin' a-comin' ter me. So hopes yo' bids good 'n' proper a-knowin' that this money a-goin' ter glorify God. Goin' ter build a fine church with this money, right in Brownsville. Goin' ter have the bes' church here north o' Mobile. Goin' ter be a church with a steeple, with colored-glass windows, with a bell and with a organ. Going ter have regular pews 'n' hymnbooks. This goin' ter be a church yo'-all be proud of. Place fer yore children ter come 'n' hear the word o' God. Place fer yore wives ter go ter. 'N' yo'-all a-goin' ter build it with the money yo' a-payin' fer these pore heathen servants what don' know they a-doin' the will o' God. Yes suh, these pore servants a-goin' ter proclaim the name o' sweet Jesus in Brownsville, so whilst yo're a buyin' 'em, don' be niggardly 'n' miserly 'cause the more money yo' pays fer 'em, the better church buildin' yo'-all a-goin' ter have."

There was a mild round of applause as Bart backed away. Brookins poured himself a generous drink from the pitcher on the table and swallowed it, then banged with his gavel. Shrugging, as if to apologize for the long prayer, he said, somewhat sarcastically, "Now Rev'nd Boggs done given God his orders, reckon we uns down here on earth kin git along with this here auction." The audience tittered mildly, but Boggs took no notice of the speaker's sarcasm. Brookins proceeded to specify the terms of the sale. Payment was to be in cash. All slaves to be sold were sound, and sold for no fault. All were free from scars of the whip and vigorous and healthy, as they had been able to see through their examination. All sales were final. No slave might be returned for refund or any adjustment of price unless some condition might be discovered in violation of the warranty given by the owner.

Brookins turned to one of his own slaves, waiting at the foot of the steps, telling him, "Carry me here one of them young varmints waitin' over there. That stout black one. It good 'nuff ter commence on. We'll see how yo'-all 'preciates a clean, young, likely piece o' nigger-meat."

The attendant escorted the black youth to the steps—one from the Romp Pasture. As they were leading him up the steps, an agreeable young man, only a little the worse for liquor, turned to Warren Maxwell, reached out his hand, and introduced himself.

"I'm John O'Neal o' Clonmel Plantation over Orion way. Heard tell yo' Mista Warren Maxwell from Falconhurst. Kindly like ter make yore 'quaintance, Mista Maxwell. Heard a lot 'bout yo' 'n' know yo' a good judge o' nigger-flesh. Thinkin' mayhap yo' advise me 'bout some of

273

these niggers. Aimin' ter buy some but don' want ter bid 'gainst yo'."

Maxwell shook hands with the young man, noting the richness of his clothes and his unusual good looks. The O'Neals of Clonmel were a familiar name and he accepted the fellow's hand and pumped it warmly. "Right pleased ter make yore 'quaintance, Mista O'Neal, 'n' this here's my son, Hammond. He a right peart judge o' niggers, too. Glad to advise yo'." He turned slightly to his son. "Ham, Mista O'Neal wantin' to know what we think o' that boy up there. Yo' 'xamined him yesterday. What yo' think?"

Hammond assumed a judicious tone. "He all right. Ain' nothing much ails him 'cept he ain' too smart. Bit simple, he is. Make a good fiel' hand 'n' looks like'n he might muscle out pretty good. He 'bout fifteen, I reckon. Kinda scrawny now but look'n like he have some Ibo blood 'n' if'n so he fill out good 'n' strong."

Maxwell beamed at his son's knowledge, and O'Neal thanked the boy and complimented him on his knowledge. They all became silent as Brookins started to speak.

"Yo' got a name, boy?" Brookins demanded of the youth, and the youth nodded his head, too embarrassed for speech. "Speak up, what is it?"

The boy answered weakly, "Deke—that is, Deacon."

"Ain' yo' fergettin' ter say 'masta suh'?"

The boy repeated the formula.

"Deacon, eh? Well, that right fittin'. We sells the deacon ter buy the church. Ha, ha!" It was a good extemporaneous joke and Brookins made the most of it, roaring with laughter, slapping his knee, and wiping his eyes with a soiled kerchief. "Well, yo' jes' shuck yo'self outa them trogs 'n' show the folks here that yo' all dressed in black jes' like a deacon even if'n 'yo ain' got no clothes on." He waited for the boy to slip off his shirt and let his trousers fall to his ankles. "Now ain' that a pretty sight"—Brookins waved his gavel at the boy—" 'n' ain' he 'n all-black nigger, a purentee nigger? Reckon his hide's so tough he kin take a floggin' one day 'n' work in the fiel' the next. Right good hand fer cot-

274

ton, he is; be a half-hand next year 'n' a full hand the year after, if'n he git 'nuff ter eat 'n' somethin' ter stick ter his ribs. 'N' look at how that boy built. He goin' ter have plenty o' sap in him 'n' make a good stud nigger he will. Give him a couple more years 'n' he kin take on five, six wenches a night."

Brookins told him to jump, and when he didn't jump high enough to satisfy Brookins, he wound a small whip around his legs—more of a threat than a blow. This time the boy jumped with alacrity, although his big feet were so clumsy he nearly fell off the platform. Bidding was invited and was opened at two hundred dollars, which the auctioneer scoffed at but accepted. "Two hun-'erd, two hun'erd. That all fer this fine boy? Who'll make it three? Come on, who'll make it three?"

A black-bearded man in the back nodded and raised his hand. "Three!" the auctioneer declared. "I got three, three, three, now make it four. Who'll give four. I got three, now four, now four. Thank you, suh, four it is, now five, five, five, five, who'll make it five?" He hesitated in a histrionic pause, pretending to be shocked and appalled by the apathy of the buyers. "Why, yo'-all come here ter buy niggers, didn' yo'? Why 'n yo' a-buyin' em? Jes' cain' let this fine boy go fer four hundred. His hide 'n' taller wuth more'n that. Got four 'n' askin' five. Who'll give five, five, five, five?"

A young man, dressed in well-worn butternut and a wide straw hat, edged through the crowd to the platform and beckoned to the boy. Brookins assisted him over to the edge of the platform and the man looked up at him.

"Jes' got here," the man explained. "Ain' had time ter look 'em over."

"Don' need no lookin'-over," Brookins said. "Sound, hale 'n' hearty with plenty o' sap in him come a couple more years. He blacker'n the bottom pit o' hell but he good 'n' strong."

"Four hun'erd 'n' ten dollars," the fellow said.

Brookins glared at him. "Ain' never took a ten-dollar bid in my life, mista. Ain' startin' now. Four twenty-five?"

The young planter nodded.

"Anybody four-fifty?" Brookins sensed that the bidding was over, and he realized that four hundred was a fair price for the boy. He surveyed the audience for a moment, then brought his gavel down. "Sold," he pronounced, "at four hundred and twenty-five dollars. 'N' I'm warnin' yo, I ain't takin' no ten-dollar bids. If'n yo' wants niggers yo'll buy 'em. If'n yo' don', jes' say the word 'n' we'll stop the sale now. This yere's prime merchandise; best niggers I've seen in a long time, 'n' Rev'nd Boggs a-sellin' them through no fault. Now, let's us go on." Having castigated his audience Brookins was now prepared to put them in a more jocular mood. "Reminds me, that do, of the time some Cherokee braves captured a small town over in Arkansas. They rode inter town 'n' a fine upstandin' young brave yelled out, 'We a-goin' ter scalp all yore men 'n' rape all yore wimmen.' Old maid a-standin' on the edge o' the crowd eyed him 'n' she hollered out, 'Well, come on, let's git started.' " He laughed so hard he had to lean on the rostrum, but finally recovered himself. "So I say jes' like that pore old maid, 'come on, let's git started.' "

Brookins had chosen the black boy for his first offering as a means of testing the temper of his audience—its willingness to bid and its inclination to buy. The fair price he had received for his first "lot" indicated that the crowd was in a buying mood, and he decided to offer the miscellany of boys from the Romp Pasture. One by one he had his two boys help them up the ladder and one by one he sold them, none lower than the original offering and some going as high as five hundred and fifty dollars. They sold fast, one stepping down as another stepped up, to the accompaniment of Brookins' sing-song chant. The planter in the wide-brimmed hat bought another youth and the original buyer of the first boy bought three. Warren Maxwell was tempted to buy a light-skinned boy whom he felt he had overlooked the day before, but his son whispered that he had examined him and found that he had two rear molars missing, so Maxwell did not bid.

The saplings out of the way, Brookins summoned a wench to the platform. She was about twenty-five years old and encumbered with two children, a babe in arms and one of about a year and a half. Both girls were to be sold with the mother as a single lot.

"Reckon most o' yo'-all looked at this nice fat wench 'n' her two suckers. Now I'm offerin' all three o' 'em in one lot, all sound 'n' hearty. Look 'em over, gen'lemen. Ever see better suckers?" Brookins introduced the trio and then turned to his slave henchmen. "Take the young uns 'roun' and let folks see 'em. Jes' take one apiece 'n' be careful yo' don' drop 'em o' they a-goin' ter bust right open. Yo' a-droppin' em 'n' yo' know what it means— means a good larrupin' with the cowhide fer yo', tha's what it means."

Brookins' two boys grasped the naked babies firmly had not too gently and carried them through the crowd to be looked at, poked and pinched painfully, and to have fingers thrust in their mouths. They squalled and bellowed but nobody sought to quiet them, although their mother followed them with her eyes throughout the crowd, anxious for their safe return.

"Ever see better suckers? Right peart they be. Each one worth a hun'erd 'n' fifty if'n it worth a penny. The wench already whelped four others, which show yo' she a damn good breeder. Buck jes' have ter hang up his pants 'side her bed 'n' she git knocked up. She good to have one a year from now on 'n' give no trouble a-havin' em, no more'n a sow a-farrowin' a pig. 'N' yo' kin see why." Brookins raised her skirt to mid-thigh. "Look at them big stout legs. No trouble at all fer her ter spit out her pups. She jes' a black goose what lays gold eggs 'n' she got 'nother dozen, maybe twenty in her yet, if'n yo got the buck what kin put it to her, 'n' if yo' ain' "—Brookins sniggered—"well, they's one good way ter git light-skinned suckers but I ain' a-goin' ter tell yo' if'n yo' don' know." He turned to the girl, letting her skirts drop. "Ain' yo' good fer twenty more suckers, gal?"

"Reckon I is, masta suh, if'n I has as good a man what I had here."

"Wait till yo' see the buck yore new masta goin' ter have awaitin' yo'." His hand wandered up the back of

277

her dress and undid the single button at the neck to show her back and prove the absence of wales. Modestly she held her garment before her to hide her breasts from view. Brookins began the call for bids, which began low but gradually advanced to eight hundred dollars. Finally bidding stopped at eight hundred and seventy-five, much to Bart's disgust, who had hoped she would bring at least a thousand with the two children.

One by one the slaves mounted the block for their brief moment. Some stood sullen and despairing; some were nervous and trembling; others were defiant; while a few natural show-offs grinned and enjoyed their moment of importance. So progressed the pathetic parade up and down the ladder until the last slave was sold.

Before that last unfortunate descended the ladder, however, Bart made his way up onto the platform, calling Nero to him and bidding him follow. After waiting for Nero to come up, Bart went over to Brookins and held a brief whispered conversation with him. Bart pointed twice, once to the foot of the platform and once to the open doors of the barn. Brookins listened, his lips pursed, his head nodding gravely in assent. At his nod, his two boys clambered down the ladder, grabbed the surprised Congo by both arms and pushed him up the ladder. He grunted and squealed in his high falsetto voice, calling loudly for his mistress, but Brookins' two huskies pushed him up until he fell, flat on his belly, on the platform. Having deposited him there, they departed, running out the doors of the barn and outside.

"Stop yore bawlin' 'n' git up on yore feet." Bart kicked Congo's prostrate form.

"I wan' Miz Callie, I wan' Miz Callie," Congo blubbered, the tears coursing down his fat cheeks. "What yo' a-goin' ter do with me, masta Bart, suh?"

"Goin' ter sell yo', tha's what I'm a-goin' ter do. Sellin' yo' off. Ain' got no use fer yo' no more." He turned to Nero who was behind him. " 'N' sellin' yo' too," he muttered, "yo' 'n' that piebald pinto."

"Yo' a-sellin' me?" Nero was completely taken by surprise. "Miz Dovie know yo' a-sellin' me?" Nero's face turned livid under his yellow skin. "She know yo' a-sellin' masta Tommy's Calico?"

"Makes no neverminds if'n she know o' not. Gittin' shet o' all three o' yo'." He waited impatiently while Brookins' assistants managed to free Calico from Tommy and push him up onto the platform. "These three fer sale, Mista Brookins. This here Nero—he Tom Verder's body servant. This here geldin' he bin body servant ter Miz Verder, 'n' this saplin' he play-boy fer masta Tommy. They's all trained house servants—all housebroken 'n' 'bedient. Sorry ter have ter sell 'em, but gotta."

"Yes suh, Rev'nd." Brookins was overjoyed at the extra commission he would get for the sale of these three servants. They would undoubtedly command the highest prices of those sold that day. He looked them over and chose Nero as the first to be sold.

"Shuck yore trogs off," he commanded. "Ain' no one had no chance ter 'xamine yo'."

It took a little longer for Nero to get out of his clothes than it had the other slaves. His undressing was complicated by the fact that he wore boots, socks, and underclothing. When he finally stood before the crowd naked there was a murmur of admiration. Nero was nearly fifty years old, but his body was as flat-bellied, slim-hipped, and barrel-chested as that of a man of thirty.

"Now this here's a quality nigger." Brookins got up from his chair where he had been sitting while Nero undressed and ran his hand appraisingly over Nero's light-colored flanks. "He a good man. Bin body servant ter Tom Verder all his life. Everywhere Tom Verder went this here Nero went with him. Un'erstand he sired all the yellow pups on Dove Cote 'n' he a-goin' ter sire a lot more. Still kin, cain' yo', Nero?"

"Kin."

Brookins went on to expatiate on Nero's other outstanding selling points. Down in the audience, Warren Maxwell, who had been about to leave in order to get started on his long ride back to Benson, turned to O'Neal who was beside him.

"If'n yo' a-lookin' fer a damn good nigger, Mista O'Neal, I'd recommend this un if'n he don' go too high.

279

I'd buy him myself only he a bit too old for me. Got my eyes on that young boy. But this here's a good man, this Nero. Trustworthy I'd say o' I don' know nothin' 'bout niggers. If'n he twenty years younger, he'd bring fifteen hundred. I'f'n yo' kin git him fer a thousand he's a right good buy. Make a top-wallopin' head driver fer yo'."

O'Neal nodded his thanks and started bidding. At first the bids were desultory, starting at three hundred and advancing in raises of fifty. The crowd was tired and they had thought the sale over. It was difficult to whip up their enthusiasm again. On reaching five hundred dollars, O'Neal started to bid, discovering that his only competitor was Norsmith, the banker. Norsmith topped O'Neal's bid by fifty dollars and a nod from O'Neal raised the price to six hundred, where it hung for several minutes until Norsmith raised it a fifty. O'Neal immediately bid seven-fifty. Norsmith, after careful consideration, came out with seven-seventy-five. When O'Neal offered eight hundred, Norsmith withdrew. Brookins harangued the crowd, but there were no further bids. Finally, sensing that the bidding had reached the limit, he started his familiar chant.

"Last chance, goin', goin', goin', last chance at eight hundred dollars for this magnificent nigger. Last chance." He waited a moment, his gavel poised in the air, looking at Norsmith expectantly, but the banker remained silent, and Brookins brought his gavel down. "Sold! Ter Mista Jonathan O'Neal o' Clonmel Plantation fer eight hundred dollars which, if'n I do say it myself, is a goddam good bargain."

"Kin yo' put up that boy next, Mista Brookins?" Maxwell called out. "Might bid on him but mighty anxious ter git started home."

Nero, still on the platform, took Calico's hand and led him forward. Down below, The Dummy was screaming and babbling. He tried to climb the ladder but was restrained by Brookins' boys. Poor Calico, realizing what was happening to him, stood stock-still in the middle of the platform, and Nero, filled with sympathy after his own shock had worn off, gently removed Calico's shirt and pants. What had to all appearances been a white boy was now revealed by the removal of his clothes to be piebald. Calico was a well-developed boy for his age with the promise of an impressive musculature. Brookins, still on his feet, ran his hands over the boy, displaying his genitalia with pride.

"Ain' often yo' sees a saplin' with a pecker like that. Breed this boy in a coupla years ter yore yellow wenches 'n' yo'll get pretty-nigh mustee pups outa him. Would say he's an octoroon 'n' if'n it wan't fer them spots on him yo'd swear he pure white. He right fancy, this boy, 'n' housebroke too. Eats right at the table with the white folks 'n' got good manners. If'n I a-sellin' this boy in N'Orleans, I'd git a thousand-dollar-bid ter start him. How much yo' offerin', gen'lemen? How much?"

Hammond nudged his father. "Yo' a-goin' ter buy him, Papa?"

Maxwell nodded but noticed the troubled expression on Hammond's face. "Ain' he all right?" he asked.

"He's a right nice boy, Papa. Mighty fine, but jes' one thing a-botherin' me. Ain' had no chance ter look him over."

"Ain'," Maxwell agreed, "but kin see he all right. Ain' nothin' wrong with him." He regarded his son again. "Is there?"

"Ain' fingered him. Yo' always say don' buy no buck what cain' skin it back. How yo' knowin' this un kin?"

" 'N' if'n he kin?"

"Buy him, Papa."

Maxwell raised his hand and caught Brookins' attention. "Mista Brookins, ain' had no chance ter 'xamine this boy, as yo' know jes' wonderin' if'n yo' let me see if'n he all right. Ain' aimin' ter bid on no pig 'n a poke."

"Glad ter accommodate yo', Mista Maxwell, 'n' don' blame yo'." He reached down to Calico and did Maxwell's bidding, displaying the results to the audience. He chuckled. "Ain' goin' ter have no trouble with this boy a-breedin' him."

Maxwell nodded his thanks. "Five hundred," he said.

"He wuth more'n that," Hammond whispered.

" 'N' fifty," a voice from the rear shouted.

Maxwell turned around and noticed a black-bearded man with a boy of about Hammond's age. Evidently he was anxious to get Calico for a companion to his son. "Seven hundred." Maxwell sought to establish his claim by raising the bid a hundred and fifty. His strategy worked. Other bidders were frightened out, for they sensed that Maxwell would top any bid they made. There were no more bids, despite Brookins' eloquence, and Calico was knocked down to Maxwell, who, in his hurry to depart, strode up to the platform, paid his bill, and signaled Calico to follow him. Calico clambered down from the platform, passing the weeping Dummy who tried to run after him but was restrained by Brookins' boys. O'Neal followed Maxwell's example and also paid Snodgrass and claimed Nero. The audience started to disperse, in spite of Brookins' loud pounding with his gavel.

Congo, a quivering mass of suet, brought only two hundred and fifty dollars, and that after a long struggle on Brookins' part. Gelded boys when young brought good prices, but an obese eunuch had little value. The purchaser, an elderly white-bearded man, whom nobody recognized, was evidently from a distant region.

A few stragglers who had remained to see Congo sold reluctantly departed. Men and their recent purchases milled out to the hitching rail. Some of the slaves were loaded into wagons while others had to trot along beside their new masters' horses. Good-byes were called out, and promises to meet exchanged. Two men made a hurried swap of their saplings before departing. Finally they all left and Brookins, Snodgrass, and Bart, with Norsmith sitting in, adjusted the accounts. Snodgrass read from his ledger, checking each item with Bart, who was so hopelessly confused that he could not possibly know whether he was being cheated or not. When everything was checked and totaled and Brookins' commission, along with Norsmith's, had been taken out, all expenses deducted except the whisky, the cloth from the store, and the advertising, Bart was left with something over twelve thousand dollars. It was more than he had expected and he forgot to quibble about Norsmith's commission, which he had not anticipated.

"Ain' safe, Rev'nd, ter leave all this money out here at Dove Cote. Whole county a-knowin' yo' had a sale today 'n' they's some riffraff what might pay yo' a midnight visit 'n' rob yo'," Norsmith warned. "Better if'n I take it with me 'n' put it in the bank where it be safe 'n' secure. I'll give yo' a receipt fer it so it's all legal 'n' I'll put it in the bank 'n' then when yo' a-needin' it, yo' comes in 'n' gits it from me. That way yo' a-makin' money, too. Earnin' two per cent int'rest all the time yo' keeps it there. Jes' a-earnin' more money fer yo'."

Bart agreed reluctantly. The slip of paper with Norsmith's name on it seemed a paltry replacement for the stacks of gold eagles piled neatly on the deal table. He had a desire to savor longer their yellow brightness; the table top appeared dull and lifeless after Norsmith had swept them into his carpetbag.

"We done a good day's biz'ness, Rev'nd." Brookins reached for the pitcher of whisky his boy handed up, poured a copious draught into his own gullet, and handed the pitcher around. "Good biz'ness 'n' lotsa money well spent, like the old maid said when she bought the stud nigger. Ain' nobody what could have got yo' more. Thought that Nero might of brought a higher price. Would of got a thousand fer him if'n yo' hadn' waited till the hind end. Got a good price fer that pinto, tho'. Thought fer a while we wasn' goin' ter get shet o' that goddam geldin'. Ain' worth much when they gits old 'n' fat. Ol' man what bought him a-sayin' he bought him fer his two sisters what live alone. Betcha"—he guffawed, choking on his whisky—"betcha they'd ruther of had that Nero'n that goddam geldin'." He continued to laugh at his own joke and the others joined in. He rose unsteadily from his chair, scratched under his arms, and slowly let himself down the ladder. Norsmith and Snodgrass joined him, leaving Bart up there alone. Norsmith relinquished the heavy bag to one of Brookins' boys to carry and they all departed.

It was getting dark. Dusky shadows piled up in the sooty corners of the barn. Bart stood up, opened his arms wide, and advanced to the pulpit. Suddenly he envisioned the rough interior of the barn transformed into his new church. The sun shone through the colored windows; the organ pealed; and he saw a multitude of white faces looking up at him.

"Brethren 'n' sistren," he intoned, "let us pray."

Chapter XIX

"Bart Boggs! Git down off'n there." Dovie's voice echoed authoritatively in the purple-drifted shadows of the big barn. "Where-at's that Calico boy? The Dummy a-wantin' him."

". . . 'N' may we all come ter sweet Jesus in my new meetin' house in Brownsville. May the grace o' God be there while it a-buildin' and while it a-usin' 'n' may sweet Jesus himself give me the words ter bring all the sinners right down ter their knees before the throne o' God 'n' be saved, 'n' be baptized, 'n' be glorified in thy name 'n' received inter thy bosom. Inter thy bosom, Sweet Jesus, inter thy bosom!" Bart had heard Dovie but he was so hypnotized by his own eloquence and by the mental picture of Mrs. Salsman's copious breasts that the word "bosom" had painted, that he did not comprehend the meaning of Dovie's command. For him the dusty barn did not exist. He had at long last achieved his greatest desire; he was standing in the pulpit of his own church.

"Shut that penny-whistle shoutin' 'n' listen ter me. Whar's Calico? Whar's Nero? Whar's Congo? The Dummy a-carryin' on in high-stericks; mama she a-screamin' fer Congo ter ease her headache. I bin a-seekin' Nero everywhere. Whar's they all at? Answer me, Bart Boggs, o' I'll come up there 'n' scratch yore eyes out."

The brilliant windows of the church vanished from

Bart's vision. Instead he saw again the reality of the cob-webbed rafters of the old barn. His beatific vision disappeared and he knew the dreaded time had arrived when he must break the news to Dovie about her servants. Pompously he turned and descended the ladder, all the while hearing her vituperations. When he appeared from behind the platform to face her, he raised both hands in a gesture of benediction.

"The Lord giveth 'n' the Lord he taketh away. The Lord he a-knowin' what he a-doin'. Today he jes' tooken them three niggers fer his own glory. Tha's all. Ain' nothin' ter git 'cited 'bout 'tall. The Dummy'll git over his high-sterickin'; Callie'll ease her headachin'; 'n' we're well rid o' Nero. Too uppity, he was, a-tellin' me what ter do. Jes' too bad we couldn' o' found that naked Kru 'n' gotten shet o' him too, 'tho' reckon nobody'd bid on a savage like'n him." His voice became unctuous. "It all fer the glory o' God 'n' sweet Jesus. Yo' gotta understand that, Dovie."

"What yo' mean? Yo' killed 'em? What yo' talkin' 'bout, Bart Boggs? Whar' are they? Answer me! Tell me whar' they be o' I'll sweet-be-Jesus yo' right on yore head. I'll . . ."

"Now yo' jes' calm yo'self, Dovie. Them three niggers not killed. Jes' sold, tha's all. Sold 'em today, I did, so's I could git me 'nuff money fer ter build my meetin' house."

"What meetin' house yo' talkin' 'bout? Yo' tryin' ter tell me yo' sold my servants ter build a meetin' house? Yo' sold Calico what the only one my pore son kin talk with? Yo' sold old Congo what bin with my mama since she a little girl? Yo' sold my papa's Nero what know more 'bout this place 'n anyone else? 'N' now yo' say they fer a meetin' house! Bad 'nuff ter sell them ter pay ol' man Norsmith fer papa's owin's but ain' sellin' nothin' ter build no meetin' house fer yo'."

"Yes, yo' are." Bart was anxious to get to the whisky barrel and build up more courage wherewith to face Dovie. "Now, looka here, Dovie. Yo' might's well know now 's never. Ain' bin no money a-owin' ter Mista Norsmith but what kin be taken care of come cotton crop's in. But I a-needin' money. Needin' it fer ter build me a new church in Brownsville. Goin' ter be the best church outside o' Mobile 'n' I a-goin' ter be the Rev'nd 'n' yo' the Rev'nd's wife. Doin' it jes' as much fer yo' as fer me, I am. Doin' it fer yore mama too 'n' fer the Dummy. Jes' think how proud yore mama'll be a-sittin' in the front pew, 'n' the Dummy he a-goin' ter be a Rev'nd's son. 'N' yo'll be all dressed up in black silk a-settin' there like'n a Rev'nd's wife. What two, three niggers compared ter all that? 'N' 'sides, it my right 'cause yore papa he promise me. He always a-sayin', 'Bart, when I die yo' kin have yore church.' "

"Tha's a damn lie, Bart Boggs. Papa never say nothin' like'n that. He was a-puttin' yo' out the very night he died. He a-knowin' yo' worthless 'n' a-tellin' yo' ter git off the place. Givin' yo' a horse 'n' saddle 'n' a-tellin' yo' ter skedaddle. All yo' do is lie. Yo' a-tellin' me we owin' money on papa's borrowing. Yo' a-tellin' me we have ter sell off our niggers ter pay it. Yo' a-sayin' yo' ain' a-sellin' Nero nor Congo nor Calico, but yo' a-sellin' Sippi. Jes' now saw Sippi. He ain' sold. Now yo' a-tellin' me yo' a-goin' ter build a church with the money yo' gittin' from my papa's niggers. Well, yo' ain', less'n yo' build it over my dead body."

Dovie's eyes searched through the dusk of the barn. On one wall, she spied a long leather rein hanging from a nail. In a trice she was across the floor; she pulled the strap down and came back toward Bart, brandishing it. Bart edged away from her, backing up toward the wall.

"Didn' sell Sippi," he protested lamely, " 'cause bein' a Rev'nd I needin' a body servant."

"Who yo' sell Nero to?" Dovie raised the strap and brought it down, but it landed with a quiet thud on the shoulder of Bart's coat.

"Yo' stop that, Dovie. What matter it makes whar' I sol' him? But if'n yo' wants ter know, sol' him ter that Mista O'Neal—him what I married ter Miz Salsman's daughter what lives out on the Orion road."

" 'N' who yo' sold Calico to?"

"Why ter that Mista Maxwell what bin here las' night. He treat him right fine, he will."

" 'N' Congo?" Dovie raised the strap again and this time it descended on Bart's face.

He flinched and advanced toward her but she cut at him again. "Whar's Congo?"

"Now, Dovie, why yo' a-carryin' on so? Put down that strap 'n' behave yo'self. Don' rightly know who bought Congo—some stranger what I never saw before. Yo' stop a-hittin' me. Yo' a Christian woman 'n' ain' fittin' fer yo' ter be sashayin' 'roun' like that. Yo' hear me, Dovie! Don' hit me 'gain." He lunged at her, trying to grab the strap from her hand. A shrill ululating scream from the door caused them both to turn. It was the Dummy.

His rage, which he was unable to express except in animal-like howls, was maniacal. He realized, through some obscure method of reasoning, that Bart had sold Calico along with the others, and now he saw this man whom he hated threatening his mother. With a howl like a wild animal, he hurled himself at Bart, biting, kicking and clawing. His teeth sunk deep into Bart's left hand and the pain made him release Dovie.

Now the pent-up hatred which Bart had always felt toward the boy exploded, and he grabbed the Dummy by his long hair, holding him with one hand while he cuffed him with the other. His cuffs, delivered with the full strength of his powerful hands, changed the Dummy's cries of rage into frightened yelps of pain. But Dovie, released now, dropped her strap and started mauling Bart with her bare hands. Dovie was no weakling. Her poundings and clawings had a telling effect, and when Bart released the Dummy to restrain her, the boy started in on him again. The total effect was like a bear baiting, with the roaring Bart as the bear and Dovie and the Dummy as the terriers.

But Bart was the stronger. He flung the Dummy off, and the boy skittered backward, stumbling and falling. Bart grabbed Dovie with one hand, and the fingers of the other tightened around her throat more to prevent her from screaming than to harm her, but once his fingers touched the soft flesh, they tightened convulsively. The Dummy crawled toward them, his one thought to protect his mother.

Out of the darkness behind Bart, a form emerged, black, brutal, menacing. It raised its enormous arms. Both Dovie and the Dummy saw it but Bart did not. Dovie struggled to free herself, feeling her breath choked off. All the while she could see the cudgel in the mighty hands descending, and then heard the hollow sound as it hit Bart's head. It sounded like the bursting of a ripe squash or the kerplunk of a dropped watermelon. Blood spattered over Dovie and the Dummy, and Bart collapsed like a bag of middlings thrown carelessly on the floor.

"Masta suh." Kru reached out his big arms and encircled both Dovie and the Dummy. "Masta suh."

The welted skin was warm against Dovie's cheek, and she smelled the fresh odor of bergamot leaves. The mighty arms protected her and calmed her while she gasped for breath. The Dummy's screams subsided to whimpers and he clung frantically to Kru, feeling that at last he had found security. Dovie panted in Kru's arms for a long moment. It was too dark to see much of anything now. Bart's body was merely a blacker part of the floor than the rest, and Kru's huge body blended into the darkness.

"I think yo've killed him, Kru." Dovie finally found her voice. She spoke dispassionately, surprised at herself because she felt so little emotion. The form on the floor meant nothing to her now, and it dawned on her that it never had.

"Yes, masta suh."

"I think he's dead and I'm glad yo' did it, Kru. I would of done it myself if'n I could. He might of killed me o' the Dummy. This is the secon' time I owe my life ter yo', Kru."

"Yes, masta suh." Kru's arms clasped them both more tightly.

"But nobody mus' ever know yo' did it o' they would kill you'. I cain' have them kill yo', Kru, fer savin' me." Dovie forgot that neither Kru nor the Dummy could understand her. "Nobody mus' know. Nobody." She extricated herself from Kru's arms. "Let me think."

A long silence ensued, broken only by the Dummy's whimpers and Kru's consoling clucks and utterances.

Dovie's thoughts were racing. At length she made up her mind. Having done so, she was in command of the situation.

"Yo' 'bide here, Kru, with the Dummy. Understand? Here! Don' move, Kru." To make certain that he understood her, she knelt down, placing her hands on his feet and pressing them to the floor. "Here, Kru! Right here! I'll be back in a moment."

Kru seemed to understand. He leaned forward, placing his hand on her head. "Yes, masta suh."

Dovie edged away, backing toward the door to see if Kru might have misunderstood and started to follow her, but there was no movement in the darkness. She ran toward the house, tripping over her long skirts. She had forgotten the recently erected hitching rail and ran full tilt into it. The fall stunned her but she was up in a moment.

A light streamed through the kitchen window of the big house. Dovie ran in through the door. Fronie was sitting on a chair, weeping, and Aunt Ruthie was slicing the remains of the barbecued pork for supper. Dovie could understand Fronie's tears for the missing Calico, but at the moment she could not condone them.

"Stop that bawlin' 'n' git up! Light me a lantern. Quick now! Somethin' happened. Don' know jes' what but gotta fin' out."

"Yo' fin' Calico, Miz Dovie?"

"Calico a-comin' back." Dovie waited for Fronie to slide up the glass panel of the lantern and light the candle inside with a folded paper spill. She slid the pane down and handed the lighted lantern to Dovie.

"Whar' yo' a-goin', Miz Dovie? Yo' wantin' I should go with yo'?"

Dovie shook her head. "Whar's Sippi?" she asked.

"He a-tryin' ter console Miz Callie 'n' ease her achin' head. He a-combin' her hair."

"Git him. Tell him ter saddle his horse 'n' ride ter Brownsville. Tell him ter seek out the constable. Name's Hendricks, I think, but he kin inquire at the store. Bring him here 'n' tell him ter hurry. They's bin 'n accident." She was out the door before she had finished her sentence, not waiting for the questions she knew Fronie would ask. Going back, she did not run. Her plan was only half formed, and she needed time to perfect it.

The lantern gave only a feeble light inside the vast barn, but it was sufficient to show Kru still comforting the Dummy, the black mass at his feet. He had not moved since Dovie had left. She went up to him, placed her hand on his arm and stroked it gently to reassure him that she did not hold him responsible for what had happened. The lantern showed Bart's body, curiously crumpled, at her feet. She stared down at it—the battered skull, the bloody features, the open, staring eyes. Holding the lantern high, she located the scaffolding of the platform, about ten feet away. Gently disengaging Kru's arms from the Dummy, she motioned to Kru to help her. He followed, looking to her for directions.

Dovie pointed to one of the crude benches which had provided a seat for the afternoon's spectators. She made a motion of picking it up, and Kru understood, for he picked up the heavy bench and stood with it in his arms. Dovie, her lantern held high, designated a spot on the dirt floor about six feet from the front of the platform and signaled to Kru to place the bench there. Now there was something more difficult to explain. Setting the lantern down, she picked up a straw from the floor and broke it in two, then walked to the bench and pointed to the middle of it, her eyes on Kru's. Her hands went through the same motions as they had in breaking the straw. Kru regarded her with uncertainty. Again her hands made the motion of breaking, and it dawned on Kru what she wanted. He jumped up in the air, coming down with all his weight on the bench, but it did not break. A succession of quick nods from Dovie caused Kru to jump again. On his third attempt the bench split. Dovie's nod this time was one of thanks. Seeing his mother smile at Kru, the Dummy came over and put his arms around the black, kissing his paps and nuzzling his chest.

Taking Kru by the arm, Dovie walked back to where Bart's body was sprawled on the floor. The pressure of her hand on Kru's shoulders made him bend over and her hands guided his to Bart's feet.

291

Now he divined her purpose. Straightening up, he grinned at her and muttered his only words, "Yes, masta suh."

The rapprochement between them was quite complete. Kru realized what Dovie was doing now; she was absolving him from all guilt in the matter; she was making it appear that it had been an accident. He dragged Bart's body over, lifted it, placed the cracked head face down against one of the broken halves of the bench, then spread the arms and legs apart, making the attitude even more grotesque than it had been before. Dovie watched, nodding her approbation. Kru stood back to survey his work, pointing to the platform above and grunting. Not waiting to use the ladder behind him, he jumped up, caught the edge of the platform and hoisted himself up.

With elaborate pantomime, he stood beside the makeshift pulpit, gesticulating, his hands making a swooping downward motion. He placed his hands on the pulpit and with a mighty wrench he loosened the nails that anchored it and sent it crashing to the ground beside Bart's body. Dovie had not thought of this particular refinement. She saw the logic in it—Bart might have been leaning on it and his weight caused it to topple over. Kru jumped down from the platform and pointed beyond Bart's body to the bloody mud on the floor. His hands scraped the dirt from the floor and spread it over the blood, trampling it down with his big feet until there was no trace left.

Dovie was exhausted. Watching Kru's movements, she perfected her story and knew exactly what she was going to say. Her only concern now was for the Dummy. Kru had quieted him and had temporarily displaced his need of Calico. He seemed contented to be with Kru. She ripped off her aron and tied it around Kru's waist, placed the Dummy's hand in his and beckoned for them to follow her. At the entrance to the house, Kru stopped, and his eyes, white in the candlelight from the lantern, showed his fear. Dovie quieted him by pointing to the Dummy and the door. Kru entered as warily as an animal entering a trap, but now that the Dummy divined what was happening and that Kru was coming with him into the house, he showed his pleasure by tugging at Kru's hand and gesticulating with the other while he uttered little cries of pleasure. Kru was convinced that nothing would happen to him, and all three entered the kitchen.

Callie, who had made her way into the kitchen, seeking the company of Aunt Ruthie and Fronie, looked up in fright.

"Who that big black gyascutus with yo', Dovie? What he a-doin' here in my kitchen? He near naked, he is."

"Sh, Mama, he keepin' the Dummy quiet. Cain' have him a-screamin' no more. Listen, Mama! Bart's dead. He's out 'n the barn, dead on the floor."

"He ain' dead, he jes' drunk," Callie scoffed. "Been drinkin' too much outa that barrel. Been a-layin' into it all day." She fluttered a disbelieving hand. "Git Sippi ter run out 'n' pour a bucket o' water over him 'n' tell him supper's ready. Such a day's this's bin! Whar' my Congo, Dovie? My head achin' somethin' awful, 'n' only Congo kin fix it. That Sippi, he too heavy-handed."

"I'll comb yo', Miz Callie," Fronie volunteered. "What yo' say 'bout masta Bart bein' dead, Miz Dovie? 'N' whar's Calico? 'N' whar's Nero?"

"I know," Dovie reassured her. "Knows whar' they at. Goin' fer ter fetch 'em tomorrow, onct we git Bart buried. Don' know if'n Honey sold o' not but if'n he not, git him ter make a coffin tonight, Fronie. If'n he sold, see if some other hand kin do it. Cain' move masta Bart now. Wantin' the constable ter see if'n he dead, but kindly think he is. Cain' tell tho'."

"Whyn't yo' with him?" Callie asked.

"Goin' back 'n' yo' comin' with me, Mama. Ain' settin' out there in the barn alone with no corpse."

"I'll come," Callie agreed, "but still ain' thinkin' he no more'n dead drunk."

Dovie had complete command of the situation now. She directed Aunt Ruthie to take the Dummy and Kru out to the dove cote and make up a bed on the floor for Kru, and then carry their suppers out there. She dispatched Fronie in search of a coffin maker. From a hook in the entry, she took a crocheted shawl for Callie's shoulders, then took her mother's arm to help her out to the barn. On her way out of the kitchen, she reached for a pork rib from the platter on the kitchen table and carried it with her.

She was strangely happy. Bart's death, although she had not sought it or caused it, solved many problems for her. Dove Cote and The Patch were now hers to run as she saw fit, without interference. She had Ransom Lightfoot to take care of The Patch but she would need Nero. Calico was a necessity for the Dummy because he was the only one who understood her son's jargon. She would get them both. Let people talk if they wanted to. What did she care? People's talk didn't butter her bread, and she had no intention of mourning Bart in the darkened seclusion of the parlor for a year. And—she took a long breath—she was free. She would marry again because her body demanded the proximity of a man. She knew she could have Ransom Lightfoot if she wanted him but she was not sure that she did. Certainly he was far more exciting to be with than Bart, but he was only an overseer. He would do for the interim but she aimed higher than Ransom Lightfoot, for someone like that Mista Maxwell who had spent the night at Dove Cote. She might as well have the best.

Chapter XX

THE STILL FLAME of the candle in the hurricane lantern provided only a feeble illumination that did little to dispel the abysmal blackness of the barn, but it was quite enough for Callie and Dovie to see the crumpled shape sprawled over the broken bench. One look fully convinced Callie that Bart was not drunk but dead. She lowered herself carefully onto one of the benches and pulled Dovie down beside her, taking Dovie's hand in her own. For a long time they sat in silence.

"Yo' never did love him, did yo', Dovie?" Callie asked thoughtfully.

"No, Mama, I jes' never did. Loved Tommy but never did love Bart."

"Now Bart's dead 'n' I think Tommy's dead too. Never had no word from him in all these years. If'n he was alive, sooner o' later we'd o' heard from him. Guess we'll never know 'bout Tommy nor what happened ter him but we shore know Bart's a goner."

" 'N' I'm glad, Mama. Tha's an awful thing ter say, ain' it? But papa was right. He should o' been sent away." She clutched at her mother's hand and stared at the dark heap. It was true, she had never loved him. She had enjoyed his body, yes. Fifteen years ago he had been young, handsome, stalwart and virile, and his body had been a thing of constant desire to her but she had never loved more than his body. Now that his body was gross, fat and too familiar, she no longer wanted that. It was true! She was glad he was dead.

Turning to her mother, more to hear the sound of her own voice than to confide in Callie, she told her everything that had happened. She told how Bart had deceived them into thinking that the sale was to repay Tom's loan at the bank; how he had intended to build a church in Brownsville with the money and set himself up as a preacher; how he had sneaked Nero, Calico and Congo into the sale without her knowing it; and how Kru had appeared out of the darkness to protect her and the Dummy from Bart's drunken rage. Now he was dead, and except for Kru and the Dummy, neither of whom was able to tell about it, Dovie and Callie were the only ones who knew. Yes, she was glad he was dead.

Her words trailed off, swallowed up in her thoughts. Never again would she have to tease or cajole him when she desired the gross animality of his flagging passion. Never again would she have to retch at his whisky breath or the stench of his unwashed body. No longer would he be a threat to her afflicted son or to herself. Dove Cote and The Patch were now hers and the Dummy's. And, with this certitude of possession, she determined to step into her father's shoes and continue on with Dove Cote and The Patch.

With this decision another tempting thought occurred to her. Just as her father had forsaken Callie's embraces for the greater delights of his wenches at The Patch, so could she, free now from Bart, pick and choose among other men, not Negroes of course, but white men like Ransom Lightfoot.

Yes, she would be mistress of Dove Cote, but in doing this she would need Nero to guide and counsel her. Not only would she need Nero but the Dummy would need his Calico, for Calico was his only means of communication. Tonight he seemed to be contented with Kru but, despite the affection she felt for Kru, she could not keep that naked savage around the house. Besides, Kru was as unable to communicate with her as the Dummy. Nero and Calico would have to be bought back, but how? She had no idea where the money that Bart had received for the sale might be. But it didn't matter. Tom Verder's daughter didn't need money; everybody knew that her credit was good now. The money was somewhere. She'd find it.

The sound of horses in the drive caused her to move and she took the lantern, walked to the door and waved the light. Sippi and a white man emerged from the darkness and although Dovie had never met the man before, she recognized the star of authority on his vest. Knowing that convention demanded it of her, she started to weep.

"We jes' had 'n accident here, Constable Hendricks. Thinkin' it best I send fer yo' 'fore we done anythin'. It my husband. He's dead. Oh, oh, oh!" she wailed, "it more'n human heart kin bear. Firs' my papa 'n' now my husband. Ain' nobody left ter take care o' me 'n' my poor 'flicted boy."

Callie looked at Dovie in surprise and then, cued by her daughter's performance, she started to wail also.

" 'N' Bart, he jes' like'n a son ter me. He so good 'n' religious 'n' all. Always a-prayin' fer me, he was, 'n' now sweet Jesus a-tooken him."

The constable was touched by the weeping women and the double tragedy that had struck Dove Cote.

"Jes' saw him this afternoon while I out here fer the sale. He a-lookin' right pert."

"It this sale what killed him." Dovie seemed to turn her tears off almost automatically. "He a drinkin' man, Bart was, 'tho he didn' let no one know it, him bein' a rev'nd 'n' all." She shook her head dolefully. " 'N' that barrel o' whisky what he bought fer the sale too much a temptation fer him, wa'n't it, Mama?"

"Bart a right bad drinker," Callie agreed, dabbing at her own eyes with her black handkerchief, "but he a good man, right religious he were, 'ceptin' that he loved his licker which no one kin rightly hold 'gainst him."

"How it happen?" the constable asked. "That is, if'n yo' a-knowin'."

Dovie nodded her head, valiantly holding back her tears now and getting up sufficient courage to speak.

"We had supper all ready . . ."

". . . lots o' barbecued pork left over from the sale," Callie finished the sentence for her.

" 'N' Bart he not in the house. Thought mayhap he might still be out 'n the barn so I went out ter call him. Came in 'n' see him a-standin' up there 'fore that dingus," she pointed to the smashed pulpit on the floor, " 'n' he a-prayin' 'n' a-thankin' God fer all the good prices what our niggers brung today. He see me a-comin' in the door —it not quite dark then—'n' he lean over 'n' stretch his arms out ter me. 'My darlin' wife,' he say, 'le's join our voices together in a prayer o' thanksgivin' ter Almighty God fer his wondrous blessin's,' 'n' those the las' words he say. He lean forward 'n' I see that there wooden thing a-givin' way 'n' it pitched my Bart right down onto his pore head onto that there bench. If'n he hadn' been drinkin', think he coulda saved himself but he jes' went headlong down. I ran to him 'n' tried ter help him but he daid then. Thought mayhap I'd better sen' fer yo', not knowin' what I should do, here all 'lone with nobody ter help me."

"Accidental death." The constable took the lantern and examined Bart's body. "Jes' pure accidental 'n' him right in his prime 'n' all. Kin see it happen jes' like'n yo' say it did. Ain' holdin' no one responsible. Yo' better come with me inter the house, Miz Boggs, yo' 'n' yore pore mama. Ain' fittin' that yo' stay out here with him no more. Yo' got anyone what kin help yo' git him inter a coffin?"

"Ain' nobody here now 'cept the niggers. Bart sold Nero 'n' he always take care of everythin'. Got me an overseer but he over ter The Patch 'n' cain' git him. Maybe . . ." She looked up at the constable, the very picture of a bereaved widow. "If'n yo' could send somebody over there ter fetch him fer me. 'Preciate it, I would, if'n I could have somebody here ter help me, bein' as how both my papa 'n' my husban's dead 'n' Nero's sold 'n' Mista Lightfoot what's over ter The Patch the only soul I kin call on."

"I'll go fer yo', ma'am." Hendricks was indeed touched by Dovie's tragedy, and the sight of bereaved womanhood brought out his chivalry. " 'N orphan 'n' a widder in less'n a month! I'll git the message ter yore overseer, 'n' kin I do anything else fer yo'?"

Dovie shook her head. "Not less'n yo'll be willin' ter ask the Rev'nd Soper if'n he kindly ride out tomorrow say 'bout ten o'clock ter speak a few words over pore Bart whilst we lay him 'way in the groun'. Mighty prayerful man, Bart was, 'n' he likin' a few words from Holy Writ prayed over him." Sippi and another boy entered, interrupting her conversation. They appeared in the dim light and lowered a coffin to the ground.

"When Honey made up that un fer yore papa, he made up 'nother so's it'll be ready, 'n' he a-sayin' yore mama she a-goin' ter need it mos' any day now." Sippi recognized Bart's body and shied off nervously.

"Well, she ain'." Dovie felt like slapping Sippi for his stupidity, but he was too far away for her to reach him. "Yo' bide here whilst I go 'n' git Aunt Ruthie ter come out 'n' wash him 'n' lay him out. Yo 'n' Masinissa gotta help Aunt Ruthie git him in the box."

"Me, Miz Dovie?" Sippi backed away and the other boy followed him. "Oh, Miz Dovie, we jes' cain' do that. Jes' cain' touch masta Bart, Miz Dovie. He daid! Cain' stay here with no daid masta Bart, Miz Dovie. Got ter help Djoubo in the barn, Miz Dovie. Jes' cain' stay here."

"Jes' kin if'n yo' not wantin' ter git strung up 'gain." Dovie was firm. "Took on plenty the las' time, yo' did. If'n yo' not wantin' ter git welted 'gain, yo' jes' try not stayin' here. I'm a-tellin' yo'. Yo' helps Aunt Ruthie."

Sippi was well aware that there was no recourse but pleaded that the lantern be left with him, to which Dovie acceded. She took her mother's arm, and with the constable leading the way through the unillumined darkness, they made their way toward the house. Hendricks bade them a consoling farewell and mounted his horse. Dovie listened to the hoofbeats going down the drive and then escorted her mother into the house.

Both Fronie and Aunt Ruthie, together with Dolly, wept copiously when they heard the news, but there was no real sorrow in their lamentations. Aunt Ruthie quickly consoled herself with the importance of her duties as the "layin'-out woman" of the plantation and gathered together her cloths and her bucket of warm water, while Dovie supplied her with Bart's only clean shirt and a brush to make his suit as presentable as possible.

"Him a-goin' ter have clean drawers?" Aunt Ruthie asked.

Dovie made another trip to her clothespress and got them. She also took a clean pair of woolen socks and handed them, together with the mended drawers, to Aunt Ruthie. The old woman departed, going first to her old crony, Aunt Nervy, to solicit her assistance.

Dovie and Callie, observing the proprieties, retired to the parlor, where they sat stiffly facing each other. There were no words for them to speak. Dovie at length tinkled the small bell on the table and Fronie came in, followed by Dolly. Dovie was glad that their brief spell of weeping was over. Dolly was her usual self but Fronie was sober, still mourning Calico.

"Fronie, yo' go out ter the dove cote 'n' see how the Dummy is. He got that Kru nigger with him but he like that savage 'n' he a-quietin' down. Ain' fittin' that I go tomorrow ter fetch Calico but I gittin' up early the next day 'n' goin' after him."

Again the problem of money rose to perplex her. She had no idea where the money might be that Bart had received from the sale; she had no way of knowing that it was already in the bank. It occurred to her that it might still be in Bart's pockets, so she sent Dolly out to look, telling her to bring back anything she might find either in his coat or pants pockets. Then she remembered she was not entirely without assets.

" 'N' when yo' comes back, Dolly, wants that yo' should git some wood ashes 'n' a rag 'n' clean up the 'Well in the Desert.' Want it ter shine bright's new. Lotsa folks a-comin' here tomorrow fer Bart's buryin' 'n' they all a-bringin' food 'n' wantin' ter eat. Got ter have things lookin' good." She looked at her mother and sensed Callie's approbation.

When Dolly returned she emptied her apron into Dovie's lap. Dovie saw no money, only Bart's gold watch and chain, an old Barlow knife with a broken-tipped blade, two nails, a small roll of twine, a pocket-size, well-thumbed New Testament and a folded slip of paper. It was Norsmith's receipt. Now she knew where the money was, although the total amount baffled her.

Hendricks had evidently taken it upon himself to call at several neighbors' houses on his way to The Patch, for even before Sippi and Masinissa came in, bearing Bart's body in the coffin, two rigs had driven up and deposited their loads of long-faced men and weeping women. Tom Verder had not been waked, but this double tragedy that had descended on Dove Cote demanded the full complement of mourners. The women, after greeting Callie and Dovie with the tears that the occasion demanded, took their seats in the parlor; the men assembled on the gallery for the long night's vigil. On such short notice, it had been impossible for the women to bring the funeral meats, but as more and more guests arrived, they made up for it. A self-elected group presided in the kitchen, and throughout the night the house was filled with the odors of roasting meats and the cakes, pies and hot breads that they turned out. Except for the small group in the parlor, who preserved the correct decorum, there was a carnival air about the house.

Fronie had picked a bouquet of tuberoses and placed them beside Bart. Their heavy odor filled the air and killed any stench of decomposition that might be setting in. The wound on Bart's head still seeped blood onto the pillow that Aunt Ruthie had put in the coffin, but neither wound nor scar showed on his face. Nobody seemed to question the fact that in diving headlong he had been injured on the back of his head. In death, clean-shaven, his face washed and his white shirt clean and crisp, Bart was actually handsomer than he had been in life, and his florid good looks elicited more than the usual amount of pity for Dovie.

Sometime during the night, Ransom Lightfoot came in to pay his respects to Dovie and Callie. He felt the warm, extra pressure of Dovie's hand and realized that it promised much, but his demeanor was correctly that of the plantation overseer to his mistress. He quickly ex-

301

cused himself to go out onto the gallery and, as the representative of the family, the only white male, he acted as host to the men.

The long night dragged on. Sometime in the small hours of the morning, the women served coffee and hot breads. Both Callie and Dovie had to refuse them, as it would not have been considered fitting for them to partake of nourishment.

Dawn arrived, stretching its gray fingers through the curtained windows and putting to shame the feeble illumination of the guttering candles. There was breakfast and now, urged on by the womenfolk, Callie and Dovie sipped coffee "ter keep up yore strength."

Dovie knew what consternation would be caused if Kru, probably forgetting to don her apron, stark naked, and the Dummy walked into the house. She did not dare to lock them in the dove cote as she knew the Dummy's howls would cause Kru to break down the door. She excused herself from the assemblage and went into her father's room, where she got a shirt and a pair of butternut trousers from his wardrobe. Hiding these under her dress, she slipped out the kitchen door and went to the dove cote. The Dummy and Kru were both sleeping, but Kru, instead of being on the pallet on the floor, was stretched out on the bed, the Dummy cradled in his arms. Nothing about their intimacy struck Dovie as being either noxious or untoward, and she had no word of disapproval as she awoke Kru. Pointing to the clothes and nodding her head vigorously, she made him understand that he was to put them on. To make her meaning more explicit, she pointed to the Dummy's clothes hanging on the bedstead.

Finally and reluctantly, Kru spoke. "Yes, masta suh." Dovie knew that he would not scandalize the mourning by appearing naked.

The Reverend Soper arrived about nine o'clock to find that the grave had not been dug. It hadn't occurred to anyone to do it, so Ransom, gathering together four hands, went out to the burying ground and had them dig the grave. It took the hands less than an hour to dig it and, although the sides were not very even and the grave was a shallow one, it would serve the purpose.

By ten o'clock, even more people had arrived, and the hitching rail that Bart had erected for the sale served its purpose a second time. It was probably one of the largest funerals that had ever been held in Brownsville, and the exclamations of sympathy for Dovie and Callie were heartfelt and sincere because of their double sorrow. The benches that had been used at the sale the day before were brought into the house. Callie, Dovie and the Dummy, who was so excited over the crowds that he willingly relinquished Kru for a short time, together with Ransom Lightfoot, sat in the parlor with as many guests as the room would hold. Extra chairs and benches were put in the bedrooms and the dining room, and those who could not be accommodated in the house—mostly the male contingent—stood outside on the gallery.

Soper, now that Boggs was dead and no longer to be feared as a rival, preached a long and eulogistic sermon. He painted Bart as a model husband, father and son, dwelling at length on his Christian virtues and his religious zeal although scoffing, in a gently chiding manner, at his allegiance to the Baptists and their insistence on complete immersion. As Soper had been trained in the Revivalist school, he turned the funeral oration into a plea to all those present to repent and be saved, delineating with fearsome detail the horrible tortures of Hell as compared with the Elysian fields of Heaven. With a final prayer for the departed soul and a plea to the Almighty to admit him, even though tainted by Baptist apostasy, to the presence of the saints, he pleaded for comfort for the bereaved family and concluded his tirade.

He took up his sermon again at the burying ground after six men, supporting the coffin on three fence poles, had carried it there. The cover was nailed on, the coffin was lowered unevenly into the raw red earth and the symbolic clods were thrown on it by all present. Callie, her arm around the Dummy, who was strangely silent, wept without restraint, but Dovie, supported in her pretended grief by Ransom Lightfoot, leaning on his chest, was unable to squeeze out any tears. Her closed eyes, her

303

swooning attitude and Ransom's strong arm supporting her, however, made a sufficiently impressive picture of womanly weakness and grief. But Dovie, her cheek against the male hardness of Ransom's chest, his man odor in her nostrils, was not mourning but anticipating.

After the last shovelful of dirt was thrown on Bart's coffin, the procession straggled across the field to the house. There, those of the neighbor women who had sacrificed the spectacle of the interment to prepare food for the inner man had set the rough table that had been used for the sale with the results of their night's roasting and baking. The family, with those neighbors who claimed a certain priority because of proximity or long acquaintance, ate in the dining room, where Ransom Lightfoot occupied the head of the table, resplendent with the brightly polished "Well in the Desert." Dovie, hungry now, no longer denied herself.

During the meal, the Dummy suddenly started weeping and carrying on. Calico's absence must have occurred to him, for he was inconsolable and came so close to another of his hysterical tantrums that Dovie led him from the table to his room. But nothing she could do had any consoling effect on him. Sheltering him in her arms, she led him weeping from the house to the dove cote. It was as she had expected. Kru was sitting on the doorstep, and when the Dummy saw him, he stopped his cries and ran to the big black, who appeared as happy to see the boy as the Dummy was to see him. Dovie pointed to the interior of the dove cote and they both entered. She closed the door behind them and went back to the house, where sympathetic nods and cluckings assured her that she had not overstepped the proprieties. It was right for a mother to attend to her afflicted son now that he had no father to protect him.

During the afternoon, the funeral guests departed in another orgy of tears and consolations. Dovie remembered to promise the Reverend Soper ten dollars, and although he would rather have had it in his hand than a mere promise, he accepted the offer gratefully and took his own lugubrious departure. By sundown the last guest had departed, and once again, after two days of mill-

304

ing crowds, Dove Cote belonged to the Verder family, such as was left of it.

Callie, with Dolly in attendance, retired to her room, hoping that the slave's ministrations might ease her aching head. The Dummy appeared in the yard, riding on Kru's shoulders. Kru had shed his shirt but still wore Tom's trousers, which reached just to his knees and could barely close. In the kitchen, Aunt Ruthie was salvaging the remains of the funeral meats for a cold supper. Sippi sat on a chair by the kitchen door, his head nodding on his chest. Fronie on the doorstep beside him gazed into space, thinking of Calico.

Dovie sat with Ransom Lightfoot on the gallery.

"Hopin' yo'll stay on at The Patch," Dovie said, breaking the silence. "Be needin' yo' there now more'n ever. Papa gone 'n' Bart gone, too. Not that he much good at overseein', anyhow," she added.

"Thinkin' perhaps yo'd be needin' me over here now, seein's how yo' ain' got no overseer here no more." Ransom shook back the thick shock of yellow curls from his eyes.

"Be needin' yo' in one way, Ransom." Dovie glanced up at him from under lowered eyelids. "But ain' a-goin' ter need yo' in 'nother. Needin' yo' over ter The Patch ter oversee. I kin manage here, but takes a man ter run The Patch 'cause it's bigger. Ain' no one what knows 'bout it 'cept yo'. Yo' satisfied with what papa bin a-payin' yo?"

"He kindly generous, he was." Ransom had other things on his mind than finances. His eyes were on the swelling curves of Dovie's bodice.

"Reckon as how I'll oversee Dove Cote myself. Ain' no law what says a woman cain' oversee her own place, 'n' I kin do it onct I git Nero back. Startin' out fer him tomorrow, I am, 'n' going ter fetch back that Calico, too. It's settled then that yo'll stay on at The Patch?"

Ransom was somewhat disappointed in Dovie's preoccupation with business. The continence that had been enforced upon him by his trip to Dove Cote last night and Dovie's nearness combined to relegate business to a secondary place in his thoughts. Well, at least she wanted him

305

to stay on. Perhaps, in view of Bart's funeral he should not press her too precipitately.

"Do what I kin if'n yo' needs me, Dovie." He stretched both legs out and leaned back in the chair.

His intent was not wasted on Dovie. "Needs yo', Ransom, shore do," Dovie responded, with great longing. "The Patch ain' so far from Dove Cote but what yo' could kindly come over here right often. Kin stay overnight when yo' comes, 'n' sleep in the dove cote. Cain' stay there tonight, howsomever, 'cause the Dummy he a-sleepin' out there with Kru. Now that he ain' got his play-boy, he got a hankerin' fer Kru, 'n' cain' have that gyascutus in the house. After I gits back, sort o' hopin' you'll come over often."

"Where yo' a-goin', Dovie? Yo' ain' a-settin' off ter fetch Nero yo'self! A woman cain' go 'roun' the country buyin' up niggers."

"Kin 'n' will. Gotta git Nero back 'n' ain' nobody else what kin do it. Yo' cain'. What if'n Mista O'Neal a-sayin' he ain' sellin' Nero back? What if'n that Mista Maxwell ain' a-willin' to sell Calico back? Yo' cain' sniffle 'n' take on, 'n' git down on yore bended knee 'n' beg 'em. I kin. I'm a woman 'n' a widder 'n' ain' got no papa neither. They'll do it fer me. Yo' a-knowin' where-at the O'Neal place is?"

"It over on the Orion road t'other side o' Brownsville."

" 'N' whar this place called Benson?"

"Hear tell it 'bout thirty miles. It beyond Orion 'n' Westminster. Have ter cross the river ter git there. Yo' goin' 'lone, Dovie?"

"Takin' Sippi ter drive me far 's the O'Neal place. Goin' ter offer Mista O'Neal that Sippi with some money ter boot if'n he'll let me have Nero back. Sippi's Nero's own git 'n' a lot younger so's it'll be a fair trade. If'n he don' want that, I'm a-goin' ter take that silver dingus in the dinin' room. Then I'll have Nero ter drive me on ter the Maxwell place ter git Calico. Onct we gits back, I'm goin' ter have Nero here ter help me, 'n' with yo' at The Patch, we'll manage. 'N' when yo' kin, yo'll come over ter Dove Cote . . . on business."

Ransom stood up and stretched, breathing deeply of

306

the warm night air. "Kinda long day," he yawned, " 'n didn't git me much sleep las' night. Thinkin' mayhap I'd better git started back ter The Patch whilst the moon's up. Guess that Djoubo boy gone ter bed so's I'll have ter saddle my own horse. Whyn't yo' walk out ter the stable with me, Dovie?"

She stood up, yawning herself. "Kindly like ter stretch my limbs a bit. Bin settin' all day."

Together they walked in the bright moonlight to the yawning blackness of the stable. Passing inside, beyond the silvered light at the doorway, Dovie found herself in Ransom's arms. It was what she had been waiting for. His lips met hers and his tongue found unresisting passage between her teeth. For long minutes they kissed and then he, without relinquishing her, edged crab-wise across the floor, carrying her with him. A pile of green grass, recently cut to clear the field for the sale, impeded their way, and they both sank down on it.

Dovie welcomed the warmth of his embrace, and for once she did not have to be the initiator. Tonight there was no praying, no recriminations, no struggle to arouse her partner into a half-hearted acceptance of her desire. He was already aroused and he wooed her, courted her, loved her and ravished her as Bart never had. In the dim light from the doorway he appeared as a black silhouette crouching over her, and the darkness of his shadowed skin seemed to titillate her even further. She wished . . . no, she didn't! What a strange thought to cross her mind. For a moment, there in the darkness, she had pictured him as a Negro, and the thought had made everything even more exciting.

An hour later, when Ransom arose to throw the saddle over his horse, Dovie spoke to him from her sweet-smelling bed of new-mown hay.

"Soon's I git back, I'll send one o' the hands over ter The Patch ter tell yo', Ransom. Be expectin' yo', I will."

"Be waitin' fer yo' ter come back, Dovie." He mounted his horse, whose hooves beat a tattoo on the barn floor.

Clutching her dress together, she stood up and came to stand beside him, her cheek laid against the rough cloth of his thigh. Her fingers were loath to part with him.

307

"How soon yo' a-goin' ter start pickin' over ter The Patch?" she asked him.

The utter matter-of-factness of her question startled him, coming as it did on the heels of her complete submission and her evident desire for him. It was as if he, having completed his dalliance with a Negro wench, had summarily commanded her to get up and get his breakfast. It established most definitely the difference in their stations—she was the plantation owner and he the hired overseer. He sensed now that he was to serve her in two ways—as her overseer and as her lover. Well, what did it matter? She was goddam good and he looked forward to future occasions.

"Reckon 'bout nex' week, Miz Boggs." He disengaged her hand and clucked to his horse.

"Let me know when yo' gits back," he called over his shoulder as he rode out the barn door.

"Shore will, Ransom," she replied, " 'n' hopin' yo' gits a bale 'n acre."

Chapter XXI

AN EARLY MORNING DANKNESS chilled the air; the fields were still dripping dew, and blackbirds were wheeling over the ripe cotton when Dovie departed the next morning. She had had one of her very infrequent altercations with the usually complacent Callie. That a widow, whose husband's body was not yet cold in the ground, should go traipsing off with only that Sippi was unthinkable. It was preposterous! It was without precedent! What would people say?

But Dovie's conduct, callous and immoral as it might appear to Callie, was as nothing compared with her taking "The Well in the Desert" along with her. This florid and completely useless piece of silver had long been Callie's particular pride. It, and it alone, had given Dove Cote a status far above that of other plantations. Why, complete strangers who had heard about it had stopped to admire it, and Callie took immense pride in showing it off. That Dolly had polished it so recently had not aroused any suspicion on Callie's part, but now when she saw it swathed in newspapers and tied with twine, she had, to use her own words, "a conniption fit," which did not influence Dovie in the least.

"Jes' what manner o' woman are you?" Callie waved her smelling salts in front of her nose. "Yo're hard-hearted, Dovie. Ain' got no feelin's 'tall. Even if'n yo' didn' love Bart 'n' ain' sayin' 's how I blame yo', yo' could show his mem'ry some respect, 'n' yo' ain' got no rights a-thievin' my silver what yore papa gave me."

"Just what kind of a woman am I?" Dovie pondered this question as she drove off with Sippi in the two-seated democrat wagon. What kind of a woman, with her husband buried in the morning, would have dallied in the barn with Ransom Lightfoot as she had done last night, and enjoyed it so immensely? What kind of a woman was she, to whom a man—even a man like Bart—was so necessary and so important? What kind of a woman was she, to flout convention and not give a tinker's dam for her neighbors' opinions? She knew! She knew that Dove Cote and The Patch were important to her. She needed them and she was going to keep them.

Now they were her own. She was the mistress of all these fertile black acres and the equally fertile black cattle that tilled them. What was a gaudy piece of silver in comparison to these other riches? It was the black soil itself that counted; it was the crops and the niggers; it was the sowing and the hoeing, the planting and the picking that mattered to her. It was the vigor and vitality of this land, translated in some way to the vigor and vitality of black hands that toiled to make it productive, and it was now unequivocably hers. It was the warmth of the sun on the land, causing it to burgeon and grow, as her warmth beside a man caused him to burgeon and grow.

There was some strange, inexplicable link between this land that she loved and this man, whoever he might be, that she was always desiring. She realized now that it need not be any particular man. Bart had served his purpose while he had been alive, even though his favors had been granted grudgingly. Last night Ransom Lightfoot had satisfied her, but she had felt neither love nor sentimental attachment for him. Theirs had not been a meetiig of minds but of flesh. They had wasted no time in words or kisses. She was as a field that had been plowed. Surely the soil does not love the plow that furrows it nor the black hands that guide the plow.

A new thought entered her consciousness—the strength

310

and vigor of black hands. She was aghast at the un-disciplined workings of her mind, which caused an attendant surge of hot blood in her body. They frightened her and yet she could not dispel them.

Why had she never had thoughts like this before? Was it because she had depended on Bart and his nearness and the knowledge that he was there to serve her need no matter how unwillingly he might do it? Now he was gone, and she had asserted her freedom last night with Ransom Lightfoot, but although Ransom had pleased her, he had not satiated her. There was something beyond Ransom Lightfoot, beyond anything a white man could give her—something primitive and savage that would out-rage her with a spasm of violent convulsions, and this was what she needed—what her new freedom could give her. How she wanted to lie back spent and exhausted—completely satiated. But this she had never done. Her partners had satisfied themselves but they had never com-pletely satisfied her. Perhaps . . . but of that eventuality she did not dare think.

Riding beside Sippi in the wagon, she glanced down at his dark hands clutching at the reins. Her skin crawled at the thought of those hands touching her and yet, de-spite her revulsion, they had a strange fascination for her. Sippi had never done any very hard work and his hands were smooth, firmly fleshed and strong. She wondered how many dark breasts they had fondled and how many dark thighs they had parted. Kru! Kru, just passing from adolescence into manhood, would have the look Dovie desired.

These forbidden thoughts gave her pleasure. Sometime, she assured herself, she would buy a servant of her own. She had never bought one herself, but now that she was mistress of Dove Cote she would have to buy serv-ants. That would be a duty and a necessity. With Sippi gone—she intended to use him in bartering with O'Neal or Maxwell—she would need a man servant in the house. This imagined need justified her fancy, and she allowed herself to conjure up a picture of such an ideal slave. She would, of course, have to examine him, for nobody in his right mind would ever buy a pig in a poke. Heavens!

She must not continue with this consuming fantasy but erase it immediately from her thoughts. She was Dovie Verder, no, Dovie Boggs (how she hated that name) and she was a white woman, mistress of two plantations. Such thoughts were not for her.

Somewhere along the line she had become confused, and her thoughts had strayed into forbidden paths. The land, the soil, the growing, swelling, fertilizing power of it had become inextricably mixed up with the black hands that sowed it and the sweaty black muscles that reaped it. No white women ever allowed such thoughts to penetrate her mind and yet . . . Someday she would have to buy. Every plantation owner had to buy and sell his black herds. And she knew that no matter how much she denied the thought, some day she would buy a slave, and she knew what she wanted. Oh, how well she knew.

She tucked the dream away into a far corner of her mind but not so far that she couldn't revive it, spoke sharply to Sippi to set the horses trotting, adjusted her parasol at a better angle to keep the sun from her face, lifted the heavy crepe of her veil to get a breath of pure air and sat back on the seat to enjoy her ride.

The broad acres of what is now called the "black belt" of Alabama (not because it holds a preponderance of Negroes, although it does, but because of its rich black loam) passed slowly by. Early morning files of slaves going from their quarters to the fields stopped beside the road to stare at her as she drove by. She amused herself by staring back at them, seeking, without realizing it, the personification of her fantasy. But alas, they all seemed alike! Niggers in work-stained clothes! Rough field hands who became an agglomeration of black faces and white grins. She wished she could remove the bonnet of black crepe that Callie had insisted she wear. It had a faint, musty, chemical smell which nauseated her, but she recognized the wisdom of wearing it. It hid her face from public view, kept her identity a secret and would, she was sure, ensure her that peculiar position that a widow, recently bereaved, is granted. This was her first venture away from home alone. Indeed it was almost the first time she had ever been away from Dove Cote except for excursions into Brownsville with her father and mother. Beyond Brownsville was *terra incognita*, and she gloried in the spirit of adventure and the authority and distinction that she had. She felt a wave of gratitude for Kru for saving her life; no, she must be honest with herself. Her gratitude to Kru was not only for saving her life from Bart but also for taking his. Again she was becoming confused. Better think of other things.

O'Neal, the owner of Conmel Plantation was, she knew, the husband of Mrs. Salsman's daughter Lorie, and Bart had married them. Although she felt it beneath her dignity to have social contact with Mrs. Salsman, it seemed expedient to call on the lady and inquire directions to Clonmel. Surely a brief pause in her journey, without even alighting, would not compromise her, so when they arrived at Brownsville, she bade Sippi stop at the Salsman house.

It was far more prosperous-looking now than it had formerly been, owing, no doubt, to the wealth of Mrs. Salsman's daughter, for the O'Neals were regarded as the local plutocrats. It is doubtful that the O'Neals had any more money than the Verders but they had the reputation for living in a style far beyond that of any other family around, and although Dovie had never seen Conmel House, she had heard about it. At her bidding, Sippi dismounted and went to rap on the front door. It was several minutes, followed by a clatter of bolts inside, before the door was opened by a very handsome young woman of about Dovie's own age, richly attired in a raspberry colored peignoir, her long hair curling down over her shoulders. In the bright sunshine, however, her face looked raddled with streaks of makeup. Dovie knew that this creature could not possibly be Mrs. Salsman so she lifted her veil sufficiently to disclose her face.

"I'm Miz Boggs o' Dove Cote," she said, " 'n' I'm wantin' a word with Miz Salsman if'n it not too much trouble."

"She ailin'." The young woman smiled. "I'm her daughter, Miz O'Neal, 'n' I'm a-lookin' after maw fer a couple o' days. Mayhap I kin be o' service ter yo'. Right sorry I was, 'n' my maw too, ter hear 'bout yore sorrow. If'n it wa'n't fer my maw's ailin', I'd a-come ter the funeral. Rev'nd Boggs he a friend o' the family. Please ter accept my sympathy. How kin I help yo'?"

Dovie thanked her, and although she had no inclination to enter the house, she wondered somewhat at the lack of an invitation. "Yo'll do right fine, Miz O'Neal, 'n' don' bother yore sick mama. Kin yo' tell me if'n yore husband be at home? Seekin' him, I am, on a matter o' business. Kindly important it is o' I wouldn't be out, seein' as how I'm in mournin', but it 'bout a Dove Cote servant what he bought two days ago. My late husban' he made a mistake 'n' sold him 'n' it right important now that I git him back."

Lorie O'Neal regarded Dovie carefully. It was without precedent that a widow should be abroad the day after her husband's funeral, but the very fact that she was here denoted the exigency of her errand. Although it would be considered highly improper for a woman alone to call at Clonmel in her absence, Lorie was never one to let conventions stand in her path, and she had no desire to impede Dovie's errand, which sounded innocent enough. Besides, she reasoned, a widow so recently bereaved could not attract her husband's attention. She had no compunction about her husband's seeking satisfaction with colored wenches but she was always suspicious of white women, perhaps because she allowed him so little access to herself. She realized his wealth and the prestige she had acquired as his wife, and she had no desire to lose these valuable assets. Even though she did not want Johnny O'Neal himself, except for what he could give her, she had no intention of relinquishing him to another woman.

"Who's out there, Lorie?" Dovie heard a masculine voice from inside the house, petulant, expectantly waiting and not to be denied. "Why'n't yo' come in, Lorie?"

Lorie closed the door behind her and stepped out. She gathered the thin silk robe about her and smiled up at Dovie.

"Mista O'Neal's at home, Miz Boggs, leastwise so far's I know."

" 'N' how do I git ter Clonmel?" Dovie asked.

"That's easy." Lorie forgot to clutch the robe as she

pointed down the street. "Jes' follow the Orion road 'bout five o' six miles. Clonmel on the lef'-han' side. Cain' miss it. Big brick gateposts out 'n front 'n' long lane o' trees a-goin' up ter the house. House brick with white pillars in front. Jes' cain' miss it. Shore would 'preciate it if'n yo' do me a favor. Take it kindly if'n yo' tell Mista O'Neal that I cain' git home today. Ma's tooken kindly bad 'n' needin' me here ter help her. That the doctor in there now." She jerked her thumb over her shoulder. "He 'xaminin' her, he is, so's that why I couldn't invite yo' in. Yo' tell Johnny I cain' git back till tomorrow."

"Shore hope yore mama's better right soon." Dovie was outwardly sympathetic, but she knew the vigorous, youthful voice did not belong to old Doctor Speare. "Give Mista O'Neal yore messsage, I will. Yo' a wishin' him ter come 'n' help yo' with yore mama?" This last, although said in outward good faith, was Dovie's way of letting Lorie know she had not believed the fabrication about the doctor.

"No, ain' necessary 'tall." Lorie's face flushed. "I'll git along all right. Tell Johnny I'll be home 'bout noon. Thinkin' Mama'll be better then." Her impatient finger on the latch signified that the interview was over.

"She a chip off'n the old block," Dovie said aloud as they drove off, thinking that Sippi would not even hear her, but to her surprise he answered her.

"Ol' Miz Salsman, she a whore," he said. "Masta Bart he used ter go there 'n' keep me waitin' outside fer a long time. Peeked through the back winders onct, Miz Dovie, 'n' seed 'em."

"That's 'nuff, Sippi. Masta Bart dead, 'n' cain' talk 'bout him. Yo' best learn ter keep yore mouth shut."

So Bart had visited Mrs. Salsman. What he had denied his wife he had sought from another woman. She hated him even more, remembering how often she had had to tease and excite him just to obtain his unwilling consent. Of course, she had suspected it but now Sippi's words confirmed her suspicions. But Bart was gone, drat him, and she intended to enjoy this outing even though she must view it through a crepe veil.

Well, if Bart had had Mrs. Salsman, she had had Ransom Lightfoot, and what more could a woman want than him. Maybe she'd marry him some day. The thought gave her a feeling of security. It would mean male companionship at all times, although even the prospect of Ransom Lightfoot sharing her bed did not dispel the other thought she had tried to hide. Ransom was a white man and, like Bart, could withhold his favors if he desired. She wanted someone who would be at her beck and call whenever she wanted him, someone who could not refuse her, someone whose body belonged to her "lock, stock and barrel." She settled back in her seat, opened her parasol, lowered her veil and told Sippi to trot the horses. She was anxious to get her business at Clonmel over with and get on to Benson.

It was as Mrs. O'Neal had told her. About six miles down the road, she espied the tall brick gateposts, each topped with a marble pineapple. The elaborate wrought iron gates were closed, but as Sippi halted the horses, an aged Negro hobbled out of the little brick house inside the gates to ask her business. Her widow's weeds proved effective. He answered her with a low bow, sent a half-naked urchin sprinting off to the big house to apprise his master of company's arrival, and with a flourish opened the gates, which were well-balanced and swung easily on their hinges. Prompted by Dovie, Sippi drove up the graveled lane under the spreading tupelos to the circular drive, which surrounded a formal planting of flowers, before the broad white steps. An adolescent boy, decently dressed, appeared to take the horse, but Dovie waved him away and signified to Sippi to remain in the wagon. Without assistance, she climbed down from the wagon, adjusted the hoops under her dress, straightened her veil and marched up the front steps. The front door was open, but instead of entering, she pulled the bell chain and listened to the jangle of a bell somewhere inside the house.

She had only a few moments to wait. A strikingly handsome octoroon girl, dressed in a brown and black calico, came undulating down the hall, her wide skirts, without hoops, dragging on the floor. She was adjusting a fichu around her neck and pinning it with a large brooch. Meeting Dovie in the doorway, she bowed low out of deference either to her widow's weeds or to the fact that she was a woman, but she did not stand aside for her to enter.

"Kindly sorry, mist'ess ma'am, but Miz O'Neal she ain' ter home." Her eyes tried to penetrate the black crepe.

"Didn' come here ter see Miz O'Neal," Dovie answered with a voice of authority that immediately told the servant she was not cut from the same bolt of cloth as her mistress. "Here ter see Mista O'Neal on a matter of business—important business. Please ter inform him that Miz Boggs o' Dove Cote awaitin' his pleasure, 'n' if'n I'm a-goin' ter wait, I ain' standin' out here on no gallery."

"Yas'm, Miz Boggs ma'am." The girl stood aside and permitted her to enter. "Right this way, Miz Boggs." She led her into a drawing room far more splendid than Dovie had ever known existed. Its jalousies were drawn against the sun to make it cool, and in the half-light Dovie had a glimpse of brocade-hung walls, crystal chandeliers, white wainscoting and portraits in wide gold frames.

"If'n yo'll sit here, please, mist'ess ma'am." The girl indicated a high-backed, ornately carved sofa upholstered in cherry-colored damask. "I'll tell Mista O'Neal o' yore arrival 'n' he'll 'tend yo'. Beggin' yore pardon, Mist'ess ma'am, he'll be requirin' a few minutes. May I serve yo' a cup o' coffee 'n' a light refreshment whilst yo're a-waitin'?"

Dovie suddenly realized that she was hungry and she sank down gratefully onto the sofa. As the girl departed, she glanced out through the hall, past the winding staircase with its carved spindles, into what must be a dining room where a shining mahogany table, part of which stretched beyond her vision, mirrored a cut glass epergne in its center. This house, with its size and splendor, would be a fitting place for "The Well in the Desert." She felt she had something to bargain with.

The girl returned with a silver tray holding a silver pot of coffee, an eggshell-thin cup and saucer and a plate of tiny buttered biscuits. Dovie noted that the girl had taken time to slip on a pair of hoops under her skirt, which now belled out as fashionably as Dovie's own. She drew up a tiny, spindle-legged table and set the tray on it, poured the coffee and passed the cup to Dovie. Dovie

317

swept back her veil and sipped the hot coffee slowly, eating two of the biscuits immediately. Her coffee cooled and she drank it all, poured herself another cup from the pot and ate the remainder of the biscuits, becoming impatient at the delay. She still had a long drive ahead of her.

After about half an hour, she heard footsteps on the stairs and saw a man descending, most correctly dressed in a long blue broadcloth coat, flowered waistcoat and slim stovepipe trousers. He was by far the most elegant person Dovie had ever seen. He was handsome, but in a far different way from either Bart or Ransom Lightfoot, for although he lacked the strength and powerful build of Bart and the rakish good looks of Ransom, he made up for it in fineness of features and an air of good breeding that neither of them possessed. He was, as Dovie could see, suffering from an early morning hangover, and even his immaculate toilet and clean-shaven cheeks could not hide the dissipation in his face.

"John O'Neal, at yo' service, ma'am." He advanced toward her. "I jus' heard 'bout yo' great loss last night. My heartfelt sympathy, ma'am." He bowed low and took a seat on the sofa beside her.

" 'N' naturally yo' didn' reckon on seein' me here today, me being a widder 'n' all," Dovie hurriedly admitted the impropriety of her presence. "But I'm in awful trouble, Mista O'Neal, 'n' yo' the only one what kin help me."

She was, O'Neal considered, a far handsomer woman than his wife, for where Lorie's prettiness had faded, Dovie's had bloomed. Added to his natural chivalry was the attraction he felt for her. Impulsively he reached his hand over, laid it on hers in a gesture of sympathy and protection, and found to his amazement that she did not withdraw her hand.

"Anything I kin do fer yo', Miz Boggs, anything at all will be a pleasure, I assure yo'. If'n I hold the key ter any problem o' yores, yo' have only ter ask." And, as she made no effort to withdraw her hand, he clasped it with what might have been heartfelt sympathy or merely the desire to make contact with her flesh.

318

"Day 'fore yesterday, the same day my husban' was killed," Dovie bravely forced back her tears, "yo' bought my man Nero, what was sold through mistake. Now I a-needin' him. With my papa dead 'n' my husband killed, ain' got nobody ter help me 'n' Nero he know Dove Cote better'n anybody. I reckon on keepin' Dove Cote a-goin'. It my home 'n' it my mama's home 'n' we needin' it. Cain' let it run ter weeds, 'n' Nero he kin help me. He always with my papa 'n' papa say Nero know as much about the place as he do. Needin' Nero bad, Mista O'Neal, 'n' hopin' yo' sell him back ter me. Aimin' ter pay fer him what yo' paid 'n' goin' ter give yo' something extra fer yore trouble."

O'Neal squeezed her hand a little tighter.

"That Nero a fine boy, Miz Boggs, but if'n yo' desire him back there ain' nothin' I kin do but let yo' have him. Yore need fer him is far greater'n mine."

Dovie was aware of the pressure on her hand, and she returned it in what might have been a gesture of gratitude or might have been because she wanted him to keep his hand there. He reminded her a little of Tommy Verder, and she envied Lorie Salsman for landing such a rich and attractive husband.

Smiling bravely in her sorrow and with a catch in her voice, she looked up at him. "Thank yo', Mista O'Neal. If'n yo' be so kind as ter send yore servant out to my rig," Dovie's free hand made a gesture towards the door, " 'n' ask my boy ter come in 'n' bring the package what's in the wagon, I'll give yo' yore choice. Kin either have my boy Sippi what was my husband's body servant o' if'n yo' likes yo' kin have 'The Well in the Desert,' which is a silver doodad my papa bought fer my mama when they were married. It'd look right well in yore dinin' room 'n' it solid silver, it is." She waited until the servant went out and Sippi came in, then gently disengaged her hand from his and supervised Sippi's unwrapping of the silver monstrosity and the placing of it in the middle of the dining room table. Its massiveness and opulence shone becomingly in the big dining room, and from the expression on O'Neal's face she knew that Nero was hers once more. Nevertheless, she felt it necessary to extol the other piece of merchandise she was offering as a choice.

"This Sippi here, he a right good boy. He's Nero's git, he is, 'n' trained fer a house servant. If'n yo'd like ter shuck him down, Mista O'Neal, yo' could take him out 'n the quarters 'n' 'xamine him. He younger'n Nero 'n' worth more, I reckon."

O'Neal paid scant attention to Sippi, as his eyes were on the centerpiece, which looked far more magnificent in the dining room at Clonmel than it ever had at Dove Cote. He examined it closely, noting the workmanship of the silver palm trees, the camel and the Arab.

"It the mos' beautiful thing I ever did see." O'Neal stood back to admire it better. "But it worth far more'n that nigger what I bought from yore husban'."

Dovie nodded her head in agreement. "Jes' wantin' ter git Nero back, tha's all. Ain' got no man ter help me now that my papa's gone."

" 'n' your husban', too," O'Neal prompted her.

Dovie shrugged her shoulders. "Bart never was much help. All he int'rested in were preachin' 'n' prayin'. Guess I wa'n't cut out ter be a preacher's wife. Heard 'nuff 'bout hellfire 'n' damnation ter do me the rest o' my life. Bart he had no business a-sellin' Nero anyway, nor that Calico boy what belonged to my son. Aimin' ter git him back too. Travelin' on from here ter see that Mr. Maxwell up Benson way what bought my son's spotted play-boy. Yo' willin' ter trade me back Nero fer that silver doodad? Cost my papa a thousand dollars in Mobile."

"It's shore worth more'n yore Nero, Miz Boggs. I kin buy a slave any day, but works o' art like this are seldom foun'. Kindly step inter my office 'n' we'll settle the matter."

He led the way out of the dining room and down the hall, pulling an embroidered bell cord as he passed. The same girl answered it, completely dressed now, having added long jet earrings. O'Neal instructed her to tell his overseer to have Nero report at once to the house. Inside his office, he seated Dovie in a chair beside a large mahogany desk, sat down and rummaged in a drawer for paper. A few scratches of the pen and a quick dash of the sand shaker completed the bill of sale, which he handed to Dovie. From another drawer he took a square mahogany box and opened it with a small key attached to a heavy gold watch chain hanging from his waistcoat pocket. From the box he counted out a pile of gold pieces, which he pushed toward Dovie.

"Here's two hundred 'n' fifty dollars, Miz Boggs, that I feel I owe yo'. Please ter 'cept it."

Dovie was awed by the pile of gold, and urged on by O'Neal, she transferred it to her reticule.

"Yo're mighty considerate o' a poor widder, Mista O'Neal." She was genuinely grateful.

"Only wish I could do more, Miz Boggs." O'Neal gestured toward the open door, where Nero stood.

"Miz Dovie!" Nero could not withhold his surprise and joy. "Oh, Miz Dovie, what yo' a-doin' here?"

"Come ter fetch yo', Nero."

"Yo' mean I a-goin' back with yo', Miz Dovie? I a-goin' back ter Dove Cote? Oh, Miz Dovie, jes' cain' wait ter git back, not but what this a nice place," he bowed to O'Neal, "right nice place here at Clonmel, but I a Dove Cote boy, 'n' jes' pinin' ter git me back there. Thank yo', Miz Dovie, thank yo' kindly fer comin' ter fetch me."

"That all right, Nero." O'Neal stood up. "Miz Boggs need yo' now more'n I do. Do yo' know the way ter Benson, Nero?"

"Went there onct with masta Tom, Mista O'Neal suh, ter Falconhurst ter see Mista Maxwell what live there. It up Westminster way, 'cross the big river."

"That right, Nero. Yo're drivin' Miz Boggs up there 'n' I don' want anythin' ter happen ter her. She a mighty fine woman, Miz Boggs is."

"She shore is," Nero agreed. "Ain' nobody in the world so sweet's my Miz Dovie." He kneeled down and placed her hand on his head. "Yo' cain' know, Miss Dovie, what this a-meanin' ter me ter go back ter Dove Cote. Pinin' fer it, I was. But what masta Bart a-goin' ter say when yo' comes back bringin' me with yo'?"

"Bart's dead," Dovie answered him. "We buried him yesterday. I'm the mist'ess o' Dove Cote now. We a-goin' ter fetch Calico too. The Dummy a-needin' him. He kinda contented with that Kru now, but he a-needin' Calico to talk fer him."

"Yo' ain' a-tellin' me that Kru a-stayin' with the Dummy, Miz Dovie?" Nero seemed shocked and was about to say more, but thought better of it. "Kin I go ter the quarters 'n' git my clean trogs 'n' such, Miz Dovie ma'am?"

She nodded her approval and he sped away. O'Neal took her arm and escorted her out to the gallery and helped her up into the back seat of the democrat wagon, where she waited for Nero.

"Miz Boggs," O'Neal looked at her as if asking her pardon in advance for what he might say, "I'm happy ter have made yore 'quaintance. Allow me ter say, Miz Boggs, that I admire yo' very much 'n' I know yo' will make a success o' runnin' yore two plantations. Yo're a fine woman, my dear Miz Boggs, 'n' an extremely capable one. I regret we couldn't have met many years ago. . . ."

Nero came running back, got in the wagon and pushed Sippi away from the driver's seat. "Let yore pappy handle the team, boy."

Dovie reached her black-mitted hand down to O'Neal. "I know what yo' mean, Mista O'Neal," she said. "Know 'xactly what yo' mean. Hopin' now that we're all 'quainted, yo' 'n' Miz O'Neal call sometime soon at Dove Cote. Be nice if'n we all git ter know each other better."

Nero turned around in the seat to face Dovie. "Kin I say somethin', Miz Dovie?"

"Course yo' kin."

"Want ter thank yo', Mista O'Neal, fer bein' so kind ter me. Didn' have a chance ter say good-bye ter that Katie wench what yo' gave me cause she out 'n the field. Hopin' yo'll say it fer me. If I wa'n't a Dove Cote boy, Mista O'Neal suh, I'd shore like ter live here at Clonmel. 'N' yo' good masta, Mista O'Neal suh."

O'Neal accepted Nero's words with a slight nod of his head and reluctantly relinquished Dovie's hand. The wagon wheels started to turn and the wagon sped down the driveway. O'Neal watched it depart from the gallery.

As the wagon turned out onto the main road through the open gates, Dovie turned and waved her parasol, surprised to see the octoroon girl in the calico dress standing beside O'Neal.

Chapter XXII

DARKNESS OVERTOOK them on the road, and Dovie stopped overnight at an ordinary, where she tossed and turned on a vermin-infested bed in a hot, airless room, while Nero and Sippi slept in sweet-smelling hay out in the stables. The next morning, her body covered with tiny vermilion spots, she managed to bathe in a bowl of cold water, comb her hair and dress. After a plentiful breakfast, which was surprisingly well cooked, considering the surroundings, they started out for Falconhurst, arriving there shortly after noon.

After the elegance and luxury of Clonmel, Dovie was surprised at the shabby homespun simplicity of Falconhurst. She had expected more than the weathered-shingle wooden house with its long gallery, which sat back from the road in front of a straggle of wooden barns and slave quarters. Her practiced eye, however, noted the well-kept appearance of the house and grounds. Although the house was no larger nor more pretentious than Dove Cote, its surroundings had an air of good husbandry. Flowers—tall sunflowers, roses, phlox, verbenas, tube-roses and many whose names Dovie did not know— grew in disciplined riot around the house; a row of splint-bottomed chairs was mathematically spaced on the gallery; lines of snowy sheets were flapping in the sun and there seemed to be an overabundance of black adolescents plying twig brooms and rakes on the clean-swept, hard-packed dirt in front of the house. A pleasant-faced woman, possibly ten years older than Dovie, for her hair was streaked with gray, stood on the top step leading to the gallery, talking to a commanding Negro woman who was vociferously directing the activities of the broom squad.

"Yo' thar, Cynthie, put a li'l elbow grease inter yore sweepin', 'n' yo', Billy Jo, yo're slower'n cold molasses. Thinkin' I'll come down 'n' touch up yore legs. Got me a whop in the kitchen 'n' kin use it if'n I have ter."

"Yas'm, Miz 'Cretia Borgia ma'am, we'se a-hurryin'." The response promised much, but the slowness of their actions belied the words.

The gray-haired woman put a restraining hand on the Negress' arm as she started to descend the steps to welcome the stranger. Her smile was gracious, and without having spoken a word, her welcome was warmly expressed. She advanced to the wagon and held out a hand to Dovie.

"Welcome ter Falconhurst," she smiled. "I'm Miz Warren Maxwell."

"Pleased ter make yore 'quaintance." Dovie waited for Nero to cramp the wheels and for Sippi to alight and come around to help her dismount. "Yo' ain' a-knowin' me, Miz Maxwell, but I'm Miz Boggs from Dove Cote Plantation down Brownsville way. Yore husband, Mista Maxwell, he just down to our place a-buyin' servants 'n' I a-comin' here ter see him on business. Shouldn' be doin' it 'cause I'm in mournin', but it kindly necessary. Hopin' yo' won' hold it 'gainst me, me travelin' roun' the country 'n' such-like."

"Why yo' pore thing!" Mrs. Maxwell opened her arms wide and enclosed Dovie. " 'N' yore pore sweet papa dead 'n' everythin'. Yo' jes come right up inter the house 'n' rest yo'self." She glanced up at the colored woman, who was staring with curiosity. " 'Cretia Borgia, git someone ter take this team 'roun' ter the barn 'n' git some food fer these boys. Git Memnon ter run out 'n' fetch Masta Warren 'n' Hammond 'n' ask them kindly ter come ter the house 'cause we got company. 'N'

325

put some coffee on 'n' fry up some ham 'n' eggs 'n' cut that Lady Baltimore cake." She put her arm around Dovie and led her up the steps. "Pity we jes' et 'n' cleared 'way."

"Ain' rightfully hungry nohow," Dovie was too excited to eat, "but kindly like a cup o' coffee if'n it ain' too much bother."

"Bother? Lan' sakes, it a privilege—a downright privilege fer such a pretty young thing as yo'. Yo' jes' come right in 'n' yo' stay right here at Falconhurst jes' 's long's yo' want."

Dovie was touched by the older woman's kindness. Without having to force herself, she burst into tears. "It not only my papa, Miz Maxwell, it my husban' too. He was kilt in an accident the same night's we had the sale 'n' he jes' buried yesterday."

The news of this double tragedy proved too much for Mrs. Maxwell and she wept in sympathy. Helping Dovie as solicitously as though she were an invalid, she propelled her up the stairs and into the main room of the house. With Dovie ensconced in a rocking chair, her bonnet removed, her feet on a hassock, and a young wench standing by to fan her, both women composed themselves. Dovie, anxious to justify her presence under such unusual circumstances, told Mrs. Maxwell of her desire to have Calico back and the reasons why she felt it so necessary to make the trip, even at such an early stage of her mourning.

And Mrs. Maxwell understood. Her heart went out to Dovie and to Dovie's afflicted son, and she agreed it was absolutely necessary that the poor dear child should have his playboy back. Moreover, she didn't blame Dovie in the least for making the trip even in the first days of her double bereavement. Naturally, and here Mrs. Maxwell nodded her head approvingly, the needs of the living came first, and of course the love of a mother superseded everything else. Why, she would do the same for her darling Hammond. She would see to it that Mr. Maxwell sold Calico back to Dovie.

There were too many niggers around Falconhurst anyway! Mr. Maxwell was just going out of his mind

326

about niggers, buying them up right and left until there were too many to do the work around the place. Did Dovie notice when she arrived that there were ten young ones sweeping the front yard when it could easily have been done by one boy? Well that's the way it was at Falconhurst now! Niggers all over the place. More niggers than could ever be used for planting and picking cotton. Not enough work to keep them all busy, and if there was anything she hated to see it was a nigger sitting around picking his toes.

The quarters were full, the barns were full and now Mr. Maxwell was even talking about taking over the chapel, which she had had built for the servants, just to house more niggers. Not that they used it anymore—there were too many niggers to get in it at one time. And nothing she could say would stop him. Hammond was just as bad. All he and his father talked about now was niggers, niggers, niggers, morning, noon and night until she was sick of it! Let there be a sale advertised, and Mr. Maxwell and Hammond were off like a couple of scalded cats and they always came home with a caffle. Heavens to Betsy! She didn't know where they would end up. Niggers eating them out of house and home!

Dovie felt better. With Mrs. Maxwell championing her cause, she was sure that she would be able to repurchase Calico. She was anxious to start for home as soon as possible, but Mrs. Maxwell, avid for company and companionship, would not hear of it. If Dovie started out, she'd have to spend the night somewhere along the road. It would be much better to spend the night at Falconhurst and get an early start in the morning. To this Dovie sensibly agreed.

Having made Dovie comfortable with refreshments, Mrs. Maxwell bustled out to the kitchen, where she started giving Lucretia Borgia, the cook, orders for an elaborate supper. Dovie heard a commotion in the kitchen and guessed that Mr. Maxwell and his son had returned from the fields and were washing up. She could hear scraps of conversation between Mr. and Mrs. Maxwell, with frequent interruptions by Hammond. While she sipped her coffee and waited for the family to re-appear, she looked around. Surely Falconhurst was no better than Dove Cote. It was, in fact, more plainly furnished. Woven rag carpets covered the floor. The furniture was patently of plantation manufacture—straight ladder-backed chairs (with splint seats to one or two of which rockers had been added)—with a sprinkling of heirlooms from Mrs. Maxwell's family.

She dismissed the little girl who was fanning her, smoothed her hair and adjusted her hoops as she heard the Maxwells coming through the dining room. They came in—Warren Maxwell, who had so recently been her guest, his wife, his son Hammond and, much to her surprise, Calico, scrubbed until his cheeks glowed and decently dressed. He stood behind a glowering Hammond and regarded his former mistress with suspicion.

Warren Maxwell advanced to Dovie's chair and took one of her hands in both of his, shaking his head gravely. "Sorry indeed, ma'am, mighty sorry fer yo' in yore trouble 'n' even sorrier that yo' had ter make this long journey. If'n I'd a-known 'bout how much store yore boy set by this here Calico, I'd never o' bought him, never."

"He's mine, papa, yo' gave him ter me." Hammond stood close to Calico. "Yo' tol' me I could have him fer my own 'n' breed him, come time."

"That's 'nuff o' that talk," Mrs. Maxwell interposed sharply. "Miz Boggs's here 'n' yore own mama 'n' such talk ain' fittin' 'fore ladies."

"I know, boy, I know," Maxwell tried to placate his son, "but yo' ain' needin' this boy like'n that poor 'flicted son o' Miz Boggs what cain' talk. Tell yo' what! I'll give yo' Willy Bill 'stead. He a rightly likely young boy."

"But he black 'n' Calico's a mustee."

Dovie tried to win over Hammond. "Calico the only one the Dummy kin make understand him. He bin a-cryin' 'n' a-takin' on ever since Calico left. Cain' do nothin' with him. 'Fraid he's a-goin' inter a dee-cline 'n' die from a broken heart." Dovie was sincere. Her love for her son, or perhaps it was more pity than love,

328

for Dovie had never been a doting mother, had brought her on this long journey, and she did not want to return empty-handed. "Tha's why I come here at this time. Got Nero back from Mista O'Neal ter help me 'n' now I need Calico fer my boy."

"He don' want ter go back," Hammond insisted. "He say the Dummy whop him 'n' ride him all the time. He sick o' being a horse fer the Dummy. Ain' right he should have ter carry a grown boy 'roun'. That ain' no way ter treat a nigger. Calico, he got feelin's too. He ain' no pony."

For the first time, Dovie realized that Calico might have feelings. The Dummy had ridden him for so many years, she had become completely accustomed to the sight. That the Dummy rode on Calico's shoulders had seemed perfectly natural—a boy's game—and she had been quite oblivious to the constant strapping the Dummy had inflicted on his playboy.

"If'n he come back," she promised, "he don' have ter tote the Dummy 'roun' no more. I'll give 'em each a horse. I'll be good ter him. Ain' never mistreated him, never." She lifted her head to look across to where Calico was standing. "Ain' yo' wantin' ter come back ter Dove Cote, Calico? Yore mama's there 'n' the Dummy 'n' me. Masta Bart ain' there no more. We'll look after yo' mighty good."

"This a mighty fine place, Miz Dovie ma'am," Calico found courage to answer. "Masta Warren he's a mighty fine man 'n' I'se masta Hammond's boy now. He don' whop me never. Le's me ride his geldin', he do, 'n' go everywhere he go. Le's me sleep right 'longside his bed. He a-goin' ter let me see 'em whop that Colt tonight."

Warren Maxwell laughed. "Don' misunderstan', Miz Boggs. We don' whop colts here. He talkin' 'bout a boy named Colt what I gotta whop tonight. Whops niggers if'n we have ter, but don' whop colts 'less'n they two-legged ones." He continued to laugh at his own joke.

"There yo' go, talkin' niggers 'gain." Mrs. Maxwell was exasperated. "No matter what we talkin' 'bout, talk gits 'roun' ter niggers sooner nor later. Now, Warren, Miz Boggs jes' lost her dear papa 'n' her dear husband, 'n' her only son a-pinin' nigh ter death 'cause his play-boy got sold. In all her sorrow she came all these miles alone ter fetch him back. Don' matter if'n Hammond has set his heart on him. They's a hundred boys 'roun' the place what he kin have."

"But they ain' mustees like'n Calico. I'll git me some fancies if'n I breed him 'n' I'll . . ."

"Hammond!" Mrs. Maxwell held up a warning finger.

"It's like'n yore mama says, son. Miz Boggs she a-needin' Calico 'n' we'll sell him back ter her fer what we paid fer him. Ain' askin' yo' no profit on him, Miz Boggs."

"Ain' brought much money with me, Mista Maxwell, but I got this in the bank at Brownsville 'n' guess that'll cover it." She passed him Norsmith's receipt. " 'Member how my papa useter write out on a piece o' paper fer the bank ter pay, 'n' Mista Norsmith—he's the banker —he'll send it ter yo'. Kinda hankerin' ter git Calico back myself. He six-fingered like'n the Dummy 'n' seem mos' like'n they's brothers, like'n my papa 'n' Nero what I jes' bought back from Mista O'Neal. It all right 'bout the money, Mista Maxwell. If'n yo show me what ter write I'll write it out fer yo' now."

"Plenty o' time fer that, Miz Boggs. Yo' a-goin' ter visit with us over night, I reckon. Cain' have yo' startin' back now. Git a good start in the mornin' 'n' yo'll make Brownsville come nightfall."

"Now, I'm a-goin' ter show yo' up ter yore room 'n' let yo' git freshened up a bit." Mrs. Maxwell was eager for feminine companionship and genuinely glad to have Dovie stay. "When yo' come down we kin sit out 'n the gallery where it cool 'n' visit. Mayhap yo'll know some new quilt patterns yo' kin show me. Miz Severance what was here las' year, she showed me Tudor Rose 'n' Young Man's Fancy. Right pretty they were. I reckon yo' 'n' I kinfolk, sort of. My mama's uncle, he married a Verder, I reckon, cause we always called her A'nt Vie Verder. That makin' us sort o' cousins, I reckon," she smiled at Dovie, "don' it?"

"Reckon it do, Miz Maxwell, 'n' I'll admire ter set with yo' if'n yore husban'll 'low me ter ask him 'nother favor first. My papa always say that Warren Maxwell know more 'bout runnin' a place 'n any man in the whole Mississippi territory. Well, I got ter fergit that I'm a woman now, jes' like I had ter fergit my sorrow when I started out fer here right after buryin' my husband. Cain' 'ford ter be a woman any more. Got ter run my own two places fer my son. He cain' take care o' himself 'n' I got ter be papa 'n' mama ter him now. I got a lot ter learn, Mista Maxwell. Got Nero ter help me but he a nigger 'n' he cain' make decisions. Would kindly 'preciate it if'n yo' could take me round yore place, Mista Maxwell, 'n' show me how yo' do things. Kindly want ter know jes' how ter handle servants. It all up ter me now. Ain' never been no place 'cept Dove Cote 'n' like ter git an idea o' how yo' do things here."

Warren Maxwell was astonished but at the same time he was pleased. He recognized the exigency of Dove's position, and although he did not approve of women meddling in plantation business, he saw that she was in a somewhat different position than other women. It was true that she had been left alone without any man to help her, and it was also true that her son was absolutely dependent on her. He admired her spunk. Most women would have been moping in a darkened room, bewailing their fate, sniffing at sal volatile, totally resigned to losing their plantation. She was a woman with git-up-and-git, and he respected and admired her courage.

"Now that'd be jes' fine, Miz Boggs, 'n' I'd sure admire ter do it. But this a kinda breedin' farm fer niggers. Don' do much with cotton here. Miz Maxwell, she don' take to it, 'n' she'll give me my comeuppance onct she gits me 'lone fer talkin' ter a lady like this, but that's how 'tis. Mite feared o' shockin' yo'."

"Mista Maxwell." Dovie rose and looked him straight in the eye. "I bin married fer fifteen years. I birthed a son o' my own. I lived with niggers all my life 'n' I know they don' find their suckers under a collard leaf. Now on I got ter handle 'bout two, three hundred servants. Got ter know how ter punish 'em 'n' what fer. Got ter keep the upper hand over 'em. Ain' that I jes' hankerin' ter but got ter do it. Got ter buy niggers, got ter sell niggers, got ter mate 'em up, got ter whop 'em. Ain' nobody but me kin do it. Don' want ter see yo' whop that Colt boy yo' talkin' bout but shore would like ter see him 'n' how yo' keep him till it time ter whop him so's he ain' a-runnin' while he's waitin'."

Mrs. Maxwell was scandalized, but she too realized Dovie's position. She knew that if anything happened to her husband, she would have Hammond to step into his shoes, but without that security she would be worse off than Dovie. She knew she could not do what Dovie was doing. She'd have to sell Falconhurst and return to her family. Despite Dovie's flouting of conventions, she too approved of Dovie's courage.

"Yo' feel like walkin', Miz Boggs?" Maxwell inquired, smiling now.

"Ain't done nothin' but set all day," Dovie answered. "Kin walk anywhere, I reckon, if'n only I could borrow the loan of a straw hat ter wear 'stead of this bonnet. Hot, it is," she explained, " 'n' it smell jes' like ink."

"Got two o' three hats a-hangin' up out 'n the kitchen. Jes' step out, Miz Boggs, 'n' try 'em on. Sure ter be one ter yore likin'." Mrs. Maxwell, her arm around Dovie, led her out through the dining room into the kitchen.

Warren Maxwell looked over to his son, noting his downcast face and that of Calico behind him.

"Got ter give in ter ladies, Ham. Always accommodate a lady what's in distress. Reckon yo' set quite a store on gettin' some nice light-skinned suckers outa this Calico boy, come two o' three years 'n' he got more sap in him."

"Yo' tol' me I could. Said I could have him."

"How old's he now?" Maxwell directed the question to his son but looked to Calico for the answer.

"I mos' sixteen, masta Maxwell suh. My mama tellin' me I the same age's the Dummy, 'n' he over fifteen now."

Maxwell pursed his lips and nodded his head sagely. "Yo' know somethin', Ham?"

332

Hammond caught the slight inflection of jocundity in his father's words. He looked at him expectantly.

"If'n I 'member rightly, this boy pretty well set up fer a boy his age, ain' he?"

"He hung heavy, papa."

" 'N' I'll bet he got good sap in him, even if'n he is young."

"Bet he has."

"Ain' bin no papers passed yet. He still yore boy. Mayhap yo' might git a sucker out'n him yet. Got all afternoon, ain' yo'?"

Hammond started to grin.

"Well, yo' know that Hebe wench?"

Hammond nodded.

"She always ketch quicker'n a house afire. She a-knowin' jes' how ter handle a young squirt like'n Calico. She down ter Dulcy's cabin now. Told her I was goin' ter pick out a buck fer her. Take this Calico down there 'n' tell Dulcy ter take a walk fer herself. Then yo' tell Hebe I said this the buck I picked out fer her 'n' fer her ter git ter work. He only got this afternoon, so's he'll have ter jump her two, three times if'n he kin.

"Then mayhap, if'n yo're lucky she'll ketch 'n' yo'll have yore bright-skin sucker after all. If anyone kin do it, that Hebe kin. Now skedaddle, both o' yo'. Miz Boggs 'n' yore mama comin' back. Git!"

They were both out the door like a flash. Maxwell bowed to Dovie and gallantly offered her his arm, escorting her out the door and down the steps to where Nero and Sippi awaited her.

"Yo' got a good boy here, Miz Boggs." Maxwell pointed to Nero." 'Mos' bought him myself, I did. That other boy look like him."

"He's Nero's git," Dovie explained.

"Better have the both of 'em come along. Might learn somethin'."

As Dovie and Warren Maxwell walked toward the quarters, Nero and Sippi followed. Far down the road that ran between the slave cabins, Hammond and Calico were still running.

Dovie found the tour interesting and inter-

Chapter XXIII

DOVIE FOUND the tour of Falconhurst interesting and
Warren Maxwell an experienced guide. It was easy to
see that his whole heart and soul were wrapped up in
his wife, his son and his plantation, although not necessarily in that order. Nothing else existed for him. He
did raise cotton, yes, but it had become of secondary
importance to him. His real crop—his chief interest in
life—was his Negroes. He realized that for a southern
planter cotton was the hallmark of aristocracy, whereas
raising Negroes for sale placed him in the same category
as those wandering slave traders who went about the
country with a caffle of miserable slaves shuffling along
behind the tailgate of their democrat wagons, but he did
not care.

Already the Hammond family, into which he had married, looked down their aristocratic southern noses at
him and his son, but Warren Maxwell didn't mind. The
future of his little world at Falconhurst, he felt, lay in
his strong, healthy Negroes rather than in his thin, worn-
out acres. He managed to convey some of his enthusiasm to Dovie, although he did not try to convert
her from concentrating on cotton at Dove Cote and The
Patch. But he did point out that she had just received
twelve thousand dollars merely from the sale of a few
of her servants. Surely cotton could not be any more

profitable than that, considering the risks and the amount of work involved in the production of one single bale.

Dovie found the cotton fields uninteresting and unexciting. They varied little from those back home at Dove Cote. Here were the same straight rows of plants, the ripened bolls bursting in the hot sun. To Dovie's eyes, however, the yield seemed sparser than that back home. The pickers—men, women and even children—dragged their elongated gunny sacks down the rows, their backs perpetually bent, their plaintive chant rising on the air. Black drivers, those petty aristocrats of the plantation, lorded it over their serfs, snapping the long black whips that were their badges of authority. Depending on the mood and character of the wielder, the whips either pistol-cracked in the air or stung the backs and arms of the pickers. When Dovie and Maxwell arrived with Nero and Sippi trailing behind, the singing stopped, and the drivers, who only a moment before had lorded it over their charges, became servile and fawning.

Maxwell explained his method of fertilizing the ground after each crop by burning the cotton plants and by hauling manure from the barns. He explained how cotton despoiled the soil, robbing it of its goodness until it became worthless. He advised letting the ground lie fallow for a season, then planting it to corn or millet to break the draining effect of successive crops of cotton. As he pointed out to Dovie, cotton at Falconhurst had become almost a token crop, grown only to justify Falconhurst's existence as a cotton plantation in his wife's eyes. More and more he was putting his acres into sustenance for his Negroes—corn and buckwheat, millet and sorghum, pasturage for his cattle and pigs and fowl. Negroes, like other cattle, needed good food for strong, healthy bodies. You couldn't raise a marketable buck on a starvation diet, so the Falconhurst slaves were well fed, probably better than many of the poor whites in the area.

Yes, he raised a little flax, more to satisfy his wife than anything else. From it his wenches made some of the crude tow linen which was used for clothing. It was really easier to buy osnaburg yardage for their shirts, pants and dresses, but it kept the female slaves busy and the spinning house had long been a plantation tradition. Soon, however, he expected to give it up as he required more and more acreage for food to feed his growing herd.

Dovie listened attentively, realizing how often she had overheard similar conversations between her father and Nero. Years ago this same Warren Maxwell had imbued her father with the idea of breeding slaves, but her father's efforts had been only desultory. He had remained a cotton man, and slaves to him were merely a sideline. Now, however, these facts were important to Dovie and she paid more attention for she knew that it would be her decisions that would govern the success or failure of her two plantations. Cultivation and husbandry were all very well and decidedly important, but they were an old story—an oft-repeated tale—and she took them as a matter of course. She did, however, admire those stalwart slaves which she saw working in the Falconhurt fields. Although Dove Cote slaves were a cut above average, she had never seen such fine specimens as those at Falconhurst. Careful selection and breeding were already beginning to show in the Maxwell herd. Warren Maxwell's stock had the appearance of being thoroughbred cattle. The men were taller, stronger and handsomer, the women prettier.

When they passed from the fields to the slave quarters, Dovie experienced a quickening of interest. Although most of them were out in the fields, there was really not enough work for them all and many were busied with odd jobs around the quarters. Maxwell took her to the vegetable gardens, the carpentry shop and the smithy and to the women's sheds, where wenches were tending children, weaving and sewing. He showed her the chapel —a special project of his wife's—now unused and the long dormitories where the unattached males and females slept. He explained to her his method of mating, whereby he alone selected the bucks that were to cover the wenches. As impersonally as though he were talking about cattle, he told how he chose only the best of his stock for mating, selling off any that were not up to his standard of perfection. Such matings were never permanent. He allowed no sentimental build ups to attach one man to one woman. It was merely a selective mating, with one buck covering one wench until the desired results were accomplished. Then the couple was separated, the woman going to the birthing house, the man back to his barracks until he had another assignment.

Maxwell, as proud of his stock as any breeder, called several of his wenches to him, had them turn and pose before Dovie that she might admire them. Ordinarily he would have shown off his bucks instead of his wenches but he was minded that he was talking to a woman, and he felt there would be a certain indelicacy in exhibiting his bucks, even clothed, to Dovie.

Their tour of inspection ended in the stables, where Dovie, exhausted after her long walk, sat down to rest on an old spring wagon seat in the cool darkness of the barn interior. She knew now that she wanted Dove Cote to be just a model of efficiency as Falconhurst was. She could not, she was quite certain, adapt Dove Cote to slave breeding as Warren Maxwell had done, but she was determined that she would breed some prize specimens for herself. A few fine slaves sold off occasionally would certainly add to her profits but she knew she had no really outstanding examples with which to start breeding. She did have some good wenches—her father and Nero had seen to that—but certainly none of the males compared with these at Falconhurst. Therefore, and she blushed at her own thoughts, she would have to buy at least one to start with, and that one would have to be a male. Its sex was predetermined in Dovie's mind.

While she was sitting, fanning herself with Mrs. Maxwell's big straw hat, she heard the slave bell tolling to bring the workers in from the fields, and almost before its peals had died away, she saw the Negroes who had been working around the quarters running toward the open barn doors.

"Ain' yo' quittin' work early, Mista Maxwell?" she

asked. "Sun's still up. We don' quit at Dove Cote till sundown."

"Ain' 'nuff work here ter keep my hands busy nohow," Maxwell answered. "Usually quits early. Gives 'em a chance ter go down ter the river 'n' git clean. Clean niggers is always healthy niggers. But yo're right, we a-quittin' a mite early tonight. Got a whoppin', tha's why. Don' whop much 'roun' here but when I do, it's fer all the hands ter see. Hates ter whop less'n I have ter, but sometimes it's necessary. So when I do whop, I teach 'em all a lesson. 'Member, I said we was a-whoppin' that Colt boy?"

The tolling of the bell and the commotion caused by the assembling slaves had set off a loud wailing inside the barn. Dovie could hear it plainly now and could make out the words which interspersed the sobbings.

"Don' whop me, masta Maxwell suh. Oh, please don' whop me. Ain' never goin' ter do it no more. Won' never pester no wenches less'n yo' says I kin. Won', masta Maxwell suh, if'n yo' jes' don' whop me this time."

Maxwell shrugged his shoulders and apologized to Dovie with a wry smile. "Sorry, Miz Boggs. That pore devil ain' a-knowin' they's a lady here."

"I heard what that boy said, Mista Maxwell, 'n' I ain' scandalized. Lived with niggers all my life 'n' I know 'em." She turned to Nero for confirmation. "Papa 'n' Nero talkin' 'bout it all the time. Papa mighty particular that his bucks don' go rampagin' all roun'. What's this boy done that's so bad, anyway, that yo' a-whoppin' him?"

Warren Maxwell hesitated and then stammered, "He disobeyed me, Miz Boggs. He was dead set on a gal I got but I wa'n't wantin' ter breed him to her." He ducked his head in confusion and then lifted it to look directly at Dovie. "Aw shucks, Miz Boggs, mayhap it only fittin' that yo' know, if'n yo' a-goin' ter run yore own place. Ain' never talked this way ter a lady afore 'n' never thought I would, but guess yo' got a right ter know 'cause mayhap sometime yo'll have a like case. It's this a way.

"This boy's a Fan, 'n' I ain' talkin' 'bout a palm leaf fan

338

neither. That's his Africky tribe. He's a purentee Fan.* He ain' no common Fanti. Fans are jes' 'bout as fine a breed as yo' kin find, tho' there's them that says Hausas o' Mandingos are as good if'n not better. Always been seeking a Mandingo, I have, but ain' never got one, so cain' tell 'bout them. Cain' ask fer nothing better'n a Fan though. They right handsome, strong 'n' smart. Treat 'em well 'n' they lovin' 'n' 'fectionate 's a puppy. Loyal too. But they high-strung 'n'," once again he hesitated, "they a mighty hot-blooded breed, Fans are. It their worst fault. They gotta have a wench o' they go on a rampage.

"Well, this Colt boy I got from a private sale in N'Orleans. Bought him 'bout five years 'go when he 'bout fourteen, fifteen years old from a man what come from Guadeloupe. Colt ain' the boy's right name; he come with a French name—Colosse o' somethin' like'n that, which means awful big in French 'cause he a mighty big boy even then—but I changed his name ter Colt 'cause he always so frisky 'n' high-steppin' 'n' happy-like. He a purentee Fan. Dam 'n' sire both from Africky. Seen 'em both, so I know.

"He always been kind of a pet o' mine. Liked him 'cause he's so canty 'n' sportive like tho' he cain' work worth a damn. He's strong but he too high-spirited ter work. Workin' him in the fields like puttin' a fine saddle horse ter the plow. So I jes' used him 'roun' the barn

---

* The Fans are a powerful tribe, occupying the Ogowe Basin in Gabon, where they migrated from the interior. They are distinguished from the surrounding tribes by their light color, finer features and magnificent physiques, as well as superior intelligence and beauty. Their language is seemingly a corrupt Bantu tongue. They are brave and courageous warriors but inveterate cannibals. They are a mixture of Negro and Hamitic stock with some Arab blood, which accounts for their lighter color. Members of the Fan tribe were in great demand as house servants among the English in the West Indies, but they were comparatively rare because they were not often captured, and being very emotional, high spirited and mettlesome, they often committed suicide before being shipped out of Africa. The Fans are not to be confused with the Fantis, who are an offshoot of the Ashanti tribe. In slave days, however, owing to the popularity of Fans, the word Fan was often used incorrectly to designate the much inferior Fantis.

'n' put him ter breedin'. Already he sired me five nice suckers, 'n' jes' took him 'way from his last wench 'n' sent him back ter sleep in the barn with the other boys." Maxwell paused to see what effect his words might have had on Dovie. He saw that she was listening rapt-eyed, so he continued, feeling freer now.

"Had me a little Whydah wench what we called Marvie 'n' she a-workin' in the spinnin' house. She not more'n thirteen 'n' this big Colt, he right taken with her. She shore was a cute little thing, pert 's a cricket 'n' pretty 's a picture. But he got her one night 'bout four nights 'go, 'n' he too big fer her. We foun' her the nex' mornin' up in back o' the chapel, 'n' she a-bleedin' bad, if'n yo' know what I mean."

Dovie nodded, not wishing to interrupt Maxwell, be-cause the story had turned out to her liking.

"This Colt boy, he shore awful big," Maxwell's face had reddened in spite of himself. " 'N' he jes' ripped that child all ter pieces. Guess he reckoned he'd done her in but she was still 'live. She lingered on fer 'bout three days, then tooken up with a fever 'n' died. Jes' 'fore she died, she tell 'Cretia Borgia, who a-nursin' her, that Colt he the boy what did it. Didn' want ter tell but 'Cretia Borgia got it outa her. So now I got ter larrup him good. Shore hate ter do it, 'cause like'n I say, he kind of a pet o' mine 'n' he a mighty fine-lookin' boy. Cain' git much fer him with a welted back, but cain' let things like that go on here. Got ter make a 'xample o' him, seein' as how every nigger at Falconhurst a-knowin' 'bout it."

Dovie agreed. "I understand, Mista Maxwell. Yo' got ter hold an iron hand over 'em. Tha's what my pap al-ways said. But if'n this boy so handsome like'n yo're sayin', it do seem a pity ter welt him up. Ain' nothin' else yo' could do ter punish him?"

Maxwell shook his head. "Sometimes we keeps 'em on short rations fer a week. jes' bread 'n' water, but that don' do much good. This time we got ter make a 'xample out o' this one. 'Less'n I whop him, he'll do the same thing right over 'gain 'n' so'll other bucks. That wench worth 'bout eight o' nine hundred dollars come another three o' four years."

"Never do it 'gain, masta Maxwell suh, if'n yo' don' whop me. Cain' take no fifty lashes, masta Maxwell suh. Kill me it will. Not my fault, Mista Maxwell suh. That Marvie she jes' a-chasin' after me alla time. I'll be a good boy, masta Maxwell, suh, if'n yo' don' whop me."

Dovie listened. The soft richness of the voice, a certain mellifluous resonance and deepness that glided over the consonants and lengthened the vowels, aroused her sympathy more than the pitiful pleas. She had a desire to see this boy Colt before he was ruined by the whip. Already a plan was forming in her mind.

"Kin I see this boy, Mista Maxwell? Yo've told me so much 'bout him I'm downright interested, 'n' 'sides, I ain' never seen a purentee Fan."

"Yo' ain' a-wantin' ter see him whopped! Ain' right fer no lady ter see that. It ain' a pretty sight, Miz Boggs, 'n' I wishin' I didn' have ter see it myself."

"No," Dovie shook her head, "ain' wantin' ter see him whopped. Jes' kindly curious ter see what he looks like 'fore he all welted up. Consider it a favor if'n yo'd let me."

Maxwell inwardly cursed the day that he had been placed in such a situation. He grabbed an empty gunny sack from the floor and handed it to Nero. "Go in that stall there 'n' tie this 'round that boy." He waited until Nero returned and then, quite unable to hide his disapproval, he conducted Dovie through the big barn to where the horse stalls were. At the end was a box stall with a heavy wooden door. It was from here that the wails were coming. He opened the door and signified that Dovie was to enter.

A small barred window in the wall made the stall lighter than the rest of the barn. Dovie saw a pile of straw on the floor, a box with a tin plate and cup on it, and a man standing against the wall. His hands were manacled, and a short chain attached to his spanceled ankles gave him some movement. At Maxwell's entrance he came forward as far as his chain would allow and fell down on his knees, raising his manacled hands.

"Don' take me now, masta Maxwell suh, don' take me now. Heard the bell a-ringin' but that don' mean yo're goin' ter take me now. Don' let Cajun whop me. Oh, masta Maxwell suh!" He clawed in the air, trying to reach Warren Maxwell's hands.

"We a-goin' ter whop yo' shore 'nuff, Colt, so stop yore beggin'. Yo' ain the first ter be whopped at Falconhurst nor the last, neither. Git up! Stand up so's this lady kin see yo'."

"Don't let him whop me, mist'ess, ma'am," the fellow pleaded with Dovie. "Ain' don nothin' bad, I ain'. Ain' runned nor nothin' bad like'n that. Yo' such a pretty white lady, mist'ess. Yo're the prettiest white lady I ever did see. If'n a pretty white lady like'n yo' asks masta Maxwell not ter whop me, he won'. Ask him, mist'ess ma'am, ask him not ter whop me." He slowly rose from his knees and faced Dovie.

The light from the small window fell directly on him, its golden-moted light gilding his body. Dovie gasped as she looked at him. He was like nothing she had ever seen before. Compared to him, her own slaves at Dove Cote were mere cattle. Even Nero, standing beside her, was dwarfed by this young giant. He towered above them all, and Dovie, who was not a small woman, reached only to his chest. His color was not light enough to proclaim any admixture of white blood, yet it was not the blue-black of the real African. Instead it was a warm tobacco brown, alive with golden highlights and wine-dark shadows. His body was so large that his head seemed small in proportion. Dovie noticed the wide forehead under the "V" of the cap of hair. Thick brows that arched upwards at the end defined the widely spaced eyes, in which black islands swam in murky whites. The nose was short and widely bridged, but the nostrils were not overlarge nor flattened, and as she looked at them, they quivered with fear, like an animal that senses danger. A sharply defined indentation below the nose divided the upper lip which, although wide, was well-defined and colored a dark burgundy like its lower twin. The cleft in the chin relieved its squareness and produced a look of boyish petulance in the otherwise strong face. The thick neck column descended from two small, close-set ears, lying flat against the clinging cap of hair, which was mat-black and crinkly but not peppercorned. Sloping muscles joined the neck to the wide shoulders and flowed into the swelling curvature of the pectorals, each of which, sharply defined and well rounded, blossomed with a sculptured bronze rosette. The flat belly fell in smoothly from the chest and lacked the swollen umbilical hernia that so often disfigured the Negro, caused by the dull knives or midwives' teeth that severed the cord at birth.

Here Dovie's inventory was forced to halt, for the soiled sack hung down from the slave's waist, and she bitterly regretted the propriety that had impelled Maxwell to adorn this bronze colossus with such a dirty rag. It seemed to detract from his savage beauty by hiding his maleness. Below the soiled rag, however, she saw the swelling thighs, the bulging calves and the huge feet, firmly planted on the floor. She moved, quite unconsciously, a step nearer to him, undeterred by the powerful musk from his unwashed body. He, interpreting this as a gesture of compassion on her part, ignored his master's command and dropped to his knees again, clutching at her hand, his thick fingers hiding hers.

"Oh, don' let 'im whop me, mist'ess ma'am. Didn' mean ter hurt that li'l Marvie. She a-wantin' me jes' as much as I wantin' her. She a-comin' ter me 'n' plaguin' me till I say I would. Ain' my fault she so little 'n' I couldn't stop. Never do it no more, mist'ess ma'am, if'n yo' ask masta Maxwell not ter whop me. If'n he whop me, mist'ess ma'am, I a-goin' ter die, 'n' I don' want ter die."

Her free hand stroked the wiry pate, feeling a strange vitality in this springy hair that resisted her touch. Ignoring the eyes that pleaded with her, she turned to Maxwell.

"How much yo' figure this buck worth if'n yo' sold him 'thout any welts on his back?"

"Could git me 'bout thousand fer him up in Natchez, I reckon." Maxwell was ill at ease, wishing now he had never brought Dovie into the stall. "If'n I sell him in N'Orleans, ought ter git more, mayhap twelve o' fifteen hundred. Maspero in N'Orleans what deals only in fancies'd ask two thousand fer him."

" 'N' how much he worth if'n yo' welt him up with fifty lashes?"

"Buyers don' take ter a welted nigger. Shows he's stubborn 'n' bad. Lucky if'n I git five hundred fer him after he takin' all those lashes, if'n they don' finish him off."

Colt, who had been listening, turning his face from Maxwell to Dovie and back again, started to sob. "I a-goin' ter die. I a-goin' ter die." Dovie patted his head.

"Well, Mista Maxwell, I'm a-offerin' yo' fifteen hundred dollars fer him right now, 'n' I'm a-throwin' in that Sippi boy what out there in the barn. He's this here Nero's git 'n' he a good boy, housebroken 'n' everythin'. He my husband's body servant. Yo' sell me this Colt 'n' then he's mine 'n' yo' cain' whop him if'n he's mine. He the finest nigger I ever did see 'n' it a pity ter ruin him. So what do yo' say, Mista Maxwell? We makes a deal. Yo' make money 'n' yo' git Sippi ter boot. I gits me a good buck so's I kin start a little breedin' on my own place. Got me some good light-skinned wenches, 'n' Nero kin pick 'em out fer this boy."

Maxwell hesitated. He stood to make considerable money on the deal yet he was undecided. Having passed judgment on Colt, he felt duty-bound to carry out the punishment, yet as Dovie had pointed out, if he did sell Colt his jurisdiction was over and he was relieved of all responsibilities. The offer was a generous one and with the inclusion of Sippi he would not only get full price for Colt but be reimbursed for the death of Marvie. Still he hesitated.

"Yo' buyin' this boy sight unseen?"

"Kin see him right good now," Dovie answered, " 'n' what I cain' see, Nero kin. Yo' guarantee he right fer breedin', I s'pose."

"Well, he all-fired big but he full o' sap. Got me five nice suckers already, 'n' yore man kin 'xamine him 'n' see that he all right." He halted, looked a long time at Colt and then nodded his head. "It's a deal, Miz Boggs. Glad in a way that I don' have ter welt him up. He 'bout the finest boy I ever had, 'n' if'n yo want ter quiet him down, yo' kin put saltpeter in his food. Won' hurt him none 'n' cool him off some." Maxwell extended his right hand. "Mos' said 'gentlemen's 'greement,' Miz Boggs. Fust time I ever sold a buck ter a lady. My wife's cousin, she bought a little wench two, three years 'go but never sold a lady a buck afore."

Dovie shook his hand, withdrawing hers from Colt's frantic clutch.

"Thank yo', Mista Maxwell. Thank yo' fer sellin' me this boy 'n' thank yo' fer treatin' me so kindly. Got ter make my own way in the world from now on." She looked down at Colt's upraised face.

"I jes' bought yo'," she said, without a trace of the emotion she was trying to hide, " 'n' yo're mine now. Want yo' should behave yo'self 'cause I kin whop jes' as well as Mista Maxwell here, but I don' think yo're goin' ter give me no trouble. Yo' a-wantin' ter leave Falconhurst 'n' go with me?"

"Oh, mist'ess ma'am, I go anywhere with yo'." Colt was crying and laughing all at once. "I happy yo' bo't me. I be a good boy 'n' yo'll never have ter whop me. I'll work hard fer yo'. Chop cotton all day 'n' git yo' good suckers, too."

"He mine now?" Dovie turned to Maxwell.

"He your'n. Passin' papers won' make him any more your'n than he is now."

"Then cain' he be unspanceled?" Dovie asked.

Maxwell turned from Dovie to Colt. "This lady jes' saved yo' fifty lashes 'n' mayhap saved your life. If'n she say ter unspancel yo', I do 'cause yo're her'n now. Yo' goin' ter be a good boy o' yo' goin' ter run out tomcattin' tonight jes' 'cause it yore las' night here?"

"Ain' a-goin' ter do nothin' bad ter my new mist'ess, masta Maxwell suh. Ain' a-pesterin' none o' yore wenches neither. Yo' a good masta 'n' I sorry 'bout Marvie. It wa'n't my blame, masta Maxwell, 'n' I a-sayin' it now jes' like I said it afore yo' goin' ter whop me. That Marvie she jes' don' leave me 'lone, a-runnin' after me even when I with Rhody, 'fore yo' tooken her from me. I not a-knowin' she never been busted. Ain' a man's fault when a woman starts hankerin' after him. No suh, masta Maxwell suh."

Maxwell was willing to admit to himself the extenuating circumstances. He knew that any wench who had the good fortune to be paired off with Colt was the envy of all the others. Undoubtedly Marvie had set out to capture Colt, not knowing that she would be getting more than she bargained for. Now that the necessity for punishment was over, Maxwell was willing to pardon Colt. Once again, his words assumed the bantering kindness he had always used with the boy previously.

"Yo're a black devil, Colt! Yo' promise ter behave yo'self fer yore new mist'ess. She yore mist'ess Boggs, Colt."

"She my sweet new mist'ess Boggs." Colt, his fear gone, was himself again, archly provocative, slightly mischievous, eyes twinkling. His whole body was such a bundle of nervous energy that he could not keep still but danced, flexed his muscles and postured, knowing full well his own magnificence and glorying in it. "She shore a sweet mist'ess 'n' I her boy now. Ain' I, mist'ess Boggs?"

"Miz Dovie," she corrected him. "Yo' a-goin' ter be my coachman, Colt, so yo'll be a house servant 'n' call me Miz Dovie."

"Ain' that a pretty name fer a pretty mist'ess, tho'? Miz Dovie! My, oh my! I'm shore a lucky boy." He reached for her hand and pressed it to his cheek.

Dovie withdrew it, not daring to look at Colt any longer. She turned to Nero. "I'm leavin'. Goin' up ter the house. Yo' stay here with Mista Maxwell 'n' look this boy over good. Soon's yo' come up ter the house, Mista Maxwell, we do business. Kin give yo' two hundred 'n' fifty in cash 'n' yo' kin help me make out the papers for the bank ter pay yo'. That is, if'n yo' trust me."

"Trust Tom Verder's daughter any time." He smiled and offered her his arm to conduct her from the stall. Nero, who remained behind, seemed entirely satisfied with Dovie's transaction.

Later that night, Dovie signed the necessary papers and received bills of sale for both Calico and Colt and gave one for Sippi. Hammond and Calico arrived at the house just before supper. Dovie heard Hammond telling the cook that Calico was to have white men's vittles, before he came in to take his place at table. After supper, Dovie asked permission for Calico to run out to the barn to fetch Nero, saying that she wished to give him instructions to leave early in the morning. Excusing herself from the Maxwell family, Dovie waited on the gallery until Nero materialized out of darkness and came up the steps.

"We a-goin' ter git started soon's we kin after breakfast," she said. "Think we kin make Dove Cote by nightfall. Yo' be ready ter start?"

"Yes, Miz Dovie."

"Sippi knowin' he not goin' with us?"

"Yes, Miz Dovie. He carryin' on somethin' awful, but I a-tellin' him he got a good place here with Mista Maxwell."

"Yo' better keep track o' that Calico tonight. Ain' wantin' him ter run."

"Ain' no need ter spancel him. Masta Hammond he say Calico a-sleepin' in the house. He don' mind goin' back if'n the Dummy don't ride him."

"The Dummy old 'nuff ter have a horse, 'n' Calico kin have one too. That'll put an end ter the Dummy ridin' him. Now, how 'bout that new boy, Colt? Yo' 'xamine him like'n I told yo'?"

"Uh-huh! He a right fine boy, that Colt."

"I knowin' that. What I wantin' ter know if'n he all right fer breedin'."

"Shore is, Miz Dovie ma'am. Shore is."

Dovie realized Nero's reticence in speaking to her. She did not blame him but she was impatient. "Yo' got ter learn ter speak ter me jes' like'n yo' talk ter a man, Nero. If'n I got ter run things, got ter know 'bout things. If'n yo' tellin' my papa 'bout him, what'd yo' say?"

"Would say he 'bout the best buck I ever did see. He got a lot o' sap in him 'n' he mighty big, but he cut."

"Cut? What yo' mean, cut? Cain' be cut if'n Mista Maxwell say he gotten five suckers outa him. If'n he cut, I ain' a-buyin' him." Dovie grasped the railing for support.

"He ain' gelded. No, Miz Dovie, he ain' cut like'n that.

He jes' cut like Kru. Mos' Africky niggers they cut jes' that li'l bit. Heard tell it make 'em breed better when they ain' got that li'l bit o' skin. But we got ter be mighty careful with him, Miz Dovie. He cain' break in no wenches o' he kill 'em jes' like'n he did this wench here. 'N' he a Fan too. Always heard they high-strung 'n' hard ter manage."

"I'll manage him." She half turned to go up the steps. "He glad ter go with us?"

"He mighty happy, Miz Dovie. Say he do anythin' in he world fer yo', seein' as how yo' saved him from gettin' whopped. He right loyal, he is." Nero stopped for a moment, reached out and took Dovie's hand. "It's good ter be back with yo, Miz Dovie. Feel like'n I kin talk with yo' jes' like masta Tom. We a-goin' ter run Dove Cote right well, Miz Dovie. Learned some things at Clonmel 'n' learned more today here at Mista Maxwell's. Don' yo' worry, Miz Dovie. We git things goin' right well. Grateful, I am, Miz Dovie." He released her hand and disappeared into the darkness.

Dovie turned to go up the steps toward the square of light that marked the doorway. Never in her life had she felt happier. She fought down the exhilaration so it would not show on her face when she entered the lighted room. She wanted to run and scream and jump and holler. She was brimming over and couldn't contain herself. She wanted to jump out of her skin. She wanted . . . oh, she didn't know what she wanted and yet she did know. Yes, she did know and it was hers. It belonged to her. She had bought and paid for it.

She halted for a moment before the door to compose her face. After all, she was in mourning. She stood for a second, eyes cast down, hands folded demurely in front of her before she stepped into the room, bracing herself for Mrs. Maxwell's motherly arms and her clucks of sympathy.

Chapter XXIV

IT WAS NEARLY MIDNIGHT the next night when they arrived back at Dove Cote and they were all too tired to do anything but stretch their aching bones, cramped from the long confinement in the wagon. All of them, that is, except Colt, who bounced down from the front seat and jigged up and down, first on one foot and then on the other, to get the kinks out of his muscles. The whole plantation was sleeping, but the noise of their arrival and the lighting of lanterns awoke Fronie and Dolly in the big house who roused Callie. She, although vehemently insisting that she hadn't closed an eye since Dovie left, had been snoring soundly. Dovie dispatched Calico to awaken the Dummy in the dove cote and detained Nero for a few words before he left.

"Where yo' bin sleepin' 'fore Bart sold yo'?" she asked him wearily.

"Where I al'ays sleep—my own cabin."

"I knowin' that, but who with?"

"Letty, my woman what masta Tom give me 'bout five years back after Belinda tooken the fever 'n' died."

"Yo' wan' ter go back ter her?"

"She my woman. She be right happy ter see me back, 'n' my chil'ren too. Think she bin a-mournin' me kind o' hard, Miz Dovie."

"What'm I a-goin' ter do with this here Colt? Got

some plans ahead but too late tonight ter do nothin'. Yo' think it right what Mista Maxwell say 'bout him bein' a Fan 'n' him havin' ter have a wench?"

"Don' rightly know, Miz Dovie. We ain' never had no Fans here. Think mayhap he right, tho'. That Colt, he right high-strung 'n' mettlesome. Jes' look at him now."

Colt had helped Djoubo unharness the horses and was now waiting to be shown where they were stabled, but instead of standing quietly he was performing a restless shuffle with his feet and snapping his fingers in time to some cadence in his head. He seemed to be as fresh and frisky as though he had just rolled out of bed.

Dovie observed him. "Thinkin' mayhap we'd better keep him happy this first night here. Kin yo' find a wench fer him 'n' take him to your cabin where yo' kin keep 'n eye on him? Jes' fer the time bein'.."

"My oldest gal, Serena, she right pretty 'n' ain' had no man since she birthed her sucker las' summer. Masta Tom a-sayin' he goin' ter give her one but didn' git 'roun' ter it. Thinkin' she admire ter have this Colt boy. She bin a-hankerin' fer a man."

"Jes' fer the time bein', tho'. Got me other plans fer him. Show him the horses' stalls 'n' yo' run down ter yore cabin 'n' tell Letty you're back 'n' see if'n Serena there. No tellin' where she traipsin' ter with nobody here ter keep 'n eye on her. Then yo' come back, 'n' if'n Serena there, yo' take Colt back with yo'. I'll stay here with him till yo' come." She turned and listened for a moment, hearing a hulloo from the house.

"Yes, Mama, I'm comin' right in," she said loudly, and then to Djoubo, "Go ter the house. Tell Fronie ter make me some coffee 'n' git me somethin' t'eat. I'll be right in," and then louder, "Yo' all right, Mama?"

She waited to hear her mother's affirmation and listened to Nero's footsteps die away, and saw Djoubo's shadow appear in the kitchen door. Taking one of the lanterns, she walked down to the stall where Colt was slipping a halter over the horse's head. She waited for him to finish and when he came out from behind the horse, she confronted him and told him to stand still.

He halted, looking down at her and grinning. "Yes

350

ma'am, Miz Dovie. Yo' say stan' still 'n' I stan' still. Yo say jump up 'n' touch the moon 'n' I jump fer it. Yo're my pretty Miz Dovie 'n' I right happy ter be here with yo'."

Dovie looked up at him, his dancing eyes, his gleaming white teeth and his good-natured grin. She felt almost maternal toward this hulking giant. Perhaps that was why she wanted to gather him in her arms and press his head against her breast and be good to him. Yes, that was it! She wanted to be good to him, to make him happy that he was here at Dove Cote. But rather than let any trace of emotion show in her voice, she spoke brusquely, even sharply.

"Didn' have no chance ter 'xamine yo' over ter Mista Maxwell's. 'Sides, ain' fittin' fer a woman ter finger a buck if'n other people lookin' on. But we 'lone now 'n' it only right that I see what I bo't. Shuck down yore pants."

"Why, yes, Miz Dovie ma'am, if'n yo' wants me ter. Yo' shore got a right ter know 'cause yo' bo't me. I'se yore boy now, Miz Dovie. I'se yore boy." Unabashedly he undid the big wooden button which held up his osnaburg trousers and let them fall down around his bare feet. With a gesture of pride, completely lacking in pruriency if not in exhibitionism, his hand reached down, grasped and displayed.

"I awful monst'ous."

She wanted to touch him. Oh, how she wanted to, but she couldn't. He was a Negro; she was a white woman. Never had she heard of such a thing as a white woman touching a Negro *there*. She could nurse him if he were sick; bathe his body if he had a fever; even pat him on the shoulder or give him some such flesh-touching-flesh token of approval, all with impunity. She might slap him if he offended her. But a meeting of white flesh and black flesh such as she had envisioned was forbidden by all the training she had ever had.

She could pet a dog; she could fondle a cat; she could kneel beside a foaling mare and try to express her sympathy by stroking the animal's neck; but she would not think of touching any animal *there*. And, to her way of thinking, this handsome happy fellow before her was only an animal. He was not a human being like herself. True, he looked like a man, except for his color, he spoke like one and she rather had an idea that he thought like one, and yet, he was not one.

Or was he? She looked at the face smiling down at her and sensed something like love for her in his eyes. It was a love she had never experienced before. It was more worship than love, for certainly there was no lust in it. He was aware that there was not now and could not ever be any conceivable bridge between them except that one flimsy, jerry-built structure linking a mistress and her servant. His touching her would be as unthinkable as her touching him. And yet she wished he would, she wished he would reach out and take her in his arms. But all the time she was wishing, she knew if he dared do such a thing, she would scream until she awakened the whole plantation and would have him whipped for it.

His smiled faded. "Ain' I all right?" he asked, previously so accustomed to words of admiration and praise. "Yo' sorry yo' bo't me, Miz Dovie ma'am? Ain' my fault I so monst'ous. Cain' help it, Miz Dovie. If'n yo say so, I'l take an axe 'n' . . ."

She shook her head violently, her lips pursed so she would not be tempted to say anything.

"Then wha's the matter, Miz Dovie ma'am? What'd Colt do ter make his Miz Dovie mad? Kin whop me if'n I bin bad, Miz Dovie. Don' min' if'n yo' whops me."

She shook her head. "Ain' aimin' ter whop yo', Colt. Yo' ain' done nothin' bad. Jes' that I a woman, tha's all, 'n' ain' never bo't me no buck before. Heard what men do if'n they buys a buck 'n' thinkin' I should do it too, but ain' never done it afore. Ain' seemin' right."

"But yo' bo't me, Miz Dovie. Yo' bo't all of me. Yo' got that right. I knows what men do if'n they buy themselves a servant. Look, let me show yo', kin I?" Her nod gave him courage to take her hand. He guided it to his mouth. "Fust they puts they finger in the buck's mouth to see if'n he got all his teeth." He opened his mouth and guided her finger inside.

She felt the sharp-pointed hardness of his teeth and

352

the moist wetness of his tongue, and once her finger was inside, she investigated carefully, going from tooth to tooth to ascertain that they were all there. She found it a particularly satisfying sensation, this contact of her finger with the strong hard teeth and the warm slippery smoothness of his mouth.

"Guess yo' got all yore teeth." She smiled back, feeling less alien toward him.

"Shore have." He was proud of his perfection. "Now yo' wants ter feel my muscle." He drew off his shirt and guided her hand down to the bulge on his arm. "Feel there, Miz Dovie ma'am." He flexed his arm, making the biceps stand up hard and round. "Got good muscle I have. I'se strong. Squeeze it hard, Miz Dovie, yo' cain' make no dent in it."

She couldn't. The bulging arm was like a piece of iron. "Yo shore are strong," Dovie agreed.

"But a boy have more muscle 'n' that what's in his arm." His hand steered hers across his chest, halting it at one of his paps. "These here are eyes," he explained, and his tone was serious. "My pappy tol' me that these eyes mo' 'portant 'n those I got in my head. These eyes see things other eyes cain' see. They Africky eyes 'n' kin see good 'n' bad, kin see if'n a person good in de spirit. He call 'em *yews day Dew,* that meanin' 'eyes o' God,' 'n' I kin see with 'em."

"They tellin' yo' if'n I good o' bad, Colt?" Dovie found she could smile at him.

"Yo' good, Miz Dovie ma'am. Yo' all good 'n' I all yores." His hand pushed hers down over his hard belly to his groin. Instinctively her hand pulled away but he held it, gently bringing it back. He pushed it farther down and removed his own hand. "That yore's too, Miz Dovie. It goin' ter make a lot o' good suckers fer yo!"

Every fiber in her being, every insane thought in her mind, pleaded with her to keep her hand there. The warmth, the strength and the vigor hypnotized her. This phenomenon so possessed her that she could not remove her hand. Instinct and desire bade her grasp tighter, fondle and caress; she knew she must relinquish her hold. Such glory was not for her; it was for that Serena. What had that stupid girl ever done to deserve this happiness? What? Nothing, except that she was black, and black could enjoy black when it was denied to white. But was it denied to white? No! White men had their black wenches. Nero was living proof of her grandfather's lust for black flesh, and down in the cabins of the quarter there were a number of light-skinned manifestations of her own father's enjoyment of that same flesh.

Yes, men could do it! They could enjoy themselves and forget it because the mores of the time permitted it. But not a woman! Not a white woman! Not Dovie Verder! Never! She could not demean and endanger herself by planting a black seed in her womb. Ah, but there were other ways—all those pleasurable ways that Bart had so inveighed against but finally submitted to. Yes, she could enjoy herself without danger. She leaned forward and her hand clasped tighter. Oh no! Whatever was she doing. She must not. She must not. She snatched her hand away and straightened up, knowing that if she did not do it in that instant of sanity she would never have the courage to do it.

Now, without the actual physical contact it became easier. Once more she could forget that she was a woman and remember that she was a *white* woman. She must terminate this excursion into the forbidden and act in a businesslike manner, as if all along she had been merely a plantation owner interested in a new piece of property. The moment of her temptation was over. She raised the lantern to see better.

"How come yo' bin cut?" she asked.

"My pappy done that when I was a young boy. He say all proper Fan boys gotta be cut. 'Nother man hol' me 'n' my pappy cut me. Did hurt me somethin' awful when he done it 'cause I never forget it. My pappy say a man cain' give his juice proper less'n he bin cut 'n' that it make a Fan boy more better'n a Ibo o' a Dahomey o' a Yoruba." He cocked his head on one side, listening. "Nero a-comin', Miz Dovie ma'am." He jackknifed down, clutching his shirt and pulling up his trousers. He buttoned them hastily.

Nero came down the length of the barn to them and

354

looked long at Colt and then at Dovie. There was no trace of either surprise or guilt in their faces. He decided from Colt's appearance, which he hoped Dovie had not noticed, that Warren Maxwell was right. This Fan boy sure was hot-blooded, and from all appearances he needed a wench—the sooner the better.

Nero was apologetic for having taken so much time. "Seems like Letty a-bawlin' more 'cause I come back 'n when I lef'. Jes' wouldn't let me go, 'n' all the chil'ren a-jumpin' over me. Didn' mean ter take so long. Spoke ter Serena 'n' she kindly grateful ter yo', Miz Dovie, fer sendin' her this Colt boy."

"Then take him 'way with yo', Nero. Get yo'self some good sleep. We a-goin' ter start workin' tomorrow. Ain' bin much done 'roun' here, what with papa dyin', gittin' ready fer the sale, Bart's buryin' 'n' me traipsin' 'roun' the country. This here Colt he a-goin' ter be my groom. Ain' goin' ter be no field hand. He kin stay at yore cabin till we get things settled." She turned to Colt. " 'N' yo' take care with that Serena. Yo' mind. Yo' be careful with her."

Dovie took the lantern and walked out of the barn. There was one thing more she must do before she went to the house. She must look in at the dove cote and see how the Dummy was. She was just beginning to realize she had a problem on her hands with the Dummy's attachment for Kru, but that too was something she would have to settle later. She trudged toward the dove cote. The door was open and she peered into the room, seeing the bed as only a white blotch in the darkness. There was a quick movement on the bed that caused the bed cords to groan. She held the lantern high, both the Dummy and Calico, lying flat on their bellies, turned their heads to look at her. The Dummy was smiling.

"He all right, Calico?" Dovie asked. "He glad ter see yo' home 'gain?"

"He right fine, Miz Dovie," Calico answered. "Right glad ter see me. Soon's I came in, Kru left. Dummy kind of mad ter see him go but he so 'cited 'bout me bein' back, he didn' take on too much. The Dummy he right fine, Miz Dovie. He a-sayin' he glad I'm back 'n' that we a-goin' ter ride horses now. He like that."

" 'N' yo', Calico? Yo' wishin' yo' were back at Falconhurst?"

"At Falconhurst, Miz Dovie, masta Hammond he treat me like'n I'm a man. He teach me things 'bout the plantation. Wishin' I could learn more. He make me feel I'se more'n jes' a playboy. I like the Dummy, Miz Dovie. He jes' like my brother 'n' I love him, but I cain' be a playboy always, Miz Dovie. Got ter be a man some day."

"We'll see." Dovie lowered the lantern and stepped out.

It seemed a mile to the house but she made it, drank the coffee and ate the bread and butter which Dolly had prepared for her. Callie, her hair in two braided cables, sat opposite the kitchen table, watching Dovie.

"Yo' bring back 'The Well in the Desert,' Dovie?"

Dovie shook her head, almost too tired to speak. "Used it fer gittin' Nero back, Mama. He worth more'n that to us now. 'Thout Nero we cain' run this place. Which'd yo' rather have, mama, Dove Cote o' that useless piece o' silver?"

Callie's lower lip trembled but she recognized the truth of Dovie's words. "Reckon yo' did right, Dovie girl. Hate ter lose it 'cause yore papa he gave it ter me, but admire yo' fer takin' hold like yo're doin'. Couldn' do it myself but yo' kin." She reached across the bare boards of the table and patted Dovie's hand. "Loved that piece o' silver, I did, but love yo' 'n' Dove Cote more."

Suddenly Dovie wanted her mother. She wanted to be a little girl again, entirely innocent of all the strange desires that were plaguing her. She wanted to be held in her mother's lap and be comforted, to know that somebody loved her and cherished her. She slipped from her chair and stumbled around the table, falling on her knees before her mother, resting her head in Callie's ample lap.

"Oh, Mama, I'm so all-fired tuckered out. I bin so far 'n' I seen so much 'n' did so much 'n' talked so much, 'n' they all strangers. Now I'm back home 'n' I'm glad ter be here. Missed yo', I did, Mama." Without knowing why, she started to sob. "I got so much ter think 'bout, Mama, 'n' I don' know where ter start 'n' I'm jes' too tired ter think."

"Yo' don' have ter think tonight, baby. Yo' must have had a hard time, jes' a pore woman all 'lone a-tryin' ter do a grown man's work. Yo' go 'n' crawl in Mama's bed jes' like'n yo' useter when papa gone ter The Patch. Mama'll look out fer her Dovie baby. Mama'll undress her 'n' put her ter bed. Come now." She guided Dovie down the hall to her room and started to remove her clothes.

Dovie watched the pudgy white hands unbuttoning the little jet black buttons, and she wished, oh how she wished, that those fumbling fingers might be strong black ones. How she envied Serena for being black and how she hated her. Yet somehow, with her mother fussing over her, she felt safe. She was safe. Oh God! Keep her safe from herself, from wanting things that she knew she shouldn't have but realized that eventually, fight as she would against it, she would finally succumb to and take.

Callie ballooned one of her nightgowns down over Dovie's head.

"Bo't us a servant, Mama. Right likely buck named Colt. Needed him 'cause I sold Sippi."

"Know yo' did right, Dovie baby. We needin' more servants now. Wishin' I had my Congo back. Bart had no right ter sell Congo. We gotta git more niggers, Dovie. Dove Cote always have fine niggers. Now go to sleep. Tomorrow's 'nother day."

Dovie slept, her head pillowed on her mother's arm.

Chapter XXV

DESPITE HER UTTER EXHAUSTION the night before, Dovie was up early the next morning. Although she had slept but fitfully, resenting the soft femininity of her mother beside her and wanting the hard maleness of a man, she awoke rested, looking forward to the day ahead. She had dreamed—horrible but exciting dreams of black incubus that had a startling resemblance to Colt—but morning brought a certain amount of sanity. Her first thought on awakening was that she had successfully resisted temptation the night before in the barn. Please God, she would always have the strength to resist such strange and incomprehensible desires.

After a hearty breakfast of fried ham, eggs and grits, to which she did full justice, she told Fronie to go out and ring the plantation bell, calling all the hands from the quarters together with their women and children, even the adolescents from the Romp Pasture, to assemble around the kitchen door. Here, with Nero beside her, she outlined future rules and procedures for Dove Cote in emphatic and definite terms. Before all the assembled servants she conferred authority on Nero. His word was to be law, subject, of course, to her veto. For herself she reserved the right to mete out punishment on Nero's recommendation, and she threatened punishments for various misdemeanors—laziness, inattention to duty, stubbornness, surliness and lack of respect to her drivers or to Nero or herself. Also for running, although this last was quite unnecessary, as it had never happened at Dove Cote. Dove Cote niggers had always been contented with their lot. She formulated regulations respecting males and females and their relationships with each other. Each man would continue with the woman that he already had, and each family group would be allowed to occupy the cabin in which it was living. New cabins would be built from time to time as new matings occurred. She was firm in her restriction of promiscuity. If, however, at any time a man became dissatisfied with his woman or a woman with her man, that person was to come to Dovie and discuss the matter. If Dovie felt there were sufficient grounds for separation, it would be arranged. Mothers were to be allowed to keep their children. The Romp Pasure would continue to take care of progeny from The Patch.

Then, singling out Colt, who was standing in the front row beside a good-looking, light-colored wench whom Dovie recognized as Nero's daughter Serena, she called him to her and bade him stand by her side. By conferring on him, in public, the title of her groom, hostler and coachman (even though she did not possess anything more ostentatious than a democrat wagon), she raised him in the hierarchy of the plantation to the rank of house servant. As she spoke, she noted the fleeting look of disappointment on Serena's face. The wench was already madly in love with him. Well, let her be! Her time with him would be short.

After dismissing the servants, she scarcely knew what to do first; there were so many problems facing her. She dispatched Nero to the barn with instructions to saddle her father's fine stallion for Colt and her own mare but, instead of putting on the sidesaddle she had always used, he was to saddle her horse with a regular man's saddle. She had already made up her mind that her voluminous skirts and petticoats were out of place in her present life.

Calling Colt to follow her into the house, she led him to her bedroom and opened Bart's wardrobe. Bart had

359

been buried in his only decent suit, but she found an old pair of his black trousers, a white shirt and a black string tie, along with his new broad-brimmed black felt hat. It was his one new possession and he had not been able to wear it in his coffin. Shooing her mother, who was curious about the new man, out of the room, she had Colt remove the sweat-stained osnaburg trousers and the tow-linen shirt that were his only articles of apparel, and bade him dress in Bart's clothes. Seeing him naked again brought back the temptations she had had the night before, but once again she summoned up sufficient courage to resist them. She knew there had been no necessity for her to watch him or for him to change his clothes in the house. It had been merely an excuse to soothe her conscience to have him change his clothes in the first place.

Bart's trousers proved too big in the waist and too short, reaching midway between Colt's calves and his ankles. In order to hold them up he had to cinch them around his waist with one of Bart's wide leather belts. Once dressed, however, with the white shirt and black tie and felt hat, Colt was far better clad than any of the other servants, even Nero. Bart's boots, big as they were, were tight for Colt, but he managed to squeeze his enormous feet into them. Although he limped painfully at first, his pride at being shod for the first time in his life overcame his discomfort. Dovie led him to a mirror and had him take a look at himself. He was properly awed and thanked her profusely, grasping her hand and carrying it to his lips, where she allowed him to keep it longer than she would have let any other servant. Then she cuffed him lightly on the head to make him relinquish it.

He grinned back at her. "You's my pretty Miss Dovie," he said.

"Soon's we git time, we'll go inter Brownsville 'n' git yo' some proper trogs," she said to him and then remarked more to herself than to him, " 'N' aimin' ter git me one of them there barouches like 'n Miz O'Neal had. Yo'll look mighty fine a-sittin' up there all dressed up."

"In proper trogs with brass buttons, Miz Dovie

ma'am?" Colt had seen such accouterments somewhere and had remembered them as the acme of splendor.

"With brass buttons if'n I like," Dovie answered. "Now stir yore stumps 'n' git out ter the barn 'n' see if'n Nero's got them horses saddled, 'n' if'n so, bring 'em 'roun' ter the side door 'n' wait fer me. I'll be out in a minute."

In her parents' room, she donned her father's trousers and one of his shirts, scandalizing her mother, who, now that Colt had left, followed Dovie from room to room.

"Yo' ain' goin' traipsin' 'roun' dressed like'n a man in your papa's clothes!"

"I am. Got me a man's work ter do now 'n' cain' flounce them skirts 'n' petticoats 'roun' a cotton field. Git all wet 'n' draggled. Ain' nobody here ter see me but the niggers, 'n' don' make me no neverminds if'n they like it or not. I'm masta 'n' mist'ess o' this place now 'n' I gotta do it. Promise yo' I won't go off the place 'thout I'm dressed up, tho'. Soon's I kin, I'm a-goin' inter Brownsville 'n' git me some trogs fer workin'. Goin' ter git some fer that Colt boy too. If'n he's a-goin' ter be my groom, want that he looks good."

"He's shore one pretty nigger boy, that Colt what yo' bought. Yo' git him from Mista Maxwell? He 'bout the prettiest nigger boy I ever did see, but always heard yore papa say that Mista Maxwell he have the best niggers o' anyone. Yo' goin' ter mate him up?"

"He's already with that Serena wench what's Nero's git 'n' lives in his cabin. Goin' ter keep shiftin' him 'roun' 'cause he too good ter waste. Wantin' ter git me some good suckers outa him so that I kin sell 'em in a few years. Slave prices a-goin' up, 'n' that's a good way ter make money, so Mista Maxwell say. That's why I bought him. Make jes' as much money with niggers as with cotton, but we a-goin' ter stick ter cotton. Niggers jes' a sideline. If'n I was a man, tho', I'd breed niggers jes' like Mista Maxwell, but it mighty hard fer a woman."

"Oh yo' pore chile, yo' pore chile!" Callie could not envisage herself in such complexities. "Ter think my baby had ter come ter this. Don' know how yo' a-goin' ter hold up yore head, ridin' 'round astraddle in men's clothes, breedin' nigger bucks, overseein' 'n' all. Jes' hopin' none of the womenfolks 'roun' git wind o' it. Yo'll be disgraced ferever."

"Be more disgraced if'n we paupers," Dovie countered, " 'n' sides, ain' nobody a-butterin' our bread 'cept ourselves. Got ter go now. Goin' ter see what's bin done 'roun' here. Mighty little, I reckon. Ain' been nothin' done, 'n' nobody 'roun' here ter see that them lazy critters a-stirrin' they stumps, but they shore a-goin' ter hump from now on."

With Callie behind her, she went out onto the gallery, where she found Nero mounted on his horse and Colt waiting to help her mount. The Dummy and Calico were also on the gallery, engaged in a violent altercation. The Dummy, angry and stamping his feet, was mouthing weird sounds, and Calico was answering him with a series of gestures that were meaningless to Dovie but that the Dummy seemed to understand. Eyes blazing, he clawed at the air, trying to tangle with Calico, who evaded him. Turning and seeing his mother, he shouted the first intelligible word he had ever uttered.

"Kru!"

Dovie stared at her son, looking from him to Calico in astonishment.

"What he say, Calico?" she asked, unable to believe her ears.

"He say, 'Kru,' Miz Dovie. Kin say it good, too. Don' know how he learned but he say it 'cause he a-wantin' Kru back so's he kin ride him. Tol' him he cain' ride me no longer 'cause yo' said not. He don' see why, 'n' he a-wantin' Kru back."

The Dummy turned and came toward his mother, his eyes brimming with tears. His having spoken one word caused her to regard him in a new light. He was indeed a handsome youth with his long, shoulder-length hair that curled in ringlets, and framed his face like a girl's. Indeed, except for his shirt and trousers he looked more like a girl than a boy. His skin had the fine texture of femininity; no sign of a beard appeared on his lips or chin. His cheeks were red-flushed from anger; his eyes, large, brown and expressive, swam with tears. He was not quite as tall as Calico, finely boned, compared with Calico's ruggedness, but there was a similarity in their facial expressions that Dovie had never noticed before. Looking at them both now, she was reminded of Tommy, gone these many years, and it seemed inconceivable that Calico could resemble Tommy, but he actually did. The two boys looked enough alike to be brothers; Calico's skin was as white as the Dummy's and no negroid features were apparent in his face, which further heightened their fraternal resemblance. She seemed to see them both in a new light—Calico not as a slave and the Dummy not as an infant who could neither understand nor speak.

Dovie spoke the word "Kru" slowly, shaping her lips to the syllable and pointing to her mouth.

The Dummy, watching her intently, echoed her speech. "Kru," he said, and although the inflection was uncontrolled and the tonality high-pitched it was definitely a word.

Dovie pointed to herself and then to her lips again. "M-ah m-ah," she said slowly and distinctly, her lips closing on the "m" and opening wide on the "a."

The Dummy regarded her, wiping the tears from his eyes. "Ma-ma," he repeated, again with a strange tonality, but none the less intelligibily. "Mama, Mama, Mama." He repeated the word several times, pointing to his mother and gesticulating for Calico's attention. "Mama, Mama, Mama!"

"He a-talkin', Calico. My boy he a-talkin'. Think o' that. If'n he kin say 'Kru' 'n' 'Mama,' he kin talk. Try ter git him ter say yore name. Make him look at yo' 'n' make yore lips go slow, like this! 'Ka' " she spread her lips wide, "Li," the tip of her tongue extended beyond her front teeth, "Co."

She turned the Dummy's face to her own and went through the lip motions again. It was too complicated for the boy the first time but he did manage to make a sound that approximated "Cali."

"Make him do it, Calico. Thinkin' he learn fas' once he git started. Promised yo' both horses 'n' yo' kin have them. Git Djoubo ter saddle up that little chestnut mare fer the Dummy 'n' yo' kin have the black geldin'. Don' wan' no fast ridin'. Yo' jes' keep 'em at a walk till the Dummy he know how ter handle a horse."

The miracle of the boy's talking brought her son closer to Dovie and she felt, for the first time, that he was something more than a child. Perhaps if he could reproduce sound from seeing lips move he could understand in the same way. Again she took his face in her hands and made him look at her. This time without making any sound, she grimaced the word "Mama." To her satisfaction the boy understood. He pointed to her. Then she mouthed "Calico," and he pointed to the other boy. Finally she said "Kru," and he shrugged his shoulders, shook his head and pointed away to the distance. A thought had been communicated to him and for the first time he had understood and answered.

"The Dummy a-talkin', Mama." She fitted her foot into Colt's palm and swung her trousered leg over the saddle. "He a-talkin', now."

"He shore is, Miz Dovie." Nero nodded in agreement. "Heard him say Kru 'n' Mama jes' as clear as could be. Mayhap he learn, Miz Dovie. Mayhap some day he learn ter hear 'n' learn ter talk. Ain' never heard o' no dummy ever talkin' afore, but this one shore a-doin' it. Whar we a-going' now, Miz Dovie?"

"Goin' ter see 'bout gittin' that cotton in what's needin' ter be picked fer more'n a week. We goin' ter work past sundown tonight 'n' if'n they's a moon we's goin' ter pick so long's we kin see a hand afore our eyes. These niggers had it too easy, a-loafin' 'roun' doin' nothin'. Now they a-goin' ter work. Don' wan' ter hear no complaints outa them. Goin' ter ride the fields today myself. I takin' the west forty with Colt 'n' yo' take the south fields. Want every buck 'n' every wench 'n' all those younguns from the Romp Pasture ter git out there. Git Djoubo 'n' Honey 'n' all the others 'roun' the house. Don' take Dolly nor Fronie 'cause we a-needin' them fer cookin'. Ain' no time fer the wenches ter cook today so's Dolly 'n' Fronie got ter git vittles ready fer dinner 'n' supper fer all the hands. Git all the work yo' kin outa everybody.

Tell the drivers ter touch 'em up if'n they a-laggin'. Yo' in charge here, Nero. Up ter yo' now."

"What 'bout The Patch, Miz Dovie?"

"Hopin' Mista Lightfoot got that near picked. If'n he ain', we'll see to it jes' as soon's we git things started here. This place goin' ter start workin', Nero, 'n' so's The Patch. Got me big plans, I have. Someday I'm goin' ter have a place jes' as nice as Clonmel. Now git goin'."

She sent her mother into the house with instructions to have Dolly and Fronie cook up enough black-eyed peas and fatback to feed all the hands, and when the door had closed behind Callie, she turned to Colt.

"Yo' a-lookin' mighty pert this mornin'. How yo' like that Serena wench what I gave yo' las' night?"

"She right pretty li'l gal, Miz Dovie ma'am. If'n yo' wants I should like her, I like her. If'n yo' don', I don' fancy her none at all. It jes' howsomever yo' say, Miz Dovie ma'am."

There was just the slightest trace of familiarity in Colt's voice, which Dovie resented. She wondered if he could possibly surmise how much she had wanted him last night and how difficult had been her struggle to resist him. Familiarity must be only on her part. Any attempt of his would be resented and punished. He must know his place.

Her voice was sharp. "Don' make no neverminds ter me if'n yo' like her o' if'n yo' don' so long's I tell yo' ter be with her. Yo' ain' a-goin' ter bide with her long nohow, so don' go gittin' no ideas in that burr head o' your'n. She ain' yore woman now 'n' she ain' never goin' ter be. Yo' ain' never goin' ter have no steady woman. Didn' buy yo' fer that. Yo' a stud nigger, Colt. Yo' know what that means?"

"Shore do, Miz Dovie, ma'am, 'n' if'n that what yo' wants yo' done bo't the right boy," he giggled. "Studs all the wenches yo' kin give me. But like'n yo' say, they ain' my women. Ain' never goin' ter have no woman o' my own. Ain' needin' none cause I got my own pretty Miz Dovie mist'ess, 'n' that all I wan'."

"I yore mist'ess jes so long's yo' behave yoreself, tha's all. Yo' try gittin' smart-alec 'n' I kin sell yo' tomorrow.

365

Kin sell yo' down in N'Orleans ter one of them cane-raisin' plantations. Heard tell a nigger down there don' las' more'n four, five years."

"Yo' ain' never goin' ter have no cause ter sell me, Miz Dovie." Suddenly he lost his smile and became serious. "Yo' jes' say what yo' wants 'n' I does it. We go out 'n the field now 'n' if'n yo' wants that I picks, I pick. Kin pick more 'n' an hour 'n' other niggers kin all day. Kin do anythin' better'n any other nigger. Kin chop more cotton, plant more corn, 'n' pester more wenches 'n' any other nigger 'cause I a Fan boy, Miz Dovie ma'am, 'n' Fan boy's better'n other niggers. Anything yo' wants me ter do, Miz Dovie, I does it fer yo'." He wet his lips, and the scarlet point of his tongue, brilliant and glistening against the raisin color of his lips, darted out like an adder's tongue.

Again she thought she detected a hidden meaning in his words, but there was actually nothing for which she could reprimand him. His tone, his demeanor and the words themselves were subservient enough. He was only volunteering to please her. Perhaps it was her own desire that made her read double meanings into all his words.

"Yo' ain' fer pickin'," Dovie answered, "but got ter find somethin' fer yo' ter do. Cain' have yo' gittin' fat 'n' lazy. Now on, yo' a-goin' ter saw 'n' split all the wood fer the big house. That use' ter be Sippi's job, now it your'n. 'N' yo' takes care o' the horses with Djoubo. If'n yo' ain' servin' some wench what I gives yo, then yo' sleeps in the barn. But yo' goes where I go. Yo' eats in the kitchen 'n' yo' eats white folks' vittles. Goin' ter dress yo' up 'n' make a show nigger outa yo'."

"Like that fine, Miz Dovie ma'am, 'specially the part where yo' say I goin' ter be with yo' all the time. Ain' nothin' I like better'n that. I shore a lucky boy, Miz Dovie. One day I spanceled up at masta Maxwell's a-thinkin' 'bout how I'm goin' ter get fifty whops 'n' maybe die, 'n' the next day I yore boy."

She did not answer him, but as she saw him sitting astride his horse—a veritable centaur—she wondered which of them was the luckier, Colt or herself.

366

Chapter XXVI

THE PATCH HAD come to be Dovie's greatest problem. She was certain that she could manage Dove Cote capably with Nero's help, but The Patch, located as it was at some distance from Dove Cote, necessitated a white overseer and was more or less out of her direct supervision. Ransom Lightfoot had discharged his duties with some efficiency and success under the supervision of her father, but Dovie realized that no hired hand, if left to himself, would take sufficient interest to get the maximum amount of labor out of the slaves and the maximum return from the soil. A man had to own something to make it prosper. She owned The Patch but, being a woman, there were limitations on her. It was impossible for her to journey back and forth as frequently as her father had, impossible for her to live at The Patch, because of her deeply ingrained fear of its miasmic dangers and its lack of a suitable dwelling house.

However, she did have Ransom Lightfoot. Yes, she had him. At one time this had meant a lot to her and she had been happy to have him around but Dovie was dispassionate enough now to realize that Ransom had very little to offer her. To be sure, he did have one important asset and that was his overwhelming maleness. But Ransom Lightfoot was her own age and she was not blind to his waning virility, the slight accumulation of fat

367

around his once slim waist which would increase with the years, the already apparent sag to his muscles and the unattractive pallor of his skin. The thick head of blond hair was beginning to thin and there were lines in his face. Lately she had been, albeit unconsciously, comparing all men with Colt. Unfortunately none of them measured up to him, with his youth, his strength and, although she would not admit it to herself, his beauty.

She could marry Ransom Lightfoot, that she knew. He would jump at the chance to be master of two such plantations as Dove Cote and The Patch. But if Ransom Lightfoot became master of her plantations, she would be relegated to second place. Legally they would belong to him; he could do as he pleased with them; he would supersede her in everything and her voice would no longer have any authority. On the other hand she saw certain advantages in marrying him. For one thing, it would solve the problem of The Patch. As her father had done, he could journey back and forth and undoubtedly, with the impetus of ownership, he would take a greater interest in it and make it pay. She, with Nero's help, could manage Dove Cote.

Yes, there was some wisdom in taking Ransom Lightfoot for a husband. Physically he was still attractive, at least more so than Bart had been. On the occasions when she had bedded with him, he had satisfied her far more than Bart had ever done. Even now, on her way to The Patch, she was anticipating the night she would spend with him—the culmination of a week of yearning in her lonely bed at Dove Cote.

She turned to Colt, who was following her, and urged him on to a quicker pace. As she looked back at Colt, she became more uncertain about Ransom. Did she really want him? The question tormented her. Her fingers ached to touch the soft skin at Colt's throat, to glide over the smoothness of his arms, to unbutton his shirt. But no! Never! White women did not have such desires, and she must realize that they were only what she might feel toward an animal. There was a certain sensuous satisfaction in stroking a dog, a certain fingertip titillation in touching the smoothness of a horse's neck or in caressing a kitten. That must be all she desired. It must be! She would marry Ransom Lightfoot and put an end forever to these strange desires for Colt. Then she would be strengthened by Ransom's constant nearness and his availability. When she had been married to Bart she had never had such longings. To touch a nigger! And that's all that Colt was—a nigger! A black animal, despite his good looks. Yes, she'd marry Ransom Lightfoot and put an end to all her problems, not only the management of her plantations but these strange desires which she had felt ever since she had seen Colt in Warren Maxwell's barn.

Wherever she went, he accompanied her these days. When she finished breakfast, he was waiting for her in the kitchen, accoutered in his new white coat and trousers, black boots and wide straw hat. Every morning his clothes were gleaming white, starched and creased from Fronie's iron, for Dovie had given orders that he should don clean clothes each day. She admired him in white because it set off the rich color of his skin, and the red bandanna he wore around his neck gave him a fillip of color that made his appearance almost theatrical. He was within calling distance throughout the day until she left him to eat her evening meal and saw the shadows engulf him on his way to the barn.

Yielding to her common sense and not to her emotions, she had supplied him with a series of bedmates, changing them frequently so that he would form no lasting attachment to any of them. In proof of his puissance, three of his companions were now pregnant, and Dovie hated them so intensely that she banished them to The Patch so she would not have to look at them. But, she argued with herself, that was the reason she had purchased Colt. He was there solely for one reason—to breed suckers for her—and breeding them he was.

Today she was going to The Patch and tonight, as was usual on her visits, she would not return to Dove Cote. Oh, how she looked forward to these weekly visits! Dove Cote, without her father and Bart, seemed so arid and barren with only her mother to talk to. The nights there with only an empty pillow for company in her big bed were so long, so dark and so lacking. But tonight would be different. Although Tom's cabin was available for her at The Patch, she never occupied it, preferring to stay with Ransom, for with nobody but the slaves there, she did not have to hide their liaison. These nights with Ransom were her only surcease from torment since Bart had died. Without them, she felt she would have died. The nearness of a man was as vital to her as food or drink. Strange that no man had ever completely satisfied her —neither Tommy nor Bart nor Ransom. Perhaps Tommy had most of all. If she had married Tommy everything would have been different. She had never ceased to think about him. An aura of romance surrounded her memories of him. Perhaps some day he would return. Should she go on waiting for him or should she marry Ransom? No, she could wait no longer.

It was beginning to get dark as she and Colt rode down the last long hill which led to The Patch. While she waited for Colt to let down the rails of the fence that marked the entrance to the motley collection of cabins and barns, she saw the slaves returning from the fields, trudging in a cloud of dust that rose to settle in the hanging moss of the trees. They were singing, and she could detect a note of jubilation in the song. The long day of heat and sun and work was over. Now had come the time for them to sit on their cabin doorsteps, lean tired backs against the rough walls and enjoy a short time of blessed rest before they sought their pallets on the floor.

Ransom, riding at the head of the plodding procession, espied her and cantered over to her.

"Wa'n't lookin' fer yo' tonight, Dovie."

"Jes' couldn't stay 'way no longer, Ransom." She walked her horse alongside his, looking over her shoulder to see that Colt was following. "Hope that yeller wench o' your'n kin fry up some ham. Starved." She jerked her head toward Colt. "'N' so's my boy. Put in a hard day at the Cote afore leavin'. He'll bed down in papa's cabin but want ter be sure he's fed."

"Nice yo' could come, Dovie," Ransom's greeting was more or less perfunctory, lacking the enthusiasm that Dovie always anticipated but somehow never received. "Tired myself. Niggers bin a-cuttin' brush all day 'n' I've bin with 'em. 'Cept for that Kru, who kin do three men's work, I cain' git a lick o' work out'n them niggers less'n I stand over them."

He yawned as he dismounted and then came over to Dovie's horse and helped her down. For that one moment when his arms encircled her, she felt happy and protected.

Inside the cabin, which contained only the bare essentials for living—a cord bed, a plain deal table, two plantation-made chairs and an old chest of drawers—she sat in one of the chairs, watching Mintie, the yellow girl who lived with Ransom, while she stirred up the fire, set the table with its crude crockery and started to cook the supper. Dovie was anxious for her to get her work done and leave. She knew that the wench would sneak over to the other cabin and bed herself with Colt. She was certain that on these nights at The Patch, Colt did not sleep alone, but she would rather not know definitely whether he did or not. Sometimes, even in Ransom's embrace, she found herself thinking about Colt.

She and Ransom ate their meal together—a meager supper of fried ham, eggs and pone—and then watched the girl put clean sheets on the bed before she cleared off the table. Rather than wait for her to wash the dishes, Dovie dismissed her, but she might as well have kept her to finish the chores because Ransom pushed his chair away from the table and got up, stretching and yawning.

"Tired's a dog," he said, his words lost in his gaping, "but got ter go down ter the barn. Promised one o' the boys a larrupin' 'n' cain' disappoint the bastard. Sons a bitches got ter git larruped every so often o' cain' git nothin' outa them. Don' spose yo' wants ter come?" he questioned Dovie. "Mighty comical sometimes how they carries on 'n' might be a good thing if'n them black runnions a-seein' yo' down there. Might git some o' the lead out'n their asses if'n they know yo' 'roun' like'n yore paw use ter be."

Dovie's head shook in negation. "Ain' never seen no nigger whopped 'n' ain' a-wantin' ter. Cain' yo' put it off, Ransom lover, 'n' yo' so tired 'n' all? Don' want that yo'

371

go. Thinkin' we kin git ter bed early." She smiled an invitation.

"Won' take long." He started for the door, taking the cowhide whip that was coiled around a nail on the wall. "Let it slip by onct 'n' they a-thinkin' I forgot. Be back soon's I kin. Whyn't yo' pop inter bed 'n' wait fer me. But don' drop off." He winked at her, clutching at his groin.

After he left, Dovie started to disrobe. Her riding habit with its long skirts was hot and stifling after the freedom of trousers. There was hot water in the kettle and she thought she would wash—just enough to get some of the dust and dirt off her skin. She dipped the water out into a wooden trencher, found the crock of soft soap and looked around for a towel, but the only one she could find was the badly soiled one hanging on a nail. It was stiff with dirt and repulsive to her touch. Ransom must have others, and she remembered the wench going to the chest of drawers for the clean sheets.

It was an old chest made of grained pine, and when she tried to open the top drawer, it stuck. When she yanked on it, it came open about an inch and she could see that there was something inside which held it. By inserting her fingers into the crack, she found a wooden box. When she pressed its cover down, she could open the drawer. Among the litter of soiled shirts and dirty socks, she located a towel, but in order to close the drawer it was necessary once again to press down the cover of the wooden box. It caught her attention. It was of mahogany or some other hard wood embellished with brass corners, and at one time there had been a lock on it.

She wondered what kind of valuables Ransom might have to keep in a box of this kind and her curiosity prompted her to open it. There was not much of value in it. Two gold eagles and some silver coins, a curiously round white pebble, two collar buttons, one set with a piece of red glass, a pearl-handled penknife and a silver watch. Something about the watch seemed familiar, and she picked it up to look at the engraving on the cover, which showed, centered along a convolution of rococo scrolls, a little scene of a house and a tree. Somewhere she had seen a watch like that before, but where? Idly she opened the hunting case and held it to the candle to read the inscription engraved on the inside of the cover.

> To Tommy Verder on his
> 18th birthday from his
> uncle Thomas Verder.

Now she remembered! Once again she saw the watch in Tommy's six-fingered hand. She remembered that day in the grove when he had implored her to save his life. After it was all over, he had reached over to his trousers, abandoned on the ground, and had drawn out the watch from the watch pocket.

She had taken the watch from him, thinking of how much had happened to her in those past two hours, and watched him while he stood up and pulled on his trousers. Then he had reached down and taken the watch from her and put it back in his watch pocket. Tommy's watch! And now, after all these years, she was looking at it. What connection was there between her beloved Tommy and Ransom Lightfoot? There must be some and she would have to find out. Could be that Tommy was still alive and Ransom knew.

She had undressed and was in bed, the sheet drawn up over her, when Ransom returned. Two tallow dips and one wax candle were burning, and there was still a remnant of fire on the hearth. He sat down in one of the chairs, fumbled under it for a bootjack and drew off his boots, watching her while he did it. He smiled at her while he unbuttoned his shirt and let his trousers slither down over his legs.

"Wash yo'self, Ransom," Dovie said, without taking her eyes from him. "Seems like'n yo' smell o' nigger sweat."

"Musta rubbed off on me." Ransom poured some water into the pan. "That son a bitch sure sweated whilst we larruped him. Did yo' hear him? Yelled like'n a painter. God a-mighty, but I'm tired. Bin lookin' forward ter crawlin' in beside yo' Dovie."

"Yo' ain' too tired?"

"What yo' think?" He pointed down at himself. "Standin' up right pert, ain' it?" He threw the towel on the floor and came over to the bed, threw down the sheet and stretched out beside her.

"Le's talk a minute, Ransom." His arms around her were provocative but there was something she must know first. She hardly knew how to start, but if there was any possibility of Tommy's being alive after all these years, she did not intend to marry Ransom Lightfoot.

"Le's do some lovin' 'n' talk afterwards." He almost convinced her, but she held him off.

"What in hell's the matter with yo' tonight, Dovie? Ain' never seen yo' like'n this before."

"Curious 'bout somethin', Ransom. Somethin' bin a-botherin' me all day. Jes' wan' ter talk 'bout it, tha's all."

"What's so 'portant it cain' wait till we gits through? Feel more like talkin' then."

"Then yo'll want ter go ter sleep. I know yo', Ransom. Onct yo' finishes yo' cain' even kiss me good night. Yo' jes' starts a-snorin' no matter if'n I had 'nuff or not." She pushed his hand away.

"How many times I got ter tell yo'? A man ain' like'n a woman. Onct he shoots his load, he's through. All right, what's bin a-makin' yo' so worrisome?"

"It's that playboy o' the Dummy's—that Calico."

"Him? I'll come over ter the Cote 'n' larrup him if'n he's fashin' you'."

"No, it ain' that he's bad o' nothin'. Jes wonderin' how come he got six fingers on his hand if'n he yore git from Fronie like'n yo' say. Ain' nobody six-fingered but us Verders. My grandpappy he had six fingers, my pappy had 'n' my cousin Tommy. The Dummy he got 'em 'n' so's Calico. Cain' figure it out."

"That all that's vexin' yo'? Thought it somethin' 'portant. What yo' so worrisome 'bout a servant fer? If'n yo' wants ter talk, le's talk 'bout somethin' 'portant. Like yo' 'n' me gittin' married up, Dovie. Tha's somethin' I bin wantin' ter talk ter yo' 'bout. Seems like'n we hit it off kindly well, yo' 'n' me."

"Bin thinkin' the same thing myself, Ransom. Likes yo', I do, 'n' likes the way yo' do things. Never did love that

Bart, never. But I got ter confess yo' one thing. That Bart he not the father o' Tommy. No, my cousin Tommy Verder what disappeared was the real papa o' the Dummy. Never loved anybody but Tommy 'n' he went away 'n' never come back. Tha's why I married up with Bart, so the Dummy wouldn't be a woods colt. But I still love Tommy 'n' ain' a-goin' ter marry up 'gain 'cause I thinkin' mayhap Tommy he come back some day 'n' if'n he do, I shore want ter marry up with him."

"He ain' never comin' back." Ransom made the statement with conviction while his hands started their caresses again. "Don' wait 'roun' fer him. Yo' loves me now. Ain' no man livin' kin pleasure yo' like'n I kin, Dovie."

Dovie longed to respond to him but she must settle something else first.

"How yo' know he ain' a-comin' back? How yo' know, Ransom? Been thinkin' 'bout it 'n' it awful funny. That there Calico with his six fingers 'n' he the spittin' image o' Tommy. Could be that somehow Tommy sired him off'n Fronie. Goin' ter make that girl talk onct I gits back ter Dove Cote. If'n she won' talk, Nero'll touch her up with a whip. Goin' ter make her tell me if'n Tommy ever pestered her somewhere. Don' believe yo' ever sired Calico, 'cause he got six fingers jes' like'n all the Verders."

Ransom was silent for a long minute. Even his fingers were still. If Dovie were to question Fronie, the cat would be out of the bag, although he was hopeful that Fronie would not remember the name of the stranger who had fathered Calico. He wanted to marry Dovie; he wanted her two plantations and, to give him credit, he wanted her too. He pushed Dovie's hand down, feeling it grasp and hold tightly.

"Yo' like that, Dovie?" He was sure of his hold over her.

"Always did, Ransom, but my mind jes' a-fumin' 'n' a-frettin' 'n' cain' git it on pleasurin'. Thinkin' I might even git up 'n' ride back ter Dove Cote so's I can question Fronie. Worrisome I am, thinkin' 'bout Tommy Verder."

He held her hand tightly, hoping its contact would change her way of thinking, but he realized that for the first time she did not respond. His desire to marry her was not purely mercenary. Dovie was the first white woman he had ever lain with and he enjoyed her more than any of the wenches who had been under him. Marriage not only offered him the uninterrupted delight of her body but a respectability and affluence he had never envisioned. He craved that position as much as he craved her. He could not allow a Tommy Verder to stand between them. If Dovie knew that Tommy was dead, his ghost would be laid forever.

"Guess mayhap I'd better tell yo' what I know 'bout yore cousin, Tommy Verder." He pulled her closer to him, whispering in her ear, confident that his nearness would lend credence to his story. "Reckon Calico's his git. One day he come a-ridin' up ter the crossroads store close by my maw's plantation. I was there. He all dressed up in a purty coat with a cape on it 'n' a-ridin' a fine horse a-sayin' he goin' ter Natchez. Come up a rainstorm 'n' he come inter the store fer shelter. I was a-settin' there 'n' Fronie she jes' a young girl what ain' never bin busted yet. This Tommy he kept a-buyin' corn 'n' he got hisself pretty much lickered up. Ol' man Bannion, him what kept the store, he tol' as how Fronie ain' never been busted 'n' Tommy he jes' a-hankerin' fer ter bust her. He a-sayin' that that one thing he always a-cravin'—ter bust a wench fer the first time 'n' he jes' finished bustin' one 'n' hankerin' fer another. He offer ter pay ol' man Bannion twenty dollars if'n he let him bust Fronie. So we went outside while he did it.

"Then after 'bout 'n hour, Tommy he come out 'n' he more lickered up'n ever. Bin a-helpin' hisself ter the jug, I guess. Got on his horse 'n' rode off. Hear tell they found a skeleton down in a ravine what bin killed by a painter 'n' folks 'roun' there a-sayin' that's him. Ain' never spoken 'bout it 'roun' here 'cause not wantin' ter cause yo' nor your pappy no worriment. But I kin tell yo' that he's daid. He ain' never comin' back 'n' no reason fer yo' ter think 'bout him no more. He's daid."

"How come yo' a-knowin' he's dead, Ransom?" She glanced around the room, and saw Ransom's rifle against the wall. Before he could stop her, she had crawled over him, jumped out onto the floor and grabbed the rifle, aiming it at him. "Did yo' kill him?"

"Git back inter bed, Dovie, 'n' stop this foolishment. Course I didn' kill him. Now put that gun down afore it goes off 'n' shoots me." He laughed and held out his hand to her. "If'n they's goin' ter be any shootin' here tonight, I'm the one what's goin' ter do it."

"Might jes' shoot yo', Ransom, if'n yo' don' tell me the truth. Did yo' kill Tommy Verder? If'n yo' didn', how come yo' got his watch in yore box over there?"

"Why Dovie, he jes' gave it ter me, tha's all. Jes' made me a present o' his watch."

"Tha's a lie, Ransom. Tommy he set a lot o' store by that watch 'cause my papa gave it to him. He wa'n't givin' it away ter nobody." Her finger sought the trigger. "Yo' tell me, Ransom."

"That gun loaded, Dovie. Yo' be careful how yo' finger that trigger. Yo' don' wan' ter kill me."

"No, I don' wan' ter kill yo', Ransom, 'cause I likes yo'. Guess I loves yo'. Know I wants yo'. But I got ter know the truth. How come Tommy Verder died 'n' yo' got his watch? Ain' puttin' this gun down till yo' tells me."

The assurance that she loved him and wanted him gave Ransom courage. Her desire for him and her need for him would, he was sure, outweigh her sorrow for the departed Tommy. He would lay Tommy's ghost once and forever.

"Well, yo' might say as how it was accidental, Dovie. Didn' have in mind ter kill him. He asked me ter ride down the road with him ter put him on the right road. He all lickered up 'n' fightin' drunk. Soon's we about a mile down the road, he got ter abusin' me, callin' me names 'n' such like. I answered him back 'n' the more we talked, the madder I got. Yanked him off'n his horse I did, 'n' we rassled in the road. He was all set ter kill me, he so mad 'n' so drunken 'n' all. Killed him in self-defense, I did, 'n' threw him down inter that ravine. Man got a right ter kill in self-defense."

" 'N' yo' robbed him too. He a-totin' a lot o' money, Tommy was. Yo' took his money 'n' his watch."

"All that a long time ago, Dovie sweetheart. Yo' loves me 'n' I loves yo', 'n' we a-goin' ter git married up. Now le's jes' fergit 'bout the whole thing. What's done is done 'n' it is so long ago it don' make no neverminds anyway. Put that gun down 'fore it goes off 'n' shoots me. Won' be no good ter yo' if'n I'm daid."

"Nor live neither. Cain' never bed me with yo' 'gain 'n' my pore Tommy's blood on yore hands. Don' never want ter see yo' 'gain, Ransom."

"Now, Dovie." Ransom's voice dropped to a honey-tongued register and he reached down and grabbed himself. "Yo' ain' never goin' ter find nothin' ter pleasure yo' so purty 'n' so nice's this. Yo' goin' ter miss it if'n I leaves. Goin' ter start thinkin' how yo' a-wishin' yore sweet Ransom back. Goin' ter be wishin' yo' had yore sweet Ransom back so's he could pleasure yo' every night. Come on, Dovie, put that gun down 'n' come back here 'side me. Goin' ter love yo' like'n yo' never bin loved before. Then come mornin' we rides inter Brownsville 'n' gits Ol' Man Soper ter marry us up. What say, Dovie?"

She almost relented. The rifle wavered in her hands but she did not take her finger from the trigger.

"Mayhap yo' tellin' the truth, Ransom. But somethin' between us I cain' forgit now. Better yo' gits yore trogs on 'n' gits out. Yo're welcome ter yore horse 'n' yore saddle 'n' whatever yo' wants ter take. Yo' got money in that box, but leave me Tommy's watch. Yo're mighty lucky I don't shoot yo' o' turn yo' over ter the sheriff, but jes' might if'n yo' don' git out. Ain' denyin' that yo' got what it takes ter pleasure a woman 'n' come tomorrow night I'll probably be wantin' it. But Tommy's blood between us now. Cain' never bed me with yo' 'thout Tommy be 'n' there too. Like'n yo' say, it a long time ago but ain' never loved no man but Tommy, 'n' now I cain' see yo' but I see my pore Tommy 'longside yo'. Won' do no good ter talk, Ransom. Ain' goin' ter change my mind. Now yo' git up 'n' git."

He saw that further pleading would be useless. His

world had suddenly collapsed about him. He had lost a wife, a position in life and two plantations, and there was nothing he could do. He swung his legs over the side of the bed and went over to where his clothes were strewn on the floor. Slowly he pulled on his trousers, buttoned his shirt and slipped his feet into his boots. While Dovie watched him, still aiming the gun at him, he piled some of his clothes into a saddlebag and took the money from the box. He had ridden back from the barn in his haste to join Dovie and had tied his horse just outside the door.

With his finger on the latch, he regarded Dovie, but he could see no signs of her relenting.

"Mayhap some day yo'll be wishin' I was back," he said. "Yo're a-goin' ter miss it. Bet yo're wantin' it right now. Jes' say the word, Dovie, 'n' we kin be back in bed in two minutes. Huh?"

He was right; she did want him. Oh how much she wanted him but she would not give in to him. Yet she could not let him go out of her life entirely. She might have to have him back.

"Owe yo' wages, I do. If'n yo' tells me where ter send them I'll have Mista Norsmith send yo' yore money."

"Send 'em ter me care o' Marysville. Shore yo' won' change yore mind?"

"Wish I could, Ransom. Jes' wish I could but I cain'. Yo' better git, Ransom. Fast!"

He opened the door, standing for a moment on the threshold, but Dovie was still pointing the rifle at him, her finger on the trigger. Even after he mounted his horse, he half expected her to call him, but her figure, outlined by the candlelight inside, remained silhouetted in the doorway. He clucked to his horse and rode off.

She listened, hearing the horse's hooves on the dusty road and then hearing them stop. She supposed he had dismounted to open the bars of the gate and she had a wild impulse to rush down the path, naked as she was, and intercept him. She would beg him to come back. What did it matter if he had killed Tommy? She wanted him. Good God, how she wanted him, but she closed the door and went back inside the cabin.

Placing the rifle against the wall, she regarded the

empty bed. The indentation on the pillow marked where his head had been, and now he had gone. She had driven him away and she was alone. What a fool she had been! Oh, why had it mattered to her what had happened to Tommy all those years ago? And damn him for taking Fronie the very day after he had left her. Damn him! Damn Bart with his psalm mouthing and his unwillingness! Damn Ransom, too! Damn them all! And now she must go through the rest of her life aching for a man, reaching out in the night and finding nothing but the emptiness of a pillow. What would she do? Oh, oh, oh, what would she do? She collapsed on the bed, burying her face in the spot where Ransom had lain, giving way to a fit of hysterical self-pity and longing that her tears did not assuage.

How long she remained there, her body racked with sobs, she did not know, but she cried until there were neither tears nor emotion left and she felt completely drained of everything but her loneliness. The candles were guttering and she was cold in her nakedness. Without conscious effort, she went to the fireplace and piled on some logs of pine, watching the flames burst up. The warmth of the fire felt good. She went back to the bed, but instead of lying down she wrapped the sheet around her and then shuffled across the floor until she located her shoes and slipped her feet into them.

"Goddam 'em all!" She brought her fists down on the table, pounding it again and again. "Don' need none o' them, I don'. Goddam spindle-shanked, fat-bellied, goddam good-fer-nothin' bastards. Goddam white-livered bastards what call themselves men 'n' think a woman got ter crawl on her belly jes' ter get 'em ter pleasure her. I'll show 'em. Show 'em what a man really is."

She ran from the cabin out into the darkness, stumbling, falling, rising and running again until she came to the other cabin. Pushing the door open, she stepped inside. No candle burned, but the dying embers on the hearth gave out enough light so she could see the tangle of black limbs on the bed. The motion ceased as she came closer and stood over them.

"Colt!" She did not realize until she heard the stridor

of her voice how much it expressed her urgency. "Git up! Leave that wench 'n' come with me."

"Yas'm, Miz Dovie ma'am." Colt extricated himself and stood up, the ruddy light making glistening highlights on his moist skin. "Gits on my trogs 'n' comes with yo', Miz Dovie."

She reached out and grabbed him by the arm, pulling him in her frenzy.

"Git 'em on!"

She felt him tremble under her grasp.

"Yo' a-goin' ter whop me, Miz Dovie? Ain' don' nothin' fer yo' 'n' Mista Ransom ter whop me. Mintie done say yo' ain' mindin' if'n she bed here."

"Ain' goin' ter whop yo' if'n yo' hurry. Mista Ransom gone 'n' I fearful o' stayin' over there all alone. Want yo' should sleep 'cross the doorstep." She added the latter for the benefit of the yellow wench on the bed.

He pulled on his pants and stretched his arms into his shirt. She motioned him to go ahead of her and he stepped out into the night. She slammed the door behind her and stood beside him.

"Carry me, Colt! Pick me up 'n' carry me over ter the other cabin. Cain' walk."

His strong arms picked her up and she pillowed her head on his chest, feeling the warmth of him through the thin cloth. Her arms reached up and fastened themselves around his neck. In the darkness she could not see him, but his strength and his warmth enfolded her.

Chapter XXVII

COLT CARRIED Dovie into the cabin. The candles had gone out but the blazing logs on the hearth gave a dancing light. Dovie regretted that light now. What she was about to do would have been easier for her to accomplish in darkness; the light was an enemy for that shamelessness she was about to perpetrate. It was unthinkable and it should, like some vile crime, be carried out in darkness. She trembled not only from her great need but from her positive revulsion at the step she was about to take. Yet dread it, fear it, decry it as she would, she knew that no power on earth could stop her now. She had planned too much on tonight, anticipated it too eagerly and now, with Ransom gone through her own doing, she must find some substitute or lose her mind. Colt was the only substitute available and she did not dare to admit to herself that she desired the substitute the more. Perhaps, Colt's availability had prompted her to dismiss Ransom. She did not know. She only knew the demands of her flesh.

Colt and Colt alone could satisfy those demands, and although the step she was about to take was not one she could take easily, it was necessary. Colt was an animal, and bestiality, by whatever name she called it, was revolting. She knew he was just as much an animal as a stallion or a jackass. Yet, withal, he was an animal with human lineaments, and except for the color of his skin, he could well be human. She must close her eyes, blot out the color of his skin, and then tomorrow she could forget all about it. She could forget that she, Dovie Verder, had yielded her body to such horror. Tomorrow she would be a white woman and he would again be an animal that she had bought and that she owned.

She closed her eyes and slid from his arms but her determination to keep her eyes closed weakened and she was tempted to open them. He stood in the middle of the room, spraddle-legged and hands on hips, his outline black against the flickering light. The exaggerated shadow of his immensity reached across the floor and climbed part way up the wall, magnifying his presence and dominating her. She felt her teeth chattering, not from the cold but from her high-strung nerves. She could see that he was nervous too, for he was shuffling and ill at ease and the fingers of his hands clenched and straightened.

"What yo' a-wantin' me ter do, Miz Dovie ma'am? If'n yo' skeered ter stay here, we kin ride back ter Dove Cote, but nothin' goin' ter happen ter yo'. Gimme a blanket 'n' I'll sleep outside on the do'step. Not even a booger git by me."

"No, Colt, we not ridin' back ter Dove Cote 'n' yo' ain' needin' no blanket. We goin' ter bide here fer the night. Tell me! Yo' bin a-pesterin' that Mintie wench?"

"Bin wantin' ter, Miz Dovie ma'am, but she ain' lettin' me. She a-sayin' as how she won' let me 'cause she kindly 'fraid o' me. She a-sayin' I too big-like fer her. After what I did ter that Marvie wench, I skeered too. Skeered I'd hurt her, so we jes' bin frolickin' 'roun', Miz Dovie ma'am. I ain' done nothin' bad, Miz Dovie. She a-sayin' yo' tol' her ter come over with me, but didn' hurt her. She ain' goin' ter have no sucker from me 'cause didn' do nothin' but play. Tha's all, Miz Dovie ma'am."

She did not answer him. Instead, she took the few steps necessary to bridge the gap between them and stood before him, so close that she could feel his warmth and smell the faint musk of his body. It did not repel her but only heightened her desire for him. Her hand reached out tentatively and encountered the smoothness of his cheeks. Slowly her fingers traced the outline of his features—the arching brows, the heavy eyelids, the short straight nose with its quivering nostrils, the thick cushiony lips and the well-defined cleft in his chin. Gathering courage, she allowed her fingers to wander up to his ears, which seemed unnaturally small and set close to his head like curiously convoluted shells. From his ears her fingers walked to his hair and discovered it to be short and wiry; it seemed to crackle under her fingers with a life of its own.

"Miz Dovie ma'am." His words were low, guttural and husky.

"Sh-h-h!" It was better for her if he did not speak. She did not want to hear his voice. It transformed him into a reality, and she desired only a chimera—an incubus that tomorrow would be just a dream.

Her fingers strayed down to his neck, lingering for a moment on a pulsing artery, then crept further down to undo the buttons of his shirt, spreading the thin garment apart so they could rest on the solid planes of his chest. Here her hands remained, for there was much to explore in the rounding curves, the distinct cleavage of muscles and the sharp protuberance of the twin paps. "The eyes of God," he had called them, and it almost seemed that they were looking at her, condemning her. She would destroy them; her fingers pinched and tweaked them, tearing at them in order to blind these twin eyes that seemed to censure her.

"Yo' hurtin' me, Miz Dovie ma'am. What yo' doin' ter me?"

The fury departed from her fingers and they became gentle, caressing softly where a moment before they had clawed and wrenched. He was breathing in short gasps now. Emboldened by the contact of her fingers, she laid her cheek against his chest, her ear reverberating with the pounding of his heart. A wave of weakness overwhelmed her and she felt the strength ebbing from her legs. Reaching for one of his hands, she placed it around her waist so that she would not collapse, but his arm seemed lifeless and his hand was shaking, affording her no support.

"Hol' me, Colt! Hol' me tight!"

"Yo' got a mis'ry, Miz Dovie ma'am?"

"Yes, Colt. Cain' stand. Mayhap yo'd better carry me ter the bed 'n' lay me down. Tha's it. I'm sick, Colt. Tha's why I come fer yo'. Mista Ransom he 'bused me 'n' lef' me here all alone. Fearful that he come back 'n' 'buse me 'gain. Cain' stay here all alone. That's why I went ter fetch yo'. Pick me up, Colt boy, 'n' tote me ter the bed 'n' sit alongside me a bit."

Now there was strength in his arms and he lifted her again and carried her across the room to where a splotch of gray-white marked the bed. He laid her down on it gently, smoothing the sheet that covered her, and then sat down gingerly on the very edge of the bed.

"Yo' wantin' drink o' water, Miz Dovie? I'll go 'n' fetch it."

She shook her head from side to side on the pillow while her restless hands sought his body again, caressing the smoothness of his skin and straying from the roundness of his chest to the ridged flatness of his belly. So far she had not committed herself. She could halt now, and she prayed for the strength to do so, knowing all the time she would never be able to stay her hands from their ultimate goal. Yet she wished she could. She was Tom Verder's daughter. She was the mistress of his plantations. She tried to rationalize that this being beside her was a black varmint and she was a white woman, but all her arguments were in vain. The warmth of the flesh under her hands was more potent than all her arguments with herself. Empty words! Nothing could stop her. Nothing!

The wide leather belt with the big brass buckle around his waist seemed adamant and immovable under her fingers. It was cinctured so tightly that her fingers could not loosen it.

"Take it off, Colt," she whispered, "take everything off."

"But, Miz Dovie ma'am . . ."

"Do's I tell yo'."

He obeyed her, and while he was struggling with his boots, she disentangled the sheet that was wrapped around her. He stood beside the bed, an immense black shadow, and she did not trust herself to speak to him. Instead, her hands reached out, touching once more the

385

warmth of his flesh and pulling him toward her with an urgency that brought him down beside her. Now, having removed all obstacles between them, she turned him toward her, raised her head and pushed his arm under it so that she could pillow her head on it. She gloried in a moment of triumph at having achieved her conquest but she was unprepared for his quiet sobbing. It did not deter her. Nothing could make her turn back now, for she had discovered the glory of his manhood and there was no retreat for either of them.

"Oh, Miz Dovie, Miz Dovie, Miz Dovie ma'am," he was crying now, his sobs choked with ecstasy. "Yo' oughtn', Miz Dovie. It a-goin' ter kill me 'n' it kill yo' too. Masta Maxwell done say so. He a-tellin' all us boys that if'n a nigger boy rape a white woman it kill him 'n' the woman too. He say white women pizen ter black boys. He a-sayin' black boys pizen ter white women too. He a-sayin' if'n a black boy pleasure a white woman, he a-goin' ter die even afore he gits whopped ter death. He a-sayin' a black boy's dooflicker jes' drop off if'n he touch a white woman. Don' wan' ter die, Miz Dovie, 'n' don' wan' it ter drop off neither. Don' wan' yo' ter die, Miz Dovie, 'cause I loves yo'.''

"Then if'n yo' loves me, Colt, yo' do 's I want. Ain' no truth in what Mista Maxwell tol' yo'. He jes' tryin' ter scare yo' so's yo' never want ter pleasure a white woman. White man pesters a black wench 'n' it don' hurt him none nor the wench neither. Black man pester a white woman 'n' it don' hurt him none nor her neither. He jes' gotta be careful, tha's all, 'cause pleasurin' a white woman ain' like pesterin' a wench. I cain' have no black chil'ren, so's yo' got ter stop."

"Cain' always stop, Miz Dovie." His sobs were subsiding.

"Yo' got ter. Jes' got ter. Tha's what Mista Maxwell meant when he said it'd fall off. Yo' don' want that, do yo'? 'N' besides, if'n yo' don' stop I'll have yo' whopped 'n' if'n yo' tells anyone I'll have yo' whopped. Yo're my boy, Colt, 'n' yo' does like'n I tell yo' 'n' nothin' bad'll happen." She pressed her lips to his, blocking any reply or further objections.

For the first time in her life, she knew real happiness in a man's arms. Through some superhuman effort he was able to control himself, and when he reached a certain pitch of ecstasy he would stop and lie trembling in her arms until he dared renew the attack.

All memories of Tommy, of Bart and of Ransom Light-foot were obliterated in the phantasmagoria of physical delight in which every sense found satiation and delight. Every sense but one! She touched him, feeling the satin smooth hardness of him; she tasted him, her lips pressed so tightly to his that the blood from his bitten lips flowed into her mouth; she listened to him and heard him; she smelled the rich muskiness of his body, which heightened her desire for him. But she did not allow herself to see him. He was a mysterious part of the darkness, indistinguishable from it. He was only the warmth, the vigor, the supreme contentment that she had always desired and never before achieved. Her eyes refused to envisage him as the servant who followed her about in the daytime, as the servant she had purchased in Warren Maxwell's barn . . . as a nigger.

During the night their positions became reversed. She was no longer the mistress and he the slave. In this close communion he became the master and she the willing slave doing his bidding as he became more emboldened and threw off all restraint. It was he who ordered and commanded and she who obeyed willingly, finding a new joy in his mastery over her. No longer did she have to wheedle and cajole as she had with Bart. No longer did she have to act with some restraint as she had with Ransom Lightfoot, that she might keep up the pretense of being a white woman, who should not entirely enjoy such things.

With Colt there were no barriers, no recriminations, no reservations. With him she felt natural, uninhibited and unrestrained, worshiping and adoring him in his entirety. Whatever he proposed she acceded to; whatever she inaugurated he accepted willingly. Their personalities were forgotten and they merged into a single completeness, recognizing themselves as a unity and not as separate components. She was not Dovie Verder and he certainly was not Colt. She was not white and he was not black. She was no older nor younger than he and he was no more experienced nor adept than herself. It was a complete communion of bodies and flesh, entirely divorced from mind or soul. It was not love; it was of the earth, and no idealism mingled with their pure enjoyment. There were no whispered words, no endearments, no restful dallying with protestations of affection. The fires within them consumed their consciousness. Colt's virility did not wane nor did she become entirely satiated until physical exhaustion quieted them, and they finally rested in a half-sleep of little stirrings and movements.

The square of light in the window grew darker as the stars faded and then lighter with the coming of the dawn until Dovie's eyes could discern the etched outline of tree branches against the window. Now she must look at him. He was sleeping, and in the still dark cabin his face was only a black blotch on the pillow. His arm across her made a black smudge on the whiteness of her skin and she gently lifted it from her, recoiling now as she touched this flesh that was so patently alien. She extricated herself from his warm closeness, feeling the stickiness that cemented their limbs together. Quietly, so as not to waken him, she stood up and picked up her clothes from the welter of his and her own on the floor. She felt strangely modest, as though it would be a sacrilege for him to see her body this morning, and she hastened to get into her clothes before he woke up. But he slept soundly, apparently not missing the warmth of her body.

When she was fully dressed, she walked toward the bed, glad of the shadowed corner and the still uncertain light. Reaching down, her fingers touched the warmth of his arm and for some reason, this morning it seemed too smooth, too glabrous, too warm.

"Git up, Colt!" Her words were peremptory, leaving no doubt that she was the mistress, he the slave. "Git up 'n' git out! I'm a-goin' ter fetch a pail o' water 'n' when I gits back I want ter see yo' gone. Git yo'self down ter the barn. Saddle up yore horse 'n' ride over ter Dove Cote. Git Nero 'n' bring him back here. Tell him I need him. 'N' remember! Yo' keeps yore mouth shet 'bout everythin' if'n yo wants ter keep the meat on your back."

He swung his long legs over the edge of the bed and stood up.

"Yas'm, Miz Dovie ma'am. Like'n yo' say. I goes ter the barn, but kin I say jes' one thing, Miz Dovie ma'am?"

She hesitated, fearing what he might say. He must not, she felt, make any reference to last night. He must forget it, as she was trying so hard to do. It was over and done with, and she was certain it would never happen again. Never! But even as she made the resolve she knew she would break it. Yet he must not presume. He must not attempt to equate himself with her. He could never be her peer. This was daytime, the darkness was over, and once again she was white and a mistress, he was a Negro and a slave.

"What yo' got in mind ter say?" She asked the question grudgingly.

"Jes' that yo' don' have nothin' ter worry 'bout, Miz Dovie. I mighty keerful las' night. Be just so keerful tonight, too. Yo' won' never have ter fret yo'self none. Thinkin' howsomever 'fore I goes ter the barn I wakes up that Mintie wench 'n' tells her I cravin' ham 'n' aigs fer break'us'. Goin' ter ask her ter cook 'em up special fer me."

She realized he was already exerting the upper hand over her. Ham and eggs was not a slave breakfast. She envisioned it as the first in a series of petty blackmailings that would multiply as time went on. She must make her point now. Her superiority must be established without question.

"Ain' no nigger gittin' no ham 'n' eggs fer break'us' here. Yo' ain' no different from any other nigger," she announced with authority. "Now git goin'. Jump! When I come back I want ter see yo' gone. If'n not . . ."

"If'n not, what, Miz Dovie ma'am?" He walked over, grinning, to where she was standing and saw the grim lines vanish from her face. At that moment he realized the fullness of his power over her. "Yo' a-goin' ter whop me, Miz Dovie? Yo' a-goin' ter put whales on my back? Don' think yo' a-goin' ter like the feelin' o' whales on my

389

back." He turned, reaching for her hands and placing them against his back. "Nice 'n' smooth now, Miz Dovie. Yo' ain' goin' ter like it all whaled up like'n a wash paddle." He turned around to face her.

She stood still, hypnotized by his nearness.

"Boy like me, a-workin' hard all night, Miz Dovie, shore does need ham 'n' aigs this mornin'. Yo' shore dreaned me las' night, Miz Dovie, 'n' needs ter git ready fer tonight."

"Ain goin' ter be no tonight," she managed to say. "Ain' never goin' ter be no more," but even while she spoke the words she realized they lacked conviction.

"Ain', Miz Dovie?" He was close to her now, so close that his body touched hers. His arms pulled her to him. "If'n yo' thinkin *ain'*, I thinkin *is*. Nigger's a nigger in the daytime, Miz Dovie. Ain' oversteppin'. Ain' gittin' uppity. Ain' shootin' off my mouth. Ain' tellin' all the other servants that I pleasures my mist'ess. No, ma'am. This nigger ain' a-tellin' no one, he ain'. But come night, he pleasures her again. Come night he ain' a nigger no more. He better'n any white man 'n' he knows it. Miz Dovie know it too."

His lips touched hers and she did not have the strength to push him away.

"Tell that Mintie ter fry yo' up some ham 'n' eggs if'n yo' got a special hankerin' fer 'em," she whispered meekly. Her arm stole around his naked back. She was glad that no welts spoiled it. Oh, what difference did it make anyway? What difference did it make, if she had at last found happiness? What difference did anything make, as long as he belonged to her and would always be with her to do her bidding?

Chapter XXVIII

AFTER COLT HAD GONE, Dovie was faced with the dilemma of wanting to remember all the glory of last night and, at the same time, trying to obliterate it from her mind. She plunged into the activities of The Patch in an effort to do either or both. Cotton had been picked there, ginned at Brownsville, baled and sold to the factors. Despite her fears, Dove Cote had produced a good crop and The Patch an excellent one: she had a large balance in the bank as a result of a successful season.

There was a hiatus now; the feverish work of picking was over. This was the time of year that Tom had always devoted to clearing brush and trees from swampland, digging ditches and turning more acres into arable land. Ransom had been engaged in brush cutting yesterday so Dovie marshaled her drivers and had them proceed with the work, directing the various groups. She noticed that when she was present, they worked with some degree of efficiency, but she was sure as soon as she turned her back, the work slowed almost to a standstill. All except for Kru, who, when he espied her, came over and stood beside her horse, mutely assuring her by his presence that he was as loyal as ever. As far as she could see, he had not changed since the first time she had seen him, on the occasion of Tommy's birth. He was still as much of a savage as ever, still unclothed but, as always, the most willing of workers. Dovie felt that she owed him a lot, but she was unable to find any way to repay him. What could she do for him? It was something she had to think about.

At least, seeing Kru and thinking about him had taken her thoughts temporarily away from Colt. Although she had plunged into her work, she had not been able to get him out of her mind. She had purposely sent him to Dove Cote to fetch Nero, hoping that a few hours away from him would give her some perspective by which to view her actions of the night before. She had not gained this and now she regretted that she had sent him. She felt lost without him beside her and kept glancing up at the sun, watching its progress and trying to approximate the time of his return. He should, she reasoned, be back by noon, and with Nero to take over at The Patch, she could return to Dove Cote. No, she did not want to go directly back to Dove Cote. She wanted something different—a way of spending the day that would be as divorced from the usual repetitive pattern of her days as last night had been from all the other nights in her life. She wanted—oh, what did she want? She wanted the lights and glitter of New Orleans; she wanted to ride through the streets in an elegant carriage, dressed in a gown of emerald velvet with a bonnet of pink roses on her head and Colt up on the box in white livery for everyone to see. She was proud of him and she wanted to show him off, wanted others to admire him, comment on him, inquire if he were for sale so that she could refuse even five thousand dollars for him if it were offered to her.

But there was no place to go except the log walls of Dove Cote or the depressing general store in Brownsville. She might go there! She could order a new dress pattern—perhaps a rose-sprigged challis or a pale blue sarcenet—because she was determined to abandon the rusty black she was wearing for Bart and her father. Yes, she'd go to the store, and perhaps there she could find out where she could buy a new barouche like the one Mrs. O'Neal had. Mrs. O'Neal! That was a thought. She'd ride out to Clonmel. It was the nearest thing to the lights and glitter of New Orleans. At least it was more exciting than the dull-as-dishwater atmosphere of Dove Cote.

Mrs. O'Neal could tell her where she had ordered her pretty carriage. It would be exciting to sit in the cool Clonmel drawing room and sip coffee from an eggshell cup and talk with Mrs. O'Neal, even if she was that Mrs. Salsman's daughter. And when Mrs. O'Neal came out to bid her good-bye, she'd see Colt astride his horse, and if Dovie knew Mrs. O'Neal as she thought she did, she would be one person who would appreciate Colt's beauty. She might have her carriage and her big house and her rich husband but she certainly didn't have anything to compare with Colt. Nobody did, and where, oh where was he? He'd had plenty of time to return. Why didn't he come?

She surveyed her workers. "Touch up them niggers, Jabed. Git 'em ter show a little sweat. Want ter see 'em workin'. Jes' a-leanin' on their snaths, tha's all they's a-doin'." She grabbed the whip from the driver's hand and rode down the row of hands, lashing right and left. It helped dispel her anxiety to see the whip snake out and hear the yelps of pain.

By noon, however, she was rewarded by the sight of Colt and Nero riding across the fields. Her heart skipped a beat and she hoped Nero would not notice her excitement. Not that it was any of Nero's business what she did, but she had an idea that if he entertained even the slightest suspicion of what had happened last night, he would kill Colt. She must be careful.

She informed Nero that Ransom Lightfoot had departed for good and that he must take over control at The Patch, at least for the time being. In answer to her questions, he informed her that things were under control at Dove Cote; there was not much there to do. Dovie told him of her intended visit to Clonmel and asked him to think of something she could do for Kru.

After gulping down a bowl of clabber and some cold pone at the cabin, she was ready to start. Once out on the road, away from The Patch, she signaled to Colt to ride beside her but cautioned him that should anyone approach, he was to take his place a horse's length behind her. By taking a little traveled road which led over the hills, she could come out on the Orion road not far from Clonmel. This would save her some five miles of riding by not having to go into Brownsville and then out again toward Orion. They spoke little on the journey. Somehow Dovie found no subjects of conversation—there was not much they could say to each other. Colt's mentality did not attract her. Yet he held such an irresistible appeal for her that on one stretch of the road, where high banks were overhung with creepers, she halted her horse and reached over to him, letting her hand creep down inside his shirt.

"Yo' my boy, Colt." She smiled at him. "What these eyes a-tellin' you they's seein'?"

"Seein' my sweet Dovie." He grinned back at her.

She noticed the use of her first name without the usual title of respect but she could not censure him for it. Still, her fear of discovery bade her remind him. "Mustn't ever call me that if'n anyone roun', Colt. Yo' know what they do ter yo' if'n they ever find out yo' been with a white woman?"

"They kill me. Whop me ter death."

"Shore would. Even the servants mustn't know. Word git ter Nero 'n' he'd kill yo' too. This's our secret, Colt." She looked around, scanning the road for travelers, but seeing none, she lifted her lips to him.

"Better not do any more o' that, sweet Dovie, o' we not a-goin' ter get where we a-goin'." He pushed her away gently and slapped her horse's rump.

When they arrived at the gates of Clonmel, she regretted that she had been unable to tidy up. Her disheveled appearance was another good argument for getting a carriage. A lady did not go gallivanting around the country on horseback or in a democrat wagon, especially a lady with as much money in the bank as Dovie had.

Once again Colt became a slave and followed the boy who met them at the door of Clonmel around to the stables, while Dovie mounted the steps and pulled the bell cord. The same octoroon wench answered, but this time, instead of being decently dressed in calico, she sported a raddled gown of pale pink china silk whose torn flounces had been caught up with pins. Before Dovie had a chance to inquire for Mrs. O'Neal, Mr. O'Neal himself, accompanied by a stranger, appeared at the door. He seemed surprised to see her, astonished, in fact, so that he could hardly speak.

"Miz Boggs! Miz Boggs, kin this really be yo'? The mos' 'markable coincidence! Mista Wainwright and I jes' startin' fer Dove Cote ter see yo'. Jes' this moment speakin' 'bout yo'." He spread his hands in a gesture of unbelief at her presence, then recovered himself sufficiently to introduce her to the man beside him.

"Miz Boggs ma'am, this is Mista Wainwright from Boston. He the man I bin wantin' yo' ter meet. Mista Wainwright, this Miz Bartholomew Boggs, who we bin talkin' 'bout."

The man—a kindly, elderly, scholarly-looking person —seemed quite as astounded as Johnny O'Neal and extended his hand to Dovie. She touched her fingers to his and entered the house as O'Neal waved her in. Once seated in the drawing room on the same sofa she had occupied before, she inquired for Mrs. O'Neal.

"Sorry, Miz Boggs, Miz O'Neal's not here." He offered no further explanation as he rang for the servant and ordered refreshments for Dovie. "But now that yo're here, my dear Miz Boggs, we kin talk 'bout what we were goin' to Dove Cote ter see yo' 'bout. It in regard to yore son."

"The Dummy?"

"Yes Ma'am. It 'bout him Mista Wainwright and I would like ter talk ter yo'. I saw him the day o' the sale, 'n' he a handsome boy, Miz Boggs. Handsome's a picture, he is, and it shore seem a shame ter me that he was afflicted. It musta bin a heavy cross fer yo' ter bear."

She bowed in acceptance of his compliments and sympathy.

"But I got good news fer yo'. That boy kin talk."

"Know that," Dovie agreed. "He a-learnin' good. Kin say 'Mama' 'n' 'Kru'—tha's one of our fiel' hands he tooken a notion to. Surprised me, he did. Said 'Kru' jes's plain's kin be, 'n' said 'Mama' too. He watched my lips."

"That's our newest theory, Mrs. Boggs." Wainwright spoke for the first time. "I have just returned from Paris where I have been learning *The Abbé Sicard*'s methods of teaching the dumb to speak and the deaf to hear. We used to teach only the hand alphabet, but now we know that the deaf can understand by watching another person talk. We call it 'lip reading.' And we are teaching them to talk, too. No longer must deaf people go through life shut off from the rest of the world. I'm starting a school for the deaf in Boston. Mr. O'Neal thought you might be interested."

"Mista Wainwright's an ol' friend o' my papa, Miz Boggs. He jes' arrived in N'Orleans from France 'n' come up ter Clonmel ter visit me 'fore he goes ter the north. I 'membered yore son 'n' spoke ter Mista Wainwright 'bout him. Tha's why we comin' over ter see yo'."

"But he a-talkin' now." Dovie had no idea where Boston was, but as she had never heard of it, it must be a long way.

"He might learn a few words by himself, Mrs. Boggs, but there is more to it than that. He must learn to read and write. He must have an education and if, as Mr. O'Neal says, the boy is now an adolescent, there is no time to be wasted. It will require four or five years to give him the most elementary education.

Dovie did not want to betray her ignorance but she was curious. "That place far away, Mista Wainwright?"

He nodded. "A good many miles, Mrs. Boggs. You'd have to relinquish your son to us but we would take good care of him. We already have two students coming from New Orleans and there are more waiting for us in New England. The boys will be well housed in my own home and well fed, because my wife is an excellent cook. We shall also supervise their morals at the same time we educate their minds. You can rest assured your son will be in good hands."

Although Dovie had never been a particularly doting mother, she could not envisage life without the Dummy. He had been a part of it for so long. She could not make up her mind and sat staring from one to the other until finally O'Neal broke the silence.

"Yo' don' need ter decide this minute, Miz Boggs. Take some time ter think 'bout it. Mista Wainwright'll be here fer 'nother week 'n' then he goes ter Natchez 'n' will leave fer Boston from N'Orleans. Yo' kin think 'bout it fer a while 'n' if yo' decide, yore son kin join him either in Natchez o' N'Orleans."

"I'll jes' do that, Mista O'Neal. I'll jes' do that. Ain' got nobody ter advise me no more with papa 'n' my husband both dead. Suppose it cost a lot o' money, but shore would like ter have the Dummy learn. He's smart, he is, but he's never been 'way from home. Don' know if'n anyone could handle him."

Mr. Wainwright nodded slowly. "We know how to handle these children, Mrs. Boggs. Their affliction causes them to be willful and stubborn and to fly into tantrums at the slightest provocation. That's the only way they have of expressing themselves. However, we have found that kindness and understanding succeed where nothing else does. We have a real affection for them and our only aim is to help them. I have dedicated my life to this work and am not interested in making money out of my school. I will charge only five hundred dollars a year for my boarding students, and if their parents cannot afford it, I will take them for nothing."

"Kin 'ford it all right."

Dovie considered five hundred a year a mere bagatelle. It was about what she would expect to get for one of the youths in the Romp Pasture, and the place was swarming with them. If it was to be as little as that, she could send Calico along with the Dummy so that the Dummy would suffer no homesickness. But no! These northerners had strange ideas about slavery. Probably this man would not allow a nigger in his house if he knew he was a bondman. She'd have to think about it.

"I'll think it over 'cause I'd like ter do it fer my boy. Think probably I will but want ter talk it over with my mama first." She accepted his nod of approbation and then turned to O'Neal. "Kindly sorry Miz O'Neal ain' ter home today. Rode over here special ter see her. She comin' back soon?"

O'Neal regarded her with unqualified amazement.

"Haven't yo' heard, Miz Boggs? She ain' ever comin' back. I thought everyone in Alabama knew 'bout the scandal she kicked up."

"Ain' heard nothin'. Ain' been 'way from Dove Cote 'cept over ter The Patch since I got back from Mista Maxwell's, time when I bought Nero back from yo'. 'Sides, I ain' much fer women's gossip 'n' scandalizin'."

"Day after yo' were here she lit out. Took up with some drummer from St. Louis 'n' jus' skedaddled. Traced 'em over ter Natchez whar they took a boat fer N'Orleans. She took 'bout five thousan' dollars 'n' all her jewelry but I cain' say I'm sorry. Never shoulda married her, anyway. Attorney Follansbee over in Natchez he got me a divorce that day while I was there. Charged her with adultery 'n' desertion 'n' took the papers ter the court 'n' got me divorced in less'n an hour. That's why she never comin' back."

He looked so jubilant Dovie could not offer him her sympathy. Congratulations seemed to be more in order, so she merely clucked her tongue, which could be taken for almost any appropriate expression.

"Were yo' wantin' ter see her personal, Miz Boggs?" he asked.

"Reckon yo'd call it more on business," Dovie answered, at which Mr. Wainwright bowed low with old-fashioned courtesy and excused himself. She waited until she saw him walking past the window that opened onto the gallery and then continued, "It 'bout that pretty carriage she had. Wantin' ter git me one like it 'n' wantin' ter know whereat she bought it 'n' how I could git me one."

O'Neal arose and came to sit beside her on the sofa. His hand reached over and clasped hers warmly. She did not feel any particular excitement at his nearness and yet she was happy to know he wanted to be beside her.

"I haven't any more use fer that carriage now, Miz Boggs. Cain' see myself ridin' 'roun' in it. It hasn' bin touched since the day she lef'. There a matched pair o'

398

grays goes with it, too. Come from Duvallier's in N'Orleans 'n' made up 'specially. If yo'd be willin' ter ride on the same seat Lorie Salsman sat on, I'd gladly give it ter yo'."

"Laws, Mista O'Neal, couldn't 'cept it as a gift but shore would like ter buy it."

"We O'Neals don' go peddlin' our second-hand trash 'roun' the country. It ain' doin' me a bit o' good, sittin' out there in the carriage house all tied up in ol' sheets. Horses eatin' their heads off out 'n the barn. Far's I'm concerned that carriage kin sit there till it falls ter pieces with dry rot." His hand clasped hers with added fervor. "I'd really be 'bliged if yo'd take it off'n my hands, Miz Boggs."

"Dovie," she said, squeezing his hand. "Always did hate the name o' Boggs."

"Dovie?" He moved closer and put his arm over the back of the sofa so that his hand rested lightly on her shoulder. "You mean I kin call yo' Dovie?"

"Yes, Mista O'Neal. Always did dislike that name o' Boggs."

"Then you'll call me Johnny, yes?" His arm came down on her shoulders. "And if'n yo' don' like the name of o' Boggs, yo' could always change it, yo' know."

Dovie snuggled a little closer to him. "Might consider that, Johnny, but got ter wait till Bart been buried a year 'fore I starts thinkin' 'bout it. Ain' much fer what other people says, but seems kindly decent, tha's all."

"I respect yore feelin's but at leas' I kin hope, Dovie?"

She appraised him. He was indeed a good-looking man, near her own age, not young but not old either. There was a certain softness about him from too much good living, liquor and octoroon wenches, which had slackened his mouth and given him lines around his eyes. His once plentiful hair was thinning at the temples and he had a slight paunch outlined by his gold watch chain. But he was a fine-looking man, and after all what male could ever compare with Colt? No white man, unless he could offer what Johnny O'Neal sitting here in the luxury of Clonmel's drawing room could. Colt had one thing to offer, but Johnny O'Neal had something else equally important—wealth and position. So . . . why not? Why couldn't she have them both, at least for the time being? O'Neal could have the octoroon in the china silk ball gown, if he wanted, and she'd have Colt. If they should marry, as O'Neal seemed interested in doing, he'd continue to have a wench in spite of anything she could say or do. What's sauce for the gander would be sauce for the goose too. She'd find some way of keeping Colt. And . . . she'd be mistress of Clonmel! That was something to think about. She could put up with Johnny O'Neal to achieve that.

She lifted her head an inch, bringing it level with his own, and his image blurred in her eyes as his lips touched hers.

"Of course yo' kin hope, Johnny," she whispered. " 'N' so kin I. Reckon as how we ain' neither had much joy from our marriages. Mayhap it's time we got some."

"Oh, Dovie, Dovie, Dovie." He slipped to his knees and laid his head in her lap. "Bin in love with yo' ever since the day yo' come ter Clonmel. Haven' thought 'bout 'nother person but yo'. I was so happy when Lorie went. I lied ter yo', Dovie. Lorie didn' steal that five thousand dollars. I gave it ter her ter leave. But she woulda gone anyway, I guess."

She leaned over and kissed the thinning hair.

"Reckon I bin thinkin' 'bout yo' too, Johnny. Dove Cote seem mighty lonesome 'thout a man there, 'n' it too much fer a woman—two plantations. Cain' do it alone."

"Then yo'll 'cept the carriage 's our betrothal gif' till I kin sen' ter Natchez 'n' git yo' a ring?"

"Things are different now, Johnny, if'n we betrothed. 'Cept the carriage gladly. Seems like'n we ain' strangers no more."

"Ain never goin' ter be, Dovie. Some day this goin' ter be yore home. Some day yo'll be comin' down those stairs all dress' up in satin 'n' diamonds 'n' there'll be people here from Natchez 'n' from Mobile 'n' even from N'Or-leans. I'll be waitin' fer yo' at the foot o' the stairs 'n' I'll say, 'Folks, I want ter introduce my lovely wife, Dovie O'Neal.' "

It was more than Dovie had ever hoped for.

"Be right proud ter be Miz O'Neal, Johnny, come the time when we kin git married up." She surrendered herself to his embraces, but his kisses left her apathetic and devoid of emotion. Nevertheless, she returned them with a convincing display of passion.

Chapter XXIX

DOVIE ARRIVED BACK at Dove Cote that evening, lolling lika the Queen of Sheba on the fawn-colored velvet cushions of Lorie O'Neal's varnished barouche. Up on the box, Colt, who had been squeezed into the livery that Lorie's coachman had worn, which had been tailored in New Orleans to match the carriage, handled the pair of high-stepping grays, holding the reins high and flicking the tasseled whip over their ears. Behind them one of the Clonmel grooms rode Colt's stallion and led Dovie's mare and a horse of his own. Dovie had never been happier in her life. It seemed as though Bart's Good Lord had been watching over her, giving her everything she had ever wanted and doing it with a lavish prodigality she had never dreamed possible. All her problems had been miraculously solved, and solved far better than she could have anticipated.

She had eliminated Bart and gained Ransom and he had, for a time, been essential in her life. Then, as if an all-knowing Providence had sensed her need, Ransom had been eliminated and she had gained Colt. She certainly did not intend to eliminate Colt in order to gain Johnny O'Neal. She glanced up at Colt's wide back, which was nearly splitting the seams of the fawn-colored livery. She had Johnny O'Neal in the palm of her hand, and if she was careful she could have both him and Colt. Being mistress of Clonmel would not obviate the necessity of driving over to Dove Cote to visit her dear mama. Of course not, and Colt would be waiting for her at Dove Cote. Probably Johnny would welcome her absence in order to devote his attentions to his octoroon wench. As far as Dovie was concerned he could have her, but she'd not go around the house dressed in Lorie Salsman's ball gowns. No sir-ee! Not even calico with earrings. She'd flaunt her charms in plain black, once Dovie became mistress of Clonmel.

Then, as mistress of Clonmel, she would also solve the problem of Dove Cote and The Patch. Johnny would be lucky to get such a rich wife; he could look after all three plantations for in addition to being a gentleman of fashion, Johnny had a reputation for being an astute businessman and planter.

She sighed and let her hand wander over the smooth surface of the velvet upholstery. This was the way she would live from now on. As Johnny had said, she'd be standing at the top of the stairs in Clonmel, clad in satin —pale blue she thought would be prettiest—and diamonds. She'd descend that grandiose staircase slowly, pausing on each polished step, smiling down at Johnny, who would be waiting for her below.

"Colonel 'n' Miz Randolph, may I present my wife, Miz O'Neal?"

"Pleased ter meet yo', I'm shore." Dovie knew how to use good manners if she wanted to. Then they would all walk into the dining room and—glory be—she'd have "The Well in the Desert" once more. Think of that! Wouldn't Callie be happy? Oh, everything was turning out just right, even to getting back "The Well in the Desert."

But there was something else—something else that added to her euphoria. What was it? Oh yes! The Dummy! He was going north to some place called Boston to learn to hear and talk. Wasn't it wonderful that her poor boy would be able to talk? Just wonderful. And although she was really glad for him, it would at the same time make things easier for her. A bride with a fifteen-year-old son was hardly a romantic figure. She'd find a way

403

to send Calico along with him. Actually, in the light of what Ransom Lightfoot had said, they were half brothers. There was no doubt about it—Calico had six fingers just like a true Verder and so did the Dummy. The germ of an idea entered her head, but she dismissed it. Time to think about that later. Time now to lean back on the fawn velvet and revel in her good fortune. Mrs. John O'Neal, mistress of Clonmel Plantation! And Dove Cote! And The Patch! Laws, it was enough to give anybody goose pimples.

Callie, sitting out on the gallery at Dove Cote, saw the grays turn into the drive and couldn't believe her eyes. Who could be coming to Dove Cote just at suppertime in such an elegant rig? But her conjectures were cut short when she saw the carriage stop, saw Colt jump down from the high box and open the side door of the carriage, saw the elegant little flight of steps come down and beheld her own daughter descend, her hand on Colt's shoulder.

"Dovie!" She tottered down the steps of the gallery on her tiny feet and picked her way bare-footed across the gravel. "Dovie, what yo' a-doin' in that there carriage?"

"A-ridin', Mama, what it look like I'm doin'? Cain' a body ride in her own carriage 'thout her mam throwin' a conniption fit? Yo' like it, Mama? Ain' it pretty? Colt, help mama in 'n' drive us down ter the gate 'n' back."

Colt hoisted Callie up into the barouche and then helped Dovie back in. The little steps folded up, the door was closed and Colt climbed onto the box. With a flourish of his whip, the grays turned and trotted down the driveway, out onto the mail road, turned and came back.

"Purtiest carriage I ever did see." Callie fingered the fringes on the seat, rubbed her bare feet over the soft carpet on the floor, leaned out and touched the silver lamps and then settled back onto the seat. "I do declare, Dovie, it most 's nice as that one I hear Miz Dalesman's daughter what's now Miz O'Neal traipses 'roun' the country in."

"It jes' as nice, Mama." Dovie waited for Colt to open the door a second time and maneuver Callie to the ground. "Jes' 'xackly as nice 'cause this was Miz O'Neal's
404

carriage 'n' it mine now. The carriage 'n' the grays're a betrothal present, Mama, from Mista Johnny O'Neal."

It was completely beyond Callie's mental capacity to
understand. She stared at her daughter blankly.

"Tha's what I say, Mama. Johnny O'Neal just gave 'em
ter me. He 'n' I's betrothed 'n' goin' ter git married up.
'Course, not right off. Waitin' till Bart been dead a year
so's it goin' ter look right, him being a dee-vorced man
'n' all, but he jes' popped the question 'n' naturally I
said 'yes.' 'N' this's my courtin' present till he kin send
ter New Orleans 'n' git me a diamon' ring." Dovie turned
to Colt. "Take the carriage out ter the barn. Take off
them new trogs 'fore yo' rubs down the horses 'n' put on
yore ol' ones. Git Fronie ter give yo' some old sheets so's
yo' kin cover up the carriage, 'n' leave them new trogs
with Fronie so's she kin brush 'em 'n' hang 'em up. See
'at that Clonmel nigger git somethin' ter eat in the kitchen
'fore he heads back home 'n' tell Dolly ter feed him good.
Ain' wantin' Clonmel niggers ter think we don' feed good
here at Dove Cote. I'm a-sleepin' out 'n the dove cote
from now on." She looked at him searchingly, making
sure he understood her implication. " 'N' yo'd better see
me 'fore yo' goes ter bed so's I kin tell yo' what I want
yo' ter do, come mornin'.' "

"Shore will, Miz Dovie ma'am." His restless feet scattered the gravel, and the whiteness of his teeth showed
between his raisin lips. "Shore want ter say that I mighty
proud ter be driving my pretty Miz Dovie 'roun' in this
pretty kerridge 'n' me all dressed up. Mighty proud, Miz
Dovie ma'am."

"He shore look pretty, don' he, Dovie." Callie stared
at Colt with admiration. "Reckon he the purtiest nigger
boy we ever had. Now yo' come in, Dovie, 'n' le's set
down 'n' yo' tell me all over 'gain 'bout Mista O'Neal.
All sixes 'n' sevens ter me now. Cain' make head nor
tail outa it but s'pose yo' knows what yo' doin'.' She
stopped short, her face lighting up with joy. "That mean
we a-goin' ter git 'The Well in the Desert' back 'gain?"

Dovie nodded. " 'N' that ain' all. The Dummy he goin'
ter Boston what's up north 'n' he a-goin' ter learn ter
read 'n' write 'n' talk 'n' hear. Mista Wainwright what's

over ter Clonmel goin' ter take him in 'n' I goin' ter finagle ter send Calico with him, 'n' gotta think 'bout that too." She held the door open for Callie and in a burst of affection leaned down and kissed her. "Things jes' a-turnin' out right fer us, Mama."

There was so much to tell! Ransom's leaving The Patch, although Dovie did not think it wise to mention her discovery that he had killed Tommy, her sudden betrothal to Johnny O'Neal and her prospects of becoming mistress of Clonmel; The Dummy's leaving for the north; the new carriage; Lorie O'Neal's elopement; Nero's staying at The Patch; and Mr. Wainwright's school in Boston, wherever that was. Not only did she have to tell all these items in detail but she had to repeat them several times so that Callie could fully comprehend them. The conversation continued through supper and afterward in the sitting room, where poor Callie, mentally unable to grasp so many things at once, stared at her daughter open-mouthed in astonishment and wonder. Dovie finally left her and went out to sit on the gallery until it was dark enough for her to go over to the dove cote. Colt came out of the kitchon, a towel over his arm and carrying a shingle with a glob of soft soap on it. His old shirt was open to the waist and his thin tow-linen trousers outlined his thighs.

The sight of him caused Dovie to suck in her breath and she had an overwhelming desire to go with him and watch him bathe. She stifled the thought and called him over to her. When he came trotting up to the gallery rail, she leaned over and whispered.

" 'Bout an hour or so, Colt. Yonder in the dove cote. I'll leave the door open. Be sure no one sees yo'."

For one brief moment, his hand brushed hers on the railing with a silent assurance of his understanding.

"Jes' goin' down ter the stream ter wash me all over, Miz Dovie. Dust seemin' ter stick ter me."

She smiled at him, appreciating his thoughtfulness, and watched the shadows of the oaks engulf him. She needed this time alone to sort out her thoughts and she knew that she could think better knowing that he would be with her in an hour. It took away all sense of torment and frustration and left her mind calm, with the certainty that she need not toss all night from one side to the other of an empty bed.

It was wonderful to contemplate the security she would enjoy as the wife of Johnny O'Neal. Not only security, she assured herself, but wealth and riches and position. It was no more than she deserved. She was a Verder, and the Verders were every bit as good and probably as wealthy as the O'Neals, but the Verders had been content to remain in the backwater of Brownsville while the O'Neals had journeyed afar and brought back other ways of living with them. Clonmel was a small palace compared to the log-timbered Dove Cote.

With Johnny to manage her two plantations, she would be relieved of all responsibility, and perhaps now, with the knowledge that he would soon control The Patch, he would be able to provide an overseer for it so Nero could return to Dove Cote. There was just one small nagging vexation that bothered her. If she married, control of both Dove Cote and The Patch would pass out of her hands. It didn't seem right that she should not retain them, but she knew that whoever she married would have *de facto* ownership of them. And, if she should die before her husband, what assurance did she have that he would not retain them and marry again? What would become of the Dummy?

Perhaps she could arrange something. She'd go in and see Norsmith at the bank and maybe he could fix it so the two plantations could belong to the Dummy instead of herself. Then, if they were legally his, nobody would have a chance to take them away. She was quite willing to have Johnny O'Neal manage them and receive the money for them but she did not want them to go out of her family—they were Verder plantations and she wanted them to remain in Verder hands. Yes, she'd see Norsmith about it and see what he could do. Her mind was at rest on that matter.

Strange how easy it was to solve all her problems. She began to think of Colt as some sort of fetish who had brought her good luck. Surely she had never been happier in her life. Perhaps she was a smarter woman than she had given herself credit for being. But then, she reflected, she was Tom Verder's daughter, and now there were no more Verders because Tommy was dead and the Dummy was a Boggs.

How she hated and detested that name! Boggs. Ugh! It sounded like poor white trash. Even if Bart's mother had been a Verder, his father must have been a redneck from some hardscrabble farm. Boggs! Poor boy, the Dummy, to have to go through life with such a name, when Bart was not his father after all. His father was Tommy Verder. Suppose she changed the Dummy's name to Verder? Who'd ever know the difference up there in Boston? Instead of Thomas Verder Boggs, he'd be just Thomas Verder, which would sound a lot better. Then, when he married, if he ever did, his children would be Verders instead of Boggses. If he did learn to talk and hear, there'd be a hundred girls who'd want to marry him, he was such a handsome boy. Then there would be Verders to carry on Dove Cote. She'd do just that—she would change his name. Another perplexing question settled.

It would be a good thing for him to go away. She wouldn't really miss him too much, as there had never existed any real companionship between them. He'd spent practically all his life with Calico. And . . . that reminded her! Calico must go with him. The Dummy would die of fright and homesickness without Calico. Why, he'd just pine away and die! But, she was certain of one thing; even Mr. Wainwright with his kindly face would never allow a nigger slave in his school. Never was a northerner yet that wasn't an abolitionist, going around saying slavery was vile and abominable. Saying that niggers were just as good as white folks, that they were human beings. M-m-m-m! Colt had sort of changed Dovie's ideas about Negroes. Supposing . . . just supposing? Fronie claimed she was a quadroon and she might well be, she was so light-skinned. Then, if Tommy was Calico's sire, Calico was an octoroon, almost human anyway. Well, if those folks up north didn't like nigger slaves, she'd make a white boy out of Calico.

If it weren't for those liver-colored spots on his body,

nobody would ever know Calico was a nigger. Never! His face and hands were just as white as the Dummy's, his hair was brown and straight and his eyes were blue. There wasn't a single feature that betrayed his origin. As a matter of fact, he looked enough like the Dummy to be his twin brother. Well, why not? He really was the Dummy's half brother and he was the same age. Let those abolitionist northerners think that they were twins. Good enough for them if they loved niggers so much. And the Dummy would need him for companionship because twin brothers couldn't be separated, could they? She'd be willing to pay another five hundred to have Calico go along and look out for her son.

However, and this presented a problem, she'd have to arrange it so that O'Neal didn't find out, for he knew that Calico was a nigger and he also knew that she didn't have twin sons. But she could manage it. In this mood of omnipotence she felt she could do anything. She'd cut off the Dummy's hair and dress both boys alike. It would take a little lying on her part, but Dovie did not shrink from a little deception.

Calico Verder! Heavens no! Too niggery! She'd call him . . . what? Calico could be his nickname if the Dummy insisted on calling him that, but what could Calico stand for? Caleb, Calhoun, Calvert? How about Calvin? Calvin . . . Callie! That was it—one named after her father and one after her mother. Yes, there'd be two boys going instead of one, and Calico, no, Calvin, could learn along with the Dummy.

How well everything was turning out. Bart was lying out in the burying ground, thanks to Kru. And that was another thing she'd have to think about right now. Kru! Twice he had saved her life. He mustn't ever fall into anyone else's hands. Kru must be forty or more. She was aware that manumission was a difficult process but that was another thing Norsmith would have to do for her. Then she'd have Honey build him a little cabin out in the woods that surrounded Dove Cote and she'd explain to him that it was his and that he'd have to wear clothes. He'd just have to wear something to cover up. When

Kru had been a young man, he must have looked like Colt.

Now that her thoughts had returned to Colt, she could think of nothing else. It must have been an hour since he had walked away with the towel and the soft soap on the shingle. She hoped nothing had happened to him. What if a painter had got him? What if he had drowned in the river? What if he had got lost in the woods coming back? She'd die! She'd just die. Johnny O'Neal and Clonmel and the new carriage and Tommy learning to talk meant nothing to her now. Every fiber of her flesh called out for Colt. Where was he?

She stood up, peering out into the dusk in the direction he would come from, her hands clutching the railing of the gallery. For long moments she stood there, wordless prayers forming in her mind until she saw a movement in the shadows—a blacker form than the shadows—coming through the trees. There was a sliver of moon and she could tell by the height and the long strides that it was Colt. He parted the streamers of moss and stepped out into the moonlight.

Relieved, she sank back into her chair, noticing for the first time how her heart was thumping. He broke into an easy lope and she waved him toward the dove cote. They met at the door and in her eagerness for him she fell into his arms. Together they walked in, closing the door behind them.

No light appeared in the windows of the dove cote. It remained dark, but inside there was warmth and life and silence.

Chapter XXX

THE HAPPIEST DAYS in Dovie's life multiplied themselves into the happiest weeks and then into her happiest months. It was one long succession of fortuitous events which seemed foreordained to turn out exactly right. Truly, everything she desired seemed to come to her full, pressed-down and running over. Every morning when she awoke in the warm musk of Colt's embrace she remembered her supreme satisfaction of the night before and her anticipation of the night to come. He had been a good luck talisman since the day she purchased him from Warren Maxwell and, along with the good luck, he had brought her a joy in living she had never experienced before. He was there! That was sufficient for her. In the daytime he was there for her to admire. Nights he was there for her to enjoy. And, with all this physical gratification there was the expectation of becoming mistress of Clonmel.

Johnny O'Neal was pressing his suit with ardor. He was in love with Dovie—perhaps not with the hot-blooded, all-consuming desire of youth but with a more mature, calculated affection. Dovie was a handsome woman with the beauty of full-blown opulence. Her standing and background would be a credit to himself and Clonmel. And, not the least of her attractions, she was a wealthy woman with two fine plantations plentifully stocked with slaves, and not a single one of them nor the plantations mortgaged. In addition, he suspected that she was a passionate woman who would not withhold her favors from him as his first wife had done. Because they were betrothed, he limited their caresses to a chaste kiss when they met and parted. The woman he was about to marry should come to his bed untouched—at least by himself. Once a man had committed himself to marriage with a woman, she immediately became sacrosanct in his eyes—something to be placed on a pedestal and worshiped. The illusion of a virgin bride must be kept up, even though the woman was a widow and a mother.

O'Neal restricted his visits to "courting nights," Wednesday evenings and Sundays. On these visits he sat with her in the parlor, brought her bunches of flowers picked at Clonmel, which were no better than those Callie grew in her own garden, small items of jewelry—an enameled locket, a silver-filigreed bouquet holder, a tortoiseshell comb and similar trinkets. These, Dovie imagined, were items left behind by Lorie Salsman, but she did not question their origin and enjoyed them. But the diamond ring, when it finally arrived from New Orleans, was her particular pride. It was not overlarge, it was rose-cut and shone with only a dim brilliance, but it was a real diamond and as Dovie had never seen any others, it seemed to her a veritable treasure. Whenever she wore it, she made affected gestures with her left hand so that it would be plainly evident. She was continually arranging her hair, stifling a yawn or patting her dress—always with her left hand.

O'Neal had no inkling that she was bored with his presence and that she anxiously awaited his departure that she might hurry to the dove cote and Colt. Dovie displayed all the fluttering coquetries of a woman in love, flattering him, lavishing compliments on him and occasionally pressing his hand with a warm fervor. Conversation between the two was never seriously at a standstill for they engaged in earnest discussions about the management of Dovie's two plantations. She had allowed Johnny to virtually take over their management. He was supervising Dove Cote through Nero and The Patch through a young kinsman of his, Orville Stanhope, from down Biloxi way. The young man wanted to learn plantation management and he was conscientious and diligent, apparently quite satisfied with the meager accommodations that The Patch offered and the ministrations of Mintie.

Dovie was relieved to be rid of all responsibilities of administration and devoted her time to preparing her trousseau and her bridal chest, neither of which she had had for her first marriage. There was also the wedding, which was to take place after the cotton was in. Although Callie insisted that the wedding should take place at Dove Cote, she was overriden by both Dovie and Johnny, who felt that the elegance of Clonmel was more fitting for the distinguished guests who would attend.

Johnny insisted that her wedding gown and her going-away dress be ordered from New Orleans, along with ball gowns and such toilettes as she would need for their honeymoon, which was to be spent in that city. She, however, found her time occupied with morning gowns, wrappers, underclothes and nightgowns. The Dummy's room at Dove Cote was a hive of activity as Mrs. Solatia Green, the seamstress from Brownsville, with her two mulatto assistants measured, cut, draped, pinned, hung and stitched the innumerable seams that transformed the yards of fine muslin and nainsook into lace-trimmed garments. With its feminine appurtenances, the room hardly looked as if the Dummy and Calico had ever occupied it.

For the Dummy had gone and Calico with him. It had taken a bit of finagling on Dovie's part and considerable deception of both the unsuspecting Mr. Wainwright and Johnny O'Neal but, like everything that Dovie put her hand to these days, it had turned out all right. In conferences with Mr. Norsmith and later with Judge Craven over at the county seat, she had deeded both Dove Cote and The Patch to the Dummy, with herself as his guardian until he became twenty-one. She understood little of the legal technicalities, but the judge managed to convey to her that although the Dummy was now the sole owner of both plantations, she could, owing to his infirmity, renew her right of guardianship even after he was twenty-one. Naturally she told Johnny nothing about this. To all intents and purposes, the plantations were hers and she was willing to allow him a free hand with them, but she knew now that if anything happened to her, the property would remain in Verder hands.

So she had sent the Dummy away. Although she had looked forward to his leaving, at the moment of parting she had a sudden and overwhelming sense of maternal love and broke down and wept. But an hour afterward she had recovered and experienced a feeling of relief that he was gone. He had never filled any particular place in her life, as he had never seemed more than an infant.

It had taken a great amount of planning on her part to get Calico away with the Dummy without Johnny knowing about it. When Mr. Wainwright had informed her he was leaving in two days, going by stage to New Orleans, Dovie demurred at sending the Dummy with him, explaining that she could not get him ready in that short time, adding with an affectionate little smile that was intended to hide bravely the tears that were not there, that she just couldn't part with her baby on such short notice. So it was agreed that he could meet Mr. Wainwright later in New Orleans and make the rest of the journey to Boston with him.

"Jes' cain' go with him mysel'," Dovie lamented, " 'n' have ter send someone 'long with him, seein' how he cain' talk nor hear."

This seemed perfectly logical to both Wainwright and O'Neal and neither of them questioned the necessity of a companion for the Dummy. On her way home, Dovie stopped in at the tailor's in Brownsville and ordered identical dark blue suits for the Dummy and Calico. That evening after supper, she called Nero and Calico into the office. Although she addressed herself to Nero, she included Calico in her instructions.

"Like'n yo' know, Nero, I'm a-sendin' the Dummy up to Boston which is up north ter learn ter read 'n' learn ter hear. He a-goin' ter meet up with Mista Wainwright in New Orleans what is 'spectin' him 'n' will take charge

414

o' him from there on. Wants yo' should take the Dummy 'n' Calico over ter my uncle who is Doctor Verder what lives close by Natchez 'n' hand the Dummy 'n' Calico over ter him. He kin git passage fer the boys on a boat a-goin' down ter New Orleans 'n' Mista Wainwright kin meet 'em there. Calico got ter go with him 'cause the Dummy cain' go 'lone."

"Cain' do that, Miz Dovie, jes' cain' do that by his own self." Nero was sincere in agreement.

Dovie continued, "Now lissen ter me, Nero, 'n' yo' pay 'tention, Calico, 'cause this's very important. Calico he a-goin' 'long with the Dummy but he ain' goin' 'long like'n no nigger boy nor no playboy nor servant neither. He a-goin' like'n the Dummy's brother—like'n the Dummy's twin. Them folks up north don' hol' with niggers nohow. He got ter go 'long with the Dummy o' he pine hisself away. If'n he go like'n a nigger or a servant, chances are they won' take him, so he's goin' like'n a white boy. Yo' understan', Calico?"

He did, and his face lighted up. He would shed his color and his bondage as easily as a snake sheds its skin. He stood up straight, looked Dovie in the eye and when he spoke, his words had a different tone. "Yas'm, Miz Dovie ma'am."

"Then if'n yo' do, set yo'self down in that chair 'cause yo' don' have ter stand up no more. 'N' yo' don' have ter call me 'Miz Dovie ma'am' no more neither."

"Yes ma'am." Calico sat down in the chair and surveyed Nero with a superior air.

"He jes' like'n the Dummy only he a little taller 'n' a little heftier." Dovie appraised him while she addressed Nero. " 'N' he jes' so white too. Got six fingers 'n' everythin'. Same age's him 'n' they look alike. Ain' nobody a-goin' ter know if'n he keep his trogs on that he ain' white. Them spots don' show on him not even one little bit."

"They don', fer a fac', Miz Dovie. He right purentee white, that boy is. Ain' nothin' niggery 'bout him, 'tall. Don' even 'pear like'n he a mustee even."

"He got a nigger name tho'." Dovie continued to stare at Calico. "Calico jes' a name fer a servant o' a horse o'

415

somethin'. Got ter thinkin'. Goin' ter call him Callie after my mama. That's fittin' fer twins—Tommy fer my papa 'n' Callie fer my mama. Kin say his name's Calvin if'n he wants but folks kin call him 'Callie.' That yore new name now, Calico. Callie!"

"Ain' wantin' no woman's name. Ain' likin' ter be called after no woman." Calico's lower lip curled out. "How come I cain' have a man's name like'n the Dummy. He's Tommy like'n a man."

Dovie leveled a finger at him. "Yo' takes the name I gives yo' 'n' yo' keeps yore mouth shet. If'n I say yo' be Callie yo' be Callie. If'n I say yo' be Rosemary, yo' be Rosemary. Yo' ain' got nothin' ter say 'bout it. Git so yo' kin write up north there, 'n' yo' kin write yore name Calvin Verder 'n' Tommy he be Thomas Verder. Ain' havin' no more Boggses no more. We'se Verders now. Yo're goin' ter be Callie Verder, like it o' lump it. Yo' a-goin' north with the Dummy 'n' goin' ter learn readin' 'n' writin' 'n' cipherin' jes' like the Dummy. Yo' got ter look out fer him. Tha's why I'm a-sendin' yo' 'long. Yo' do like'n he say 'n' if'n yo' don', Mr. Wainwright he'll whop yo'.'"

"Yas'm."

"Yo' got ter act like'n white folks now but that ain' goin' ter be hard fer yo'. Yo' always et at the table 'n' et white folks vittles. Ain' never been treated like a nigger 'n' don' ever tell no one up north there that yo' a nigger. Yo' the Dummy's twin brother 'n' yo're white. 'N' he don' rightly know but what yo' are his brother. Yo' always been with him. Guess yo' smart 'nuff ter fool them northerners, ain' yo'?"

"Yas'm."

Some ten days later when Nero returned from Natchez he reported on their reception by Dr. Verder and the doctor's shock to hear of his brother's death. Mrs. Verder had fallen in love with the twins, saying that they were both true Verders even down to their six-fingered hands. Both the Doctor and Mrs. Verder seemed inclined to favor Calico over the Dummy but that, Nero thought,

416

was because they could communicate with Calico and not with Tommy.

Immediately on their arrival, Dr. Verder had obtained passage for the Dummy and Calico. He sent a letter advising Mr. Wainwright to meet them when their ship arrived.

Another problem had been worked out entirely to Dovie's satisfaction. She sighed and sat back in her chair. It was wonderful to have everything go so well. Johnny O'Neal never suspected a thing, and unless Mr. Wainwright should write him, which Dovie considered unlikely, he'd never know about Calico. Well, she figured, what Johnny O'Neal didn't know about Calico wouldn't hurt him and what he didn't know about Colt wouldn't hurt him either. She thanked Nero for delivering the boys safely but he remained standing before her, apparently wanting to discuss something with her, but not knowing how to begin.

"Well, what is it?" she asked.

"Don' jes' know how ter begin, Miz Dovie ma'am, but it 'bout that Colt boy what drivin' yo'."

"What about Colt?"

Nero's hands fumbled with his hat. "Ain' somethin' I should talk about with yo', Miz Dovie, yo' bein' a woman 'n' all but seein' as how yo're mist'ess here, 'pears like'n I got ter. Ain' scarcely fittin' ter talk with a woman 'bout, tho'."

Dovie was trembling inside. Anything connected with Colt was vital. Although he was with her practically every moment of the day, and his nights were devoted to her, he just might be carrying on with some other girl.

"What he bin a-doin'?" she asked, frightened yet anxious to have him answer her.

"That Mista Gullivant what live at Burnt Hills Plantation he stopped me on the road on my way home today. Said he been admirin' that Colt boy what he's seein' drivin' yo' roun', 'n' wantin' ter know if'n yo'd take a stud fee fer him. Says he cain' ask yo' but askin' me. He's got three, four wenches over ter his place he'd like ter cover. Wantin' Colt ter come over there 'n' stay a

417

week. He a-sayin' as how he'll pay ten dollars if'n yo' kin spare Colt."

Dovie was relieved and could afford now to be emphatic. "Colt ain' fer hire. We ain' a-studdin' him nor any other Dove Cote nigger. Never did it when papa was alive 'n' ain' goin' ter start it now. We kin keep him busy here."

Nero bowed his head slightly as if to apologize for having asked the question but he did not leave. When he lifted his head, he looked searchingly at Dovie.

"Serena mos' ready ter birth that sucker what he planted in her when he firs' came. She plaguin' me ter know if'n he kin give her another. Reckon she got a hankerin' fer him."

She was treading on dangerous ground, Dovie realized. She had bought Colt ostensibly to improve the breed of Dove Cote slaves. To deny his services to an outsider was one thing, to deny them at Dove Cote was another. She felt she had covered her tracks too carefully for Nero to be suspicious and she was as anxious to keep her intimacies with Colt from him as she would have been from her father.

"Reckon we'll think 'bout that when the time comes. Serena ain' even had her sucker yet." She stood up in dismissal of Nero. "Plenty o' time ter think 'bout it onct we see what kind o' a sucker he kin git outa her."

Chapter XXXI

BREAKFAST WAS OVER, and Dovie sat on the gallery with Callie, waiting for Colt to bring the horses up from the barn for their daily trip to the fields. He came out of the stable, mounted on the big stallion and leading Dovie's mare. As always when she saw him, her whole world changed. She watched him coming, walking the horses, sitting straight and proud in the saddle. Reining the horses in at the steps, he alighted in one easy movement of flowing muscles and came up the steps, drawing a letter from his pocket.

"Nero he jes' back from town, Miz Dovie ma'am, 'n' he askin' would I kindly give yo' this, please ma'am." Colt handed it to Dovie but included Callie in his smile. " 'N' kin' I ask how yo' feelin' this mornin', Miz Callie ma'am?" Colt knew that the older woman admired him and he always made an effort to captivate her.

"Jes' fine, Colt, jes' fine." She waited for Dovie to break the seal and unfold the paper. "What yo' got there, Dovie?"

Dovie read it aloud slowly, stumbling over some of the words and unable to read others:

22 Dauphin Street
New Orleans, La.

My esteemed Mrs. Verder:
This will acknowledge the safe arrival of your two sons. I was quite prepared for Calvin's arrival but did

not anticipate Thomas coming with him. However, I can understand your disinclination to separate twin brothers. Although our facilities in Boston are concentrated entirely on the teaching of the deaf, we shall endeavor to provide Thomas with an elementary education so that they will not have to be parted.

I have not had time as yet to make a thorough examination of Calvin's mentality but I believe he is intelligent and capable of learning. Naturally his progress will be slower than that of Thomas as he must first learn methods of communication. I shall, however, hope to have good reports for you on both boys.

An old friend of mine from Boston, Captain Mapes, will convey us to Boston on his ship and we plan to leave here the end of the week. I shall advise you of our safe arrival in Boston and in the meantime I thank you for depositing funds for both boys in the bank in Boston through your bank in Brownsville. Your son Thomas wishes me to send you his love and I am sure Calvin does also even though he cannot express himself.

Yours respectfully,
Jon. Wainwright

Dovie shook her head and then proceeded to read the letter over again. The second time she became even more confused than the first.

"That man ain' too smart," she remarked to her mother. "He a-thinkin' Calico the one what's deaf 'n' Tommy the one what kin hear." She sighed in exasperation at Wainwright's stupidity. "Got ter write him 'n' straighten him out."

"He jes' confused, I guess," Callie laughed. "Them northerners ain' too smart nohow. Had mos' forgot myself that the Dummy named Thomas since we ain' never called him nothin' but The Dummy. But don' yo' worry, Dovie, he a-goin' ter fin' out which one's deaf 'n' which one ain'. He'll git it all straightened out, Dovie. Ain' no need a-writin' him. He'll find out The Dummy's the deaf one."

But Mr. Wainwright never did find out. When he had met them at the boat in New Orleans and recovered from the shock of finding two boys instead of one, Calico had announced himself as Tommy and introduced the Dummy as Callie. Calico had never had any affection for Callie herself and he was determined that he would not bear her name. Besides, it was a woman's name and after his experience at Falconhurst, Calico felt that he was a man. Hammond Maxwell hadn't had to tell him what to do with that Hebe wench. He'd gone right ahead and done it, not once but twice. Hammond had told him that he had acquitted himself well. After that experience at Falconhurst, he had sickened of the things that he and the Dummy did together although at one time he had enjoyed them as much as the Dummy. He still submitted to them passively with the realization that they did solve certain problems for him. They had bought him freedom. He was a white boy now, and that was reason enough to continue to submit to Tommy when necessary.

No, Mr. Wainwright never did find out because, of course, Dovie never got around to writing to him. As far as he was concerned, Callie Verder was the deaf-mute —the slight, handsome boy—and Tommy Verder was the other—the strong manly one.

Chapter XXXII

It was to be a wedding unrivaled in magnificence!
There may have been weddings among the old Creole
families in New Orleans and possibly among the great
houses of Natchez or Charleston or Tidewater Virginia
that could have compared with it, but certainly Alabama
had never heard of anything like it. That a divorced
man and a recently widowed woman (whose husband
was scarcely cold in his grave) should plan a wedding
such as this! Flaunting their shame in public. Unthinkable! Yet who would refuse to be present? Who among
those three hundred favored by invitations would let
hell or high water keep them from seeing John Taliaferro O'Neal married to Dovie Verder Boggs? Who indeed?
Even though it was a scandal that cried to high heaven,
not a soul wanted to miss it.

Callie had at first insisted that the wedding take place
at Dove Cote. A bride should be married from her own
home. That had been laid down by etiquette and custom.
But where, Johnny O'Neal asked (for he was determined that his wedding should eclipse all others), could
they possibly accommodate three hundred guests at
Dove Cote? Why, even Clonmel would be packed tighter than a bale of cotton to get them all in. Guests were
coming not only from the surrounding neighborhood but
from far-away cities. The O'Neals were a big family and

their friends were legion—in fact, most of the invited guests were from the groom's side. Dovie had almost nobody to invite except the immediate neighbors.

There were not, Callie agreed, three hundred tea cups and saucers at Dove Cote to serve them. As a matter of fact, there were not at Clonmel either, but that did not mean that the grand caterers from New Orleans could not supply them along with everything else.

Dovie's wedding dress had been made in New Orleans and true to southern tradition, it was of satin "that would stand alone." The veil of rose point had come from Brussels and was caught up into a tiara of seed pearls. There was also a going-away dress of dove gray satin trimmed with cut-steel passementerie and a gray bonnet lined with pink chiffon that sprouted a tangle of pink rosebuds and gray ostrich plumes. Ball gowns and other dresses were awaiting Dovie's arrival at the bridal suite of the St. Louis Hotel in New Orleans. Even Callie had benefited to the extent of a new dress of lilac taffeta with flounces of black chantilly caught up around the skirt with bunches of silk violets. It was the first important new dress she had had since she was married. There had never before been an occasion to have one made.

And now it was almost time—just a few more days. The invitations had gone out—stiff white engraved cards embossed with osculating doves (what could be more appropriate?)—addressed in a florid hand by old man Patterson, who was the bookkeeper at Norsmith's bank.

Mrs. Calinda Verder
requests the honor of your presence
at the marriage of her daughter
Dovie Claradelle
to
John Taliaferro O'Neal, Esq.
At Clonmel Plantation
On Saturday the Fourth of October
At High Noon

There was so much to be done, so many plans to

make that Dovie spent most of her days at Clonmel where, under her supervision, everything was cleaned, scrubbed, polished and waxed until the whole house shone and glittered. Clonmel could not, of course, accommodate all the overnight guests so these were to be farmed out at other plantations within a twenty-mile radius.

Dovie herself—knowing that she was to be the central figure of this imposing drama—anticipated it more than all the others, almost forgetting at times Johnny O'Neal would also be a part of this new splendor. But then, Johnny was so much in love he was a most compliant person. She could twist him around her finger. Almost! He had been averse to letting Colt accompany them on their honeymoon. There was no reason for it, he said, as he intended to purchase a new carriage in New Orleans and he might just as well buy a coachman to go with it. Dovie did not care to press the point and when he gave her Roxanna, the mulatto wench at Clonmel who had been Lorie's personal servant, to accompany her, she was glad Colt wasn't going along. Better to have him remain at Dove Cote where Nero could keep an eye on him than have him pestering that Roxanna who, Dovie knew, would get her fingers onto him the first chance she could get. When she had a chance to reflect, she realided it would be better to have a new coachman. It would provide a good excuse for leaving Colt at Dove Cote to drive Callie. Then, when she came over to see her mother, which would be frequently, he would be there.

On the Wednesday before the Saturday that she was to be married, Dovie drove back to Dove Cote late in the afternoon. The knowledge that she would be sacrificing Colt in a few days made her gaze up at his broad back lovingly as he reined in the horses, cramped the wheels of the carriage and slid down from the seat to help her out. During the month that she was to be gone she intended to hand him over to Serena, Nero's daughter, who had been delivered of her child and now stared at Colt with languishing ox eyes whenever she could get near enough to him. It would satisfy Nero, divert any suspicion that she might be using Colt herself and, she felt, eliminate any possibility of Colt forming any lasting attachment, for he had been with Serena once before and as far as Dovie could remember, he had never mentioned her since.

As she stepped down from the barouche, her hand moved from his shoulder to his neck and she inserted one finger between the tight white collar and the warm skin.

"Goin' ter bed early tonight, Colt boy. Ain' got us but a couple o' nights left. Goin' ter miss yo', I am."

"Yo' mean . . ." His smile was erased and terror showed in his eyes. "Yo ain' a-goin' ter sell me, Miz Dovie?"

Her hand released its grip on his collar and gently circled his ear.

"Such foolishments! 'Course not. Go eat 'n' then wash yo'self. It too cold now ter wash in the brook. Don' wan' yo' gittin' the ager."

"Ain' too cold fer me. Like it thata way. Makes me feel . . ." He clenched his fist and stuck his arm out.

"Sh-h-h!" She shook her head as Callie came out onto the gallery, shielding the flame of a candle in her hand.

"That yo', Dovie?"

"Yes, Mama, 'n' I'm plum' tuckered out. Got mos' everythin' ready tho'. Day after tomorrow I'm goin' ter strip yore garden. Goin' ter take every posy yo' got. Goin' ter need 'em. Usin' all the Clonmel flowers 'n' those over ter Mista Gasker's 'n' Miz Clara Reeves. Them people what servin' the dinner want all they kin git ter put 'longside the staircase."

"Take all yo' want, Dovie." Callie waved a careless hand in the direction of the garden. "Ain' much there 'ceptin' chrysanthemums. Some coxcomb 'n' goodbye-summers, but it gittin' late. Should've been married in May when they's lots o' flowers."

"They be all right, Mama. Jes' goin' ter eat somethin' now 'n' go ter bed. Got us a big day tomorrow. Don' let me fergit ter take over all the linen napkins we got. Goin' ter need 'em. Nigh onto twelve dozen at Clonmel but they ain' 'nuff."

During supper Callie had to know all about the wedding presents that had been received that day; she had to know about Johnny O'Neal's health and if—she lowered her voice so the servants would not hear—he had been drinking much. Had any of the guests arrived? Then she was anxious to know if "The Well in the Desert" had been properly polished and if it was to be the centerpiece of the table. The meal would, of course, be served on long tables on the lawn but the dining room would have a punch bowl at one end for the gentlemen and a bowl of syllabub at the other for the ladies. Callie felt that nothing at Clonmel would contribute quite so much to its elegance as her own "Well in the Desert."

Dovie ate listlessly, answering her mother's questions mechanically, hardly thinking what she said. She wondered, now that the wedding was so near, if she were really doing the right thing. Life had been infinitely pleasant these past few months and she dreaded to change it. Somehow the anticipation of getting married was more thrilling than the actuality. But she brushed such thoughts away. She'd be mistress of Clonmel along with being Mrs. O'Neal and if she played her cards well, she'd have everything she had now and more too. Well, perhaps she'd not have quite as much of Colt as she wanted —not every night—but she'd make sure to have enough of him on the nights she stayed at Dove Cote to tide her over until the next time.

"Plum' tuckered out, Mama." Dovie pushed back her chair and stood up. "Jes' ain' hungry tonight 'n' thinkin' I'll git ter bed early. 'Morrow's Thursday 'n' it the last day I'll have ter git much done. Them folks comin' Friday ter git the cookin' 'n' sech done. Rev'nd Joslin, he a-comin' down from Natchez Friday too. Guess pore ol' Soper's nose out-a-joint 'cause he ain' goin' ter do the marryin'." She kissed her mother absently and with a quick "good night" went out onto the gallery and across the yard to the dove cote.

Pushing the door open, she heard the sound of sobbing from the corner where the bed was and made her way cautiously to sit on the edge of the bed. For a moment she feared that the Dummy might have come back, but her hands groping in the darkness encountered the warm flesh of a naked man, and with her intimate knowledge of Colt, she knew that it could be no one but he.

"What yo' doin' out here all 'lone a-bawlin' like a li'l pickin'? What yo' got ter cry fer, Colt boy? Ain' nobody 'bused yo', have they? Yo' jes' tell Dovie if'n they have."

She felt his head shaking in denial.

"Then what's frettin' yo'?"

"Yo' ain' a-goin' ter sell me, sweet Dovie?"

"Tol' yo' I ain'. Don' yo' believe me?"

"Believes yo', I do, but what goin' ter happen ter me, sweet Dovie? Yo' goin' ter marry up with masta O'Neal 'n' yo' goin' ter live at Clonmel. I yore boy, sweet Dovie." His hands clutched at her with a grip of urgency. "But I cain' be with yo' over ter Clonmel like'n I am here. What I a-goin' ter do 'thout my sweet Dovie? Ain' never wantin' nobody else. Ain' never wantin' no colored wenches 'gain, never."

Dovie was touched by the depth of his affection for her. True, she had worshiped him, or at least his body, but she had never realized that he had any feeling for her outside of the breathless moments they spent together in the darkness. A nigger couldn't *love*. A dog after a bitch in heat did not *love* the bitch, neither did a stallion love a mare. Love was a delicate passion reserved for whites—for humans. That Colt might love her was beyond the pale of reason. Surely, she reasoned, she didn't *love* him. Wanted him, enjoyed him, took pride in him, yes, but as to loving him, no! Well, perhaps she did in a way, but certainly not with the whole-hearted devotion that was wringing sobs from him. Yet it must be love she felt for him, or she would not feel pity now. She wanted to comfort him, protect him, give rather than take from him. For the first time since she had owned him she had no desire to touch him except with the cool fingers of consolation. She turned sideways on the bed, pillowing his head in her lap, her fingers caressing his hair.

"Pore Colt boy!" She was surprised to feel her own tears on her cheek, "Now yo' jes' stop yore frettin'. Ain' goin' ter sell yo' never. Don' never vex yo'self no more 'bout that, understand?" Her fingers circled the small shell of his ear. "Yo' al'ays goin' ter be my boy. I a-goin' ter live at Clonmel 'n' yo' goin' ter bide here at Dove Cote. But I needin' ter come over mos' every day ter see my mama 'n' goin' ter have ter spend a lot o' nights here too. Yo' goin' ter be waitin' fer me when I come. Mista O'Neal he ain' never goin' ter know nothin' 'bout it. 'Sides, I'm thinkin' he goin' ter like ter have me come over here, 'cause he mighty taken with that Roxanna wench. She even got ter go on our weddin' trip with us. He say she a-goin' like'n my servant but I know why she a-goin' 'n' it don' make me no nevermind. He kin have his Roxanna if'n he wants, 'n' I got yo'."

"How'm I goin' ter live, sweet Dovie, if'n yo' not here *every* night?" Colt broke into another fit of weeping.

"Yo' got ter pleasure that Serena wench fer a while after I go. We goin' ter be gone a month, so I want yo' should git her a sucker so's Nero 'n' Mista O'Neal ain' goin' ter start thinkin'. Then when I comes back, goin' ter put yo' ter other wenches too. Wants yo' should git some good suckers off'n 'em. If'n yo' don', Mista O'Neal goin' ter say 'What yo' got that big handsome stud nigger over ter Dove Cote fer if'n yo' ain' gittin' no suckers off'n him? He jes' eatin' his fool head off 'n' ain' earnin' his keep. Better sell him off if'n he ain' got no sap in him!" She ran her hand down over his body, " 'N' sides it time yo' had some real pleasurin' o' yo' a-goin' ter fergit how."

"Pleasurin' the way we does is jes' fine, sweet Dovie. Ain' no fun pleasurin' nigger wenches 'cause they don' do it the way we do." His hand strayed up to take the pins from her hair and let it fall down around him. "All they wantin' ter do is grunt 'n' heave 'n' sweat 'n' then it all over. Wenches don' like lovin' 'n' playin' 'n' doin' nice things like'n we do."

She moved her head and her hair swept across his face. How silly she had been to be jealous and suspicious of him all this time. Often when he had not come from the barn the moment she called him, she had pictured him with some wench in the hay. His love and his faithfulness to her she had not counted on. All this time she

428

had really had more than she realized.

"Ain' no reason fer yo' ter stop lovin' me, Colt boy. I ain' goin' away fer long. Comin' back 'n' yo'll love me more'n ever."

"Oh, sweet Dovie." He sat up and took her in his arms again. "It awful ter be black. It awful ter know that I cain' be marryin' up with yo'. Why'm I black, sweet Dovie? Why I got this black skin? Why it make me different from masta O'Neal? Nobody kin sell masta O'Neal like'n masta Maxwell done sol' me. Nobody kin whop masta O'Neal if'n they wants ter. He's white, sweet Dovie, 'n' he kin have everythin' he wants. He kin have a big house like Clonmel, he kin have black boys what he kin whop if'n he wants 'n' what he kin sell if'n he wants. Jes' 'cause he's white, sweet Dovie. 'N' I'm black. I ain' nothin'. Ain' I got no feelin's?"

"Yes, yo' have, Colt boy. Yo' got good feelin's. Yo' a good boy."

"Got feelin's, yes, but what good they do me? Man say sell that black boy, they sell me. Man say whop that black bastard, they whop me. Man say work, I gotta work. Man say git me a sucker outa that wench, I gotta do it. I got feelin's, sweet Dovie. I got feelin's but makes no neverminds how much feelin's I got. Cain' marry up with you'. Cain' have yo'. If'n I work it don' git me nothin'. Cain' have me a house nor a suit o' clothes, nor nothin' less'n yo' gives it ter me. Cain' *work* fer it 'n' git it, sweet Dovie. Yo' kin have me cause yo're white 'n' I'm black. Yo' kin say ter Masta Maxwell, 'here's some money, give me that black boy', 'n' he gives me ter yo'. But what kin I have, sweet Dovie? Cain' even have yo' what I loves so much 'cause my skin's black 'n' yores is white. Oh, sweet Dovie, why'n't yo' take a gun 'n' shoot me 'n' stop my misery?"

She loosened his arms from around her and gathered him into hers, seeking unconsciously to protect him. "I cain' answer yo', Colt boy. White men mastas, black boys servants. Tha's the way it is 'n' ain' no other way. Al'ays bin that way 'n' al'ays will be. Bart use ter say the black man here ter serve the white man 'cause the

Bible say so. White men say black men jes' animals what ain' no better'n a horse o' a dog."

"Yo' thinkin' I'm like a horse, sweet Dovie? Yo' thinkin' I jes' an animal what cain' think, what don' have no feelin's?"

She did not answer him, trying to sort out her thoughts. She must remember this was a nigger she was talking to. She had bought him, she owned him and, if she wanted to, she could sell him. She could do the same with the stallion out in the barn, and yet between that brute animal and this man in her arms there was a vast difference. What was he? Was he man or beast? No, surely he could not be a mere animal, for he thought, he spoke, he loved and he *was* a man.

" 'Course yo' ain' no animal, Colt." She was surprised at her own words but she knew now that she believed them. "Yo' a human. Mayhap that 'cause yo' a Fan boy 'n' they better'n the rest but I don' know. Nero he ain' a Fan 'n' he a good man. That Calico he a good boy too. Nero half white 'n' Calico mos' all white but that don' make 'em no better'n yo'. Ain' human blood, Colt, 'cause yo' ain' got none, that make yo' the best man I ever known. Yes, Colt boy." She rocked him gently in her arms. "Don' ever fergit what I say. Yo' the best man I ever known. Yo' good, Colt."

"Yo' mean that, sweet Dovie?" He seemed comforted.

"Mean every word of it," she affirmed. "Ain' my fault that yo' born black. Ain' my fault yore skin different from mine. Ain' yore fault neither. Ain' yore fault yore hair kinky where mine straight, yore lips wide where mine ain', yore nose flat 'n' mine not. Ain' yore fault 'n' ain' my fault. But I know this one thing, Colt boy. I bin married up with one man what was like a hog. I bin bedded with 'nother which wa'n't much better. Now I think 'bout them they seem dirty 'n' ugly ter me. Ain' no white man what so clean-limbed, so strong 'n' so beautiful like yo'. Yo' got that ter be proud-minded 'bout. 'N' yore right handsome too. Ain' no one what kin say that kinky hair ain' jes' so beautiful's straight hair o' that big lips ain' so pretty's thin ones. Yo're handsomer'n any man I know 'n' that's something else yo' got ter be

430

proud-minded 'bout. 'N' here's 'nother thing. If'n yo wants, yo' kin even be proud-minded 'bout that black skin o' your'n. It right fine lookin'. Ain' white like'n a fish belly 'n' ain' got black hairs all over it. Yo' ain' fat 'n' yore belly don' sag 'n' yore breath don' smell o' corn." She thought of Johnny O'Neal. "Wants yo' should be proud-minded, Colt. Ain' wantin' yo' ter be biggety but jes' proud 'n' I'll tell yo' somethin'. Want ter hear it? Then stop bawlin' if'n yo' do."

The sobs trembled in his throat for a moment, then died away.

"What yo' aimin' ter tell me, sweet Dovie?"

"Tell yo' this, Colt boy. Makes me no neverminds if'n yore skin white or black. I'd be proud ter marry up with yo' tomorrow if'n I could. But yo' know 'n' I know that I cain'. Anybody know yo' 'n' I together like here to-night, they'd kill yo' 'n' tar 'n' feather me. But yo' jes' hold on ter that one thing, boy. I'd marry up with yo' if'n I could 'cause I think yo're the best person I ever known in my life. Yo're clean 'n' straight 'n' honest. Yo' jes' keep yoreself fine 'n' clean fer me, Colt boy, 'cause I a-needin' somethin' fine 'n' good in my life. Never had it till I met yo'."

"Oh my sweet Dovie." He nestled closer to her, feeling in the protection of her arms that nothing could ever harm him again. "I ain' got many words. Can' tell yo' all that's in my heart 'bout how I feels 'bout yo'. Somethin' strange 'n' different. Somethin' so big I jes' cain' tell it but it's there, sweet Dovie. Wishin' I could die right now, here in yore arms 'n' never wake up no more. Here in the dark, it don' make no neverminds what color I am o' what color yo' are. Ain' no black 'n' no white. Ain' no mist'ess 'n' no servant. Ain' no nigger 'n' no white woman. Jes' us, sweet Dovie, 'n' me wantin' yo', 'n' yo' wantin' me."

"Tha's lovin', Colt boy. Tha's lovin' someone else so much yo' cain' say it. Tha's more'n jes' pleasurin' 'n' carryin' on. Deeper, it is."

"My pappy tol' me that his pappy tol' him that way back in Africky Fan people et other people. Man want ter have a lot o' brains, he et 'nother man's brains. Man want
431

ter be big 'n' strong, he et 'nother man's arms o' his legs. Man want ter be brave, he et 'nother man's liver 'n' heart. He a-tellin' me tha's what make Fan people strongest 'n' smartest o' all niggers. Wishin' now, sweet Dovie, yo' could eat me so's yo' could have me right inside yo', lovin' yo', 'n' wishin' I could eat yo' so's yo' could be right in me, lovin' me." His lips nuzzled at her flesh while his fingers undid the buttons and stays that imprisoned her.

"Ain' no need, Colt boy." She felt his mouth warm and wet against her skin. "Ain' no need 'cause we all together anyway."

"We two jes' like'n one person, Dovie. Ain' no white o' ain' no black no more."

"Jes' one, Colt boy, 'n' ain' nobody nor nothin' ever goin' ter separate us." She adjusted her body to his quietly and easily. "We got ter part fer a little while but yo' got ter promise me one thing. If'n yo' pleasure wenches while I'm gone, yo' ain' ter feel 'bout them like'n me."

"Cain', sweet Dovie, never kin. 'N' when yo' marries up with masta O'Neal, yo' ain' goin' ter love him like'n me, neither."

"Don' fret yo'self. Mista O'Neal he a fine man 'n' he a rich man. He goin' ter help me with these two places but I don' love him 'n' I never will. Respect him, I will, 'n' I'll be a wife ter him. 'N' another thing! He ain' goin' ter be yore masta. Ain' no man ever goin' ter be. Promise yo' that."

Their bodies touched, their arms enclosed each other, and for the first time they found a greater communion in this new understanding that existed between them. It superseded all other emotions. It was sweeter by far to lie here together, listening to each others' heartbeats. Passion had not died between them. It would soar to greater heights than ever before, but for this one night it was enough to lie quietly and to know that indefinable security that comes from a love so deep it needs no outward expression. Words, gestures or movements were unnecessary. Even in sleep, they were not separated.

Chapter XXXII

ON THE AFTERNOON of the day before her wedding, Dovie left Clonmel early. Everything was in readiness. The flowers from the various gardens were standing in tubs of water on the gallery, waiting to be embowered in the hall on the morrow; the French chef and his assistants had taken over the kitchen, along with the half-dozen glossy mulatto boys who had accompanied him as waiters and were already lording it over the Clonmel servants. Dovie had peeked at the soaring white wedding cake and had admired the cream-colored broadcloth suit and the shot-silver waistcoat that Johnny was to wear on the morrow.

She had allowed him to kiss her chastely on the lips before she departed. He had whispered, "Tomorrow night, Dovie darling, we'll be together," and she had smiled back at him as though to tell him that that would be the greatest joy she could imagine.

All the while she was secretly thinking, "Tomorrow this will all be mine." But when he reached in his pocket and took out a long plush box, she gasped. The pearls were large and creamy and felt cold as he hung them around her neck. They were so beautiful that she kissed him again, almost meaning it this time, for if she didn't love Johnny O'Neal, she certainly did like him and all that he represented.

"Goin' ter ask that Frenchman out 'n the kitchen if'n he cain' pack one o' them bottles o' champagne up 'n ice so's I kin take it home ter Mama. Don' think she never tasted anythin' cold in all her life. 'N' if'n he kin spare some cold turkey 'n' some o' those pretty little pink cakes, goin' ter take some 'long too. Poor mama'll be so flustered tomorrow, she won' eat a bite, 'n' want she should taste somthin'.'"

Of course, Johnny was willing and attended to the matter himself, so that when Colt drove her away, there was a bottle of champagne packed in ice and sawdust in a bucket and a big box of dainties in the carriage. Dovie had decided to stop and see Mr. Norsmith at the bank on her way home. Although she knew that Johnny would pay for everything, it would be nice to have some money of her own along—say five hundred dollars in case she saw something she wanted to buy for herself.

She directed Colt to stop at the bank and then relaxed on the cushions, realizing that her wedding would be an important milestone in her life, perhaps the most important of all. Tomorrow night she would be Mrs. Johnny O'Neal, and as such she would be entertained on their way to New Orleans at Oak Vale Plantation, then the next night at St. Helena, where Johnny's cousin lived. After that there was the city and the round of receptions and balls in her honor. It was a big step but—she looked up at Colt's back—she was going to miss him. Since Wednesday night there had been a stronger bond than ever between them. She wished, with all her heart, that she could love Johnny O'Neal as much as she loved this boy up on the box but she knew she never could.

After Mr. Norsmith had counted out the gold pieces for her, he opened the drawer of his table and took out a folded piece of paper.

"'Member yore askin' me some time 'go if'n I could get yo' freedom papers fer that servant o' yores by the name o' Kru? Jes' came through, they did. Had a time gittin' 'em cause the government don' hol' with settin' niggers free. But tol' the judge how this boy saved yore life 'n' yo' wanted ter do somethin' fer him. So, he said as how he might be willin', 'n' here it is, all made out proper-like 'n' this Kru's a free nigger now. Jes' give him this paper 'n' tell him ter hang onto it case he want ter leave Dove Cote. Paddy rollers see this 'n' they ain' goin' ter touch him 'cause it signed by a judge 'n' all."

Dovie thanked him and placed the paper in her reticule along with the gold pieces. She'd give it to Kru and although he wouldn't know what it was, it would be proof that he was free. Even if it did not change his life, it gave her the assurance that he would never be sold or forced to leave.

When she arrived home, she instructed Colt to take the bucket and the box of food out to the dove cote and to meet her there as soon after dark as possible. She wanted to lie down for a while and rest; she'd have to be up early tomorrow morning.

Her hands went to the pearls around her neck. Johnny was so good. Too bad, in a way, that she loved Colt so much. No, it wasn't! He'd given her more happiness than she had ever known before, and she didn't regret anything. Nothing! After all, she reassured herself, in all these nights they had spent together, he had never really *done* anything to her. Not once! Her conscience was clear on that point. She'd never have to fear having a nigger baby, and anyway Colt seemed to like her way better than his own. Tommy had taught her those things —poor Tommy! Bart hadn't liked them, but she had prevailed against his aversion and his constant condemnation of her as a Jezebel steeped in lust and sin. But like it or not, he'd done it. Only with Ransom had she allowed a man to do with her as he wished sometimes, but she knew he had some exciting memories of doing it her way. She hadn't seen or heard from him since the night he left and she hoped she never would. He had been the direct cause of all her suffering; through him she had lost Tommy. She had wasted fifteen years on Bart and only now, since she had forced Ransom to go, had she been happy.

Callie was waiting for her, primed with a thousand questions, but Dovie pleaded a headache and went to her

435

room, where she disrobed, glad to free her body from the stiff stays and welcoming the looseness of the calico wrapper. It was a temptation to finger the stiff satin of her wedding dress, but she was so exhausted, she fell on the bed and slept. When she awoke, she gossiped with Callie until dusk but said she wasn't hungry and couldn't eat a bite of supper. Pleading her tiredness and the demands of the morrow, she started for the dove cote. Halfway there, she turned and retraced her steps to the house. She would give Kru's paper to Colt with instructions for him and Nero to seek Kru out during her absence and try to explain the paper. Colt knew a few words of African dialect from his father and perhaps Kru would understand him. Then the thought occurred to her that she would give Colt one of the gold pieces. He was like a child in some ways, and he could spend it at the store in Brownsville for stick candy, a jackknife or the gaudy kerchiefs he so loved.

She picked up her reticule and left the house by way of the kitchen, stopping to light the candlestick with the big tin reflector. Tonight, for the first time, the dove cote would be illuminated. It would be more fun eating the good things in the box and drinking the champagne if they had a light.

Colt was not in the dove cote when she arrived. He always waited until he was sure nobody could see him when he entered, so she closed the shutters on the two front windows, leaving only the one open to cool the room. It faced out on a thicket of shrubbery and the blank wall of the barn so she was sure none of the servants would see them—they would all be in bed anyway. She had only a few moments to wait before there was a slight scratching on the door and Colt slipped in, his hair bedewed with moisture and his shirt plastered wetly to him.

"Slip outa them wet trogs," she told him. "Ain' wantin' yo' ter catch no mis'ry. Nights a-gittin' cooler now."

She patted the bed beside her, inviting him to sit down. He had some difficulty in getting the cork from the chapagne bottle but his strong teeth prevailed. The loud pop of the bottle surprised him and the frothing liquid was colder than anything he had ever drunk before. Neither Dovie nor Colt had ever tasted champagne and neither was impressed by it, but its icy bubbles were invigorating and they sipped it along with the *petit fours* and the tiny turkey and *paté* sandwiches.

Dovie's hands strayed to him and his to her. The heady wine gave impetus to their fingers, while the candle set grotesque shadows dancing on the wall. Their dalliance had a bitter sweetness never before experienced. The discovery that they loved each other gave a deeper meaning to that which had hitherto been only wanton caresses. Their dread of separation on the morrow overshadowed every thought and lent a bitter poignancy to everything they did.

But now, Colt pleaded for the ultimate fulfillment, which she had always denied.

And Dovie almost yielded. In granting him this ultimate surrender not only would she give him infinite pleasure but it would be the final glory for her too. It would put a seal upon their love. Yet even in the hot haze of wine and desire, she was able to fasten on one minuscule iota of reason. She could not spend her honeymoon wondering if some embryo of dark life were germinating within her. His weight was overpowering and he was urged on by a power that he could no longer control. She managed to push him away from her, using all her strength to disengage herself until he lay beside her moaning in his frustration. Her fingers tried to assuage him, but he disengaged them.

"No, sweet Dovie, not that way tonight. It got ter be the other way."

"Sh-h-h," she tried to quiet him. "Rest a minute. Take it easy, Colt boy."

He reached for her hand. "Got ter put me outa my sufferin', sweet Dovie."

"Not now, Colt, not now."

"But we got a whole night, sweet Dovie. Won' make me no neverminds. First time never count with me; second one neither. Yo' knows that." Slowly and stealthily, with blandishments of fingers and lips, he covered her, and the token resistance with which she opposed him gave him courage.

"Now, sweet Dovie, now," he pleaded, "jes' so's I kin remember when yo're gone."

Her resistance crumbled. "If'n yo' take care. Oh, Colt boy, kin I trust yo'?"

He did not answer her but filled his lungs with air as he buried his face in the tangle of hair at her neck. All the power of his immense body became concentrated in his efforts, which caused Dovie to scream out and clutch at him, her fingers gripping his back so that the nails dug into his flesh.

In her pain and ecstasy she did not hear the creak of the door hinges. The tattoo of marching footsteps on the floor caused her to open her eyes, but she could not see beyond the shadow of the candle reflector.

"Who's there?" Fright turned her scream into a hoarse whimper.

A hoot of derisive laughter hit her ears and when the laughter died down there were words.

"Now ain' that a purty sight, Jonas? Bet yo' never saw so long's yo' lived a white woman a-gittin' pestered by a nigger buck. Right comical, ain' it?"

"That boy shore was a-humpin' his ass, wa'n't he, Ransom. 'Pears like'n she was a-pleasurin' him jes's much's he a-pleasurin' her. Al'ays heard that onct a white woman start gittin' it from a nigger, they ain' got no use fer white men no more."

Colt, hearing the voices, used the leverage of his arms to push himself up and turned, sliding off and standing beside the bed.

Dovie had recognized Ransom Lightfoot's voice. She reached for the crumpled sheet and pulled it up over her.

"What yo' a-doin' here, Ransom, 'n who that with yo'? I put yo' off'n my place onct 'n I kin do it again."

Ransom walked slowly out from the shield of darkness into the light. The pistol barrel reflected a splinter of brilliance as he aimed it at her.

"This time *I* got the gun, Dovie. Las' time yo' had it 'n' that made the dif'rence. Howsomever, jes' come ter pay yo' a friendly call even if'n I got a pistol. Brought

438

my brother Jonas 'long with me too. Seems like yo' didn' send us no invite ter yore weddin' tomorrow, but we reckoned as how yo' jes' might of forgot, seein' as how we're part of the family, I figure. Jonas 'n' me we been a-peekin' in the winder 'n' we shore been tickled ter see yo' 'n' yore nigger buck a-carryin' on. Suppose yo' goin' ter say he bin a-rapin' yo'."

"White woman al'ays do, Ransom," Jonas said, stepping into the light, "when they gets caught with a nigger. No matter how much they a-lovin' it, onct they git found out they start screamin' that he been a-rapin' 'em 'n' the poor bugger gits whopped ter death."

"Yo' a-goin' ter say he been a-rapin' yo'?" Ransom asked.

"Ain' goin' ter say nothin', Ransom Lightfoot, 'ceptin' ter tell yo' 'n' that worthless brother o' yore's ter git out. Kin have yo' both 'rested fer trespassin'."

Ransom walked over and sat down on the edge of the bed. "Now why don' yo' jes' do that, Dovie? Yo' go right ahead 'n' have us 'rested fer trespassin'." He started to laugh again and pointed up to Colt. "That nigger sure shiverin' 'n' shakin', Dovie. He knows that if'n yo' open yore trap I'll shoot him. He cain' figure out tho', if'n he goin' ter git whopped o' whaled o' skinned 'live o' hung, 'n' he jes' don' know which one he goin' ter git. He a fine-lookin' nigger buck he is, ain' he? How much 'n upstandin' buck like that worth, Jonas?"

Jonas walked over and ran his hands over Colt. "Figures he ought ter be worth couple o' thousand if'n he sold at the Forks o' the Road over ter Natchez. Worth more down in New Orleans. Some whorehouse down in New Orleans shore pay big ter git a nigger boy built like'n him. Why he a regular fancy." He slapped at Colt playfully. "What yo' like best, boy? Yo' 'druther git skinned 'live, o' shot o' jes' plain whopped ter death?"

Ransom joined in the merriment. "Yo' al'ays was a case, Jonas, but I bin a-thinkin' it a shame ter spoil this boy. Jes' ain' worth us takin' vengeance on him. Like lightin' a see-gar with a thousan'-dollar bill. Think we better keep him 'n' sell him."

"Ain't no sellin' a-goin' on." Dovie sat up straight.

"This boy's mine 'n' this place's mine 'n' I'm a-sayin' what goes on here. Now yo' both git. If'n yo' don' I'll start screamin' 'n' Nero'll come 'n' all the rest o' the hands."

"Yo' jes' scream onct, Dovie, 'n' it'll be yore last." Ransom placed the cold steel of the pistol against her throat. " 'N' 'sides, don' think yo' want Nero nor yore mam nor nobody else a-runnin' in here 'n' seein' yo' 'n' that nigger buck both nekkid as jay birds. Ain' goin' ter do no good neither ter say he been a-rapin' yo'. Ain' nobody goin' ter believe yo' when me 'n' Jonas tell what we seen through the winder. Why, Dovie, even if'n I killed yo' 'n' him both, ain' nobody a-goin' ter say one word. Jes' say I came a-ridin' in with Jonas 'n' we heard yo' screamin' from the dove cote here 'n' we busted in 'n' foun' that nigger boy a-pesterin' yo'. Shot at him 'n' jes' accidentally killed yo' too."

" 'N' I kin witness it." Jonas was still touching Colt.

Ransom disregarded his brother, lowered his gun and hitched around to face Dovie. "Way I looks at it, Dovie, don' look like'n yo' goin' ter have much ter say 'bout whether I sells this nigger o' not. He goin' ter be mine 'n' everythin' here at Dove Cote 'n' The Patch goin' ter be mine. Yo' see, Dovie, yo' 'n' me goin' ter git married up, come mornin'."

"Yo're a fool, Ransom." Dovie's body tensed in anger. "I ain' a-marryin' up with yo'. Cain', anyway, 'cause I'm marryin' up with Mista O'Neal come tomorrow."

Ransom doubled up in laughter, joined by an even more vociferous Jonas.

"Well now, ain' that comical? Ain' that jes' too funny?" Ransom managed to get control of himself. "Mista O'Neal a-takin' yo' fer his wife when Jonas 'n' me tell him what we been watchin' ternight. Mista O'Neal he a-goin' ter be right proud o' his wife, ain' he? Mista O'Neal jes' dotin' on a wife what a nigger lover! Ho, ho! So yo're a-goin' ter marry up with Mista O'Neal. That the most comical thing I ever did hear." His laughter froze in his throat and he reached out with one hand and grabbed her. "No, Dovie! Yo' gittin' married up with me. Don' make me no neverminds if'n yo' been pleasurin' with a nigger. Don' make me no neverminds at all 'cause I wouldn' pester yo' 'gain if'n yo' paid me a hundred dollars. Ain' playin' second fiddle ter no nigger. But I'm a-goin' ter marry up with yo'. Yes sir-ee! Ain' no way yo' goin' ter stop me." He shook her violently. "Yo're goin' ter marry up with me 'n' I'm goin' ter have Dove Cote 'n' The Patch. If'n yo' don' ..."

"If'n I don'?" Dovie defied him.

"Kin use this." Ransom indicated the pistol with a nod of his head. "O' tomorrow when yo' a-gittin' married up, me 'n' Jonas goin' ter drag this nigger ter yore weddin'. We a-goin' ter make this nigger confess if'n we have ter take the meat right off'n his back 'fore all them fancy folks what goin' ter be there. We goin' ter hol' yo' up ter all them folks for jes' what yo' are—a dirty nigger-lovin' whore. 'N' they goin' ter believe us too."

Dovie knew that they would. She knew that deny it as she might, they would not believe her. Colt's denial would mean nothing, but his confession under torture would. She would suffer the worst disgrace any woman could and Colt would die. She knew she was beaten.

"What kin I say ter all them people what a-comin' to-morrow?" Whatever Ransom Lightfoot told her to do now she would have to do. Somehow it didn't seem to make too much difference. The whole beautiful edifice of her life had crumbled, and now nothing made any difference.

"That up ter yo'. We a-goin' ter Brownsville soon's it gits light. Goin' ter have ol' man Soper marry us up. Yo' kin say what yo' likes. Make it real romantical if'n yo' wants 'n' say the only man yo' ever loved came back jes' in time. Say yo' never loved nobody but yore dear Ransom. Say anythin' yo' likes jes' so long's yo're my lawful wife."

"Ain' nothin' I kin say ter change yo', Ransom? Kin pay yo' money." She looked up at him hopefully.

"Ain' nothin' yo' kin pay me worth so much's these two plantations 'n' all the slaves. 'Sides, I always hankered ter own me a plantation. Tha's why I come here ternight. I knew what yo' bin doin' with this nigger buck. That night yo' sent me from The Patch, I snuck back 'n' saw yo' 'n' him frolickin' roun'. Didn' have no witness then 'n' that's why I brought Jonas back. Got me a witness now. Jonas here kin swear on a stack o' bibles that he saw that nigger a-pesterin' yo'. Guess they ain' much yo' kin do, Dovie, 'cept do's I say."

It was true. There was nothing she could do. The scandal that her absence from her wedding at Clonmel would cause would be as nothing compared to the stigma and disgrace that would be hers if it were known that she had voluntarily bedded herself with a Negro slave. She remembered an old tale of a woman—some poor white up in the northern part of the Territory—who had been surprised in bed with a Negro. She had been tarred and feathered and ridden out of town on a rail and the Negro had been hacked to pieces with scythe blades. No, there was nothing she could do to save herself, but she might perhaps save Colt.

"What yo' goin' ter do ter him?" She pointed to Colt.

Ransom did not answer her but turned to Jonas. "Know what she a-sayin' when she bought this nigger? Sayin' she a-goin' ter use him fer a stud nigger. Goin' ter git some right likely suckers outa him. Sayin' as how he'd been recommended ter her as a first-class stud."

"He shore ought ter be," Jonas guffawed, "but sometimes these big niggers ain' got no sap. But if'n yo' goin' ter sell him, Ransom, don' make no difference if'n he got sap o' no. Ain' no buyer goin' ter find out till after he buys him. Seems a pity, tho', that yo' goin' ter sell him 'fore yo' has some o' his git here."

"Feelin' like'n I ought ter larrup him a little, but he jes' too pretty ter mess up. Cost me a thousand dollars if'n I put whales on him 'n' I ain' wastin' that kind o' money. Does seem a pity, tho', that we ain' goin' ter have none o' his git roun' here."

"Yo' a-goin' ter sell Colt?" Dovie realized it would do no good to ask. She was only grateful that they were not going to murder him, as they might well have done.

"Ain' too late, Ransom, tho'." Jonas gave Colt's rump a resounding slap. "Ain' too goddam late, feller. How'd yo' like a fine light-skin sucker outa him?"

"Yo' mean . . . ?"

"Why'n yo' let him finish what he doin'? Light-skinned

442

sucker a-goin' ter be worth more'n a black one." He winked at Ransom. " 'N' sides, if'n yo' ain' aimin' ter take no nigger's leavin's, might's well git all yo' kin outa her. Kindly like ter watch it too; ain' never seen no buck a-pesterin' a white woman afore."

Ransom walked over to where Jonas was standing. He slapped his brother on the back and they both went into spasms of uncontrolled laughter.

"Jes' a minute." Jonas disappeared out the door and came back with a coiled whip in one hand and a jug of whisky in the other. "Might's well be comfortable." He pointed to the jug and then unwound the whip and laid it sharply around Colt's legs. "Come on boy, start humpin' yore ass."

"No, masta, no," Colt whimpered.

Ransom pointed the pistol at him.

"Yo' aimin' ter git shot, boy? How come yo're sayin' 'no' ter me?"

Colt looked at Dovie but her eyes were blank. She could not help him. Jonas had the whisky jug tilted to his mouth, and Colt knew it was no use entreating Ransom.

"What yo' wan' I should do, masta Ransom?"

"Git in the saddle, boy. Yo' goin' ter do some gallopin'. Yo' 'n' yore sweet Dovie a-goin' ter town. Git goin', boy. Touch him up, Jonas." Ransom took possession of the whisky jug. "Don' lay it on heavy. Don' wan' no whales on his back but jes' nuff ter keep him humpin'.' "

Colt moved slowly to where Dovie was sitting on the bed.

The whip descended with metronomic regularity on Colt's back and buttocks. Ransom and Jonas passed the jug between them, alternating the jug and the whip until Colt sank breathless and shuddering onto the bed. The candle burned low and guttered out. There was no sound in the darkness but Colt's hard breathing until Ransom spoke.

"Come outside, Jonas. We got some plannin' ter do. This goin' ter be a busy day fer us. We gotta wake up the house. Want that Fronie ter git some coffee on. Ol'

Miz Verder she goin' ter cry up a storm but won' do her no good."

"Yo' goin' ter leave 'em 'lone?" Jonas asked.

"Why not? Ain' no place they kin go. 'Sides, that boy too tuckered out ter move." When Ransom opened the door there was a pale light in the sky. "Gittin' on toward mornin', 'n' we got ter move fast." He waited for Jonas to go out and then turned and spoke to Dovie before he closed the door. "Better git yo'self up 'n' git yore trogs on. Goin' ter ride inter Brownsville soon's it gits light. Man don' wan' ter be kept waitin' fer his weddin'."

She did not answer him, waiting for the door to close. Laying her finger on Colt's lips, she got up from the bed, ran across the room and peeked out the door. She could see the dim figure of Ransom walking toward the house and, a few feet away, Jonas standing by the horses that had brought them there. In a moment she was back by the bed, shaking Colt.

"Git up 'n' git dressed. Move fast, Colt. Cain' do nothin' ter save myself but kin save yo'. Here." She fumbled under her wrapper on the chair and found her reticule. She pulled out a paper and passed it to Colt. "Take this paper, Colt. It a freedom paper fer Kru, but ain' no reason why yo' cain' be Kru. 'N' take this." She waited for him to slip his pants on, then poured the gold pieces into his pocket. "Now listen 'n' pay heed ter every word I say 'cause I cain' repeat it. This here's a freedom paper 'n' makes yo' a free man if'n yo' say yore name's Kru. 'N' yo' got plenty o' money in yore pocket ter git away. Git out the winder there 'n' git over ter the barn. Saddle up yore horse. Ride down through the woods till yo' come out on the road, 'n' then ride fas' 's yo' kin. Don' go Brownsville way. Head south to Mobile if'n yo' know where that's at. If'n the paddy rollers stop yo', yo' jes' show 'em this paper 'n' say yore name Kru 'n' yo' a free nigger what's goin' ter Mobile on business fer yore ol' mist'ess. Now go, Colt, hurry 'n' be careful."

Her arms encircled him, her lips sought his and when he lingered, she pushed him away. She saw his dark silhouette climb out the back window. In a few minutes she heard the neighing of a horse in the barn, and then

444

she saw, in the gathering light, the dim figure of a rider come out of the back door of the barn and lose itself in the moss-hung shadows of the wood.

Listlessly she donned her wrapper and pulled it around her. She stumbled on the empty champagne bottle as she walked to the door, leaned over and picked it up. Once it had been full of promise but now, like her life, it was drained of all it had ever contained.

The first rays of the morning sun touched her as she stepped out the dove cote door. Jonas looked up at her with a sheepish smile and she managed to smile back at him. Anything to give Colt an extra few minutes. Now that it was light and she could see Jonas better, he was not too bad-looking. Older than Ransom, but not a bad-looking man.

"Yo' a-goin' ter stay here at Dove Cote too?" she asked, trying to add a hint of invitation to the commonplace words.

"Aimin' ter." He grinned now.

"Might's well," she said as she walked toward the house.

It was going to be a nice day, this day that she had so long anticipated. Soon the guests would be arriving at Clonmel, but she would not be there. They would wait at the foot of the flower-embanked staircase but she would never descend it. Johnny O'Neal would hide his face and his shame and take his Roxanna wench and himself to New Orleans or some other place. She hoped she would never see him again.

She would be married to Ransom Lightfoot. What was it Ransom had told her? He'd never play second fiddle to a nigger? No? She started to laugh as she walked to the house. Never? That's what Ransom said now, but she knew better. The time would come when he'd want her again and if he didn't, well, there was Jonas. Then she remembered. What if . . . ? Oh, God! What if she had a nigger baby? Something in the back of her mind told her that she would; it seemed that she could already feel a stirring of life inside her. Well, what did it matter if she did?

She squared her shoulders and walked on. That would

445

be the worst thing that could happen to her, so let it happen. She'd give birth to it and Ransom could sell it if he wanted to. What did she care? Nothing mattered now. Nothing! And then she started to laugh again. So Ransom thought he was going to get Dove Cote and The Patch. He did, did he? But now they belonged to the Dummy! After he married her he'd find out he was as far away as ever from owning them.

She reached the gallery of the house and walked up the steps. She knew that in all her life to come she could never suffer worse anguish than she was suffering right at that moment. One could only reach a certain depth and then things had to get better. Things were beginning to look brighter already. A yellow chrysanthemum that had bloomed since she had stripped the garden caught her eye and she bent down and picked it and stuck it in her hair. It would be her bridal bouquet.